An Untamed Land

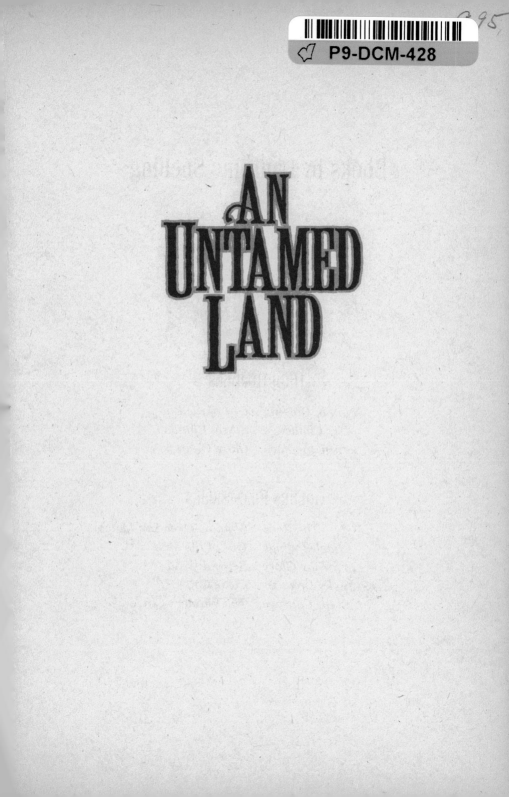

Books by Lauraine Snelling

Red River of the North

An Untamed Land
A New Day Rising
A Land to Call Home
The Reaper's Song

High Hurdles

Olympic Dreams   *Out of the Blue*
DJ's Challenge   *Storm Clouds*
Setting the Pace   *Close Quarters*

Golden Filly Series

The Race   *Shadow Over San Mateo*
Eagle's Wings   *Out of the Mist*
Go for the Glory   *Second Wind*
Kentucky Dreamer   *Close Call*
Call for Courage   *The Winner's Circle*

AN UNTAMED LAND

LAURAINE SNELLING

BETHANY HOUSE PUBLISHERS

MINNEAPOLIS, MINNESOTA 55438

Winner of the 1997 Angel Award

An Untamed Land
Copyright © 1996
Lauraine Snelling

Cover by Dan Thornberg, Bethany House Publishers staff artist.

Published by Bethany House Publishers
A Ministry of Bethany Fellowship International
11300 Hampshire Avenue South
Minneapolis, Minnesota 55438

Printed in the United States of America by
Bethany Press International, Minneapolis, Minnesota 55438

Library of Congress Cataloging-in-Publication Data

Snelling, Lauraine.
    An untamed land / Lauraine Snelling.
        p.   cm. — (The Red River of the north ; bk. 1)

    1. Frontier and pioneer life—North Dakota—Fiction. 2. Norwegian Americans—North Dakota—Fiction. 3. Immigrants—North Dakota—Fiction. 4. Farm life—North Dakota—Fiction. I. Title. II. Series: Snelling, Lauraine. Red River of the north ; bk. 1.
PS3569.N39U57   1996
813'.54—dc20   95–43938
ISBN 1–55661–576–0   CIP

Dedication

The men and women who left Norway to forge a new life in America were pioneers of deep courage and fortitude. Leaving behind everything they treasured, they faced innumerable hardships as they settled across the territories of the West. To those forefathers whose fearless valor tamed this harsh new land, I dedicate this book with gratitude and admiration. Since my heritage is Norwegian, I tell my ancestors' story—a story of all those who ventured from their homelands to pursue their dreams in another country.

The sons and daughters of those heroic pioneers are dying. To the remaining few in my family—Gilbert Moe, Clara Rasmussen, and Thelma Sommerseth—I give my love and appreciation. The pioneers helped shape us all.

Acknowledgments

Writing a book of this scope would be impossible without the assistance of many people: those who have compiled their own research, those who write their own family stories and histories, and all those who have a love of history and are willing to share it. I cannot list them all, but they are a part of this series, nonetheless.

I spent many hours in universities, historical societies, libraries, churches, and book stores researching the setting for this series—the Red River Valley. In addition, I spoke with numerous individuals in order to gain a better understanding of the people and conditions of this time in history. The books on farming and the history of the Red River farmers by Dr. Hiram Drache of Moorhead, Minnesota, were not only informational but interesting reading as well. He is a delightful person and a veritable fount of information. John Bye and his staff at North Dakota State University in Fargo, Sharon Horerson at Concordia Lutheran in Moorhead, and Sandy Slater, along with her assistant Dean Yates, at the University of North Dakota in Grand Forks all provided me with valuable material from the universities' regional study programs and from the collections of family histories. The textbook, *The History of North Dakota*, by Elwyne B. Robinson, made reading history delightful. Dan A. Aird guided us on a tour of Bonanzaville in Fargo that transported us back to the early days of this country. Robert J. Lommel at Stearns County Historical Society and Mark Peihl at Clay County added their colorful input, along with Frank Schiller, who loves to show off the collection at Minto, North Dakota, where the Walsh County Historical Museum is located.

Shirley L. Richter of the Fargo/Moorhead Convention and Visitors Bureau sent me packets of information, as did Sandy Dobmeier in Grand Forks. Thanks to the tourism magazine of North Dakota, we spent two days at the Fort Ransom Sodbuster Day, which was a reenactment of early history. What fun we had, and what wonderful people we met. Theresa Johnson and her family demonstrated soap making, cooking in a spider in a fire pit, period dress, and shared all the books and information they've collected to make the reenactment accurate. John drove the most gorgeous team of mules, and he, along with other farmers, hitched up three across to show me what it took to pull that early machinery. Thanks to all you people for your love of old-time farming practices and your willingness to answer my myriad of questions. Mr. Carter of Carter Farms in Park Rapids, Minnesota, raised and trained a team of Ayrshire steers to pull his farm wagon. Talk about a huge, beautiful team of oxen! Ardenwood Farms in Newark, California, also conduct old-time farming days, and I was quickly reminded of the reason denim overalls were worn. Wheat spears easily poke through cotton knit shorts and tank tops, with itching success.

So many others added their bits of information. My uncle Gilbert, at ninety-five, remembers it all, if I can think of the right questions to prime his pump. Rod McIntosh of Colfax, Washington, explains well the finer points of plowing and other general farming tasks.

Friends and family help any writer keep sane and on track, and mine are no exception. Thanks to Pat Rushford and Ruby MacDonald for their critiquing skills and their abiding friendship. Thanks to my husband, Wayne, who is growing as a researcher while I continue to grow as a writer. All things work better when we are part of a good team.

No book would ever make it to print without editorial expertise. Sharon Madison not only read and reread the manuscript, she cheered me on when the going got tough, and when I was running out of pages and time. Sharon Asmus has an eye for detail that is amazing and the patience of a saint. My thanks to all the Bethany House Publishers staff who put this book together when I finally got it finished.

Prologue

Norway 1877

Gustaf Bjorklund waited patiently in his chair at the head of the oval oak table for the members of his family to take their seats so the discussion could begin. He stroked his gray beard with fingers coarsened and cracked by years of heavy labor in the frigid Norwegian winter air. One curling strand caught in an open crack and he felt the small twinge of pain.

However, that pain was minute compared to the heavy pain burdening his heart. But he would show neither.

"Far, you have blood running down your finger." Roald, the second-eldest son, reached for a bit of cloth and handed it to his father.

"Uff da, what shall I do with you?" Bridget, Gustaf's wife of thirty-five years, pressed her finger against the cut until it ceased to bleed. "You haven't been using the goose grease, have you?"

With a quick frown that failed to penetrate Bridget's armor of concern, Gustaf retrieved his hand from her grasp. "Enough," he said.

From under bushy eyebrows, liberally sprinkled with gray, he slowly stared at each one seated around the table. Years before, when the children were young, they had quailed from such a look and ran quickly to do his bidding. Now, nearly all of them grown, they let their father wait as they finished their animated discussions and settled expectantly into their chairs, their mood of excitement irrepressible.

Were they so enamored with the adventures of going to the new land that they were all ready to leave Norway this very night? Gustaf shook his head at the thought. If and when they together made the decision, it would be months, possibly even years, before the needed money could be gathered. That would be part of the discussion he expected would continue for some months yet. As if they hadn't talked and argued and discussed over and over the move already— no thanks to the letters his younger brother sent home from Amerika. Perhaps he should have burned them when he had the opportunity, but what with the zealots for emigration canvassing the entire country, what chance did he have of keeping his family together here in the hills of Valdres?

Finally, silence fell upon the room, an expectant silence broken only by the snapping of the fire in the round, ceramic stove in the corner. Its windows glowed a cherry red from the heat of the fire crackling within.

Gustaf stared up at the carved shelf that followed the walls around the entire room and held his family's heirlooms of kettle and plate. He'd built that shelf with his own hands during the cold nights of a winter long past, just as he had built every piece of oak and birch furniture in the house: the tables and chairs, the spinning wheel that sang in the corner, the dry-well sink, the open-fronted cupboards in the kitchen. He had taken great pleasure in putting his own stamp of craftmanship on this house and making it truly their home.

"We are ready." Johann, oldest by two years and heir of the Bjorklund farm, touched his father's hand to get his attention. It wasn't like Far to be off in his thoughts like this. Johann shot a questioning look to his younger brother Roald.

Roald barely dipped his head, but the message was clear. Let them begin.

Gustaf flashed his eldest a look that left no doubt he was back in charge. "It is good of you to come together this day. I know you have all been talking much about the possibility of moving to the Dakota Territory of the United States of Amerika." With one finger he traced the outline of the newspaper article centered in front of him on the oilcloth table covering. Beside it lay their prized copy of an Amerika book, the cover faded and bruised by the many who'd pored over its pages. The pause lengthened. "You must all understand it is not my wish for any of you to go. Would that we could all stay here in this country we love, that there were land available and work that you might make a good living like we did in days long gone."

Had he failed them? Was it his fault that wages paid today would scarcely feed one man, let alone a family? In this year of 1877 every-thing had become so costly: the food they could not produce them-selves, little though that was, new tools, a cow to replace the one they'd had to butcher when she was so old she would no longer breed. When he looked up he saw that everyone was sitting with their gazes fixed on his face. Where had he been? *Oh, my God, my God. Is it your will my fine strong sons will cross the sea, and I will never see their faces again this side of eternity?*

He squared his broad shoulders and took in a deep breath of air redolent with the precious cinnamon Bridget had used in the röm-megrot, a flour and cream pudding, she'd made as a special treat. "Let us get on with this." His voice gained strength with every word. "Would that I could give each of you a portion of this farm, but that is not to be. Our ten acres will not support five families, as you well know."

"And in Dakota Territory, land is free for the taking." Roald's deep baritone rang with conviction. "I will go first and make a way for the others."

By his side, Roald's wife, Anna, tried to keep her gaze on her hands, but disobediently, both her eyes and her lips smiled up at him. She hugged Thorliff, their twenty-month-old son, closer to her breast, breathing in the sleepy sweet scent of him. They would do this for their children. All of this for their children. By the time they sailed for Amerika, Roald would have two fine sons to train up as his helpers. She guarded that secret deep within her, pushing away the traitorous possibility that the new seed growing within her might be a girl. Roald needed sons.

Gustaf nodded, a small movement of the head that took all his willpower to perform. "Ja, that is the best way. Now then . . ." His deep blue eyes gazed around the table, meeting the eyes of each of his children, never leaving one for the next until he had searched their intent through the window of each soul. Was it inevitable that they all wanted to leave Norway so badly? Would their hearts never yearn for home? "The money—it will cost a king's ransom to send Roald and his family to the new land."

Halfway down the table, nineteen-year-old Carl cleared his throat. "Far, I've been thinking I should go along. Two can work better than one, as you've always taught us."

"Ach." The cutoff sigh that sobbed of pain and sorrow escaped from Bridget. Gustaf turned to his wife and watched as she quickly smothered a second sigh with her hand, knowing the thought of losing yet another son to Amerika pained her deeply.

Looking back at Carl, he asked, "You'd turn a man's wisdom against him, then?" With the sharp retort, Gustaf disguised the surge of pride he felt in his fine strong sons. They *had* listened to him through the years. He knew that by the way they often quoted him.

"Only when necessary." Carl's quick answer, along with a cheeky grin, brought warm smiles from the others gathered around the table.

"Then we'll need to save the price of another ticket," Roald said, nodding to his brother.

"More like two," Carl quickly added. "I would marry Kaaren Hjelmson before we leave."

Amidst smiles of approval and a slight gasp from Bridget, Gustaf remained silent. He looked at Carl's clasped hands upon the table in front of him, hands like his father's that could shape a piece of wood into whatever he asked of it. This third son of his was gifted with many talents.

"And you can support a wife already?" Gustaf asked as he leaned back in his chair. "I understood you didn't want to farm."

"That was when there was no possibility of land. I don't want to work myself into a grave for someone else."

A murmur of agreement flashed around the table.

Gustaf felt it like an arrow piercing his side. Was this what *his* father had felt when brother Thorliff insisted on emigrating? They'd never seen him again and only received one letter from him before a friend wrote to say Thorliff had been killed in a logging accident in the north woods of a place called Minnesota. The new land everyone claimed to be so welcoming of immigrants had already extracted its own severe price.

Gustaf dug in his vest pocket and removed his favorite pipe. Even though he'd been rationing his scant store of tobacco, tonight was surely one of those times when a good smoke was needed. He cradled the familiar piece in his hand, drawing a measure of comfort from it before he tapped, tamped, and lit it, sending rings of gray smoke spiraling toward the ceiling. When it was drawing to his satisfaction, he leaned forward.

"I'm sure you have a plan in mind." He directed the comment to Roald.

"Yes, sir, with your permission." At his father's nod, Roald took a piece of paper from his shirt pocket and unfolded it. "In fact, I have several plans so we can decide what will work out best for all."

"We can decide? Wouldn't it be better to lay those plans of yours before the good Lord and let Him choose the best path?" Gustaf watched his son bite back a retort. Roald had never been one to ask for or expect divine guidance. *Where did I fail him?* Gustaf shook his head. Enough of that. Look ahead. Looking back never did anyone any good.

Gustaf wasn't surprised that Roald chose to ignore his father's question and instead continued as if he had not spoken.

"I say that I should go work on Onkel Hamre's fishing boat as soon as I can leave my work here," Roald said, laying out the first step of his plan.

"I'll go with you," Carl spoke up. "Onkel has begged us both to come and help him for the last couple of years."

"It is dangerous work," Roald reminded him.

"More so for you than me?"

Roald took in a deep breath and returned to his list. "Anna can either return to live with her parents, or stay here. That way we won't be paying rent on our house."

"And we can sell our furniture and put that money toward the tickets." Anna flashed a smile that showed she agreed wholeheartedly with her husband.

"Anna, if you stay here and help Mor, I can find a position in the city and send the money home," Augusta, the eldest daughter, added.

The discussion continued far into the night as everyone suggested possible ways they could help the emigrants prepare for their journey to Amerika.

As Bridget refilled coffee cups around the table, she relocked the door to her heavy heart. Her children would go to Amerika, and she would grieve a long, long time. Yes, they would write letters home. And yes, this was for the best. For them. Already she could feel the wrenching.

1

Ingeborg Bjorklund shifted on the hard bench and fingered the tattered newspaper article in the pocket of her reticule. She lifted her face to the offshore wind that brought a fresh breeze to nostrils filled too long with only salt-scented air.

They had safely crossed the great Atlantic Ocean. In spite of several cruel, unrelenting storms at sea and a ship that moaned its desire to join comrades now crushed in the ocean depths, they could smell the robust fragrance of land, even though they couldn't yet see it. Seagulls screeched around the sides of the ship, harbingers of the new life that waited for them. Bonanzaland, some called it.

She didn't have to reread the article. In the last months Ingeborg had read it so many times that she had every word memorized. Paul Hjelm Hanson, a Norwegian-American journalist from Minnesota, had sent his articles to newspapers all over Norway, writing of rich, flat land that lay empty, pleading for the bite of the plow. "New Canaan," as he called it, had land free for the claiming, land that promised untold wealth and farmsteads for their children. It was the promise of land that fed their dream and pulled them from the security of Norway in that year of our Lord, 1880. And Ingeborg had promised herself that once they left the shores of Norway, she would not look back. There would be no regrets, only dreams of the new life that lay ahead. Together with Carl and Kaaren, she and Roald would build a good life in a new land. God had made possible this journey to Amerika, and God would be with them here, just as He had been with them all along the way.

But she couldn't help thinking of her family—Mor, Far, Katrina, and the baby—would she ever see their beloved faces again? *No, don't think of all that's left behind,* she ordered herself sternly. *Only look ahead to the future, and all the good things it holds.*

She laid a hand on her stomach, queasy again from the constant pitch of the ship. Long rolling swells raised and lowered the prow of the complaining steamship as they surged westward. She knew for certain now that the nausea didn't come only from the motion of the sea. Ingeborg would tell Roald the joyous news after they landed. She carried within her their first child, the first Bjorklund to be born in the new country.

"Mor," called five-year-old Thorliff, interrupting her thoughts. He dashed across the heaving deck to clutch at her dark wool skirt. He'd called her Mor from the first time his father introduced the boy to his new mother, just a little over a year before. "We're almost to our new farm. Far said so."

Ingeborg couldn't resist the beaming smile on his round little face. She tucked his curly wheaten locks back under his black wool cap and cupped his rosy cheeks in her mittened hands. "Yes, my son. But you must hang tightly to your far's hand. A large wave could come and wash you into the sea. Then what would we do?"

He stared reproachfully out of eyes as deep blue as the Norwegian fjords, eyes that matched those of the man standing behind him. "But I have something to tell you."

"What's that, den lille?"

"Far said I can have a baby dog."

"A puppy?"

"Ja, for me." His eyes danced above cheeks made ruddy by the biting wind. "And a horse, and a cow and"—he scrunched up his eyes to remember—"and two sheeps."

Ingeborg laughed, the sound lilting above the hiss of the surge against the prow like the trill of a songbird in flight. From the railing, two men turned to see where the laughter came from and smiled at the tableau of mother and child.

"Land, ho!" The call passed from one eager passenger to the next, spoken in a symphony of languages. Those brave enough to face the wind crowded to the rail, hoping for a glimpse of solid rock.

In her excitement, Ingeborg leaped to her feet and started toward the rail. But when she recognized the narrowing eyes and straight brows of her husband's frown, she stopped midstep and returned to her bench in the lee of the funnel, Thorliff beside her. She clasped her mittened hands, wishing she could crowd the rail like the men. If allowed, she'd have been standing in the foremost inch of the prow, straining to catch the first sight of land. But according to

Roald, proper women didn't do such things. At least not his woman.

Ingeborg's sigh of disappointment drifted away on the stiff wind. Wishing did no good. Her mother had diligently instructed her daughter on this and many other principles of behavior becoming to a Christian woman, such as never wasting even a minute and always obeying her husband. As she'd been reminded by her mother more than once, Ingeborg, at her advanced age of twenty-two, was fortunate to have married such a fine man. An upstanding Christian, a good farmer, a man strong and brave enough to leave the old country and go to Amerika to start a new life. It didn't matter that she felt no love for him when they first married—only a deep and abiding respect. But love had blossomed later, as her mother had promised it would.

A second sigh floated on the wind after the first. If only he would smile, even once. She thought of the new life growing safely inside her. Mayhap *that* would bring a smile to his sober face.

"Mor, why are you sad?" The small voice drew her back to the windy deck.

Ingeborg drew in a deep breath of land- and sea-scented air. "Let's go see if Tante Kaaren is feeling better. We'll help her with the baby." How rich and refreshing a first glimpse of land would be rather than sitting in that fetid hole-in-the-wall they called a cabin. True, she should be grateful they weren't crammed together like the poor souls down in steerage. And she was grateful, but, oh . . .

"I want to see the new land." Thorliff dragged at the firm hand that pulled him toward the stairs.

"Me, too, but Far wants us safe from all the pushing and shoving. A little boy like you could get squashed like a bug."

"Ugh," Thorliff said, puckering up his face.

"I know. Far will come for us when it is time. We must be patient."

⚬ ⚬

Roald Bjorklund escorted his wife and son to the companionway and saw them start down before turning back to shoulder his way to the crowded rail. Amerika! The land of his dreams for far longer than he'd been married to Ingeborg, his second wife. Beautiful Anna—the love of his youth—was gone forever. Together they'd dreamed and scrimped and saved to buy tickets for passage to Amerika. But then she had died and taken his heart with her. The son she'd labored so hard to bring into this world had died only a few hours later. Sometimes he still dreamed of her, but when he awoke, it was Ingeborg's face on the pillow beside him. Comparisons did one no good.

He tugged his black felt hat farther down his forehead. Off in the distance he could see the dark shoreline of his new country. Here, he would have his own land, unlike in Norway, where only the oldest son could inherit the family farm.

Roald blew his nose on a handkerchief pulled from the pocket of his black wool pants. The time for mourning was long past. *Ingeborg is a good, strong woman*, he reminded himself again. *A woman built to bear many sons and help me face the hardships I know are coming in this new land.* And he had come to care for her as he knew he would. That was why he wanted her safely below. It was too dangerous for her and Thorliff to be in the thick-pressed crowd on deck.

Like a rock battered by the surging sea, he stood solid against the surging masses of humanity around him. Where was Carl? Tall as Roald was, he searched the crowds for his younger brother, wiped his nose again, and shook his head. Probably off swapping stories with the other group of Norwegians they'd met. Carl frittered too much time away on foolishness.

Roald had spent enough time dreaming at the rail. They would be disembarking soon, and there was much to do. He turned and left to search for his brother, for they should be gathering together their possessions. They could not afford to lose a single thing.

❧ ☙

Ingeborg carefully made her way down the steep, narrow stairs and stopped to open the second door on the left. With the porthole closed against the sea spray, the room stank more than usual. Bare wooden bunks, stacked along the walls in tiers of three, were so shallow that a broad-shouldered man could barely roll over. People had to turn sideways to navigate between them. Quilt-tied bundles, wooden trunks, and satchels of black leather filled the empty spaces where many had lain in an agony of seasickness for much of the voyage. All the others who'd shared their cramped quarters had packed their belongings and were already up on deck.

All but Kaaren Bjorklund, wife of Roald's brother Carl. Beside her lay a mewling infant, born just four days ago and three weeks earlier than they'd expected. No one had thought the tiny babe would live this long. Suffering the pangs of labor for two days had drained what little stamina Kaaren had left after her voyage-long illness. It seemed the churning sea did not agree with Kaaren, for she'd been sick all the time since they'd left their beloved homes above the fjords of Norway.

Ingeborg knelt beside the hard bunk and stroked back the tendrils of sun gold hair framing her sister-in-law's wan face. "Soon, kjaere, my dear, we will be standing on the new land. Then you will feel better. Perhaps we can remain an extra day or so before we board the train, and then you can regain some of your strength. Good cow's milk will help you, I know."

"Ja, that is good," Kaaren agreed, her words faint in the cacophony of creaking hull and slamming waves. The swaddled infant in the crook of her arm stirred and whimpered. "She is hungry again. My milk is not enough for her." Despair colored her words the gray of the walls. "Ingeborg, promise me you'll care for her." Kaaren gripped her sister-in-law's hand.

"You will raise her yourself. You must not give up hope." Ingeborg gentled the tone of her voice. "Rest easy, Kaaren. Soon we'll be on land again."

"Thirsty. I'm so very thirsty."

Ingeborg pushed to her feet and sidestepped her way to the water bucket wedged in the corner. She dipped out a cupful and sidled back to the bunk.

"Here." Kneeling again, she gently raised the sick woman's head and held the cup for her to drink.

"Mange takk. You have been so good to me." A tear slipped from the edge of Kaaren's eye. "What would I do without you?"

Precious little, Ingeborg thought as she continued to murmur words of comfort. *These men of ours are so quick to beget children, but we are the ones who bear them and care for them and each other.* She thought again of the look of sorrow on Carl's handsome face when he was informed he had a daughter. Ingeborg shook her head. *And such a perfect baby she is. Men, how to ever understand them!*

"Mor." Small Thorliff tugged at her sleeve, his eyes huge in the dim light from the hanging lantern. "Can we go on deck now? I don't like it down here."

"Soon, den lille." She stood again and studied their pile of belongings. How would they ever be able to carry all their possessions off the ship when Carl would have to carry Kaaren? She was much too weak to walk and might not even be able to sit up once they reached the dock.

Worry lined Ingeborg's forehead and drove the dimple in her left cheek into hiding. Her mother would say to leave all her worries in God's hands. But lately, with the trip as hard as it had been, it seemed that God had hidden His face from them, much as He had from His people in the Old Testament. Had their leaving home and kindred to search for new farmland been against His will? While pondering the predicament, she tucked a stray strand of hair up into the thick, honey-hued braids that circled her head like a crown.

Ingeborg stood five feet seven inches tall, and her elbows bumped against the low ceiling beams as she repaired her hair. She clamped her full bottom lip between teeth that were even, but for the slight overlap of the left front, and tilted her head, the better to reach the strands trickling down her neck. Birdlike, she called it, but others had laughed and said the bird was certainly a swan. She adjusted her skirt, the waistband now loose. Like the others on board, she'd lost a fair amount of weight on the diet of thin soup and hard bread provided by the steamship company. But at least the seasickness hadn't laid her out as it had so many others. For that she was grateful.

Suddenly the door burst open, and Carl, slender of build but wiry and an inch shorter than his six-foot-two-inch older brother, rushed in. "We'll be docking by midafternoon. The shoreline stretches north and south as far as the eye can see. Soon we'll be entering the mouth of the Hudson River." He stammered over the English "Hudson River," always trying to improve his new language.

Ingeborg rose so he could take her place by the rough bed. Excitement seemed to bristle even from his black wool coat. He took his wife's thin hand in his and stroked her limp hair with the other. "Kaaren, you must fight to get well again. Now there'll be good food and plenty of fresh air to get you back on your feet. And then we'll settle on our own land."

Kaaren smiled wistfully up at him and clutched her babe close to her side. "I will, I am." She reached up to stroke the golden strands of his full beard. "I'll be waiting right here when you're ready to go ashore."

"Take Thorliff with you, please," Ingeborg pleaded as Carl sidestepped his way to the low door.

"Come, boy." Carl stretched out his hand. "You should be on deck with the men on such an important day." The little boy's face shone with pride as he waved goodbye to his mother.

Ingeborg busied herself washing Kaaren's face and brushing and rebraiding her hair. She changed the baby and then helped Kaaren into her petticoats and thick woolen dress. By the time they were finished, the sick woman lay back, exhaustion graying her face. Ingeborg rubbed at a crick in her back from bending and lifting in the cramped quarters.

She stood in the wider central aisle and dug at the small of her back with both fists. *Oh for a whiff of the sea and a sight of the land.* Making her way to the open area of the cabin, she rubbed the glass of the porthole and pressed her nose against it to look out.

A gasp escaped before she could contain it. They were in the river, steaming parallel to the shoreline. Off toward the green coast, several ships tugged at their sea anchors. She bit her lip against the urge to dash up the companionway and over to the rail.

A glance at Kaaren showed both mother and child sleeping peacefully. Ingeborg quietly cracked open the cabin door and slipped out into the narrow passageway. She *had* to see the docking, she just *had* to. No other time in her life would there be this excitement. *Besides, I must save this story of our coming to the new world to tell my grandchildren*, she told herself. With that mission in mind, Ingeborg darted up the companionway and out onto the crowded deck.

The brisk wind tugged at her scarf and clawed at her hat with demanding fingers. She pressed a hand over the black felt hat pinned to her coronet of braids and clamped the veil between her teeth as she threaded her way toward the railing. No one paid any attention to her murmured "excuse me," as it meant nothing to many of those around her. She didn't understand their replies either.

The crowd fit together like bricks in a wall. Ignoring her mother's frequent admonition that a true woman of God was never rude, Ingeborg pushed and shoved her way through the human bricks to the railing and leaned out to see around others in front of her. There ahead lay New York City. The scene was breathtaking, more than she had imagined. Tall wooden buildings lined the long docks, crowded by ships berthed prow to stern.

The ship's horn bellowed above her. Ingeborg ignored all the ballyhoo around her, feasting her eyes on the bustling city ahead. Ferries, tugs towing barges, boats and ships of all sizes and kinds anchored, steamed, or sailed the harbor. Colorful flags snapping in the wind above the vessels proclaimed homelands from around the globe. The ship's bells clanged, and Ingeborg's ear, trained by her days at sea, heard the cutback of the engines. What glorious sights and sounds! She would never forget this day!

Knowing she needed to go below before Roald discovered her latest adventure, she stole one more long look at the city ahead, imprinting every detail in her memory. But when she turned, she bumped nose first into a familiar broad chest.

Roald steadied her with massive hands clenching her upper arms. "Leaning out like you did, you could have fallen overboard. I told you to stay below with your sister-in-law."

"Ja, that you did." Ingeborg stiffened her back and raised her squared chin to look into his stern face. "But . . . but I had to see the city. Kaaren was sleeping, along with the babe, and . . ." Why did just looking at his frown make her stutter and stammer like a schoolchild?

"And where is my son? I left him with you."

"Carl has him. Thorliff wanted to be on deck, and I was caring for . . ."

"Far, Far!" A happy voice interrupted their discussion. Ingeborg looked up to see the subject of their debate waving from the shoulders of the young man striding toward them. The little boy's chubby hand was locked in the blond curls on his uncle's head. "Did you see?" Thorliff's entire body bounced in the thrill that wreathed his ruddy face with joy.

Ingeborg looked up to her husband's face in time to see the softening of the granite features that only occurred when Roald was with his son. It was as close as she'd seen to a smile. Would he share a smile with her when *their* son was born? She shifted her gaze back to the child at his giggled, "Mor, see me."

"Let off." Carl laughed upward as he removed the boy's arm from a hammerlock over his eyes. "One of us has to watch where I'm going, and it should be me. You want us both to end up in the water?"

Thorliff crowed and bounced again. Carl reached up with both hands and swung the boy to the deck. "Now, you go with your mor so you don't get trampled in the rush to get off the ship. Your far and I will come for you when it is our turn."

"But, I want to—" At a stern look from his father, Thorliff ducked his head and cut off the words. He reached for Ingeborg's hand and sniffed.

Ingeborg clasped the boy's cold hand, wishing like Thorliff that she could remain topside to watch all the hustle and bustle. Instead, she leaned down and asked, "Where are your mittens, den lille? Your hands are freezing." Thorliff held up his arms to show the mittens dangling from their knitted yarn chain. Ingeborg shook her head as she held the mittens open for him to insert his hands. When both hands were snug again, she dropped a kiss on his nose. Hand in hand they followed behind Roald, who shouldered his way through the crowd to the companionway like a ship's prow cleaving the waves.

"Uff da," Ingeborg muttered after he ushered them into the cabin and closed the door. The urge to stamp her foot was quelled by the remembrance of the utter horror on her mother's face the last time she'd succumbed to that temptation. The thought made her laugh. Poor Mor.

"Ingeborg, is that you?" The weak cry from the figure in the bunk banished all thoughts of rebellion from Ingeborg's mind and replaced them with the nag of guilt. She really should have stayed with Kaaren. They were closer now than sisters after all they'd been through together.

"Ja, 'tis me. Can I bring you a drink or something?" she asked as she sidled down the aisle to the bunk. The thought of crabs scooting sideways in the fjords of home brought a merry smile to her face. Now, after all these days of traversing the narrow aisles, she certainly knew how they felt living a sideways life.

"Are we nearly there?" Kaaren raised her head, careful not to disturb the sleeping Gunhilde.

"Ja, the tugs are guiding the ship into its berth just like a mallard hen with her ducklings. Hear all the noise? The crowd on deck is waiting for sailors to lower the gangplanks. Roald and Carl will come for us as soon as the crush is over." Ingeborg perched one hip on the edge of the bunk. "Any minute now they'll throw out the hawsers and cut the engines. Then we will walk down the gangplanks with all the others on board and begin a new life in this new land." Ingeborg lost herself in the dream. Soon, after a long train ride and a journey by horse and wagon, they'd find land to homestead, rich flat land in the Red River Valley of the North. That's what the article, folded up and saved so carefully in her reticule, promised.

"If I don't . . . if I . . ."

"You *will* go with us. You mustn't even think of anything else. Just like we planned all those evenings around our kitchen table, this year we will build a sod house for us to live together in for the winter, and next year we will build another. Our children will grow up on farmsteads side by side, and one day we will send money for more of our brothers and sisters to come and join us. We will build a town for all the Bjorklunds with a church and a schoolhouse. You will see it, Kaaren, kjaere, you will." Ingeborg clasped the thin cold hand of her sister-in-law. "You will."

"Me, too." Thorliff leaned against her knee, his head resting against her arm. "Far said a big farm, bigger than all in Norway. Bestefar, grandfather, will come to see me."

"Yes, you too." Ingeborg circled him with her arm and patted his cheek, holding him for a moment against her. "Please, dear God, let it be so." Her whisper held a note of desperation that told of un-counted repetitions. Had she pestered God too much? Would He be like the judge in the Gospel that gave in because the woman per-sisted? Ingeborg had been accused of pestering before. When was too much? Or not enough? But, she knew that for all the needs of those she loved dearly, there could never be too much prayer. *And, God, please give this sister-in-law of mine strength again. Bring the roses back to her cheeks and the laughter to her lips, so she can raise this beautiful child you have blessed her with.* She dipped her head. *Amen.*

The baby whimpered and stretched; her mouth opened and closed with tiny lips circling a pink tongue. She turned her face toward her mother's chest, already nuzzling and seeking the breast that nourished her.

Kaaren undid her dress with shaking fingers and turned so her daughter could nurse more easily. As soon as the little one was suck-ing contentedly, her mor readjusted the quilt in gentle modesty.

"She is so perfect." Ingeborg watched the age-old process with delight. In seven months or so, she looked forward to doing the same. Fall would bring the arrival of her son. So certain was she, she'd already chosen a name—Carl Andrew. Since Thorliff was named after Roald's uncle, they could choose what they liked. Couldn't they? Couldn't she?

Thorliff stuck his first finger in his mouth, his eyes drooping in weariness. The sucking of the nursing infant sounded peaceful in the gloom.

"Listen." Ingeborg sat ramrod straight.

"What?"

"The quiet. The engines are still." She leaped to her feet, grab-bing Thorliff up in her arms, and sidestepped her way to the porthole. "Look, Thorly, the wharf. We are docked." She spun him around in the small open space. "We're here. We're finally here."

"In 'merika. In 'merika. Me see." She lifted him to the tiny window, where he banged his hands against the wall as he peered out. "People, lots of people." He wriggled in her arms to be let down and ran to the door. "Far come now."

Ingeborg snatched his hand away from the handle. "Soon, den lille, soon."

The minutes stopped, dragged, and stopped again. In what seemed like forever, Ingeborg retied the quilts for the third time and rechecked under every bunk in case they had left something precious.

Finally she heard Carl's voice and the low rumble of Roald's answer. The door flew open, banging against the wall as the men strode through.

"Our first stop will be Castle Garden, where we must go through immigration. Ingeborg, I'll take you and Thorliff first, along with as much baggage as we can carry. Then I'll return to help Carl with the rest. An official from the dock warned us not to leave anything unattended. There are thieves who prey on new immigrants." Roald handed one satchel to his wife and loaded himself with others as he spoke. "Now, Thorliff, you hang on to your mother's hand and don't let go, you hear?"

"Ja, Far, I'll be good." The little boy danced in place, already leaning against the restriction.

When they cleared the companionway to the deck, Ingeborg stopped still. "Oh, hutte meg tu!" The words were whispered in awe. Buildings rose so high they blocked out the westering sun and numbered beyond her time and ability to count them all.

"Come, come." Roald turned around and frowned at her when he realized she wasn't right beside him. Ingeborg put her feet in motion, though her mind remained suspended in disbelief. Could men really build anything so tall? Or was New York like the Tower of Babel, and God just hadn't gotten around to crushing them down yet?

Roald grunted under the weight of the load he carried. Not bothering to excuse himself, he pushed and shoved through clusters of jabbering immigrants who swarmed the docks like flies. The sight of huge black men, naked to the waist, lugging crates and barrels up a plank to a neighboring ship gave him pause. "Uff da," he muttered, shaking his head. But it didn't slow his pace.

He stepped out of the way of a horse-pulled cart when the driver yelled at him. The tone and sneer of the man told him the words were lacking in hospitality.

"If you'd speak Norwegian like any decent man, I'd have moved sooner," Roald responded, returning glare for glare until man and beast passed by.

So much for a warm welcome to his new land. He clapped his mind shut against the thought that the newspaper articles had been less than honest about Amerika welcoming all newcomers with open arms and free land.

After three long years of planning and saving, he was finally here. That was enough. And his family was safe. He flinched again at the memory of Ingeborg leaning so far over the rail. One accidental shove and she'd have flown overboard. Uff da. Yet the merry smile that crinkled around her gray eyes made his mouth twitch in response. *Ingeborg, Ingeborg. What am I to do with you?*

He stopped when he reached the head of the pier. Now he stood on solid land. *His* new land. His dream had come true! He set the bundles down and rubbed the shoulder where the box had dug a furrow into a muscle. "Ingeborg, just a . . . ." But when he turned, she wasn't there.

⚓ ⚓

Ingeborg followed the laden Roald down the ramp and up the cobblestone pier. Teems of immigrants from other ships and stevedores surged around her, carrying them along like twigs on a stream newly released from the bondage of winter. She hurried to keep Roald in sight. God help them if they got separated now.

Strange languages flowed around her, people shouted above the noise of the crowd, and ships' whistles bellowed out their calls—all blending into a mishmash of sounds that crashed against her eardrums. And she'd thought the ship's engines loud! She wrinkled her nose and tried to breathe in small sniffs at a time. Rotting vegetables, horse droppings, smoke, unwashed bodies—the pungent smells assaulted her nostrils as intensely as the sounds did her ears.

Roald strode on ahead of her.

"Come, Thorliff, we must hurry." She pulled him closer to her side and tried to move faster, but the carpetbag on her other arm weighted her down. A brisk wind snatched at the veil of her hat, threatening to carry it over the edge and into the oily water below.

Roald disappeared in the surging mass ahead of her. She could no longer see his tall hat above the others.

Fear clutched at her chest, driving the air out and cramping her belly. "Hang on to my skirt," she commanded Thorliff, her voice breathless. She set the carpetbag down with a thump, reached up with both arms, and unpinned her precious hat, stuffing it in the bag at her feet. At least she wouldn't lose that. She hefted the bag again, grasped Thorliff's hand, and determinedly set forth. Roald would be waiting up ahead.

When they reached the juncture of wharf and pier, Roald stood amid their pile of belongings, his arms crossed. His eyebrows formed a straight line, and his scowl cut deep slashes from nose to chin.

"I thought you were right behind me. What if I lost you?"

Ingeborg bit back a reply. She knew that Roald's concern always came out gruff. "Ja, I know. But we're here now, and we're safe." Her hand twitched with wanting to smooth away the worry lines on his face. But one did not do such a thing in public. And with Roald, one didn't do it at all.

Roald hoisted his load again and strode past the wide doorway of a warehouse. "Castle Garden is ahead of us. We'll go through the immigration process there. They say there are doctors too, so there will be help for Kaaren."

Ingeborg saved all her breath to keep up with his long strides. And poor Thorliff practically had to run as he held on to his mother. Besides, the fear that Kaaren would be considered too ill to enter the country left Ingeborg with no spit to swallow, let alone breath to respond.

Roald nearly disappeared again in the crush of immigrants when he set his bundles down in a square open area. On the land side of the point, a wooden fence with tall vertical posts protected a circular building. "That's Castle Garden. There is help for us there," he said as he finished mounding their belongings. He pointed to a wooden box. "You sit there and wait for us. I'll return as soon as I can. Once we have a bed for Kaaren, we'll get our trunks out of the hold."

Ingeborg nodded as she gathered her dirty skirts about her and sank down on the box. Thorliff stared wide-eyed at the commotion around them. Two boys, whose pants were held up with twine, chased each other around the flag pole. Young, old, and all ages in between—the lines of immigrants stretched four abreast out of the gate and curved around the courtyard. If only she could take a place in line, but then who would guard their belongings?

Shortly after Roald disappeared back into the throng of disembarking passengers, a broad-shouldered man in a dark blue wool uniform stopped in front of her. Ingeborg shook her head when he spoke to her, then shrugged. She had no idea what he'd said. He leaned closer and raised his voice. At her shrug, he pointed at the gate. "Norwegian?" The one familiar word brought a smile to her face that lit up the dimming square.

She nodded. "Ja, Norwegian," and continued in a stream of her own language.

He shook his head, disgust visible on his square-jawed face.

Fear clawed again at her throat when he picked up the roll of quilts and a box. "Nei, nei!" Ingeborg leaped to her feet and grabbed for his sleeve. He shook her off and nodded to the fence with his chin. When he reached the wooden pillars, he dropped her box and returned for more.

Ingeborg breathed a sigh of relief. He was not a thief waiting to run off with her things. He was merely helping to move them out of the way. She carried the carpetbag over and smiled her thanks. "Mange takk." But her gratitude only bounced off his disappearing back. With a sigh, she sat back down on the box. "Thorliff?" The second call rose to a near scream. "Thorliff!" She searched behind the stack and all around her. Roald's son was nowhere in sight.

2

I don't want to die! I don't want to die!"

"You won't, don't even think such a thing." Carl stroked the limp strands of hair back from his wife's pale forehead. "We're here in New York now; wait until you see it. Roald and Ingeborg have already gone ashore. They'll be back for us soon."

Kaaren reached up with a quivering hand and locked her fingers into his rough black lapel. "You'll care for Gunny, promise me." Her voice, in sheer desperation, sounded strong for the first time in days.

"Kaaren, Kaaren, don't even think of such a thing."

"Promise!"

"Yes, I promise. Now never talk of dying again. We've come to Amerika for a new life. This little one here was just too impatient to wait." With a gentle finger he brushed the cheek of his sleeping daughter lying secure in the crook of her mother's arm.

Kaaren studied the strong face of the man sitting on the edge of the narrow bunk. Wind and sun had burnished his cheeks with a ruddy glow. His blue eyes, Bjorklund eyes they called them at home, smiled tenderly down at her. Back in grammar school, she'd fallen in love with his eyes first. And she'd been in love with him ever since. She released the fold of his coat and reached up to the crinkled lines radiating from the corners of his eyes.

"But . . . but those stories of people being turned away. What if they won't let me in?"

"You're not ill with tuberculosis or something contagious. You just had a baby and a rough voyage. That's all. Many were seasick; surely the authorities will understand that. I will tell them you've never before been sick, not a day in your entire life."

"That is true." She attempted to return his confident smile. *But why, then, have I nearly died? Women have babies all the time and get right up and go back to baking bread or whatever else they were doing.* She shook her head. "I'm just not very good at riding on a ship, I guess."

"Roald and I should have taken you fishing on Onkel Hamre's boat so you could have gotten your sea legs. Riding out a raging storm in the North Seas will take the seasickness out of anyone."

She transferred her hand from his face to his fingers. On his left hand he carried the badge of a fisherman: a missing finger. He'd lost it in the rigging during a bad storm one night. She shuddered at the thought. "And you think farming will be any safer?"

"At least you can't be washed overboard." When he smiled that way, she could refuse him nothing. He leaned forward and touched his lips to hers. "Think, my love—our own land. Crops to feed our children and sell to a hungry city. Wheat for bread, hogs to fatten, cows to milk, butter and cheese to make. A white house of our own with sunlight streaming through the windows. A great shiny black stove where you can bake and cook anything you want."

Kaaren closed her tired eyes and let him paint the pictures on the back of her eyelids. She would be the mistress of her own home, not at the beck and call of the lady of another house. For the last three years she had worked hard as a hired girl. Now *Kaaren* would be the lady of the house, and one day mayhap they would have their own hired girl. And hired men to help Carl and Roald work the fields. She could almost see the golden wheat swaying in the wind.

"Are you ready, then?" Roald's deep voice cut into her daydream.

She turned her head to brush a kiss across her daughter's forehead. *God of heaven and earth, give me the strength to make it through the inspection. May your heavenly angels be with me now.* She gently laid the infant down beside her. "Please help me with my coat, Carl. Ingeborg has all our things gathered together."

"I found a handcart," Roald said, entering the cabin. "A good man on the dock loaned it to me." He began to load their valises and bundles onto the two-wheeled dolly. "Once we've been through Castle Garden, we'll come back for our trunks that are stored in the hold."

Kaaren could sense Roald's excitement, even though his face was set in its normal sober lines. Sometimes she wondered how the two men could be brothers, they were such opposites in temperament. She looked into the eyes of her husband as he carefully slipped the buttons of her coat through their holes. She gave him an answering smile when he winked at her, his full lips tilting up in the grin she loved.

"Ready?" he whispered.

She nodded and picked up the still sleeping babe. "Ja, I'm ready."

Slipping his strong arms around her shoulders and under her knees, he lifted her and Gunhilde in one smooth motion. "Ready or not, Mrs. Bjorklund, we have arrived in Amerika!"

Sheer terror cut off the scream choking Ingeborg's throat.

The blue-coated officer loomed in front of her. "Ma'am, what is wrong?" His voice sounded clipped, gruff, like a soldier's.

If only she could understand what he was saying. "Thorliff, I must find Thorliff!" She broke away from his restraining hand and darted down the side of the wooden pillars to see if the little boy had hidden there. If only she could make them understand. "I must find my son, Thorliff." She screamed his name again, the desperation of her voice turning many heads.

"Here, now. Calm down. Acting crazy will get you nowhere." The officer grabbed her arm again, this time with no doubt that he planned to hang on to her.

By then a crowd had gathered, their various languages rising in discordant noise.

"She's looking for something—or someone." A man in a black wool coat stepped forward. "I think she's speaking Norwegian, or maybe Swedish. Have you someone around who can speak the language?"

The officer looked at the stranger, then shrugged and loosened Ingeborg's arm. "Mayhap we do. If ye'll keep track of her, I'll go inside and ask around. Can't have a crazy woman disrupting the proceedings, now, can we?" He gave Ingeborg a little push that sent her bumping into the tall man.

Ingeborg broke free and headed for the other end of the log fence. "Thorliff! Thorliff!" A ship's whistle echoed her plaintive cry, sobbing along with her. Her heart pounded so hard she could barely hear herself crying. Where had he gone? How could he have gotten away so quickly? *Why? Oh, dear God, why?*

"Fraulein, how may I help you?" the man asked.

She spun around. So near her own language—German, the man spoke. "Thorliff, my son, so little." She held her hand about waist high from the packed dirt beneath them. "He's gone. Disappeared. I was right there with our things and he—why would someone take so little a boy?" Her Norwegian words tripped over themselves, hastening for expression like a creek bounding down the mountains of home.

"You must calm down"—he held up a soothing hand—"for I cannot understand you." He spoke slowly, enunciating every word clearly.

A woman wearing a white bibbed apron came running out of the gate. "How can I help? I hear you need someone who speaks Norwegian."

At the sound of her own language, Ingeborg swallowed her tears and drew herself erect. "My son, Thorliff, is missing. Mr. Roald Bjorklund, my husband, said for us to stay here with our belongings, but when the man in the blue uniform made us move closer to the fence, Thorliff disappeared. I . . . I . . ."

The woman clasped Ingeborg's icy hands in her own. "We will find him; you pray." She turned and gave orders in English to those around her. Then turning back to Ingeborg, she asked, "Now what does this Thorliff of yours look like?"

Ingeborg drew in a deep breath. "His hair is gold like the summer wheat, and his eyes are blue like his father's. He is five years old and wearing a black coat with a cap I knitted myself." Her hands moved swiftly, describing height and size.

The aproned woman quickly translated the description of the boy and sent people scurrying in different directions. "Now then, my dear, you and I will wait right here so they can find you when they need you."

"No, I must go look, myself." Ingeborg tried to pull away, but another aproned woman blocked her path.

Ingeborg sniffed back a fresh onslaught of tears. What was the matter with her? She knew that crying never did any good. They must think she was a hysterical female, one who couldn't even keep track of a small boy. She drew her shoulders straighter and dug in her reticule for a handkerchief. And she'd been worried earlier about losing her hat!

"I'm better now." Ingeborg straightened her back as she spoke to the kind woman beside her. In the distance, she could hear voices calling out her son's name. *Dear Lord above, watch over your wayward lamb. You, who said a lost sheep was worth searching for, please help these good people find my Thorly.* While she wasn't sure how closely God was listening, nevertheless, the prayer made her feel better. Could even the eye of God find one lost boy in all this confusion?

A few minutes later a shout went up some distance away, and Ingeborg turned her head in that direction. What were they saying? Oh, to be able to understand the language!

"Come, I think they may have found him." The woman in the apron pointed down the street bordering the enclosure.

Ingeborg looked up the street and then back at the pile of belongings stacked against the wooden posts.

"I will care for your things." The other aproned woman smiled and gave her a bit of a push. "Go now."

With a hasty "mange takk," Ingeborg followed the woman's advice and darted down the cobbled street. Tall wooden buildings rose on either side of her, blocking the sun. She could hear the sounds of a crowd up ahead and made for the noise. As she ran, her mind kept time with her feet. *Please let him be all right, Lord. Please.* She pulled up short at the sight of a small boy snagged in the clutches of a blue-coated officer. The ruddy-faced man was handing the squirming child to an officer wearing a uniform and badge.

Thorliff clutched an apple in his hand.

"Thorly!" Ingeborg's screech could have crossed the North Sea.

"Mor!" The little boy reached for her with open arms.

She grabbed the child away from the police officer and hugged him close.

"E's a thief, that's whot 'e is." The man brusquely took ahold of her arm above the elbow.

Unable to understand the man's words, but sure of the look on his face, Ingeborg thrust Thorliff behind her and turned on him like a banty hen defending her lone chick.

"You leave him alone! I don't care who or what you are, you leave my son alone."

At that moment, one of the apron-garbed women from Castle Garden puffed into the intersection. "Now then, missus, what seems to be the problem?" She spoke in the dialect of Oslo that Ingeborg could well understand.

The policeman crossed beefy arms over a chest broad enough to dance on and glowered down at them. "Blasted furiners! When they gonta learn to speak the king's English?"

His scowl made Ingeborg stutter. "He . . . he had Thorliff."

"And what did the mite do to bring your wrath down on his

innocent head?" The woman in the apron planted her hands on hips that well filled out the gathered garment.

"He stole that apple, he did." The officer jabbed an accusing finger in Thorliff's direction.

The man from behind the corner fruit stand joined the growing crowd. "There were three of them hoodlums. One distracted me while the other took my apples and tossed them out to others. Then they all ran off."

"All but this little one," the woman said, planting herself in front of Ingeborg.

Behind his mother, Thorliff took another bite of his apple. Ingeborg heard the crunch and instantly turned around. Bending over, nose to nose, she demanded, "Did you steal this apple from that man?"

"No, no. The nice boys . . . they gave it to me." His chin quivered and a single tear hovered on the tip of his blond lashes. "Mor, they gave it to me. I promise." He tried to hide the evidence behind his back.

"Give it to me." When she had the apple in her hand, Ingeborg tried to hand it to the stern-faced policeman. "He did not know he was doing wrong, sir. Surely you can understand that. Where we come from, when someone gives you a gift, you say 'mange takk' and enjoy it. When my husband comes . . ." At the thought of Roald, her heart dropped to her ankles. She caught her breath and continued. "He will pay for the apple."

The woman acting as interpreter finished conveying what Ingeborg said to the police officer. "And where are the ruffians who actually did the stealing?" She glared at the tradesman and the officer. Then laying a hand on Thorliff's head, she asked, "Why aren't you chasing after them instead of scaring this poor innocent?"

Ingeborg looked from one to the other, trying to follow what was happening by the expressions on their faces and their tone of voice. If *only* she could speak Amerikan; the thought hardened into resolve. She *would* learn to talk right. There had to be a way. If only they had learned to speak Amerikan before they came. She just hadn't realized how important it would be.

Her protector kept on talking, jabbering so fast that Ingeborg thought no one would understand the torrent of her words. But before her very eyes, the storekeeper threw his hands in the air and strode back to his fruit stand. The policeman shook his head and, after giving what sounded like a serious warning, headed back toward the wharf area.

"Come, dear, it is all right now." Taking Ingeborg's arm and Thorliff's hand, their newfound friend led them back across the busy street and down another.

The buildings on either side of them appeared totally unfamiliar to Ingeborg. Where was she taking them? Ingeborg could feel her stomach tie itself up in knots again. Whatever had she done to deserve this? She had not even had time to thank God for saving Thorliff, and they were off again. She planted her feet on the cobblestone walk and refused to go any farther.

"My things, I must get back to guard them."

"Oh, my. I didn't tell you. We are just taking a shortcut to get there sooner," their guide said. "I'm sorry."

"Oh." Ingeborg felt as she had when scolded as a child by a schoolmarm. But the woman wasn't scolding her; the smile that turned her cheeks into round buns assured them of that. "I'm so sorry."

"Never you mind. I know this has all been terrible for you, not understanding a single word of what's going on and all. You just come with me, and we'll get you back to Castle Garden and to your husband."

Please let us get there before Roald does. Ingeborg's plea drifted heavenward. But when they turned the final corner, she knew her request had fallen on deaf ears.

"Far! Far!" How could one small boy shout so loud? Ingeborg wished she'd been able to clap her hand over his mouth before the shout. The thunder gathered on her husband's brow left her in no doubt of his state of mind. If only she could back up time and pretend this all hadn't happened.

Roald strode across the street, the crowd parting before him like the Red Sea before Moses. "Where have you been? I left you to take care of our belongings. You know what they've said about people stealing from immigrants. How could you leave?"

"Now, Mr. Bjorklund, your belongings are—" Their angel of mercy cut short her words as Roald quelled her with a stern look.

When he directed that same withering glare at Ingeborg, she ignored the urge to hang her head and let the tears flow. Here she had risked life and limb to find *his* son, had snatched Thorliff away from the police, and then returned to find his father on a rampage.

"We will discuss this later." She grabbed Thorliff by the hand and marched over to the wall where Carl had set Kaaren and the baby down on the mound of bundles and satchels. "Thank you for watching our belongings," she said to the aproned woman who still hovered by the stack. Ingeborg turned to her guiding savior and extended a work-worn hand. "Mange takk." She closed her other hand over their clasped fingers. "You have been so good to us. God bless you."

All the while, she wanted to throw herself into the motherly woman's arms and bawl like one of the newly weaned calves in the pens back home. Home. So far across that turbulent sea. Another world, another lifetime.

She could feel Roald, his barely contained anger an ominous presence, by her side. As if she would walk away from all their earthly possessions without good reason, when she knew the mound of belongings may mean the difference between life and death when they reached their new home. The thought of his accusations caused a spark to smolder in her midsection. Her mother's frequent admonition resounded in her ear. *A calm and gentle spirit, Inge. Pfft with the anger and the talking back.*

Ingeborg deliberately released the tension in her jaw. She looked up to see Carl watching her, compassion evident in his eyes and half-hidden smile.

"You are all right?" he asked quietly.

"Ja, God be thanked." She could feel a tremor begin in her chin. If she wasn't careful, someone being nice to her would be her undoing.

"I'm going inside to determine how we are to proceed," Roald said over his shoulder. "Are you coming, Carl?" When there wasn't an immediate answer, the tall man in black paused. "Well?" He turned to face the small group clustered for comfort amidst the sea of pushing and yelling alien bodies. When Carl shook his head, Roald grunted a sound of disgust and merged with the swirling crowd, only his black felt hat visible above the masses.

"Well, Thorly, you certainly caused a stir, didn't you?" Carl swept the boy up in his strong arms and looked him in the eye. "Didn't your far and mor tell you to stay right here?"

Thorliff nodded. His lower lip began to quiver.

"And what did you do?"

Thorly hung his head. "I went after those boys."

"Why?"

"I don't know." A tear beaded on an eyelash and meandered down his cheek.

"Little boys are to obey their parents. You won't do such a thing again, will you?"

Thorliff shook his head.

"I should have kept hold of his hand, but . . ."

"It is not your fault," Kaaren said from her place among the bundles. "It was an accident, but all is well now."

Ingeborg shot her sister-in-law a grateful look. "How are you feeling, den lille?"

"Stronger. Being off that . . . that heaving ship helps." She looked up with lines of worry creasing her forehead. "How will I ever pass the inspection?"

"With God's strength. He wouldn't have brought us here if we weren't supposed to come." Ingeborg put all the confidence she could muster into her words. "Tomorrow, we will be all together on our way west."

A woman's wailing snapped their heads up.

"I'll see what is the problem," Carl said before pushing his way through the crowd. When he returned only seconds later, they could see he carried bad news.

"What . . . what is it?"

"She is being sent back to Norway. She has tuberculosis." Carl reached for Kaaren's hand.

"Oh, dear God, dear God." Kaaren leaned her cheek against his arm. "Father God, not us. Please, please. I could not bear the return voyage. Please, no more ships." She rocked back and forth, wasting precious strength in her fear.

"Kaaren!" When the babe began to whimper, Ingeborg spoke again, even more sharply. "Kaaren! Enough!" Ingeborg saw Carl frown at her sharp reprimand, but he kept silent when Kaaren's cries turned to sniffs.

"Like I told you, you are not sick, only weak from having the baby and being seasick. Surely they will understand this. They are not ogres after all," Carl said as he stroked his wife's head.

"Not to be afraid, Tante Kaaren." Thorliff crept closer to her side. "Far won't let the bad mans get you."

Kaaren smiled through her tears. "Mange takk, Thorly. You help Far, all right?"

The little boy nodded and grinned. "I big help."

"Carl, Carl." Roald's shout caught all their attention. "We'll gather what we can for the first trip inside with you and Kaaren. Then you can wait in line for all of us. Once we have our things there, we can purchase something to eat." He hefted bundles and valises as he spoke, loading himself up more heavily than had the black stevedores they'd seen on the docks. "Ingeborg, you and the boy stay here." He shot Thorliff a stern look. "And you obey your mor, hear me?"

Thorliff nodded and ducked his head. He studied the top button on his coat until his father strode off.

For the next half hour, Ingeborg waited and watched as hundreds of anxious immigrants filed past her into Castle Garden for inspection. Then above the crowd she saw Roald's black hat as he fought his way back through the crowd to get them. Silently she thanked God for her husband's tall height.

Once inside, Ingeborg looked up in awe at the ceiling arching high over their heads, supported by tall white columns. The din of hundreds of petitioners entering the new land echoed around the vaulted ceiling, increasing in volume on its journey. Ingeborg felt like clapping her hands over her ears, for the roar was worse than the mightiest breakers pounding the rocks of the Norwegian coast. Even the tallest waterfall hurling its spume to the river below failed to match the thundering sound. For this river carried a powerful riptide of fear and agony. An undertow of apprehension.

Roald returned from his mission for food and handed each of them a pasty of potatoes and carrots baked in a golden crusty dough. He also brought a jar of milk and gave it to Kaaren. "For you. The man said it was fresh this morning."

"Thank you, Jesus, for this food for our bodies." Ingeborg murmured the prayer before biting into the tantalizing pie. She closed her eyes, savoring both smell and taste. After stew or soup for all the meals during the voyage—often consisting of more water than sustenance—she bit into the flaky crust with relish and chewed slowly, delighting in each mouthful.

When she opened her eyes, she looked around at the four adults in their party and the small boy who'd let out a shriek of delight at his treat. If her face looked like the others, this first bit of food in their new land spoke well of it. And she was certain she saw a tinge of color coming back into Kaaren's cheeks after only half the milk was gone.

At that moment, as if afraid she might be missing out, the baby let out a wail that made others in the snaking line turn their way.

"Our baby's hungry," Thorliff announced to all within earshot.

As Ingeborg looked at those waiting patiently around them, she was greeted with nodding heads of understanding and gentle smiles. Gone were the frowns and impatient mutterings—a baby always seemed to bring out the best in folks. She looked down at Kaaren, nestled on their mound of belongings. She had a worried look on her face, but her cheeks now blossomed with color.

"How can I feed her here?" Kaaren whispered to Ingeborg. The baby wailed louder, in spite of Kaaren's rocking and shushings.

"We cannot leave the line," Carl replied.

"But we can gather around her and make our own wall." Ingeborg motioned for the men to join her. They stood facing out, arms crossed over their chests, as if daring anyone to make a comment.

When Ingeborg looked up at her husband's face, his expression was blank. But the nearly invisible twitch hadn't yet left his right eye. That twitch alone told her he was still angry with her. Knowing him as she did, she knew he would never mention the incident again.

How would she find a way to pay the shopkeeper? Could she find him at all?

By the time they reached the inspectors, Thorliff was whiny, the baby refused to be comforted, Ingeborg felt a pounding in her head, and Roald's left eyelid had begun to twitch in earnest again. Only Carl could summon a smile or an encouraging word.

The woman who had rescued Ingeborg earlier appeared at the doctor's right side, ready to interpret. Her smile bathed them all in warmth. As she asked the questions and translated their answers, a man perched on a stool at a tall desk wrote swiftly in a huge ledger.

"He's just writing down the information," the woman assured them.

After all the questions had been answered, the man in charge excused himself and walked across the tiled floor to speak to another official.

A mewl of fear escaped from Kaaren, who was propped upright between the strong arms of Carl and Ingeborg.

Ingeborg gave her a comforting squeeze. Only a few minutes to wait. They would pass—they *must* pass—all of them! *Please, God, let not all our hardship be for naught.*

3

*W*ill *they let me stay in Amerika?* Kaaren knit her fingers together in worry, then placed one hand in Carl's.

"Do not fear. God is faithful," he whispered.

Her head lying weakly on his shoulder, Kaaren heard the tenderness in his voice as he pressed his lips to her ear. She knew Carl was trying to be strong for her sake.

Kaaren wanted to believe him with all her being, but her heart raced like waves before a wind, and her knees trembled until she was sure they would buckle beneath her. *Father God, if you bring us past this barrier and into the new land, I will honor you all my days; I will dedicate one of my sons to serve in your house; I will . . .*

She looked up and saw the doctor coming toward them.

My Lord and my God, I...

The aproned woman accompanying the official bounced in her effort to match the man's long strides. While her face kept the prescribed sober demeanor, the wink of one blue eye said it all.

Kaaren trapped the rising sob in her throat. *Could it be? Could it really be?*

"I've discussed your case with my colleagues, and we agree that your wife's weakness is due solely to childbirth and a difficult passage. Since she does not seem to be running a fever, we will overlook her illness." He directed his remarks to Carl. "I recommend, however, that you allow her time to rest before you begin your journey west. Mrs. Amundson, here, will give you details regarding places to stay."

At Carl's nod, the man stepped back to let them pass and raised a hand to beckon the couple behind them. "Next!" he called.

Kaaren released the breath she'd been holding. She gripped

Ingeborg's hand with all her strength to keep the sobs locked within her breast. "We are here. God be thanked. We are here. God be thanked." She repeated the words over and over, first in her mind and then in a whisper. When Carl and Ingeborg had settled Kaaren on one of their bundles, she reached for the infant Ingeborg held snugly against her bosom.

"Mange takk." When Kaaren folded back the quilt to see her sleeping daughter's face, she could hold back the sobs no longer. She buried her face in Gunhilde's coverings to stem her wild weeping.

Ingeborg stood beside her sister-in-law, clasping the woman against her waist with both hands. Kaaren transferred her wet face from the blanket to Ingeborg's skirts. While tears of joy poured down her cheeks as well, Ingeborg kept her back ramrod straight. *One more hurdle surmounted*, she thought to herself. "It's all right now, kjaere, you needn't worry anymore."

Ingeborg reached for Thorliff, who was tearing up also. He too buried his face in her black wool skirt and mingled his tears with those of his aunt.

"If you two keep on like this, soon I will be too soaked to walk out in public. I will have to go change my skirt," Ingeborg said, drying her own tears.

Kaaren looked up, a smile fluttering at the corners of her mouth. She sniffed and swallowed before sniffing again. "We are a sorry group, are we not?"

"Ja, but these are tears of joy, healing tears, as Tante Gunhilde would say." Ingeborg referred to a dear old aunt of Carl and Roald's who had adopted and counseled her entire village. *Ach, I will miss her wisdom so. Hers and Mor's—together they tried to make me the kind of woman I should be.*

Ingeborg refused to let herself think of home, even for a moment. If she did, her tears would quickly turn to those of sorrow and mourning. It was joy they needed now.

She turned to see Carl and Roald standing behind them with matching looks of consternation on their faces. They'd retrieved all the bundles and chests, and now the mound around them looked more like a mountain.

"Come, we are blocking traffic." Roald shook his head, the expression on his face revealing his impatience.

Ingeborg knew that look. It always made her feel as though he thought she had no more sense than a goose. Truly, he just didn't understand.

"Mrs. Amundson gave me a map showing where to find an inexpensive rooming house. While she said it is not far, I'm afraid we must rent a cart to transport all our belongings. We have been fortunate so far that nothing has been stolen."

"I will go on ahead with Kaaren and the baby so we do not waste our money on carts and wagons. That is what God gave us strong backs for—to carry things." Carl looked up at his older brother. *You will not blame me and mine for spending our precious gold. We all agreed to carry our share of the burden.* "Now that we are here, I know Kaaren will get better quickly. One day and two nights of rest is all I ask."

Carl watched as Roald locked his arms across his chest and dipped his chin so that his blue gaze beamed piercingly from under his hat brim. The silence stretched.

We are partners, and I will act so. Carl straightened his shoulders. All his life he'd deferred to the wisdom of his older brothers. But now he had a family of his own, and they were *his* responsibility. "Agreed?" Carl thrust forward his right hand.

With only a momentary hesitation, Roald took it. "Ja, we are agreed."

Carl did not miss the slight hesitancy on his brother's part but chose to ignore it. Proving his manhood was no new thing. He'd been the younger brother all his life, with two elder ones to keep him in his place. But here in Amerika, things would be different. He and Roald would work as equals, starting now.

"Come, kjaere," he said for Kaaren's ears alone. "Can you hold the babe, while I carry you? We will find you a good bed and another jug of cow's milk to rebuild your strength. Mayhap there will even be fresh eggs to go with the bit of flour and sugar we have left."

Kaaren shifted Gunhilde in her arms. "Ja, we will be fine. I could walk some, though, I think."

"No, you must save your strength. Soon there will be roses in your cheeks, and I will hear you laugh again." He scooped one arm beneath her knees and locked the other behind her shoulders. "See, you are so light I could carry you with one arm."

"There is no sense in my waiting here. I will come with you to carry one of the trunks." Roald shifted one of the bags off the smaller of the trunks. "Ingeborg, you will remain—you and Thorliff." The big man swung the trunk up to his shoulder and, once it was balanced, grabbed two valises in his other hand.

"I want to go, too," Thorliff pleaded, his bottom lip quivering.

"Nei, you stay right here, and no more chasing after ruffian boys. Did you not learn your lesson?" Roald's thick eyebrows nearly met between his eyes.

"Ja." The little boy twisted his coat button. A single tear slipped down his cheek.

"We will be back soon." Carl sent the child a private smile. "Then you can help us carry our belongings to the boardinghouse."

Thorliff brightened at the promise. "You hurry, then."

"Ja, sure. We will hurry." Settling Kaaren more comfortably in his arms, Carl strode off after his brother, who was already a few strides ahead of them. They exited the sandstone block building by a small door in the side. Once out on the Battery walk again, the two men headed up Broadway, dodging milling immigrants, hawking peddlers, and seamen free on leave.

If Carl had his way, he'd have stopped in a doorway just to watch the seething crowd and try to decipher the cacophony of all the languages. Instead, he had to watch where he stepped and try to keep Kaaren and the baby from being bumped into. He glanced down at her, pleased to find her cheeks brightening with the chill wind, and her eyes showing interest in her new surroundings for the first time in days.

The baby started to fuss, her mewling whimper threatening to turn into a full-throated cry. How could one so tiny make such a large noise?

"I'm afraid she is hungry again," Kaaren said apologetically.

"She is always hungry." Carl could feel his arms growing weak already, and they had only gone three blocks. How far had that map said?

"I'm sorry," Kaaren whispered.

"You needn't be sorry." Carl tried shifting her weight so he could breathe more easily. "Babies are supposed to be hungry. Now if we can get you eating like she does, you'll be back on your feet in no time." His straining breaths punctuated each word.

Roald strode on ahead of them, seemingly unaware of his brother's discomfort.

Carl sagged against a brick wall, letting the rough surface hold him while he caught his breath. *Roald, can't you have the decency to wait—or at least look back to see if we are still following?*

"Let me sit on those steps for a bit." Kaaren nodded to the entry of the building.

"No, just give me a moment." Carl grinned at her around his

efforts to inhale. "Now, if I could just sling you over my shoulder like a sack of wheat, I could carry you for half a day with only a tiny backache."

"I am . . ."

"Nei, don't say that anymore. I've heard enough sorrys to last a lifetime." He hefted her higher in his arms and started off after Roald. "If we don't catch up to that brother of mine, we'll both be sorry, for I don't know the way."

Right then the baby let out a wail, drawing the attention of several people walking by. Carl shrugged when he caught their inquisitive gazes and walked on. Where in heaven's name had Roald gone? Why couldn't he have the heart and sense to wait for them? Carl stopped at the corner and looked both ways. There, off to the left, he could see the top of his brother's black hat, bobbing above the bustling crowd. *Thank God we're so tall*, he thought. *Otherwise I'd just have to wait for him to realize we were left behind.*

✕⊛ ⊛✕

When both families and all their goods had been transported to the boardinghouse, they ate a simple meal of bread, milk, and a bit of cheese before collapsing onto their beds.

Kaaren and the baby had fallen asleep long before Carl was able to shut off his thoughts and let his body succumb to the comfort of a real bed with a straw-filled pallet. He rolled to his side and wrapped one arm around the waist of his sleeping wife. They were in Amerika and soon would be on their way west. *God be praised!* How strange it felt to be on solid ground again after twelve days on a pitching sea. Were it not for the months spent on his uncle's fishing boat, he might well have suffered as miserably as Kaaren did. On the first fishing trip, it had taken several weeks for him to gain his sea legs. What good would sea legs do him in this new land, he wondered. Better that he be grateful for a strong back to plow all the acres he would soon claim as his homestead.

He fell asleep with another *Thank God, God be praised* pacing the hallways of his mind.

In the other bed, Ingeborg let her thoughts roam back over the events of the day. If someone had told her she would go through such a harrowing time as she had, she would have thought them ready to be locked in shackles. She turned her head upon the pallet. And the losing of Thorliff—God be thanked, they had found him.

"Oh." She stifled the sound, fearful of waking her sleeping husband.

"What is it?" Roald lifted his head, speaking in a bare whisper.

Ingeborg bit her lip. He hadn't been asleep, after all. How could she tell him what was wrong?

He shifted on his side and rolled over to face her. "Are you in pain?"

"Nei, I mean, not really. I have a problem is all." She could feel the strength of his gaze upon her face. Even in the dark, she could feel the heat of it.

"Ja, don't we all?"

Ingeborg breathed in deeply and let it out, being careful not to sigh. Sighing wasn't done; it might show weakness. And heaven forbid that anyone in this man's family should show weakness. She cut off her troubling thoughts, the weight of his attention feeling heavier than a millstone.

"When Thorliff took that apple . . ."

"I thought you said the boys gave it to him."

"Ja, well, they did. But since they stole it from the grocer, I felt it was my duty. . ." She paused to summon the courage up from wherever it was hiding. "I . . . I promised to pay for the apple."

"And how were you going to do that?" The breath of his whisper tickled her nose.

"To be precise, I promised you would pay the man." There, it was out.

"Is that all? He probably didn't even understand a word of what you said. Forget about it. Those things happen to fruit sellers all the time. They are used to it." He turned over with a snort of disgust.

"But . . . but I . . ."

"Forget it! Good night!"

How could just a whisper convey such command? Ingeborg wished she would have a good night too. But how? All her life she'd been taught that once she gave her word, she must live up to it. *God in heaven, what am I to do? I said I would pay—no, I said my husband would pay, and he refuses. I gave my word. Mor said, "Listen to your husband." But he is wrong. And it is my word.* She could hear the slight snore that told her Roald was finally asleep. Here she was, wide awake with a body aching to sleep, and all she could think of was the apple. *Oh, Thorliff, what trouble you have caused.*

The baby whimpered. Within moments she heard a rustling, and then the sound of the infant nursing. Quiet, homey sounds. If only she could forget the apple. Just before falling asleep, she knew what she would have to do.

In the morning, Carl crept out of the bed, left his sleeping wife and daughter, and followed Roald down the stairs. The sun had not even cracked the horizon when they stepped outside onto the front stairs and discovered a world blanketed in white. Gone were the filthy streets and cluttered sidewalks. Even the streetlamps wore white caps.

"Well, I'll be a . . ." Roald looked up the street and saw a milk wagon stopped at the curb. Even from where they stood, the two men could see the clouds of steam billowing around the horse's nostrils.

"You thought it didn't snow in New York?" Carl rubbed his hands together.

"Nei, just that yesterday was more like spring, and today we are back in winter."

"Most of this will disappear with the sun." Carl stepped down to the sidewalk. "I'm for getting another jug of milk, and mayhap he carries eggs also. I don't want Kaaren going out today; she needs to rest."

"You are right." Roald looked at his brother, as if trying to discern the change in him. "I saw a bakery down that way. They should be open soon. Fresh bread will bring back a failing appetite."

"She *is* trying."

"I know that. Now let's just see if we can find the kind of food we all need after that slop they served aboard ship. Those last days were enough to make anyone leave off eating." Roald shoved his hands in his pockets. "I'll be back soon. After we eat, we'll look for the office Mrs. Amundson told us about, where we can apply for citizenship. No use waiting until we reach Dakota Territory." He nodded to his brother and started up the street, long strides eating up the distance.

Carl stuck his hands in his pockets, setting the coins to jingling. He was thankful to God that Mrs. Amundson had shown them an honest place to exchange their Norwegian currency for Amerikan. They'd heard terrible stories of immigrants being bilked out of their hard-earned cash by dishonest money changers, only hours after stepping off their ship.

"Not much different than in the Scriptures," he muttered, thinking about the exchange. "The money changers seem to always be out to rob the innocent." But at least he had the coins to pay for the milk, even though he had no idea how he would know the man's price and which coins to use. "God dag." He greeted the milkman after he stepped from his wagon.

"Aye." The man tipped his head in acknowledgment.

"I would like to buy milk."

The man shook his head. "You'll have to speak English if you want me to understand you."

Carl smiled and shrugged. He pointed to the bottles of milk, the cream golden at the top of the glass necks. He held up two fingers.

The man nodded and named the price.

Carl dug the change from his pocket and held it out on the palm of his hand.

The milkman smiled, showing one missing front tooth. The twinkle in his dark eyes showed he understood. He took some change out of his own pocket and held up two copper coins. "You need two like this."

Carl nodded and handed over the matching coins. *Now, how do I ask for eggs?* He scratched his beard in thought. "You have eggs?"

The man shook his head and shrugged. Then he motioned Carl to join him at the rear of the covered wagon. When he showed his wares, Carl pointed to the eggs filling a wooden basket. He raised six fingers.

The milkman smiled again and counted out the number requested. As before, he showed Carl the proper amount of money needed.

"Mange takk," Carl said with an answering smile, sensing the man's honesty. He carefully placed the eggs deep in the pockets of his black wool coat and crooked his left arm around the milk jugs. He stepped back to let the man make his delivery to the next house, watching as the milkman set three full bottles on the stoop and retrieved the empty ones. The clink of glass on glass sang its own song as the wagon continued down the street, stopping here and there.

Carl shook his head. Did they deliver milk like this in Oslo? He shrugged. For certain, everyone who lived in cities couldn't have their own milk cows as they'd had on the farm. Ja, they had much to learn about life in Amerika. He strode back to the entrance of the boardinghouse, impatient to eat and then explore this New York

City. If only Kaaren were strong enough to be up and about to enjoy the sights and sounds with him.

Both women were up and dressed, and Ingeborg was braiding Kaaren's long hair when Carl walked in the door of the third-floor room. He looked around and noticed the room had been tidied as much as possible with their belongings taking up so much of the space.

"Onkel Carl!" Thorliff threw his arms around his uncle's knees. "You went away."

"But not for long, and look what I brought." Carl dug in his pocket and held up two brown eggs. "I'm going downstairs to ask madame house owner, Mrs. Flaksrude, she said her name was, if she will let me boil them. Then we'll each have one now, and Tante Kaaren will eat another later."

"Oh, how delicious. Just think, to eat fresh eggs again." Kaaren smiled up at her husband.

Thorliff let loose of his uncle's knees and reached up to pat the other pocket.

"Careful. It wouldn't do to break these precious things. Come, you can help me get them cooked." Carl removed his hat and, with great care, placed each egg in it. With hat in one hand and Thorliff's hand clenched in the other, he left the room, childish chatter floating back from their departure.

"Something is bothering you," Kaaren said to Ingeborg as she lifted a hand to smooth back a wisp of hair that refused to remain in the coronet of braids.

"Nei, it is nothing." Ingeborg placed the hairbrush and comb on the washstand by the sturdy white pitcher in which she'd fetched warm water for their morning washing. Her hands refused to remain still. Instead, she placed the pitcher in the matching bowl and then set the bowl exactly centered on the oak stand.

"Is everything to your satisfaction?"

Ingeborg could hear the teasing in her sister-in-law's voice. She clamped her hands together to stop their telltale busyness, moving to look out the window instead of facing Kaaren. "Did you see the snow? There's a man setting up a stand of some kind across the street."

"Ingeborg, what is it?" Kaaren persisted.

Ingeborg hesitated only for a moment, and then the words came out in a rush. "I promised to pay the grocer for the apple Thorliff was given, but I have no money, and Roald insists it is nothing. He refuses to go back and pay, and I gave my word." She sighed and turned her back to the window. "What to do?" She felt the weight of the worry sitting right on her shoulders. How could one red apple cause so much trouble?

"I have some money. I will give you what you need," Kaaren offered.

"You do?"

"My mor believes a woman should have something of her own for times of emergency. She made sure that when Carl and I married, I had a bit also."

"But that is yours. I cannot take it."

"Ours. With all that you have done for me, I now can give something in return." Kaaren started to rise from the chair, but Ingeborg waved her back. "I know, save my strength. There, in the bottom of that black leather valise is a drawstring purse. Carl changed the money for me at the Castle Garden."

"He knows you have it?"

Kaaren nodded. "But he won't mind in the least. In fact, we can ask him to go pay it."

Ingeborg shook her head. "No, he and Roald have much to do today. I will not bother him." She pulled the jingling bag from the valise and poured the coins into her palm. "Surely it can be no more than two or three of these copper coins." She slipped them into her own pouch and, after pulling the strings closed, buried the small bag back in Kaaren's valise. "Mange takk. I can't tell you how much. I will return these as soon as I am able."

"Don't be silly. Maybe we'll find that street paved with gold and fill the poor bag right up." Kaaren crossed her ankles and clasped her hands in her lap. "Oh, the luxury of being on land again. I don't think I'll ever even want to go out in a rowboat on a lake." She paused and stared at Ingeborg. "How will you return to pay the grocer?"

When Ingeborg refused to look at her, Kaaren swung her feet to the floor. "You cannot think to be going yourself!" The sound of her fear set the babe to whimpering.

"See now, you must not get all upset. We will talk about that later." At the conversation, the baby screwed up her face and let out a wail that nearly covered the sound of the door opening.

"It appears to me someone around here feels plenty better," Roald said while handing two crusty loaves of still-warm bread to Ingeborg. "I see Carl was able to buy some milk."

"And eggs." Kaaren's soft sigh floated like a prayer.

"Carl and Thorliff went downstairs to see if Mrs. Flaksrude would let him cook them in the kitchen." Ingeborg lifted one of the loaves to her face and inhaled the aroma. "They'd best hurry back or I shall eat all of this myself." The temptation to break off just a bit of one end made her fingers twitch. The fragrance tasted of heaven. Soon she would be baking her own bread again, in her own house, on their own land.

She glanced up to see Roald watching her with his eyebrows nearly meeting in a straight·line, a line that always spelled a scolding. What had she done wrong now?

"That is for everyone and should last until supper tonight." Roald removed his coat and hung it on one of the nails by the door.

Ingeborg caught her reply before it passed her lips and nodded instead. "Of course." Didn't he understand she was teasing? When would she learn that her husband, fine man that he was, didn't make jokes? And didn't seem to appreciate it when others did.

She glanced at Kaaren and saw her grin before she ducked her head in the baby's blanket. At least *someone* else could see some humor in their situation.

"Far, Far, we cooked the eggs." Thorliff burst through the door and flung himself at his father's pant legs. "Onkel Carl said we each get one. A whole egg!" He stared up at his father, his round little face beaming in delight. "No more of that nasty porridge, like on the ship."

"Now, you must be grateful for all our food." Roald disentangled his leg. "God is good to give us what we need."

"Ja, I will." Thorliff let loose and, bowing his head, sneaked his thumb into his mouth.

"Only babies suck their thumb," Roald thundered like the voice of God himself.

Thorliff whipped the thumb behind him and buried his chin in his sweater.

"I brought something else." Carl drew his hand from behind his back, a hand that held a steaming pitcher.

"Coffee. I thought I smelled it but didn't trust my nose." Kaaren held out her hands. "Here, let me pour."

Ingeborg rummaged in one of the satchels and withdrew the cups they'd used on the ship. Eggs, bread, coffee, and milk with real cream—a veritable feast. Thanking God for their food was certainly easier today than it had been on board the ship.

As soon as their feast was set before them, Roald bowed his head and offered grace. His mumbled "I Jesu navn går vi til bords . . ." stampeded to a close. They fell to as if they hadn't eaten for days.

Ingeborg looked up at Roald from under her eyelashes. Dare she ask him again if he would pay the grocer? He seemed in a good mood at the moment. She wiped her mouth on her handkerchief and tried to find either the words or the air to speak. Neither came to mind or being.

She felt akin to a child lost in the fog and hoped it wasn't a portend of things to come. Ingeborg squared her shoulders. She would find a way. She would keep her word and pay the man. *Please, God, don't let Roald come back before I do*. For if he asked her, she could not lie to her husband, no matter how angry he might become. She shuddered at the memory of the glaring look on his face when he thought she'd lost Thorliff.

But he hadn't said *she* couldn't go. He had just said he wouldn't. The thought consoled her as she nibbled at her last crust of bread. Strange how it didn't taste quite as good now.

When the men left, promising to be back as soon as possible, she cleaned up their crumbs and rinsed out the cups. Then settling Thorliff next to Kaaren for a story, Ingeborg donned her black wool coat, tucked a blue muffler around her neck and, bending over to see in the mirror, pinned her bit of a hat on top of her head. She tucked her braids into a bun at the base of her skull so her hat wouldn't look like a sail in full wind. All the time she bustled around, she could feel Kaaren's gaze penetrating her back.

"Just don't say anything." Ingeborg nodded toward Thorliff, who had watched all the goings-on with curious eyes.

"Can I go?" Thorliff asked the question as if he already knew the answer to be no.

"Not right now, den lille. Maybe later. Tante Kaaren will tell you about the boy who got thrown down the well for teasing his brothers."

"Will you?" Thorliff snuggled closer to his aunt's side.

"Ja, I will."

Kaaren's eyes were so full of concern that, for just a moment, Ingeborg wavered. But only momentarily. She checked her pockets for her mittens and then opened the door before she lost her courage.

"You do as Tante Kaaren says, now," she instructed Thorliff. Ingeborg straightened her back and walked out the door as if she were on the way to a firing squad and square shoulders might earn her a reprieve.

When she stepped down onto the snowy sidewalk, she turned left and began retracing her steps from the day before. If only she had paid more attention to all the turns they had made. But surely, finding the Castle Garden again wouldn't be difficult. She looked up at a word on the signpost at the corner. If only she could read it. Glancing back up the block to the boardinghouse, she imprinted the scene in her mind. All she had to do was find Castle Garden, walk to the grocer, pay him, and return to this street. That was all.

An hour later, with no Castle Garden in sight, she wondered if Roald had not been right. Was paying the grocer really that important?

4

urely they couldn't have moved the place overnight. Ingeborg wound the strings of her reticule tightly around her fingers. Where had she gone wrong? She glanced up at the tall building on her left. Had she seen it before? Was it today—or yesterday? How could she, who had never in her entire life gotten lost in the mountains or forests of home, be so confused in this maze of dirty buildings and even filthier streets?

She could feel her nostrils twitch at the foul stench that rose from the open sewer running by the curb. While the snow had temporarily whitened the world this morning, now the streets were full of passing carts and carriages that splashed mud all over everything, including her skirts.

She thought back to one of the Bjorklund family's heated discussions on the new land. Some had said the streets were paved with gold. If New York, the largest city in Amerika, was any indication, the only gold to be found lay in the dreams of the immigrants.

She looked up and down each street of the intersection, praying for a glimpse of the immigration center. Castle Garden was far too large an edifice to hide behind anything. It had to be here somewhere.

Where was she? Nothing looked familiar to the streets they had passed yesterday.

A shiver of fear added to the chill from the wind that had been kicking up ever since the sun disappeared behind scudding gray clouds. If the weather here acted like that at home, more snow was imminent. If she couldn't find the center, how would she ever find her way back to the boardinghouse?

Another shiver chased the first. Fear made her mouth dry.

She paused an instant too long on the curb. A tall man, looking even taller with his beaver hat, jostled her on the right.

Caught just as she was stepping out with her right foot, the bump made Ingeborg stagger. Coming down hard, a patch of ice under the snow sent her sliding into a portly gentleman on her other side, and straight toward becoming an ignominious heap on the cobblestones.

But as quickly as she slipped, the first gentleman spun around and grabbed her arm, literally lifting her back to her feet and safe onto the sidewalk. It all happened so quickly that Ingeborg only had time for a tiny shriek. But in that instant, her imagination had her huddled in a puddle on the streets of New York City.

"Mange takk," she whispered at the same moment he asked her a question. At least it must have been a question because of both the inflection and the questioning look on his handsome face.

"I asked if you are all right?"

Ingeborg looked up at him, certain the shock of hearing her own language on the lips of a fashionably dressed gentleman on the sidewalk of New York must be registered on her face.

"You speak Norwegian?"

"Yes. Since birth." The smile that lifted the corners of his mouth lacked the stiffness of those passersby she'd noticed in her travels of the morning. "But I must know, did you injure yourself in the slip?" he persisted.

Ingeborg shook her head, making her hat bounce alarmingly. As the black brim tipped slightly forward over one eyebrow, she wished for a pit of quicksand beneath her feet, rather than the icy, rounded cobblestones.

"But you talk like an Amerikan." Ingeborg ignored the voice of her mother echoing in her ears, the voice that warned her against speaking with a man to whom she'd never been formally introduced.

With a gentle hand on her arm, the tall stranger drew her back out of the melee of rushing pedestrians and against the protection of a brick wall. "I am an American, but my nursemaid was a fine Norwegian girl, straight from the old country. By the time I could talk, I spoke either language easily."

As he talked, Ingeborg tried to unobtrusively push her wayward hat back in place. The stubborn thing tipped even farther, and the feather, of which she'd been so proud, now tickled the end of her nose. She batted it away with one impatient finger, all the while trying to stifle a sneeze. Failing in that effort, she sneezed hard enough to splatter his lapels. Instant mortification stained her cheeks. She could feel the heat as if she'd just stuck her head over a bubbling wash boiler.

"Bless you." He whipped a white handkerchief from his breast pocket and handed it to her.

"Mange takk." Was that all she could say? Between her hat, her now throbbing ankle, and his handkerchief, the earth opening up and swallowing her could happen none too soon.

"Mange takk, again. And for your kind assistance." She started to hand him back the used handkerchief, but better sense prevailed. How could she possibly return a dirty handkerchief? Where were her manners? If only she could run down the street and hide in a doorway. But if she started to run, where would she stop? And how would she ever get back to the boardinghouse? Visions of Roald roaring through the streets looking for her made her chin start to quiver.

She smiled bravely up at her savior and thanked him once again. Then turning on her right foot, she tried to make a graceful exit. And failed. Or at least her foot did. Walking was extremely difficult, if not impossible, for a sharp pain sliced clear to her knee. She bit back the groan but failed to hide the flinch.

"You are hurt." Instantly he appeared at her side again.

"It is nothing. I am fine."

"It is more than nothing, and it is my fault. I bumped into you." He tucked her arm in his. "Now, you must tell me where you are going, and I will take you there." As he spoke he waved at a passing hansom cab.

"Nei, nei, you mustn't." Ingeborg tried to draw back but, as in everything else so far this day, failed miserably. Before she could protest any further, he had lifted her into the still swaying cab and stepped in after her.

"Now, where do you need to go?"

Ingeborg knew an angel when she met one. She just didn't expect to see one wearing a rich gray topcoat and a black beaver hat. She gave a sigh of surrender and told him all that had happened since their arrival.

". . . and so I came out to pay the grocer and lost my way." She clasped her hands in her lap and raised her gaze to meet his. The genuine concern in his warm brown eyes made a lump form in her throat.

"Would you recognize the place if you saw it again?"

She nodded. "I feel sure I would."

"Good. Then we will return to Castle Garden and proceed from there." He leaned forward and gave what Ingeborg assumed to be instructions to the driver. Not understanding the language was proving to be a greater barrier than she had ever dreamed it would be. As the driver clucked to the large black horse, she made herself a promise. She would learn the language sooner rather than later. All the reports they had received in Norway had said that immigrants could live in this new land without taking time to learn to speak Amerikan. But Ingeborg now knew differently. All that had happened since they stepped off the boat had proved that. She would learn Amerikan, and she would learn it well.

As the horse trotted down the street, she leaned back against the leather seat. She could hear Roald, like her mother, saying she must get out immediately. Who knew where this stranger was taking her? After all the admonitions she'd heard about immigrants being robbed and suffering other unthinkable things, here she was riding the streets of a bustling city in the company of a man whose name she did not even know.

What does one do? The thought nagged at her sense of propriety. In all her life, she'd never done such an outrageous thing as this. What would Roald say?

He's not going to know. The thought flitted through her mind and lodged securely in a corner as though made for that place. *And what he doesn't know won't hurt him.* She raised her chin and straightened her spine. *So I will enjoy every moment, for such a time shall never come again.* She watched out the window as the round stone fort filled her vision. She could go inside and find Mrs. Amundson. Surely she would be able to help. She would remember where the grocer's fruit stand was located.

But something inside Ingeborg rebelled at the thought. Would she forever be needing others to help her accomplish the slightest thing? *That* wasn't why she had braved a turbulent sea and homesickness to come to the new land.

"Let me see, I'm sure it must be up that way." She pointed to a street angling off from the one on which they approached the Battery. Her escort gave the driver instructions, and off they went. *What is this man's name? Who is he?* Would it be too forward to ask?

She gave a tiny shake of her head, sending the hat into its final dislodgement. The contrary thing slid forward and completely covered one eye. She sneaked a peek at the man sitting across from her, hoping against hope that he was looking out the window rather than seeing her discomfort.

He averted his eyes politely, but the smile that tugged at the corner of his shapely mouth didn't hide quickly enough.

Ingeborg could imagine what she looked like. A bedraggled kitten wouldn't be too far off, she knew. She tried to ignore the hat, the close confines of the cab, and the handsome man close enough to touch with her knee. She tried, really she did. But it was too much. A giggle stole past her iron will.

One look at her escort and they were both laughing like children let loose at recess. When the hat gave up entirely, she raised her arms and unpinned the silly thing.

"There now," she said, laying the black hat in her lap. "Now it can fall no farther."

"You'd best hang on to it tightly; it seems to have a mind of its own."

"Rest assured, I will." Ingeborg leaned forward and pointed out the window. "There it is, the grocer's. We found it." She pulled open the strings of her bag and dug inside for the coins Kaaren had given her. Removing the two copper pennies, she held them out. "This will be enough, don't you think?"

"For one small apple, I am sure." He ordered the driver to stop in front of the apple cart that took up the same space on the corner as it had the day before. When Ingeborg started to rise, he stopped her with a shake of his head. "I will do this for you."

"Mange takk." But when he started to step down without her money, Ingeborg pressed the coins upon him.

He rolled his eyes upward as if looking for consolation and took one of the coins from her hand, obviously against his will.

Ingeborg watched as he spoke with the grocer and, with a nod, indicated her sitting in the cab. When the aproned tradesman started gesticulating and raising his voice, her angel pressed the coin into the man's hand, spoke in a sharp tone, and spun on his heel. The straight line of his mouth told Ingeborg something the grocer said had irritated him.

"What did the man say?" she asked when he swung himself back in the cab.

"He demanded I also pay for the apples the ruffians stole."

Ingeborg waited until he settled himself in the seat and repositioned his beaver hat, knocked slightly askew by the doorway.

"And what did you answer him?" Guilt for involving someone

else in a brew of her own making made Ingeborg twist her fingers together.

"I told him to move the cart back to where he could keep better track of his produce and quit trying to take advantage of immigrants like yourself. For all I know, he and those two hoodlums are in cahoots."

"Oh." All of a sudden the enormity of her situation rolled over Ingeborg like a thick fog coming in from the sea. Whatever had possessed her to think she could just waltz right out of the boarding-house, find her way back to the Battery, find the grocer, and then return to the only place that right now seemed like a haven of comfort?

"Hutte meg tu," she muttered as she pinned her hat back in place. The simple words could be used as a sigh of disgust or an expletive of the proper manner, whichever one chose. Ingeborg could think of stronger words to call herself but stopped in time. *Oh my, what a dolt I must seem.*

"My mother has a favorite saying, 'All's well that ends well.' I think we can apply that bit of wisdom here. Now, can you tell me the address or at least the name of the place where you are staying?"

Ingeborg nodded, pleased that she at least had the wits to do that before venturing out. "I wrote it down." She dug the bit of paper out of her bag and handed it to him. "How can I ever thank you enough for all that you have done?" She raised her eyes filled with gratitude to meet his.

"You will do a kind deed sometime for someone in your life, then they will do so also, and thus the circle continues. Now, let me show you some other sights of my fair city as we return to your starting place."

"Mange takk . . ." Ingeborg paused. "But . . . I don't even know your name."

"Nor I yours. I cannot keep on thinking of you as my 'Norwegian in distress.' " The twinkle in his eyes invited her to enjoy every moment. "My name is David Jonathan Gould, and please don't believe everything you'll hear about my family. We were immigrants once, too, and now my father is encouraging people like you to come help settle the West so we can push our railroads out there." He leaned forward. "And now, I know what a fine sense of honor you have, but I do not know your name either."

"Ingeborg Moe Bjorklund. My husband's name is Roald, and we are journeying to Dakota Territory to homestead there with his brother and wife." Ingeborg could feel questions welling up like an artesian spring, but she quickly put a cap on them.

David tipped his beaver hat. "I am pleased to make your acquaintance, Mrs. Bjorklund."

His smile made her want to say something witty and wonderful to keep that glorious smile in place, but, as usual, words deserted her. When he turned serious, she felt as though a gray cloud had blocked the sun.

"If you ever need something, you can write me here." David reached into the pocket of his topcoat and pulled out a small white card with black embossed letters, which he offered to her. "No matter where I am, your letter will find me."

Ingeborg bit the inside of her cheek and swallowed quickly. What could she say to such a kind offer? Fearing the inanity of words, she just nodded and took the card, placing it carefully in a pocket in her reticule. Whatever made her accept it? She blinked quickly and pointed to some tall posts that held up a metal framework.

"What is that?" She felt relieved that the quiver vibrating in her throat stayed put.

"The el, or elevated train. One of our modern wonders. By elevating this type of transportation, the streets are then free for all other types of conveyance, including that streetcar over there." He pointed to a long, horse-drawn car filled with riders, many of them reading newspapers. "New York is known for its modern methods of transportation."

"Well, I never . . ."

As they continued, David pointed out the copper-domed courthouse and various mansions that made Ingeborg wonder at the wealth that allowed people to live in palaces such as these. Had the people here indeed found the streets that were paved in gold, and then harvested it all? He also showed her Columbia College and St. Paul's Cathedral. Even Ingeborg, with her totally confused sense of direction, realized they had not returned by the shortest route.

By the time they arrived in front of the boardinghouse, she knew a seed of a different kind had been planted in her fertile mind. While farming was to be their livelihood, Ingeborg was beginning to realize there was more to Amerika than crops and cows.

She looked out the window of the cab and felt her heart drop. Two tall, very familiar men were approaching from the opposite direction. Whatever made her think she could get away with something this momentous without Roald discovering her duplicity?

5

Ingeborg recognized storm warnings when she saw them. Apparently David Jonathan Gould did too, for she could see his assessing look as Roald and Carl approached.

"Do you know that man?" he asked. "Your husband?"

Ingeborg nodded. While Roald had a hard time smiling, the anger on his face and in his stride was visible for all the world to see. *Why, Lord, couldn't you have timed this better?* She felt like crawling under the carriage seat, but experience had taught her the ineffectiveness of trying to hide. Like a good soldier, she understood the value of a strong offense.

"Roald, you have arrived just in time to thank Mr. Gould for assisting me." She extended her hand for her husband to help her down from the cab. When he ignored it, she smiled at Carl, who, tongue securely nestled in the curve of his cheek, took her hand as if he'd been assisting ladies from carriages all his life.

With her feet planted firmly on the sidewalk, Ingeborg ignored her husband's glower and turned to smile her farewell to the man who'd become her guardian angel. "Mange takk. Go with God."

"Velbekomme." Gould tipped his beaver hat and turned to speak to Roald. "Mr. Bjorklund, may I wish you and your family success in your homesteading endeavors. My father is a partner in several of the railroad ventures in the West. If you are ever in need of employment, please feel free to contact me." He handed Roald an embossed card, tipped his hat again, and motioned for the cabby to drive off.

Roald looked from the card in his hand to the departing cab and back again. He took one step forward as if to follow, checked the card one more time, and, apparently making a decision, placed it carefully in an inner pocket of his wool coat.

But when he turned to Ingeborg, all traces of confusion had vanished. The thunder on his brow matched the lightning in his eyes. "So . . .",

But before he could continue, Ingeborg, too, made a decision. She held up a mittened hand. "I kept my word, as I always will. I paid the grocer." She spun on her heel and marched up the three steps, back straight and strong as an iron bar.

Roald started after her. "You will . . ."

She stopped in the act of opening the door. When she turned, her air of calm authority stopped him midword. "You are correct. We will not discuss this any further."

The look on his face made her want to beat a hasty retreat, but instead, she mustered every ounce of courage she possessed and, nodding to both of the brothers, stepped through the door and headed for the stairs, stubbornly ignoring the pain in her foot. Feeling his eyes drilling into her back, she took each step with perfect posture, as if she carried a gallon jar atop her head. However, the tension felt more like ten gallons.

All the way to their room she could feel the thrust of his unuttered words like arrows thudding against her armored back.

"Mor." Thorliff catapulted into her skirts as soon as she opened the door.

"How did it. . . ?" Kaaren stopped as soon as she saw Roald directly behind his wife. "Mrs. Flaksrude said there would be hot coffee ready whenever you returned." She reached her hand out to Carl. "Before you ask, yes, I am feeling much better. The good food and rest have given me some strength back. Thorliff has been making me laugh, and that always helps."

"I'm glad, for we have our tickets to leave tomorrow. We will take a ferry across the river to Jersey City and board the train there."

"More walking?"

"No, we have a wagon coming at dawn."

"Far, I . . ." The small boy broke off his words after a look at his father's face.

Ingeborg looked up in time to see Carl wink at his wife and to catch the smile he gave her as he followed Roald out the door to get their coffee.

The steel rod of resolve that had been keeping Ingeborg upright melted in relief as soon as the men were gone. She collapsed in a boneless bundle on the bed.

"Did you find the man?" Kaaren whispered.

Ingeborg nodded and tugged open her reticule. She handed Thorliff the remaining copper coin. "Here, take this to your tante Kaaren. There's a good boy."

"What man?" Thorliff asked, doing as he'd been told.

"None of your business." Kaaren took the coin and looked across the room. "You don't have to give this back, you know."

"Just as well. We may need it another time. But let me tell you, I will do just as my mother did. The egg money will be mine." Visions of milk cows and laying hens flew through her mind. Roald dreamed of land and more land, but her dreams were more specific: food for her family and enough extra to sell in the nearest village. Townspeople always were in need of butter, cheese, cream, and eggs. And if their garden did well, some of that could be sold, too.

Feeling Kaaren's gaze upon her, Ingeborg drew her attention back to the room. "I will tell you of my adventures another time." Taking off her coat and mittens, she busied herself with transferring things from one satchel to another. What had happened to her? In all her life, she had never felt as though she'd stepped into another world as she had with David Jonathan Gould—and so comfortably. Where had she learned to act that way? What on earth had possessed her to allow a strange man to drive her about in a city that certainly was foreign to anything she'd ever known? And what about Roald? Would he ever forgive her?

But why do I need forgiveness? I did nothing wrong. And if Roald had lived up to his responsibilities, none of this would have happened. With that thought, and feeling totally justified, Ingeborg snapped the catch closed and dusted off her hands. Maybe the arrival in a new land had acted as a spring tonic and purged her of past behaviors. Men! Uff da!

She looked up in time to catch Kaaren's intent stare. Thorliff stood in the crook of his aunt's arm, eyes the same color as his father's, studying her as if he wasn't quite sure that she was truly his mor. Ingeborg held out her arms.

"Come to mor, den lille, and I will tell you about the train that ran on tracks high above my head."

"Like a bridge?" Thorliff darted to her side and twined his fist in her skirt as if to tether her to the ground, then leaned his head against her bosom.

"Like a bridge that goes on forever."

Roald burned his tongue on the coffee. He kept the pain to himself and, before the next sip, poured the liquid in the saucer and drank from that. The scalding coffee had nothing on the fury thundering in his head. What on earth had gotten into Ingeborg to think she could ride around in a horsecab with a total stranger? And after he had explicitly told her to stay in the boardinghouse. He knew he had made himself clear. Yet she seemed to have a mind of her own.

Her insistence during the night upon paying the grocer twinged the edge of his conscience like a sore tooth. He *could have* said he'd pay. But an apple was such a trivial item compared to all the important things they had to do before leaving New York. What was the matter with her? Couldn't she understand all the responsibility he was shouldering for all of them? On top of that, Ingeborg had deliberately disobeyed him. She'd never done such a thing before. Was this a portend of things to come?

Roald was brought suddenly out of his musings by the snapping of Carl's fingers in his face.

"Roald, Mrs. Flaksrude has asked you two times if you'd like a doughnut."

"Oh." Roald paused as he always did before answering. "Mange takk, Mrs. Flaksrude." He dipped his head in acknowledgment. "Excuse me for letting my mind wander."

"These are for your womenfolk and that charming little son of yours."

The woman's smile made him feel even more guilty as she placed a full plate in front of him. Where had his manners gone?

"And I will have a basket packed with food for your journey before you leave in the morning."

"But we cannot—" Roald started to protest.

"No, do not try to change my mind. The basket goes along with the price of your room, so say nothing about it. You will have enough on your mind without worrying about how to feed your families." She placed both hands on her ample hips. "And besides, those robbers who sell food to the immigrants at the stations charge prices that would bankrupt a rich man." She shoved the plate of doughnuts closer to the two men. "It's the least I can do for good folks like you."

"You've done so much already." Carl thanked her further by biting into the sugared treat. "Mange takk is far too small a word to say for all you've done for us."

"Ja, well, I want to help my fellow countrymen get a start here. It is not so easy as those agents led you to believe. I could tell you stories that would curl your toenails." She shook her head dolefully.

"I'm sure we've heard them all. We didn't start this venture with our heads in the clouds." Roald wiped the sugar from his fingers. "We knew long before we chose to immigrate to Amerika that there would be no streets paved with gold. The gold we are looking for is the rich black soil of Dakota Territory." Roald reached for another doughnut and thanked his hostess when she refilled their coffee cups. "That is all the gold we need."

"You mark my words, that golden dirt ain't as free as they say either." She took her coffeepot and headed back to the kitchen. "I'll pour up some hot for your womenfolk."

When Mrs. Flaksrude returned with the full coffeepot, Roald and Carl thanked her and headed back to their room bearing doughnuts and coffee for them all.

Thorliff's eyes popped out in wonder at the sight of the full plate of sugary doughnuts. "For us?" he squealed. "All that for us?"

"Ja, but not to eat up in one sitting," Roald answered in his usual stern manner, though the gleam in his eye reflected his own appreciation of Mrs. Flaksrude's generosity.

After they all enjoyed a respite of coffee and doughnuts, Ingeborg began sorting, organizing, and repacking their belongings in preparation for boarding the train tomorrow, while Kaaren and the children took a much needed rest. Roald and Carl spent the remainder of the day discussing the trip ahead of them, planning and dreaming of their arrival to their own land.

In bed that night, Roald had a difficult time getting to sleep. The dawn would bring the beginning of the next leg of their journey. In four days, five at the most, they would arrive at Glyndon, the final stop of the St. Paul, Minneapolis & Manitoba Railway. It was hard to imagine a land so large that one could spend four days on the train and still not reach the other side. This was like traveling from the southern tip of Norway to the northern.

He listened to Ingeborg breathing easily beside him. When he thought back to the events of the day, his jaw tightened. What had she been thinking of?

The next day, saying goodbye to the New York skyline from the ferry to Jersey City didn't bother Ingeborg a bit. But much to her surprise, the thought of never seeing Mr. Gould again brought a twinge of sadness. Their hurried wagon ride to the ferry dock on the Hudson River had passed with prescribed stern orders from Roald, encouraging murmurs from Carl, and fussy cries from the baby. Thorliff kept his thumb in his mouth, despite his father's command to stop that babylike behavior.

In the interest of trying to help things run smoothly, Ingeborg tried to anticipate her husband's needs, but her efforts only seemed to make him more demanding. When she took Thorliff's small hand in hers and went to stand at the rail, she could ignore Roald's black looks and muttered comments. She knew very well what was bothering him: she hadn't told him she was sorry for leaving the boardinghouse the day before.

But she wasn't sorry. Not one whit.

If Roald had done as she asked, she never would have ventured forth. She never would have met David Jonathan Gould, her guardian angel. His kindness made her feel like . . . like . . . Ingeborg couldn't come up with a word to describe her feelings. Imagine her, an immigrant only one day off the boat, riding around New York City in a horsecab. The day before, she'd been dragging bundles through the streets. Riding in a horsecab with leather seats was certainly far better.

She tried to not think about what it must have cost, but it was like trying to stop a windstorm. Imagine, having the money to hire a cab to assist someone you'd never before met and never would see again.

"Mor, Mor," Thorliff cried.

She ignored the sudden pang brought by the thought of never seeing her guardian angel again and bent down to answer Thorliff's question. She could tell by the way he tugged on her skirts that he'd been trying to get her attention for a long while. "What is it, child?"

"Look, we're almost there. Far called us." He pointed to the squared-off prow of the dingy white ferry.

Now Ingeborg did feel a stab of guilt. She should have been helping Kaaren with the baby and their valises. "Mange takk, den lille. You are good to remind your mor this way. Now let's go see what we can do to help. We have lots of things to carry."

By the time they transferred their belongings to a cart, crossed to the Pennsylvania Railroad station, and boarded, a thick silence, punctuated only by the grunts of the two men stowing their belongings, had fallen on the group. Even Thorliff, creator of a myriad of questions, had discovered that staying out of his father's way and keeping quiet made good sense.

Ingeborg kept him close to her, finding little things for him to do to ease the tension and pass the time away. She slipped him a cookie out of the well-filled basket provided by Mrs. Flaksrude and winked to let him know he should keep the treat a secret.

Kaaren had done her part by shooing other passengers away from the facing double seats. Carl had claimed them for his families when he carried the first load on the car. When they finally could all sit down, they sighed in unison.

"Thanks be to God." Kaaren shifted little Gunhilde in her arms to free one hand to clasp that of her husband.

"Ja, you have said that right." Carl leaned his head on the seat back. "Why is it that we who have so little right now seem to have so much?"

"It will seem like blessed little when we reach our homestead." Roald drew a long list from his breast pocket and studied it for the hundredth time. "The way our funds are dwindling, I don't see how we will ever buy all that we need to get started. The money slips away like grain draining out a hole in the sack." The frown deepened above his bushy eyebrows. He shook his head and traveled one finger down the paper. "We are going to need all of these things if we're going to get crops in next spring."

Ingeborg knew the list by heart, having been a part of all the family discussions around the oak table on what to bring with them and what to buy when they arrived in Amerika. But there had been no more money to be found anywhere in the family. All the relatives had donated everything they could earn, beg, or spare. The immigrants would have to make do with what they had. There was nothing new in that.

Ingeborg glanced up at the sound of angry shouting. At the far end of the car, a huge man in black pants and a once-white shirt held another by the jacket front; he lifted him clear off the wooden seat. A frightened woman beside the strung-up person appeared to be pleading for mercy. Ingeborg was beginning to realize how much she could tell about others just by watching them and listening to their tone of voice.

She placed her hands over Thorliff's ears and bent her head to rest her cheek on his curly hair. After the early morning rising and all the excitement of the streets of New York, he lay curled in her lap, sound asleep, his forefinger and thumb slipping out of his mouth. Ingeborg felt her heart swell with love for the child. One day he would have land of his own because of the long, hard journey they had endured. The struggle was for their children, for a new life for all of them. She had to remind herself of their dreams, for at the present moment, if offered the chance, she would climb right back on the ship and head home to Norway.

Oh, to see Tante Maria again, her far and mor, brothers and sisters, the hills behind their house, covered with pine trees still trimmed with snow. To breathe the clean, nip-your-nose air. She unintentionally drew in a deep breath and carefully hid a cough. The smell of damp wool, unwashed bodies, wet babies, and burning coal was almost more than she could bear.

The whistle blew and the train jerked forward. As they pulled out of the soot-stained station, Ingeborg craned her neck for one last look at the large city across the water. When a fleeting thought of a tall man in a gray wool topcoat intruded upon her reverie, she quickly shut the door on that particular memory. She had met him, enjoyed their brief time together, and would be forever grateful for his generous treatment of a lost immigrant. And that would be that.

Carl reached for the basket. He removed the jar of coffee and poured each of them a small cup. He handed them all a cookie and said, "I propose a toast." He held his coffee up. "To our new life in our new land. And to a change. We have been spelling Amerika with a *k*. That is not the way it is spelled in this country. America is spelled with a *c*. We will learn many other new words, and from now on, we will be Americans."

Roald shook his head but added his "here, here" to the others.

Kaaren and Ingeborg clanked cups and drank their treat, letting Thorliff dip his cookie in their coffee. He giggled and said, "Here, here," raising his cookie just as the adults had.

Ingeborg leaned back against the seat. *Bless you, Carl, for giving us some joy on this journey. We all need to be reminded about the joy.*

By late afternoon, they all felt as if they'd been on the train forever. If Thorliff had asked, "When will we get there?" once, he'd asked it a hundred times. And they were stiff and sore from hours of sitting on the hard wooden benches.

"Here, you take the baby, and I'll entertain Thorliff." Kaaren roused herself from the much needed nap she'd collapsed into and extended the closely wrapped infant to Ingeborg. "I need to go to the necessary, anyway."

Ingeborg watched as the younger woman adjusted to walking down the swaying aisle. Despite the few days of rest, Kaaren still looked a little pale, and Ingeborg recognized the flinches of pain, no matter how hard her sister-in-law tried to disguise them. While Ingeborg had never had a baby herself, she'd watched her mother massage her stomach in that same way when she thought no one was looking.

The infant in her arms whimpered, so Ingeborg set to rocking against the back of the seat. "Hush now, den lille, your mother will be back soon, and it wasn't that long ago that you ate, anyway." She looked out the sooty window to see the outskirts of a small town before the train passed clickety-clack by. A blanket of snow covered the ground, and it appeared to be falling again. Maybe they should have waited until spring to travel, as they'd been advised. But Roald had insisted they be on the land, their own land, by the time the snow melted.

She caught back a sigh. Right now, spring seemed as far off as eternity.

By evening, Thorliff had made friends with the two dark-eyed boys across the aisle, and the car rang with the merry shouts of children. Ingeborg smiled at the boy's mother, for, unlike the playing children, their only method of communication was to smile at each other.

Roald and Carl returned in time to share the basket of food Mrs. Flaksrude had fixed for them. But other than that, they spent most of their time with a group of men from the next car who were also heading west to homestead. When the train stopped, as it so frequently did, Ingeborg could see the men striding up and down the station platform, their breaths creating puff clouds as they walked and talked.

"Next time they are going to take Thorliff with them," Ingeborg muttered.

"You know men, they don't like to be bothered with small boys," Kaaren said, then shifted on the hard bench, trying to get comfortable.

"Humph." Ingeborg settled herself more securely into the corner, a blanket she'd drawn from their valise folded behind her. She rubbed her stomach and swallowed carefully. Was this queasy feeling gnawing in her stomach from something she'd eaten, or was it because of Roald's babe she carried?

"Are you all right?" Kaaren leaned forward to look more closely in the gloomy light. Kerosene lamplight gave everyone a yellow tinge and deep shadows.

"I will be." Ingeborg gritted her teeth.

"You look terrible. See, you are even perspiring, and it is not that warm in here."

Ingeborg bolted to her feet and flew down the aisle, careening off the seat backs in her desperation. She shoved open the door of the necessary and threw up.

"Are you all right?" Ingeborg heard Kaaren's concerned voice as she knocked on the door.

"Ja, I will be," Ingeborg called out.

"What?" Kaaren said, leaning her ear against the door.

Ingeborg raised her voice and repeated herself.

"Can I get you something? Water, perhaps?" asked Kaaren as she shifted Gunhilde to her shoulder.

"Nei, there is some here." Ingeborg wet the bit of muslin she kept tucked in her sleeve for a handkerchief and wiped the beads of moisture from her forehead and her mouth. If only the train would stop swaying.

"Are you running a fever?" Kaaren asked when Ingeborg finally made her way back to their seats.

"Nei, I am not sick in that way. Remember when you were in the early months with her?" Ingeborg nodded to the infant sleeping in Kaaren's arms.

"O-o-h." Kaaren's face lit up like a brightly burning candle in the dark. "You are with child. Oh, Ingeborg, I am so happy for you." Kaaren clasped one of Ingeborg's frigid hands in her own. "No wonder you . . . you . . . ." Her mouth formed a perfect O. "Does Roald know yet?"

Ingeborg shook her head. "I planned to tell him as soon as we stepped foot on our new land, but you know what the last few days have been like. It slipped my mind in all the moving." She shook her head. The guilt of keeping something this special from her husband made her squirm. To be honest, she just hadn't felt like telling Roald. While there had been no good time, she knew she could have found a way.

She laid her hand on her still-flat belly and gazed at the sleeping babe in Kaaren's arms. This certainly wasn't the best time to be suffering from morning sickness, but maybe this one episode would be the only incident. She couldn't afford to be sick now. There was so much to do when they reached the end of their journey. And what would Roald say?

A day later, after countless trips up the aisle, Ingeborg thought maybe she really did have some intestinal disorder. But if so, it hadn't seemed to bother anyone else, at least not as far as she could tell.

The train slowed and ground to a squealing halt. She stared out the window, but as for the past several hours, all she could see was blowing snow. The flakes glistened like flashes of white in the light from the kerosene lamp.

The uniformed conductor entered from the rear door and called out commands in what Ingeborg was beginning to recognize as American.

Several of the men got to their feet and, after donning heavy coats, caps, and gloves, followed the conductor out the door. A gust of wind sent a swirl of flakes into the car.

Carl and Roald reached for their coats.

"Where are you going?" Kaaren asked softly.

"I think they need help. We were told that passengers should assist the crew in shoveling when the snow drifts too deeply over the tracks." Carl wrapped a long scarf around his neck and pulled on his mittens. "You sleep for a while. We'll be back."

Ingeborg watched the exchange from the warmth of her quilted cocoon. Snow or not, right now she felt deeply grateful that the train had ceased its swaying.

For what seemed like hours, the train intermittently waited, pulled forward a ways, and then waited again. Each time they cleared a drift away, the men came in, gathered around the potbellied stove at one end of the car to get warm, and then, when the train stopped again, headed back outside to clear the track.

While the men labored in the biting cold, a woman at the end of the car kept the stove stoked with coal and a large coffeepot boiling on top. They counted the hours from one drift to another.

Ingeborg awoke to another heaving attack. Afterward, in the necessary, she discovered bright stains of scarlet.

6

Please, God, no, I want this baby. Don't take it away before it even has breath. Please," Ingeborg pleaded. She hadn't even told Roald the good news yet, and now it may be too late.

After adjusting her clothing, she poured a few drops of water from the bucket into her handkerchief and patted her mouth, wishing for the pure, clear water that flowed in the mountain streams back home. The thought of drinking out of this communal pail made her gag again.

By now, most everything made her gag: eating, not eating, the smell of other people's food, the sway of the train, the stench of drying wool from the coats hung about the stove. Grabbing the backs of the seats, she slowly made her way back to their seats. Fear settled in the middle of her breast and wrapped its tentacles around her heart.

Was this a harbinger of things to come? She shuddered at the thought.

She tried to put a composed look on her face, but when she sat down, she couldn't help noticing Kaaren's worried look.

"What is it? What is wrong?" Kaaren whispered urgently.

Ingeborg glanced at the sleeping men and children and shook her head, placing a finger on her lips. "I'll tell you later," she whispered back, so softly that she wasn't certain Kaaren had heard her. The younger woman nodded but didn't take her gaze off Ingeborg's face.

Ingeborg slipped into a troubled sleep, with Thorliff leaning against her. It seemed only moments before she awoke with a start, sure that the scream she'd heard had been her own. The dream had been so vivid she could still feel her heart pounding. In it, Roald

LAURAINE SNELLING

had been furious with her. He had even raised his fist.

His voice still echoed in her ears. "You never told me, and now you lost the baby. I need more sons. What is the matter with you?"

She glanced to his sleeping form beside her, soft snores puffing his lips. When could she tell him? Here? Amidst all the restless immigrants and their squalling children?

Ingeborg closed her eyes again, hoping to stem the queasiness already welling within her. Like all else she'd tried lately, that too failed. Gently moving Thorliff, she headed for the necessary once again.

As she staggered down the aisle, she thought of her mother. Had she been sick like this when she carried her babies? Oh, to be at home and feel her mother's gentle healing hands on her forehead.

She shoved against the closed door. Locked. Someone was in there. She swallowed hard and tried to concentrate on the vision of their home high above the fjord. The snow lay crystalline about the house, bending the pine boughs low with the weight. The air sharp, clean. Her attention jerked back to the railcar. She must have breathed deeply by accident, for the heavy odors from the car started her to gagging again.

Oh, would this journey never end?

Roald awoke to find his wife curled in her corner of the seat, pale and shaking. "Ingeborg, what is the matter?" He laid a hand on her forehead to check for fever, but she shook her head. "Are you ill?"

Ingeborg shook her head again as tears leaped up her raw throat and threatened to spill from her eyes at the kindness and concern in his voice.

"Then, what is it?"

"I . . . I wanted to tell you at a better time, but this child of yours seems to be causing all kinds of problems."

"This child of . . ." The light dawned on his face like that of a bright sun rising. "You are carrying my son?"

Leave it to a man. Ingeborg shook her head and smiled in spite of her misery. "Bear in mind that this one could be a daughter. But yes, we will have a baby before fall." *If I carry it that long.* She refused to allow the thought to take root. She would bear this child. She *would.*

She watched her husband's strong face as he thought through the news. He nodded his head, and when he turned to look at her again, the smile she'd always dreamed of lifted the corner of his mouth.

"That is good." He nodded again. "That is very good."

Ingeborg's tide of emotion burst, but she hid her tears in his shoulder. He had smiled! A smile that rode an arrow directly to her heart and spread throughout her chest. Within moments, her stomach settled, and she fell back asleep, exhausted, but peaceful.

They reached Chicago six hours past the designated morning arrival time. Coming in, they'd passed acres of stockyards filled with thousands of cattle raising a cloud of steam on the frigid air.

"Look, Far. See all the cows. We are going to have cows on our farm and sheeps, too." Thorliff bounced in front of the window as if during the night someone had filled his pant legs with springs. "So many cows. Why are they all in the pens?"

"They are ready to be butchered so people will have meat to eat." Carl set the child back on his feet after a particularly hard jolt of the train sent the boy careening into his uncle's knees.

"We will have milk from our own cow. I'm going to learn how to milk it, Far said."

"Don't you want meat too?"

Ingeborg watched the wheels turning in her small son's mind. He'd been part of the butchering that fall before they left and understood that to have meat, the animal must die.

"Ja, but"—a grin stretched his rosy cheeks—"we will have to have two cows and calves too."

"You are a smart one, you are." Carl tousled the boy's curly hair. "How about we go out on the platform so you can see better? Get your coat and hat; it's cold out there."

Ingeborg watched them go, grateful for the reprieve from Thorliff's unending questions.

"Now, you will tell me what frightened you so terribly." Kaaren had shifted Gunhilde to the opposite arm and was carefully keeping the nursing infant covered with a quilt over her shoulder.

"I found bleeding." The stark words stabbed anew.

"Has there been more?"

Ingeborg shook her head.

"Then you needn't worry."

Ingeborg shot her complacent sister-in-law a look of total disbelief.

Kaaren shook her head again. "I know, I know, it's frightening.

But many women show spots sometimes. You must take life easier for a time."

Again, the look, this time accompanied with raised eyebrows.

The train slowed, and the women glanced out to see the brick station looming ahead of them, the tiled mansard roof thrusting above the surrounding area. A huge American flag, flying high above the flat roof, snapped in the wind off Lake Michigan.

Bedlam broke out in the car, with children racing from one end to the other, passengers grabbing their belongings from the overhead shelves and from under seats, and a cacophony of languages, all shouting to be heard.

Baby Gunhilde jerked in her mother's arms and let out a wail fit to be heard above all the noise. Thorliff, returned by Carl, clutched Ingeborg's skirts with one grubby hand and watched the goings-on from the safety of his mother's skirts.

"You sit right here." Ingeborg picked him up and set him on the seat. "And don't you move. I'll not have you wandering off again." The finger she shook in front of his eyes made him cower back against the seat.

By the time they had all their belongings gathered, unloaded, and reloaded on a four-wheeled handcart with Kaaren and baby perched on the side, Ingeborg wished desperately for a cup of coffee. They had run out of food the night before, with only a crust left for Thorliff's breakfast. Her stomach growled in protest.

She straightened her spine by rubbing her lower back with kneading fists. At least she wasn't throwing up, thank God for that. To take her mind off the hunger gnawing in her belly, she studied the vaulted room with its marble floor patterned in alternating square black-and-white tiles. Long wooden seats, set in orderly rows and filled with waiting passengers, took up the center space, while the ticket booths were all off to the sides of the cavernous station. If only the voice calling over the loudspeaker spoke Norwegian so she could understand what was being said. Perhaps they'd missed the train they were to take and would have to wait overnight. Would they stay here and sleep like some of the others stretched out on the hard wooden pews?

"Carl should return soon with something to eat." Kaaren patted her own midriff to still the growling that dueted with Ingeborg's. "He said he'd bring coffee too. Surely he will find a loaf of fresh bread that won't cost so dear."

Ingeborg snorted. Everything edible anywhere near a train station cost enough to make the angels cringe. She could tell by the look in Roald's eyes that he hadn't been prepared for quite such robbery, no matter how many people had warned him.

"How long do you think we'll have to wait for our next train?" Ingeborg asked.

"Too long," Roald said. "I will go and see."

As Roald walked off, Ingeborg studied the picture on the front of the handbill Carl had handed her. If only she could read American. Pictures of birds and plants were covered by a white scroll with words on it. She traced the letters with her finger.

"Next stop, Minneapolis." Roald strode back across the marble floor toward them, his boots ringing against the stone. "We won't leave until four o'clock in the afternoon, so we might as well find a place to be comfortable." He picked up the T-bar iron handle and leaned into pulling the cart. "I saw some empty seats over in that other section."

Before Thorliff could ask, Ingeborg lifted him onto the few remaining inches on the wagon so he could ride. The grin on his face more than thanked her.

When Carl finally arrived, dusted with snow but with a bundle under his arm, they fell to the simple meal with the hunger of a twenty-four-hour fast. Ingeborg closed her eyes in bliss. Without the constant rocking and smells of the train and its occupants, the bread and milk settled in her stomach, and its contents stayed where they belonged.

⚓ ⚓

The next thing Ingeborg knew, Roald was shaking her gently. "Come, our next train is here, and we can board now."

Ingeborg blinked her eyes and raised herself from the carpetbag she'd nestled against. "Thorliff?"

"He's with Carl." Roald hefted the remaining bags and strode over to the cart, tossing them aboard, making Thorliff laugh.

Ingeborg struggled to get her bearings. She must have slept for hours. How could that be? She licked her dry lips and smoothed her hair back into the coronet of braids that had needed rebraiding for the last two days. She had wanted to use the necessary in the station to get herself back into some semblance of order, but now it was too late.

She thought of the unfinished letter in her reticule for the families left behind in Norway. She'd started it at the boardinghouse in New York and planned to finish it on the train to mail in Chicago. One thing for certain, she had plenty of exciting news to share. She would have to write later, that was all.

"Are you coming?" Roald returned to her side.

"Of course." Ingeborg got to her feet, only to feel the queasiness in her middle join forces with the dizziness in her head. She took the cup of cold coffee he handed her and sipped, hoping the liquid would settle her stomach. Where was the necessary? Could she make it to the passenger car and use the one there? If only she could read the signs.

By the time they found Carl, who was stowing the remainder of their baggage above two facing seats, Ingeborg felt her knees buckle. She clamped her fingers around the back of the seat with the force of a drowning victim around a life preserver. She *would not* collapse here in front of all these strangers.

So much for force of will. When Ingeborg came to, Kaaren was wiping her brow, and Ingeborg was lying on a seat padded with their own quilts. If she hadn't felt so terrible, she might have appreciated the comfort more.

She reached a trembling hand out to Thorliff, who looked as if he'd been crying and might burst into tears again at any moment. "It is all right, den lille, Mor will be better soon." The whisper rasped on the raw surface of her throat. She smiled as reassuringly as she was able and let her eyes drift closed. *This must be one stubborn baby*, she thought, *to be causing such an uproar*.

When they reached Minneapolis, they would have to change trains again. Ingeborg awoke to hear Carl and Roald discussing the move. The thought of solid ground under her feet made her cautiously lift her head.

"Good, you are awake." Kaaren leaned forward from across the seat. "Here, I have some flatbread for you. A woman several seats up said if you eat this before you move, it will help the sickness."

Ingeborg looked at the offered treat. At this point she would try anything. Is this what Kaaren had felt like on the ship? No wonder she'd moaned about turning around and going home to Norway. Ingeborg nibbled on the dry bread, gratefully keeping her eyes closed and her mind off the bustle of passengers preparing to disembark. She should be helping, not lying here like an invalid.

"Don't even consider moving." Kaaren leaned forward again. "It is our turn to care for you."

Ingeborg felt so much better, she smiled in return. "You will make a good schoolteacher someday. Who could not do what you say when you sound so stern?"

"Please, God, that I may." Kaaren shifted the baby in her arms and, getting to her feet, placed the sleeping infant beside Ingeborg. "Here, if you must feel useful, mind Gunny. Then I'll have my arms free to carry something."

For a change, Ingeborg did as she was told. As she cuddled her tiny niece to her breast, she closed her eyes to better experience the joy of it. Soon she would have her own baby to hold, to nurse, and to love.

Dawn had barely tinted the gray sky when they pulled into the station at Minneapolis. By this time, each station on this halt-and-hurry journey had run into the next in her mind, all of them a dissonance of huffing trains and human misery.

As soon as they entered the vaulted waiting room, she looked around for the necessary.

"Over there," Carl pointed, correctly interpreting her distress.

"Mange takk." Ingeborg pushed Thorliff toward his uncle and told him to hang on to Carl's hand. By the time she found the necessary after traversing a long marble-floored hall, she also found fresh stains.

Panic returned with a vengeance. So easy it was for others to say that if a babe didn't go full term, surely the loss was God's will. So easy to say—except when it is your own. A son that your husband has dreamed of, counted on. A son to inherit the land they were striving for, crossing continents to discover, and giving up home and family for the chance at a new life.

All these thoughts passed through her mind as she unpinned her hair and let the braids fall to their full waist length. The thoughts continued to thunder through her mind while she unplaited the golden ribbons, brushed out the waves, and rebraided her hair. By the time she pinned the coronet back in place, the thoughts and fears had calmed to murmurs, and except for the ache in the small of her back, she felt more like herself than she had for days.

She could hear her mother's voice as clearly as if she stood right behind her shoulder. *This too shall pass, Ingeborg.* What she would give for her mother's wise presence right now.

"Are you all right?" Kaaren came up behind her and laid a hand on Ingeborg's shoulder.

"Ja." Ingeborg kept the fearful secret deep in her heart. She'd have to trust the baby to God's will, for Kaaren didn't need any more to worry about than she already had. Their gazes met in the mirror—two women trying with all their strength to endure an arduous journey that sent weaker sisters screaming for home. Or just plain screaming.

Ingeborg raised her hand and, with gazes locked in the mirror, patted her sister-in-law's comforting hand. "We will make it. The end of the journey isn't too far off now."

Sitting on the wooden seats in the waiting room, Ingeborg took out the letter. Maybe writing would keep her mind off the queasiness in her stomach. She reread the page she had already written. Yes, she had told them of the difficulties of the voyage but made light enough of it that others wouldn't be too afraid to come. A smile quirked the corner of her mouth at the recounting of her adventure in New York. Mor would be scandalized, but it made for a good story. She dipped her pen in the small inkpot and continued the tale of their adventures so far.

"We are in St. Paul, Minnesota, now, and the end of the journey is in sight. Roald is anxious to find our land so we can begin planting as soon as the snow is off the ground. Our good news is that we will have another member in our family come fall next year. Of course, Roald plans on our having a son.

"I miss you all terribly"—Ingeborg felt the tears fill her eyes—"I cannot tell you how much. Greet each one for us, and please continue your prayers in our behalf, as we do for you daily. Your loving daughter, Ingeborg."

She blew on the ink and folded the flimsy paper carefully, inserting it in the envelope she had already addressed. If only she had the money herself for the postage, so she wouldn't have to ask Roald for it. He had already made it clear that letters to home were a luxury.

She sighed.

"What is it?" Kaaren looked up from nursing the baby.

Ingeborg held the letter up.

Kaaren reached out and took it. "Say no more. Carl will mail this for us. You know that all of our families will pass it around until the letter is worn out." She called Carl over and explained what she wanted.

Carl looked up with a smile and a wink. Both of them warmed Ingeborg's heart. He slipped the envelope in his pocket and strode across the marble floor to ask a question of the man behind the ticket window.

Thank you, God, for that man who goes out of his way to make the journey easier for us.

Roald was nowhere in sight.

⨯⊛ ⊛⨯

Later that afternoon, with snow still falling, they boarded the St. Paul, Minneapolis & Manitoba Railway for Fargo, Dakota Territory, by way of Glyndon, Minnesota.

Carl and Roald settled their families in the facing seats and excused themselves to join a group of men gathered around the stove in the rear of the car. Most of the men spoke Norwegian and were comparing the weather outside to the storms back in the old country.

"You think it will turn into a blizzard?" asked one of the men, a wad of snoose ballooning his cheek. He sent a stream of amber liquid toward the brass cuspidor at the base of the stove. Most of it landed in the right place.

"The way I hear it, blizzards in Dakota Territory make any others look like mild snow flurries. The winds come down from the north, and there's nothing to stop them."

Roald nodded. "Ja, that is what I hear too. But we came through some heavy snows before Chicago, and we did just fine." He scratched the side of his nose with one finger. "What have you heard about land in the Red River Valley?"

The discussion continued for a time, but when no new information was forthcoming, Roald excused himself and returned to his family. Ingeborg sat staring out the window, gently stroking the curls of the little boy who lay asleep with his head on her lap. She had some color back in her cheeks and looked to be about half asleep herself. Kaaren and her babe both slumbered in the seat facing him.

Roald lifted Thorliff, so he now held the sleeping child in his lap. After nodding to the question on Ingeborg's face, he lay his head back on the seat and closed his eyes. Like Ingeborg, Anna had been ill with their second child. Would Ingeborg suffer the same fate? He shuddered at the painful memory and jerked his eyes open. He turned to study the profile of the sober woman beside him. Where had her smile gone? With a pang, he realized he missed it.

But the Bible says women are to suffer in bearing children; that is their lot. He sighed. He wanted sons so badly, strong sons and beautiful daughters. *Lord God, keep this woman of mine safe. And our babe.* He stroked Thorliff's leg and his shoe. *And thank you for this fine son I have.*

Roald placed his hand palm up on the seat between them. He watched as Ingeborg looked at him, glanced down at his hand and back to his face. A ghost of a satisfied smile touched her pale lips, and she placed her hand in his. Roald curled his fingers over hers and squeezed them gently.

Roald glanced back when peals of laughter burst forth from the keepers of the stove. Carl straightened from inserting another chunk of coal, and the laughter on his face told Roald who it was that was entertaining the small gathering of men. Unclasping her hand he laid his hand on his wife's shoulder but put a finger to his lips when she looked up at him with a question on her face. For a change, those around them were either sleeping or knitting. One grizzled man leaned over a growing pile of shavings, industriously carving and smoothing a handle for a hand tool.

I should be doing the same, Roald reminded himself, thinking of the carving tools his father had so carefully shined and sharpened before packing them in the flat wooden box. Chisels and knives, rasps and planes that had belonged to his father before him. All things that he could eventually pass along to his own second son, since the land always went to the first. Roald glanced out the window. He could see nothing but driving snow, so dense that it made the interior of the car darken like night.

The conductor pushed open the rear door and began lighting the lamps—a large one swaying from the overhead hook and smaller ones on the walls between the windows. The bite of lighted kerosene added to the already ripe odors of unwashed bodies, drying wool, and wet babies. Someone had brought Limburger cheese, its strong smell rising above the others.

Roald felt his stomach rumble at the odor of cheese. If only they had some of their good gammelost left from home. As soon as they owned a cow again, Ingeborg could save some of the milk and make cheese. She made such good cheese that surely they could sell the extra and perhaps pay for a second cow. He rubbed the side of his nose with a cracked finger. So many things to buy and do. And here they were slowed down by the snow again. Surely their plans of being on their own land by the first of March were as elusive as summer clouds hugging the mountaintops above the fjords of Norway.

The train ground to its first halt well before midnight.

"All you strong backs get bundled up. We've got some shoveling to do." The conductor stopped and threw another chunk of coal in the fire, then turned to address the women. "Make sure the coffee stays hot and the fire keeps burning extra smart to warm these fellas up when they come back in. It's cold as the arctic out there."

Carl and Roald staggered to their feet, shrugged into their heavy coats, and wrapped hand-knit scarves around their necks, ready to pull up over their faces to protect their skin and lungs from the biting cold.

The wind pummeled them and sucked their breath away as soon as they slid open the door. Snow pellets stung their exposed skin even as they wrapped their scarves tighter. They took snow shovels from the train attendant and plodded in a single line through drifting snow to the front of the train, broken into the semblance of a trail by the three men in front of them. Roald could see one of the men, but the two five feet in front of him had disappeared into a swirling white wall.

"Better rope up." A man at the head of the engine screamed to be heard above the screeching wind and puffing train. Carl and Roald dutifully tied the ropes around their waists and stepped from behind the protection of the huffing black engine. The wind caught them and tried to hurl them back against the steel cow catcher on the front of the engine.

Roald said something to Carl, but the words were ripped from his mouth and flung to the far reaches of the icy prairie. Instead, he pointed ahead and dug his shovel into the waist-deep snow. He had a feeling the drifts would only get deeper the farther they went.

He dug until the bitter air sent his lungs into a coughing frenzy, and then he threw his weight into the shovel and dug some more. Hoarfrost beaded on his heavy brows and blocked his vision—what little was left from the snow swirling and driving in front of his eyes—until it was easier to dig with them closed. A shout beside his ear and a tug on his rope told him they'd finally broken through the first drift.

"You go on back inside," the train employee shouted when the train pulled up even with them. "We have another crew to do the next one. If it gets much worse we'll just have to shut her down and wait it out."

Worse? Roald brushed his sleeve across his forehead where the sweat had turned instantly to ice. Never in his life had he seen a blizzard like this, and Norway was known for having some of the worst winter weather in the world.

When the men stumbled into the warm car, Kaaren and Ingeborg brushed off what snow they could with a broom and shook the ice coating off the men's clothing as soon as it was removed.

"Ach, what has this storm done to you?" Ingeborg took a handful of snow from the back of Roald's coat and rubbed the white spots on the crest of his frozen cheeks. Even in the short time he'd been out there, frostbite had already set in.

"Enough, woman." He drew back, the sting making him flinch.

"Nei, you hold still. You want the gangrene to set in, near as we are to our land?" Her smile showed her concern, in spite of the sharpness of her words. She scrubbed away with a second handful of snow.

The tingle soon turned to piercing pain, but Roald held himself still. He'd had frostbite worse than this on the fishing boat last year, but then he'd nearly lost a toe.

It took two shoveling shifts before the train broke free again. While the drifts slowed the struggling engine, the engineer pushed on through. An hour later, they slammed to a halt again. Once again, the cold air and a swirl of snowflakes rushed in as the conductor opened the door a few moments later.

"I hate to do this, but we need you poor fellows again."

Roald and Carl looked at each other and shook their heads. Would this night never end? When the next crew relieved them and they staggered back into the safety and warmth of the car after what seemed like hours, defeat stung as hard as the snow that had pelted their shivering bodies. When the storm seemed to gather more strength, the engineer decreed they'd have to wait it out and ordered the rest of the men to return to their cars and get some hot coffee to warm up and then some rest.

"Pray God they've put in plenty of coal," Carl muttered when the shrieking wind had been dulled by the slamming door.

"Pray that this storm blows itself out before we run out of food. We didn't buy that much in St. Paul because we were supposed to be in Moorhead by now."

"I've heard the storms can last for days," Carl said.

"I know. I've heard the same." Roald held snow to his cheeks and the bridge of his nose. "Right now, I've got to have some of that coffee to warm up my insides. Never have I been so cold as this."

The two men made their way to the back of the car where a smiling woman poured them up two tin mugs from the large coffeepot on the stove.

"Be careful, it's hot," she warned them.

Roald attempted to close his hand over the cup handle, but his stiff fingers refused to obey his command. The cup clanged on the rim of the stove, throwing scalding coffee over Roald and the man standing beside him.

A curse split the air as the cup hit the floor. Roald threw the man a withering glance, while at the same time he pulled his own wool clothing away from his body. The extra sweater Ingeborg had forced upon him earlier now stood him in good stead. Instead of being burned, he just had wet clothing. At least they wouldn't have to go back out into the blizzard again. He picked up the cup with his left hand, stretching and clenching the fingers on his right at the same time.

"I'm sorry," he said to his neighbor. "Are you all right?" When the fellow muttered an agreement, Roald held out his cup again. "Mange takk. I think this time I can be trusted to hold my cup."

The men stood around the stove until they'd all warmed up, both inside and out, some accepting whiskey added to the steaming cups by one of the immigrants. Carl and Roald declined the liquor booster. Soon the noise around them grew in direct proportion to the amount of drink consumed.

"Uff da," Roald muttered when one of the men bumped into the two brothers. He apologized by lifting his mug with a bleary grin. "If we have to go out and dig again," Roald said, "they'll all freeze to death."

"They'll fall in the snowbank because they can't tell up from down." Carl turned from the fire and headed back to the seats where their families still slept in spite of the racket.

Hours later, the train hadn't moved. A fistfight finally ran out of steam when the two men couldn't see each other well enough to land their punches. Now all the revelers snored instead of shouting and singing. The women and children huddled quietly to keep from disturbing them.

"Come." Roald signaled Carl with a brief nod. "We will return soon," he whispered to Ingeborg, who sat knitting while telling Thorliff the story of Daniel in the lions' den.

"Me too?" Thorliff asked hopefully.

Roald shook his head, which brought a frown to his son's face.

The two brothers made their way the length of the car and pushed open the door leading to the front of the train.

"Where are we going?" asked Carl.

"There is a man named Probstfield riding in the first-class car who's supposed to know all about farming in the Red River Valley. I think we should ask him some questions and learn all we can from him."

"Can he speak Norwegian?"

"I don't know, but maybe someone around him will. This could be our one opportunity to talk with someone who's been farming in the valley for some time."

The brothers passed two cars full of stoney-faced passengers before pushing open the door to a car filled with the rich odor of cigar smoke and a soothing quiet made possible from the absence of noisy children and drunken men. Instead, four men, dressed in suits, were sitting at a table playing a quiet hand of poker by the stove. Another gentleman sat reading by the light of the kerosene lamp, while two elderly women napped in the rear seat. Lamplight disappeared into the red plush furnishings but reflected off the windows dulled by the approaching evening. On the north side a drift covered part of the car.

"I am looking for Mr. Probstfield." Roald stopped at the seat where a full-bearded man sat reading. He had a pad of paper beside him on which he'd been writing.

"I am he."

"You speak Norwegian?"

"Only a bit. I speak fluent German though. We shall be able to converse if we both talk slowly." He spoke in German, doing as he suggested. "Can you understand me?"

Roald nodded, a frown of concentration wrinkling his forehead. "Ja, mange takk. I have heard that you know much about farming in the Red River Valley. Men say you have tried many things and that you are willing to share your knowledge with immigrants such as my brother Carl and me. I am Roald Bjorklund from Valdres, Norway. We want to homestead in this valley we hear so many good things about." Roald found himself watching Probstfield's face, seeking the smile of comprehension.

Probstfield nodded. "I am glad to hear that more strong Norwegian farmers are coming into the valley. Where did you hope to find land?"

"That is what we wanted to ask you." Roald looked at Carl, who nodded. "That and for any other advice you think we might need."

Probstfield began gathering his papers and stuffing them in a carpetbag at his feet. "Here, sit down so we can talk without giving me a crick in my neck." At the puzzled look on Roald's face, Probstfield rubbed and stretched his neck in pantomime.

Carl chuckled as he took the proffered seat. He rubbed his neck too. "Ja, a sore in the neck." When the two men were settled, Probstfield leaned forward, elbows on his knees.

"You're aware, of course, that the bonanza farms have taken all the acreage around Fargo, although some was homesteaded also?" He repeated his comment when he received no response from the two brothers.

"How far north?" Roald finally asked. He'd been afraid of that when it took them so long to prepare for the trip. All the good land was probably already taken.

7

What if there were no land left? The thought left Roald with a rock in his belly.

"You mean the Red River Valley is all taken up?" Carl leaned forward, his consternation evident in his furrowed brow.

"No, no. Just the area around Fargo and up toward Grand Forks. There's still plenty of land in Pembina and Grand Forks Counties. If you're fortunate, you might even be able to get a stake of land with river frontage there. And if you want, there are thousands of acres available to the west. You know, we have steamboats shipping up and down the river, and they need wood for fuel. Many farmers along the river cut wood in the winter to sell to the steamships and to haul to the grain elevators."

"What are elevators?" Carl asked.

"That's where the farmers take their grain to sell."

"And the elevators need firewood?" Roald wondered at the strange habits in this new land.

"No, no. After they deliver their grain, they pick up wood for the trek home. There aren't any trees for firewood away from the rivers and creeks."

"How do they heat their houses, then?" Carl asked.

"Oh, cow chips, grass twists, corncobs, some coal, when they can get it. You'll see more and more coal brought in, mark my words. Used to be buffalo chips aplenty. . . ."

"Cow chips, buffalo chips?"

"Dried manure, burns long and hot. We use what we have out here. Your son, he could look for that. Children learn to make hay twists too."

"Ja, my Thorliff, he will be a hard worker. He will guard the sheep and the cow."

"You have to guard young children out here. They get lost in the prairie grass real easy." At the look of doubt on the two brothers' faces, the portly man chuckled. "You might have grass on your land that grows taller than your head. Some parts of the valley grow like that, others only up to your chest. You must be able to tell direction by the sun, or not only the children will lose their way. I heard of a man who set out for town, got turned around, and they found his pack miles from home a few days later. By then the wolves had pretty well taken care of the body, but there was enough left to tell what had happened."

Roald had a hard time imagining grass that grew taller than his head. Knee-high grass had been a good harvest back in Norway. He caught Carl's look of consternation. It was a good thing they both knew plenty about navigating by the sun or stars. Their time on Uncle Hamre's fishing boat had been good for more than just the money earned. *I will guard my family well*, he promised himself. *From the tall grass and the wolves.*

The train lurched, and Roald glanced out the window. Dawn had come and with it an ending of the blinding blizzard. The conductor stuck his head in the rear door of the car. "We'll be moving out fairly soon, Mr. Probstfield. A good crew is out front shoveling the track free."

"We should go help." Carl started to get to his feet.

"No, no. If he'd needed you, he would have asked. What other kinds of questions can I answer for you?"

"We are in need of many supplies: a team of horses, a span of oxen, wagons, a plow. Do you know where we can buy these with as little money as possible?" Carl clasped his hands between his knees.

Probstfield dug a piece of paper from the breast pocket of his tailored woolen jacket. "Here's the name of a man I am acquainted with. You might ask him if he's aware of any homesteader who has decided he can't take the hard life out here and wants to leave. That's one of the best ways to get supplies cheap. There's some who just can't stand the loneliness of the prairie or the hard labor required the first couple of years to break the sod and wrest a living from the land. One thing though, you take good care of your land here, and it will take care of you. Richer soil you won't find anywhere on God's good earth." He finished writing and handed Roald the paper. "Tell Henry I sent you and said for him to give you a good deal."

"Ja, that I will do." Roald carefully folded the paper and placed it in his inner coat pocket. "Does this Henry sell oxen also?"

The train lurched again, and this time it started to move slowly forward.

"No, but he will know someone who does. You ever driven a team of oxen before?"

Roald and Carl both shook their heads. "But our book says they are better than horses."

"We really need a team of horses and one of oxen, too," Carl added. "If only we can pay for them."

"Are you aware that banks are loaning money to homesteaders? Loans are not too hard to get, once you have proved up your land. Until then, it is up to the local banker, but many are pretty good about it."

"Ja." Roald nodded. "I know, but we don't want any more debt than is necessary."

"Good idea, but keep in mind you need to get that sod broke so you can get a cash crop as soon as possible."

"True." Carl nodded also. "I saw a picture of a plow that you can ride on—no more walking behind the horse and pushing the plow. That would make breaking sod much easier. And faster."

"Yes, all the bonanza farmers are using them. I have ten myself."

"Ten? And ten teams?"

Probstfield nodded, a twinkle in his blue eyes. "I am not a bonanza farmer by any means, but I plant around two hundred acres in wheat."

"Two hundred acres." Carl shook his head. "I have a hard time imagining such a large farm."

"Between the two of you, you'll be able to homestead an entire section, that's three hundred sixty acres. And from what I can see of you, that won't be enough in a few years." Probstfield dug in his coat pocket and pulled out a cigar. "See this? I raised the tobacco myself, cured it, and hired a man to roll 'em. I've tasted better, but this just goes to show you can grow about anything in the Red River Valley." He dug out two more and handed them to the brothers. "Here, try them. You smoke, don't you?"

Carl and Roald shook their heads but lifted the cigars to their faces to inhale the pungent aroma. Roald looked up. "What else do you grow?"

"I have what you might call a diversified operation. I grow hay and oats to feed my beef and milk cows. I have chickens and hogs, and I raise corn to feed them. I plant barley, an acre or two of garden, and I have a small orchard with some fruit trees. Everybody teases me about my hothouse, but we had tomatoes in December last year."

"Hothouse?"

"You know, a glass-covered building to keep plants growing in the cold season."

Will wonders never cease? Roald thought. *As Carl always says, "only in America."* He fingered the cigar he still held. The smooth texture felt good and fit right between his first two fingers. Maybe he would take up smoking. He'd quit chewing tobacco when Ingeborg made such a fuss about it. That had been a nasty habit, anyway. Someday he'd have such a hothouse for Ingeborg as well as a grand home with glass windows to let in the sun, a huge black cookstove where she could bake to her heart's content. There would be beds all around for her beloved flowers. Someday he'd have plenty of things they both needed and even wanted.

"Anything else I can tell you?"

"Would you mind if I come to you for advice sometime?" Carl asked.

"Not at all. Either one of you a blacksmith?"

"Ja, our father made sure all his sons could handle a forge and make furniture, as well as farm. He said that way we would never go hungry. There will always be horses to shoe and plows to mend, and every woman wants a fine cabinet for her kitchen." Carl looked over his shoulder at Roald. "We learned well."

Roald nodded in agreement. "If we can locate a forge and some scrap iron, we would be assured of hand tools and sharp scythes."

"Your father is a wise man, and taught you well, I see. But mark my words; it won't be too long before steam engines take over the work of the horse."

Roald kept the surprise from showing on his face. Surely the day would not come when horses did not plow and pull wagons. Surely a matched team for the buggy would always be something a wealthy man would enjoy. Of course, he'd never told anyone of his secret dreams of prosperity. In Norway, dreams were an idle indulgence in the fight for living; dreams were only for the wealthy. Now, in America, he would have as good a chance as anybody to make his dreams a reality.

In New York, he'd seen the telephone and telegraph lines, the gas lights in the houses and on the streets—was there no end to American inventiveness?

"Mange takk for all your time and information." Roald rose to his feet and reached out to shake the hand Probstfield extended.

"Let me know how things go; my address is on that paper I gave you. Pay attention to what's happening with the railroads. They're going to change the face of commerce in this part of the country, just as they have back east. James J. Hill with the St. Paul, Minneapolis & Manitoba Railway might run a line right through your land—if you should be so fortunate."

Roald dipped his head in acknowledgment. So much to think about.

"Alexandria coming up," the conductor called out as he slid open the door. "All you folks going into Moorhead and Fargo must change to the Northern Pacific in Glyndon."

Roald and Carl shared a look of anticipation. Only two more stops, and they would be there. Dakota Territory—their new home. Carl clapped his hand on his brother's shoulder and nodded to Probstfield. "We thank you again for your time and advice, sir. You have taught us much." He led the way out of the car and battled the wind to hold the door open for his brother. "That was good. Only we better learn the American language quickly."

"Ja, my mind feels like it has wrinkles in it from trying so hard to understand him." They made their way through the next two cars, excusing themselves as they brushed past passengers taking their belongings out of the overhead rack and bundling things together. How many of them planned to homestead in Dakota Territory? The brothers knew that time was of the essence.

By the time they'd unloaded, changed trains, and gotten settled again, Roald was so keyed up he couldn't sit still. He paced the aisle and let his mind run with all he had learned from Mr. Probstfield. With weather like this, how could they continue north to find their homestead? Buying supplies would take time too. Probstfield had suggested they take the train and purchase their goods in Grand Forks, but they were fast running out of money.

He fingered the small card with embossed letters in his pocket. Should he use it and contact Mr. Gould for work for himself and Carl on the rail line? He rubbed the cleft in his chin and continued to pace. Where would they live in the meantime? And on what? How would they save to buy horses and wagons, let alone a plow and seeds for planting? How? How? How? The pounding questions kept rhythm with the clacking wheels of the train.

8

Roald felt like kissing the ground when they stepped out on snow-covered Dakota land. He looked up and down the street that ran next to the train station. While this wasn't New York, there were thriving businesses, both horse and foot traffic on the street, and buildings as far as he could see. This was Fargo, the largest town in Dakota Territory.

Within three days, the Bjorklunds had settled into their new life. Without being forced to contact Gould, Roald and Carl had asked around and managed to find work on the bridge the St. Paul, Minneapolis & Manitoba Railroad was building across the Red River between Fargo and Moorhead. Ingeborg found immediate employment in the kitchen of the Headquarters Hotel, the largest hotel in Fargo. And Kaaren cared for the children in their two rented rooms in one of the boardinghouses on Broadway Street. The proprietor promised board and room in exchange for labor as soon as Kaaren felt strong enough.

Every morning at dark, Roald and Carl left to begin working on the trestle for the bridge. The huge round piers, formed of curved sandstone blocks, had been set the previous summer and fall, along with the wooden pier posts of the trestle. The billowing steam engine had pounded the round timbers into the mud before the ground and river had frozen. Carl and Roald worked as a team with the whipsaw to trim the tops of the timbers that had been splayed by the pounding, so another team could come behind later and lay the roadbed.

The chug of the steam engine, thudding hammers, and the commands hollered on the frigid air, combined with the ring of pounded metal, made it difficult to hear their soft grunts as each pulled the

LAURAINE SNELLING

saw toward himself. Frost formed on Carl's beard and Roald's eyebrows from their puffing exertion. It was hard work, but they were both glad to be earning money for their needed supplies.

A curse rang out behind them from one of the other workers. Carl and Roald stopped for a moment and straightened to stretch their tiring muscles.

"Another broken handle?" Carl tipped his hat back and rubbed a gloved hand across his brow, causing ice to break free.

"Ja, when spring comes there will be quite a harvest of hammer heads down between these piers. No one seems to care much, for the railroad just provides new ones. They say it's a waste of time to stop and fix them."

"If no one cares, why don't we go dig them out? We can carve our own handles."

"And trade the extras," Roald said, picking up on his brother's idea.

"Or pound them out and use the iron for scythes and plowshares."

The two brothers finished each other's sentences in their excitement.

That night, lit only by the full moon overhead, they kicked the loose snow in the forest of wooden piers and uncovered ten large hammer heads and several small ones. Loaded with their treasures, they made their way back to the boardinghouse.

In the kitchen of the Headquarters Hotel, Ingeborg wiped the perspiration from her brow with the back of her hand. Scrubbing pots in steamy water in a room already hot and stuffy from the two cast-iron ranges that were always kept hot to provide the food for the dining room would make anyone sweat.

"Are you all right?" asked Mrs. Johnson, head cook and commander of the kitchen, as she stopped on her way back from the pantry.

"Ja, I will be done in a bit. Then I will get to the bread like you asked." Ingeborg kneaded her aching back with her fists and rolled her shoulders forward. She put the last dirty kettle in the water and set to scrubbing it. She'd never known there were so many pots and dishes in the world. Her hands were red and sore from the hot water. By the time she finished, they would be ready to prepare another meal, and she would have to start all over again.

"I forgot to tell you, I hired a young boy to scrub and clean. You are much more valuable as a cook."

Ingeborg raised her head and looked over her shoulder. "Mange takk." She hadn't realized the cook was still standing beside her. "I am glad to hear that."

"Ja, well, just see you continue like you have been. A good day's work is all I ask." The aging blonde trundled off toward the dining room, and Ingeborg returned to her labors with renewed energy. She would rather bake breads and make stews any day. And she'd only been working here for a little over a week. She paused when she heard the now familiar train whistle. Since the track lay directly alongside the hotel, everything shook when the train chugged by, and no one could hear themselves think for a few moments.

Ingeborg was not afraid of hard work. She'd helped on the farm back home since she was a child. But the continual ache in her lower back was beginning to worry her a bit. She thanked God daily there had been no more telltale spots of blood to signal trouble, and, besides, anyone would be tired after the long days she'd worked, slaving over the steamy sinks. She left for work early in the morning, even before the men did, and when she returned, all of the others were sound asleep.

That night she crawled under the covers nearly frozen after walking the six blocks home. The heat radiating from Roald's slumbering body made her feel as though she were lying next to the stove.

"Uff da," he muttered when she accidentally touched one icy foot to his wool-covered leg. He rolled over and laid a hand on her shoulder. "You are a chunk of ice. Come here and let me warm you." He turned her over and pulled her into the warmth of his body, carefully tucking the quilts around them again. "Are things going well at the hotel?"

"Ja." She started to tell him about her change in status, but a gentle snore told her he'd already fallen back to sleep. She fit her body, spoon fashion, against him. Morning would be here long before she was ready for it.

By the end of three weeks, Ingeborg had tackled and accomplished every task in the hotel kitchen, much to the surprise and delight of her employer. The two women worked well together and kept mounds of delicious food flowing out the door on the trays of two hustling waitresses, neither of whom spoke Norwegian.

"No, I said we was wanting the fried chicken, not the steak." Pearl, the elder of the two waitresses, planted her hands on her hips. "Ingeborg, you said you understood."

Mrs. Johnson translated from across the kitchen and finished with, "You know you have to be more careful. It's your fault as much as hers, Pearl."

Pearl made a face, and with her back to Mrs. Johnson, she could get away with it. Her glare included Ingeborg.

"Ja, the mistake is mine." Ingeborg hurriedly dished up a new plate with the fried chicken in place of the steak. "I am sorry." Those words she had learned quickly. She handed the plate back with an apologetic smile. "Chicken." She said the English word carefully. Her language would improve; it had to. Thank the good Lord the recipes were written in Norwegian, and Mrs. Johnson could speak Norwegian, English, some German, and a bit of French.

"Do not speak Norwegian to me anymore," Ingeborg said when they were clearing things away for the day. The potato water had been mixed for the bread starter, and the already kneaded dough had been set near the stove to rise overnight. The sourdough made a wonderfully light bread that Ingeborg delighted in forming into loaves and rolls.

"I'll go along with this when we have the time, but during meals and such, repeating the words and making sure you understand would be too much. I do admire your gumption though." Mrs. Johnson turned to Ingeborg and spoke in English. "Now you must go home or you will meet yourself coming back."

Ingeborg shook her head. She only understood a few words, like "you," "home," and "back."

"Say again, please." That phrase she had learned well.

Mrs. Johnson slowly repeated the words.

Ingeborg nodded. "I go home." The rest didn't really matter. She wrapped her scarf around her throat and pulled on her mittens. Clutching the collar of her black wool coat around her neck, she stepped out into the frigid night air. At least there was no new snow, and during the day icicles had been dripping outside all the windows. The moon lighted her way, turning each breath into a miniature cloud in front of her. In spite of her aching weariness, she felt like skipping. She had two dollars and fifty cents in her coat pocket to add to the growing fund. Wages for one week, more than one earned for several months in Norway. And the men were earning two dollars a day—each. She could scarcely wait to write home. God had truly blessed them, just as all their family had said He would.

A twinge of guilt made her catch her breath. She hadn't mailed a letter since they arrived in Fargo. The last one she'd sent was from Chicago, to let the families know all the immigrating Bjorklunds had arrived safe and were well. Maybe she would have time on Sunday afternoon to write, for Mrs. Johnson had said Ingeborg could leave after the noon meal.

She tiptoed into their room and, after putting two dollars of her wages into the leather bag they used as a bank, undressed for bed. As she removed her petticoats, she contemplated what she had done. Safely tied in a handkerchief lay the remaining fifty cents. Now she had some money of her own. Never again would she have to plead for a penny or a nickel. What would Mor say about this? Or Roald?

She folded up the thoughts and carefully tucked them away, much like she did her undergarments. Kaaren's mother was right. A woman needed a bit of her own no matter how good a man she married.

In her nightgown, she knelt by the pallet in the corner where Thorliff slept and touched his rosy cheek with the tips of her fingers. "Good night, my son. Soon I will talk to you in English, and we will be able to speak with everyone in our new country."

Ingeborg was reaching for her coat to go home the next afternoon when a knock sounded from the back door. She glanced at Mrs. Johnson, who nodded for her to open it.

A man and a boy stood on the back steps. The man took his hat off and dipped his head in a motion of servility. "Please, ma'am, can I talk with the person in charge here?" Watery blue eyes gazed up at her from beneath nearly white eyebrows. Deep lines gashed from nose to chin and wrinkled his forehead.

"Ja, of course you may." Ingeborg stepped back and motioned them in out of the cold.

The young boy trailed behind the man, as if trying to disappear in the coattails, of which little remained. The man's tattered coat looked as though it had been caught under a plowshare.

"Here, come close to the fire. You look half-froze." Mrs. Johnson beckoned them close to the big range, already banked for the night.

She pulled a pot of coffee from the back where it warmed and poured two cups.

The two did as she ordered, looking as though anything else would be too much effort.

"Ingeborg, fetch some cream from the larder. These two look as if a little wind might send them bouncing like tumbleweeds across the prairie. Now, my good man, what can I do for you?" She plunked the two cups down on the table as she spoke.

The man turned his backside to the range and twisted his hat in his hands. "My name is Mainwright, David Mainwright, and this here's my son Daniel. I took up a homestead about four miles from town, but we ain't doin' so good. My wife died just before Christmas, her'n the babe she was bornin', and I don't have nothin' left. I thought as maybe Daniel, here, could work for his room and board. He's a good hard worker—for fetchin' wood and scrubbin' and such." His voice died away when Mrs. Johnson failed to comment.

Ingeborg looked from the man's tired face to the young boy who stood hunched close to the stove, wiping his red dripping nose on his tattered sleeve. He glanced up from time to time, his gaze darting from his father to Mrs. Johnson and back.

"And what are you planning on doing?"

"I'm going to sell out as fast as I can and take the train back to Ohio where I belong. I never shoulda come out here to Dakota Territory, free land or no. That land ain't free. It sucks ever bit a life outen a man." For the first time, a bit of fire sounded in his strained voice. "All I'm wanting is for to go back home before the prairie kills us all."

"You have other children?"

Mainwright nodded. "I thought leastways Daniel, here, would get something hot in his belly regular like. He's a good boy, like I said."

Mrs. Johnson nodded toward the pantry again, and Ingeborg flew to do her unstated bidding. She cut two thick slabs of bread and spread an ample amount of butter and jam on them. There were two sausage patties she had planned to use for the soup, but it seemed these two needed them worse. When she placed two plates with the bread and sausage in front of the Mainwrights, the boy looked at her as if she'd given him a bit of heaven. The look on his face when he bit into the bread made her want to weep.

Would the prairie do this to the Bjorklunds, also? She banished the traitorous thought before it could take hold and become more of a fear than those she already carried. She'd heard so many horror stories from those who came and went in the hotel.

"Thank'ee, ma'am," Mainwright said and prodded his son, who nodded around a mouthful.

"Well, I reckon I can find work for Daniel, here, and a place for him to sleep. Would you then be taking him with you when you went?"

Mainwright shrugged. "'Pends on how much money I get for my team, and iffen I can sell the homestead. I gotta pay up at the bank and the general store. They won't let me have no more credit, as if I wouldn't pay whens I could."

Ingeborg's interest picked up instantly. She'd have to tell Roald right away. With the money they'd all been saving in the last few weeks, maybe they could strike up a deal and purchase a team at a good price.

Mrs. Johnson fingered the ring of keys she kept in the pocket of her floor-length white apron, a sure sign she was thinking over the man's proposition.

"You got anything to feed those children still at home?"

Mainwright bowed his head and shook it slowly from side to side.

"Then we better give Daniel here an advance on his wages. Ingeborg, fetch a sack of beans and a bit of cornmeal. That might help for a few days. Wish I could do more for all the starvin' farmers who come by here, but this is better than nothing."

Mainwright blinked rapidly and sniffed. "Thank'ee, ma'am. There'll be stars in your crown for sure. I'll pay you some when I sell my stock, I will."

With a smile, Ingeborg came back from the pantry and handed him the sack. If only she could talk with him. If only she could talk with Roald before this man headed back out across the prairie. What would her husband want to do?

Mainwright pulled his hat down over his forehead and stepped out into the fading sunlight.

Mrs. Johnson returned from the hallway and handed a quilt to the boy. "Now, you can make yourself a pallet behind the stove for tonight, and tomorrow we'll decide where you will sleep. You get your rest now, because our morning starts mighty early."

Ingeborg hurried home, excitement with her news lending wings to her tired feet.

When Carl and Roald returned from another hard day of work

on the bridge, they found Ingeborg laughing and playing Find the Thimble with Thorliff, and Kaaren turning the heel on the gray wool sock she was knitting. Baby Gunhilde lay asleep in the center of the bed, snuggled under a quilt.

"Now this is what I like to see." Carl hung his coat on the peg by the door and crossed to the potbellied stove in the corner, where he rubbed his hands over the heat. "That bridge has got to be the coldest place on earth. The wind blows across the frozen river and right up through us."

Roald followed suit. "We could jump off the bridge, and the wind would carry us right back up."

Thorliff ran to his father. "The wind could do that?"

Roald shook his head. "No, son, but it is bad." He turned to look at Ingeborg. "It is good to see you. I was beginning to doubt I still had a wife, except when her cold feet tell me she is home."

Ingeborg smiled. What had gotten into this man of hers? She poured each of them a mug of hot coffee and, raising the pot, glanced at Kaaren. Kaaren shook her head. After pouring a cup for herself, Ingeborg joined the men around the small wooden table, her secret bubbling inside her.

"I think, and Carl agrees, that a week after the thaw comes, he and I should buy our team of horses and ride north to locate a place to homestead. You and Kaaren will stay here, and when we get back, if spring is really here, we will buy a team of oxen and the rest of our supplies, and then drive to our new home." He stopped and looked around at the three.

"Where will you go?" Ingeborg asked, carefully keeping her secret safe, waiting for just the right moment to tell them.

"North of Grand Forks to Pembina County. We've heard there is still land there for homesteading."

"Wouldn't it. . . ?"

"Ja?" Roald looked at her as if she'd spoken out of turn.

"Wouldn't it be better to wait until the weather is safer?"

"Safer?" His tone made the word sound incredulous.

"Come, Inge, remember you are talking to two Norwegians who have lived through winters in Norway. We know how to take care of ourselves." Carl grinned, his shoulders hunched forward from his elbows propped on the table.

"Ja, I know, but . . ."

"And besides, if we don't hurry, someone else might take the land we want." Carl sipped his coffee.

Ingeborg shook her head. She knew she shouldn't have said anything. Now they would be more stubborn than ever about leaving in a week.

"I've heard it said that spring storms can be most vicious here. They were talking about the weather today at the hotel, among other things." She wrapped both hands around the cup of coffee. This wasn't going the way she had planned. "They told some terrible tales of travelers trapped in whiteouts, even after the grass had sprouted."

"Ja, tomorrow night we will go look at those horses Mr. Probstfield told us about." Roald continued talking as if he'd never heard his wife or her concerns. "If we wait too long, there may not be any horses for sale either."

What would it take to make them listen to her? Ingeborg studied the dregs in her coffee cup. She could feel her anger straighten her backbone, give it the iron it needed. It was now or never.

"A man came into the hotel kitchen tonight to see if his boy could work there so he would be fed." Her words came out clipped and sharp.

The men turned to her with questioning looks.

"Ja, so?" Roald asked.

At least she had their attention.

"The man said he was selling out and going back east somewhere. He has horses and machinery also. I believe he will take any reasonable offer."

Roald stopped and turned to look at her. "Why didn't you say so sooner? We can go see him right now. What is his name, and where do we find him?" He rose to his feet as he spoke and headed for the door. "Come on, Carl."

"You can find his son Daniel at the hotel. I'm sure he will show you the way."

"You could have told me sooner; look at the time we've wasted." He reached for his coat and scarf, the weariness of a hard day's work gone from his face. "We will do what we can."

Ingeborg bit back the answer. She had tried—they just didn't want to listen.

"But you haven't had supper yet." Kaaren put down her knitting.

"We can eat anytime. You go ahead, and don't wait up for us." Carl waved as he followed his brother out the door.

Ingeborg could feel the anger leaving as fast as it had come. She and Kaaren ate their soup in silence. Even Thorliff left off his normal chatterbox ways and kept yawning between bites of the bread and cheese.

Ingeborg bid her sister-in-law a quiet "good night" and tucked little Thorly into his pallet bed. Together they folded their hands and began their prayer. "Nu lukker seg mitt øye, Gud Fader i det høye, i varetekt meg tag, og takk for denne dag. Amen." Thorliff drifted off before the amen.

Ingeborg sat with her back against the wall and her arms around her raised knees. She rested her cheek against the wool fabric of her skirt. *Father in heaven, please protect Roald and Carl on their way tonight. I know they are impatient to find our land, and I am too, but here we are safe from the wind and snow, and our money is being replenished. Is it wrong to want to keep them safe?* She paused in a rare moment of introspection. Was it because they were earning more money than any of them dreamed possible? Was she putting money and safety above owning their own land? She scraped her cheek back and forth on the fabric, comforted by the warmth. *Thank you for all you have given us. Amen.*

The cold from the unheated room seeped through her clothes, making her shiver. She'd not started the stove because she knew they would be in the other room. Now she wished she had done so, or that she could take her pencil and paper in the other room and write the long overdue letter home. Had Kaaren written? If so, that letter would have been passed around to all the relatives. She'd ask tomorrow. With a sigh she undressed and crawled under the quilts. She could have brought in a warmed brick to put by her feet. But before she could make the effort, she'd fallen asleep.

When Ingeborg awoke in the predawn chill to get ready for work, she reached beside her and panicked. The place beside her was empty and had not been slept in. Where was Roald?

9

What had happened to Roald and Carl? Ingeborg threw back the covers and grabbed her wrapper from the bottom of the bed as she shoved her feet into her slippers. When she entered the other room, Kaaren and the baby were still sleeping.

Had she slept only a short time and something had awakened her? But the room was chilled and the fire nearly out, so it must be morning. Where were the men?

God in heaven, protect them. Her mind played the phrase like a litany without end. She tiptoed out of the room and back to her own. She had to be at work, and there was no sense letting Kaaren worry longer than necessary. Ingeborg dressed quickly with the lamp on dim and, picking up Thorliff's slate and chalk, wrote Kaaren a message.

"When the men return, ask them to let me know they are all right." She set the slate just inside the door and hurried out into the darkness.

Her litany for their protection kept time with her feet as she headed toward the hotel. Had they found the farmer? Did they stay there because it got too late? Were they lost on the prairie? *Oh, dear Lord, be with them.* The black sky, pinned in place by a myriad of stars, brought a cold comfort of its own; at least there hadn't been a snowstorm to trap them. To the north, the aurora borealis flared and subsided in a dance of celestial splendor, all the colors of the rainbow more brilliant against an ebony sky.

Ingeborg kicked the snow off her feet outside the back door of the hotel kitchen and gratefully stepped into the warmth that penetrated even out into the enclosed porch. "Good morning." Ingeborg pronounced her greeting in English carefully. But she had to revert to Norwegian to ask the question burning in her mind. "Is the boy Daniel here?"

Mrs. Johnson shook her head. "And to think I trusted that young whelp. Here it is the first morning, and he is already gone."

"Nei, it is not his fault. Roald and Carl took him back out to his father's farm last night so they could talk to Mr. Mainwright about buying his horses. They have not returned."

Mrs. Johnson stopped in the act of adding more coal to the fire-box in the larger of the two stoves. "Oh, land." She finished what she was doing and turned to Ingeborg. "You needn't worry. There was no storm. It probably got late, and so they spent the night. Mark my words, they'll be by here on their way to the bridge. Those men of yours wouldn't miss a day's wages less'n they were dead or nearly so."

While the words were meant for comfort, Ingeborg didn't need a reminder about the alternative. She clutched the message of hope to her breast and tied her apron around her waist. As her mother had always said, "Busy hands keep the mind at peace."

Soon the bread was in the oven and more set to rise; a large pot of oatmeal simmered on the back of the stove, and she was slicing thick slabs of ham when the door banged open and Daniel burst through.

"Please, I am sorry I weren't here to start the fires. My pa said we was to spend the night so the Bjorklunds and me wouldn't freeze to death on the way back to town. We started way before daylight."

Ingeborg listened with surprise and a sigh of relief. Last night the young fellow hadn't said one word.

Right then Roald stepped in behind him. "I'm on my way to the bridge. Carl has gone to tell Kaaren we are safe." He nodded to Mrs. Johnson. "God morgen."

Worry died as soon as Ingeborg saw her husband's face. Questions bubbled like the porridge on the stove. "Mange takk, did you. . . ?"

"I will tell you tonight." He touched a mittened hand to his cap. "Goodbye." With that he was gone out into the silvering blackness.

Ingeborg shook her head. He was not a man to waste words, that one. But she had to know how they fared. Would asking Daniel be discussing their private business with strangers? As if Mrs. Johnson was a stranger, for that matter.

"Here, have something to eat and warm you up before you start your chores." Mrs. Johnson handed Daniel a thick slice of bread and butter, which seemed to disappear into the boy's mouth in one bite.

As if sensing her curiosity, Daniel continued. "Mr. Bjorklund, he bought the horses offen my pa and said he'd take the wagon too, after my pa kin haul everything to town. My pa said those Bjorklunds are sure good men." The words were a bit difficult to understand, mixed as they were with half-chewed bread, but it was enough.

Ingeborg heaved a sigh of joy and relief and gave the oatmeal an extra vigorous stir. The men were safe, Roald now had his team of horses, and . . . and they would leave any day for the north to find land. Her relief was short-lived at best. She straightened and dug her fists into her lower back. Here the morning had barely started, and already it was aching something fierce. Did she really want spring to come?

When she arrived back at the boardinghouse that night, the men had just finished eating and were sitting at the table enjoying their final cup of coffee.

"You are home early." Roald greeted her.

"Ja, that young Daniel, he made the clearing away go so much faster today." Ingeborg hung up her scarf and coat on the peg near the door. "Is there any coffee left?" She crossed the room to rub her hands over the heat of the stove.

Kaaren handed her a half-filled mug. "I could put some water in it. Most likely it is pretty strong by now, anyway."

Ingeborg shook her head. Questions about the men's trip the night before warred for first place. She turned to smile at Carl. "I heard the two of you made life easier for that poor man and his family last night."

Carl nodded. "Ja, Roald made sure everyone came out ahead on that deal. I never would have thought of a plan like that."

"Like what?" Kaaren asked the question Ingeborg had been dying to ask.

Roald gave a faint shake of his head, as if discouraging the discussion, but Carl ignored him and went on.

"We went out there to buy the team, you know, and perhaps some other tools and such if they were in good enough shape." He leaned back in his chair, ever the storyteller. "Well, we got there, thanks to Daniel's guidance. We never would have found the homestead without that young man, since it was already dark and all. Probably would have gotten lost and frozen to death."

"Carl, get on with the story." Kaaren grinned back at her husband. They all knew how he could stretch out a good tale. Roald snorted and shook his head.

"Ja, ja, I'm getting there. Mainwright invited us into his soddy, and you'd of thought they were animals living in a burrow. No wonder the man can't wait to get them out of there. But at least they'd had some supper that night; we could smell the beans he'd cooked. Daniel admitted they were nigh unto starving to death."

Ingeborg clutched her elbows in both hands and stepped closer to the stove. Here in Fargo they had heat and food. Who was to say such a thing couldn't happen to them? She shivered and leaned forward, wishing Carl would hurry.

"Ja, it was bad," Carl said with a nod. "Can't blame the man for wanting to move back east."

Roald bent over and fished his sack of carving tools out from under the table. He drew a half-formed piece of oak from the sack and, knife in hand, began to shape the ax handle he'd been working on the last few days.

"First, he showed us his horses," Carl continued. "The team needs some feeding up, but they look sturdy. His wagon will need a good bit of repair, and some of the equipment . . ." He wrinkled his forehead in thought. "There was a plow in bad shape but fixable—come to think of it, no wonder that man didn't make it as a homesteader. He didn't keep up his machinery. Right, brother?"

"Ummm." Roald nodded and eyed the curve of the ax handle that was taking shape.

"So what did you do that made such a good deal for everyone?"

"We bought all he had," Carl said matter-of-factly.

Ingeborg felt her body reel as if struck by a giant hand. Where would the money come from?

Carl smiled from one woman to the other. "But we only paid him a hundred dollars now, and we will pay the rest when he is ready to leave. For now, he will keep his wagon to load the things he plans to keep. We will have the horses for our trek north, and when we get back, we will hitch them to the loaded wagon and haul what's left of his family to the train. He has food and money to pay off his debts, we have the horses when we need them, and everybody is happy."

"Pity you didn't buy the cow and chickens, too." Ingeborg couldn't resist the jibe.

"We would have, but they'd already eaten them all."

"Not to worry, Inge, we will still have some money to start with.

And Mr. Adams on the bridge assures us that getting a loan at the bank in Grand Forks will not be difficult. Not once we have land to prove up. Credit is easy here, he said. Mr. Probstfield said the same."

Ingeborg shuddered. She could hear her father's voice as if he stood in the room. *Owe no man but the debt of love.* What were they getting themselves into?

"I thought the land here was free."

"Ja, homesteading is. But we will need seed and oxen. And if we pay a portion, the land will be ours sooner." Roald spoke slowly, as if explaining something to a wayward child.

That is why I think we should stay here longer; we need more money. The thought never made it to the door of her lips. Squelching thoughts was a habit she'd developed years ago.

The warming weather held, and the following Sunday, Roald and Carl took the sacks of food Kaaren had packed for them, tied rolled quilts across their backs, and swung aboard their heavy-footed mounts. The two horses—one bay and one white—snorted in the predawn cold, sending clouds of steam into the air.

"Now, you are not to worry," Carl reminded his wife for the third time. "We will return as soon as we can, but don't begin to look for us before ten days have passed."

"Be careful." Kaaren clutched her elbows with both hands. "Go with God."

Ingeborg looked up at Roald, who, like Carl, rode bareback with a wool blanket for saddle. "You have extra socks now?" She knew he did, for she'd tucked them in herself, but the question hid the words her heart wanted to say. Words she knew he'd not appreciate. Words such as "come back soon," "I love you," and "wouldn't it be better to stay right here and keep adding to our savings for a while longer?"

She stepped back, pasted a smile on her mouth, and waved good-bye. She refused to think about the possible dangers that lay ahead for them. As they trotted up the street, Ingeborg turned the opposite direction and headed for the hotel as Kaaren hurried back inside to check on the sleeping children. Someone in this family had to be earning money.

⁂

"Ingeborg, you'll have to help Pearl in the dining room today," Mrs. Johnson said a few hours later. "Amelia just went home sick;

we couldn't have her contaminating the food."

Ingeborg swung around from the stove where she'd been turning out flapjacks as fast as she could flip them. She needed to make new batter, too. Everyone in town must have come to the Headquarters Hotel for Sunday breakfast.

"But I can't speak English well enough," Ingeborg made excuse.

"You will deliver the food to the tables, and Daniel will clear away. We are short handed and will have to make this work." Mrs. Johnson broke eggs into a large bowl to make more batter. "You'd best put on a clean apron and wipe that smudge of flour off your nose. I knew I should'a hired another girl when I had the chance."

For a while there was a lull in the arrival of customers, allowing Ingeborg to keep up with her cooking. She put two hams in the oven for the noon meal and set Daniel to washing the pots and pans. But it wasn't long before she was dishing sausage, eggs, and pancakes onto the plates as fast as she could flip the eggs in the pan.

"You help serve now." Mrs. Johnson took over the position at the stove. "Table three."

Ingeborg lifted the tray full of plates of food and backed out the kitchen door into the dining room. She turned and headed to the right, where four men sat around the cloth-covered table, all wearing shirts and waistcoats that spoke of the East. She carefully placed a plate in front of each guest, then looked up to find a pair of familiar brown eyes studying her.

"Mrs. Bjorklund?"

"Ja." She felt her heart leap within her breast. "Mr. Gould!"

10

The weather held clear for the trip north. Roald and Carl followed the well-worn trek up the east side of the frozen river. The first night, they reached Georgetown and asked at the livery if they could sleep in the hay in the barn. Rolled close together in their quilts and covered with hay, they slept comfortably through the night.

In the morning, they ate cold bread from the sack Kaaren had packed and welcomed the hot coffee the livery owner had brewing on the back of his forge. Thanking the man for his hospitality, Roald and Carl gathered their things, mounted, and headed out.

Long before the sun reached its zenith, the men dismounted and walked for a time, both to warm themselves and to save the horses. The wind kicked up snow granules to sting their faces even as the sun warmed their backs.

When they mounted again, Roald let his thoughts return to Ingeborg. Would he ever understand her, or was it man's lot to . . . he shook his head. She sure had gotten her dander up. All she had to do was tell them about the Mainwrights when she first walked in the door. Would have saved a heap of time. He looked over at Carl, who appeared half-asleep. Keeping their eyes closed enough to not become snow blind and yet stay awake took some doing.

They stopped that night in an abandoned soddy. "Why you suppose these folks left?" Carl asked when he came in from caring for the horses.

Roald blew on the bit of flame he'd finally coaxed from his flint and the pile of tinder he'd shaved so carefully. He added other sticks and gradually some larger pieces they'd broken off a tree. Soon they had a nice fire crackling. They both held out their hands to the heat.

"Maybe they got sick or just didn't want to work hard enough.

Like Probstfield said, not everyone is cut out to prove up a homestead in Dakota Territory."

"Maybe we should look into this one." Carl turned around to get some heat on his backside.

"Nei, too close to the neighbors. We couldn't add enough land to our original section."

"Ja, you are right." They boiled some of their dried meat in the coffeepot and drank the broth too. Along with the cornmeal mush they made, they both were filled. Exhausted from the long ride and warmed by the hot food, they rolled up in their quilts in front of the fire and, quickly drifting off, passed a peaceful night.

Late the third night, cold clear through and wishing for some hot food and coffee, they crossed the bridge into Grand Forks.

"We should have stopped back at that soddy," Carl said as he slid off the horse in front of the livery stable. He clutched the horse's mane to keep from crumbling to the ground. "My feet have no feeling whatsoever."

"Ja, perhaps we should have waited out the cold." Roald tried moving his own toes but couldn't even tell where his feet were. They should have gotten off their horses and walked more often. He shuffled his boots on the ice-packed snow. The horse snorted and stamped its feet.

"Ja, you are hungry too. As soon as I can move, you will go inside and be fed." Slowly the feeling came back, burning and piercing like miniature knives cutting his flesh. He ignored the pain, grateful he had the feeling back in his feet. Many men had lost their feet from frostbite, as well as other parts of their faces and hands. They would have to be more careful.

Roald pounded on the stable door, waited, and pounded again. Surely the owner had at least a hired man sleeping on the premises.

Finally the door slid open a crack, and a tousled young man eyed them balefully. "Yer out kinda late, ain't ya, mister?"

Understanding the tone but not the words, Roald answered, "Our horses need feed and hay."

"All right." The boy switched to Norwegian and pulled the door back on its runners just far enough for the horses to come through.

The warmth of the barn felt like a summer's day compared to the frigid air outside. Roald inhaled both the heat and the smell of horses, hay, and manure, overlaid with the acrid odor of the now silent forge. He led his horse after the boy and tied the weary animal in the appointed stall.

"That'll be two bits for each horse. You can pay Jorgeson in the morning."

"Ja, that will be good. And might my brother and I sleep in your haymow?"

The boy dumped a mound of oats in each feedbox and added a forkful of hay. "I guess, but don't go lighting any lamps or smoking. Jorgeson has strict rules about smoking in the barn."

"We do not smoke," Carl assured the boy, then turned and shook out the quilt he'd been sitting on and folded it over his arm. "Do you have hot coffee? Or food? We will be glad to pay."

"No, the fire went out hours ago." He pointed to a ladder leading to a square hole in the ceiling. "You can sleep up there."

"Coffee would have been mighty good." Carl pulled more hay over their quilt-padded bodies. His rumbling stomach said more than his words.

"Ja, that it would," Roald replied.

Finally, with the combined warmth of their bodies, along with the quilts and the hay, they fell asleep.

In the morning, they brushed the hay off their clothes, and after asking directions of the blacksmith who owned the livery, they headed for a small building up the street. When they had stuffed themselves full of pancakes, eggs, and ham, they continued on to the land office.

To their frustration, no one in the office spoke Norwegian.

Roald clenched his fists and jaw. The morning was wasting.

"I'll go get Jorgeson," Carl said. "He can interpret for us."

Roald nodded and turned to study the map of Dakota Territory hanging on the wall. He located Fargo and traced their route up to what he knew was Grand Forks. Beyond that, few towns dotted the prairie land. At the northern border lay Pembina, too far north for his liking. He traced the rivers that flowed into the Red Valley. Land along the river with trees and good prairie to turn under for wheat; that was what he wanted. There looked to be plenty of it available.

Time seemed to drag like a dull plowshare. When Carl and the blacksmith finally returned, Roald had reminded himself of the virtue of patience more times than he wanted to count.

"He needed to finish shoeing the horse first," Carl said by way of apology.

"Mange takk. I'm grateful to you for coming."

"Us Norwegians, we must stick together." Jorgeson brushed a clump of manure and straw off his leather apron. "Glad to be of some help. We need good farmers up here."

But when they asked about homesteading the land to the north, the clerk simply shrugged. "That land is not platted yet, so if you find a piece you like, you cannot file on it. You'll have what's called squatter's rights."

Squatter's rights? The question burned in Roald's brain. Squatter's rights wasn't enough. "So, how do we make it legally ours?"

"When the surveyors go through in the spring, you'll have to come back here and file your claim. You'll pay your fourteen dollar fee at that time, and we'll draw up your documentation. You'll get your final deed when you've proved it up."

"In seven years."

"Only if you do all the improvements you're required by law to do."

"I know that I am to build a house, break ten acres, and live on the land."

"Yes, that is what the law says, but you must keep in mind that . . ."

"I must do more than that to live."

Roald shot his brother a quick look and saw the small grin that indicated he recognized Roald's heavy sarcasm. That mouse behind the window surely didn't understand the Bjorklund brothers.

"We each want a quarter section of prairie and the same amount for a tree claim. All that is permissible?" Roald's eyebrows were dangerously close to meeting, a sure sign he was not pleased with the tone of the official. "And yes, I know we cannot have all of that at once."

"Yes, that is permissible . . ."

"Mange takk. We will find our land." Roald turned and headed out the door. He was glad he didn't understand what the man sputtered after them. Officious little prig. From the look of his hands, he hadn't done a decent day's work in his entire life.

The three men strode up the street to the smithy without a word, snow crackling beneath their boots and their breaths staining the crystal air for brief seconds. The sun turned the melting snow to flashing diamonds.

"Mange takk for your assistance." Roald thrust out his hand and shook that of Jorgeson's. "I will not forget that you took time to help a newcomer."

"That is what the Good Book says—to befriend strangers. And anyone who comes from Norway is not a stranger, but a brother from the past. I will look forward to shoeing your horses in the future."

"Ja." Roald nodded and dug in his pocket for the feed money.

Jorgeson shook his head and waved the coins away. "You keep that. You will need it more than I do right now."

"But . . ."

"No, you do something good for a stranger, and he does something good for someone else, and the cycle goes on. Go with God." The smithy left them standing by the stalls of their horses and went to pump the bellows on his forge.

"That is a good man." Roald lifted down his bridle from the peg on the stall post and patted the big bay on the rump. "Easy, boy, now we must get back on the trail. Move yourself over like a good boy."

Within a few minutes, bits jingling and hoofs crackling the icy road bed, they headed northward out of town, following the stagecoach road to Manvell.

Three days later, after having scouted the Turtle and the Forest Rivers, they still hadn't found the perfect place. Some of the land they wanted was already taken, and other sections had too many settled farms already in the vicinity. Each night they found a soddy, or in a rare case, a log or frame house to beg shelter. And in the ways of the prairie, they were always made welcome. In some places they found fellow Norwegians and could talk and share the news they'd heard. In others, nods and smiles were the best form of communication, but the people freely shared what they had, proud to show off what they'd accomplished.

Late one afternoon they could see black clouds building on the western horizon, and the wind no longer teased their horses' manes but tried to tear the hair from their necks. While the men hadn't planned to stop so soon, they turned their horses to the east. Off over the rolling snowdrifts, they could see a corral. As they drew closer, they knew the two largest drifts around the corral must be the sod house and the barn. The horses whinnied a welcome that was difficult to hear over the rising wind.

A dog barked at their approach.

Before they could dismount, a man who made Roald and Carl look like growing boys stepped from under the mound of snow connected to the corral.

"God dag." His voice rolled around in a barrel chest and came out like thunder, but the smile that stretched from earflap to earflap made them forget the clouds had eaten the sun.

LAURAINE SNELLING

"God dag to you." Roald stumbled a bit on his nearly wooden feet but met the man in between the house and the barn. The giant looked so familiar that Roald took a moment to study the rough-hewn face. "Do I know you?"

"The name's Ole Haugrud, and I left Oslo just two years ago. My brother, Swen, is planning on emigrating this summer. Where are you from?"

"Valdres. Did your brother work on a fishing boat in the North Sea?"

Ole chuckled deep in his chest. "He did and still does. You knew him, then?"

"We met." Roald shook his head. "Who'd think in all this space we'd meet someone from so close to home."

"Grace of God, my friend. How do you think my sea-loving brother is going to like this flat land of ours?" The three men studied the horizon now smothered in black clouds. The restless wind blew shards of ice and jerked on their coats as if seeking warmth itself. "Here, let me take your horses, and you go on up to the soddy. Marte will be so glad to see a new face. She's probably already set the table. The coffee's always hot."

"Can I help you?" Carl asked.

"Nei, nei, I did the chores early when I saw that cloud begin to swell. I'll feed your horses while you get warmed. We might be snowed under for a couple days again."

"I thought spring was here." Carl handed the reins to the giant. "Could have fooled me."

"It'll come, but winter has to battle back a few times yet. The first year we was here, we had snow flurries on the first of May. But by mid-May the garden was up. You'll find that when the sun shines and the ground thaws, things grow so fast you can see it, just like they do at home."

The biting wind whistled through the bars of the corral and moaned at the eaves of the sod barn. "You two go on now. Marte and the little ones will skin me alive for keeping you out here." He turned and clucked the horses to follow.

Carl and Roald, quilts and bags bundled under their arms, made their way to the solid wood door, the slabs obviously having been cut by a hand that knew wood and knew how to form it. One knock and the door flew open as if by itself.

"Company!" A little girl, with braids so white they nearly matched the snow and a grin that showed one front tooth missing, danced in place, one arm waving them in while the other tried to keep the door from banging all the way open.

A woman's voice from the dim interior ordered with a laughing tone, "Don't just stand there letting the storm freeze them and us, invite them in." A tall woman, still tying a clean white apron in place, met them as they ducked under the doorframe and stepped into the soddy. Two candles on the table and the flickering flames from the fireplace lit the dark room. As Carl and Roald had already learned, the black windowless walls deepened the gloom, making one feel as if they were closed in a box.

"God dag. We are Roald and Carl Bjorklund, recently of Valdres, Norway, and we know your brother-in-law. We worked on the same fishing boat."

"Well, imagine that." Even before the introductions were finished, she had poured two cups of steaming coffee and set them on the table. "Here, let me take your coats, and you make yourselves to home. Supper will be ready as soon as Ole finishes with the stock."

The two brothers took places at a plank table lined by benches on both sides. The little girl who greeted them drew her younger brother from behind his mother's skirts and plopped him down beside her on the bench next to Carl.

"Do you have children?" Her blue eyes crinkled at the corner exactly like her mother's.

"A baby girl born on the boat over, and my brother has a five-year-old boy named Thorliff. How old are you?"

"I'm six, and when we get a school closer to home, I will go to it."

Roald looked at his brother over the rim of his cup. Children were always drawn to Carl, and not only children, but adults as well. He looked around the sparsely furnished room. A rope bed covered with quilts and a buffalo robe sat in one corner, and the narrow bed in the other was obviously for the children. A spinning wheel sat next to a bag of wool with carding paddles on top of it. Looped and tied skeins of yarn hung from the rafters, as did bunches of dried herbs and bags of food, to keep them away from the varmints. Shelves lined one wall above a trunk decorated with the rosemaling of the Valdres region. Every inch of space showed the hard work and ingenuity of the couple.

Our house will look like this next winter, Roald promised himself. *And we will hang a bed from the wall, like we do on the ships. Between us, Carl and I will accomplish much.*

Discussion over the delicious deer stew and thick bread Marte served ranged from life on the prairie to what they had heard from home. When Carl asked about land to be homesteaded, Ole nodded around the wreath of smoke from the pipe he clenched in his teeth.

"Ja, there is good land to the north and to the east of us. The Little Salt River is about eight miles to the north, and we are about four miles from the Red. The town of St. Andrew is located on the north side of the mouth of the Little Salt. There aren't very many settlers in the area yet. This part of the country was a no-man's-land between the warring Indians.

"Indians? I thought they were all on reservations." Roald propped his elbows on the table.

"They are, but folks have been slow to settle here, anyway. We see some Metis and a wandering brave or two."

"Metis?"

"They're neither Indian nor French but a combination of the two from the days of the fur traders."

"Half-breeds."

"Yes, but you don't want to call them that. I don't see no harm in them. I heard tell that the Metis shot all the buffalo around here, but I don't always believe everything I hear. I traded wheat for that buffalo robe you see over there. Robes like that help keep out the cold better'n any quilt or blanket I've seen."

In the pause of the conversation, Roald could hear the wind howling at the door and the chimney. The cold outside made him appreciate both the warmth of the stove and the warmth of the family that welcomed strangers.

"We do appreciate your taking us in like this. I'd hate to be caught out on the prairie in weather like that." He nodded toward the door.

"Ja, I learned early to string a rope from the house to the barn when a blizzard blows up. Men have been known to wander off and not be seen or heard from again. If the wind don't get you, the wolves will."

Roald felt Carl shudder beside him. As a young boy, Carl had had a run-in with a wolf. The wolf had taken the lamb they fought over, but Carl had saved the remainder of the flock.

Later, when he and Carl were bedded down on a pallet in front of the fireplace, visions of home blew through his mind. He could see it as if he were standing right in front of it—the two-story log house built securely into the hillside, grass growing from the roof, and the lower level held up by a solid rock foundation. Here the wind would blow away a house like that. The mountains of Norway stood tall and white, and the fjords were deep and blue, reflecting the white clouds passing overhead and the pines and aspen in the high pasture. He tucked the quilt more firmly around his shoulders. This was home now, this windblown prairie, and here he would stake out his land.

Two days later, after the storm had blown itself out and the sun returned to melt the snow, they found their land.

Mrs. Bjorklund, is it really you?"

Ingeborg felt the tray shake in her hands at the same moment she heard the dishes rattle. She watched the man stand and, with a very private smile, remove the heavy tray from her hands and set it on an empty table.

"I am glad to see you again, Mr. Gould." She stopped her hands from twisting in her apron. "Welcome to Headquarters Hotel. I hope your business is going well." Only through a supreme act of will did she keep her voice steady. That same act of will kept her from reaching up to tuck a wayward strand of hair under her coronet of braids.

"Yes, it is. But if you are still in Fargo, you must not have found land to homestead yet?"

"My husband and his brother Carl are out looking for land now." Ingeborg heard mutterings from the waitress and guests at other tables. "Excuse me, I have work to do." She whirled around, took up her tray, and headed for the door to the kitchen.

"My land, child, what's gotten into you?" Mrs. Johnson looked up from stirring more batter. "You look as though you've seen a ghost."

"No, just a friend. No, I mean an acquaintance, a . . ." Ingeborg could feel herself making the situation worse. She picked up two plates and hustled back out to the dining room. No one liked to have cold food, not for the handsome prices they paid at Headquarters Hotel.

While placing the plates in front of two men, she scolded herself for acting like such a ninny. With a smile she pointed to their empty coffee cups and went to get the pitcher to refill them. She kept her gaze away from the table where David Jonathan Gould sat with three other men.

Now, straighten yourself up and go fill their coffee cups. That is your job today, so do it. She went from table to table, pouring coffee, nodding when someone said something to her in English. They could have been talking Russian for all she knew. All the English she had so laboriously learned had suddenly flown right out of her head. What was Gould doing here? Had he been here for sometime, and she didn't know it? This kind of gentleman did not look in the kitchen for his friends.

"Mange takk," he said softly.

"Velbekomme." She let herself steal a glance at him and remembered New York, the cab ride, and his gracious helpfulness to a foreigner. Her spine straightened, her shoulders squared, and her chin lifted just enough to become . . . to be . . . "More coffee?" Her English returned and with it a smile that set her heart to thrumming and her feet skimming the floor.

He held out his cup. "Thank you."

She filled his cup and the others at his table. "More food?"

The older man to his left nodded. Ingeborg took his plate back to the kitchen, filled it, and returned with a plate of biscuits hot out of the oven.

"Thank you, that looks delicious." The man tucked his napkin back in his vest and helped himself.

"You are welcome." A slight nod from Gould, along with the twinkle in his eye, let her know she was doing well.

By the time the early morning rush was over, Ingeborg was well into preparing food for the dinner menu. Stuffed chickens were in the ovens baking, potatoes were in the pot and ready to boil, and another batch of bread was rising. They had baked the pies and cakes the night before, so these stood ready on the sideboard.

"Here, sit for a moment and drink this." Mrs. Johnson pointed to the chair opposite hers and handed Ingeborg a cup of coffee. "What was it that flustered you earlier this morning? You'd of thought you stole Pearl's beau, the way she looked daggers at you."

"Uff da, it was nothing. The kind man who helped me find my way when I was lost on the streets of New York was here to eat today." Ingeborg sipped her coffee and leaned gratefully against the back of the chair.

"Um-m-m."

"He was very good to me. I . . ." Ingeborg snapped her jaw shut. She was explaining too much.

"Um-m-m, I see."

Ja, well I'm certainly glad you do, for I don't at all. Ingeborg rotated her head, trying to pull the kinks out. Those trays were heavy.

"Did Mr. Bjorklund get off this morning?"

Ingeborg nodded, a nagging guilt making her wince inwardly. Except for telling Mr. Gould the men had left, and after praying them into God's hands for safe keeping, she hadn't given them a moment's thought. She drained her cup. "I better get back to the oven and check on those chickens. I'll start the venison steaks too. They can simmer on the back of the stove." When she rose to her feet, the familiar ache in her back twinged enough to make her dig her fists in it for relief.

"I have a personal question to ask." Mrs. Johnson set her coffee cup down. At Ingeborg's nod, the older woman continued in a soft voice meant only for the two of them. "Are you in the family way? What with your back so sore and all? I know'd you to turn green and run for the bucket a few times."

Ingeborg nodded. "But that part seems to be over now."

"And you're fixing to drive north to homestead in the next month or so?"

Ingeborg nodded again.

Mrs. Johnson shook her head. "You heed my words. You need to take better care of yourself, so you can bring a healthy babe into this world of toil and tears. I seen you rubbing your back some, and I knows what it's like." She nodded again, her double chins bobbling with her motherly scolding.

"Thank you for your concern." Ingeborg felt tears sting at the back of her throat. Mrs. Johnson had sounded so stern when she'd first started working here. Now, she'd become a dear friend. "I try to be careful."

Mrs. Johnson snorted and rolled her eyes. "Ja, and I'm a German princess."

The door to the dining room flew open and Pearl came into the kitchen, took a piece of paper from her apron pocket, and thrust it at Ingeborg. "This here's for you. That swell you was talking to left it for you."

Ingeborg glanced at the paper, grateful it was written in Norwegian so Pearl couldn't read it. *Please tell me what time you will be off work so we may talk before you leave for home. Sincerely, D.J. Gould.*

She looked up to find both Mrs. Johnson and Pearl studying her. She could feel the heat flaming into her cheeks. "Thank you," she said in careful English and stuffed the bit of paper into her pocket. Whatever did he want to see her for?

"You didn't answer my note."

"Why, you startled me." Ingeborg raised a hand to her throat. She stepped down from the rear porch of the hotel and headed around the corner of the building. What could she say?

He fell into step beside her. "Fargo is booming, is it not?"

"Mr. Gould, what is it you want?" Ingeborg, in her forthright fashion, came straight to the point.

"I want to learn how a friend of mine is surviving in the wilds of Dakota Territory. I think of her often, and here she is waiting on my table, and I am grateful. Friends are important in life, are they not?" He took her elbow for an instant to keep her from stepping in front of a team of fast-trotting grays.

"Mr. Gould, it takes more than the little time we've spent together to become friends. My family is waiting, and I must hurry. My sister-in-law has been with the children all day, and she will have supper waiting." Ingeborg looked straight ahead, walking swiftly on the board walkway.

"I will not slow you down, only visit with you as we go. Now you must ask me how I came to be in Fargo, and I will tell you that my father sent me on a trip to look over his railroad investments. Then you will say that you hope my trip is successful, and I will . . ."

Ingeborg could no longer keep the smile she felt in her heart from showing on her face. "And then I will say you are being ridiculous and thank you for walking me home, but here is where I live." She stopped and looked up at him, her smile making her gray eyes dance. She extended her hand. "Thank you, Mr. Gould. It has been a pleasure to see you again, and God bless."

They shook hands, with Gould bowing slightly over hers. "God bless you, my friend. Even though I leave on the morning train, I will see you again, I promise."

Ingeborg climbed the stairs and turned at the top. He tipped his hat to her and strode up the street, a cheery whistle floating back over his shoulder.

"Who was that?" Kaaren asked as soon as Ingeborg entered their rooms.

"The man from New York, remember? I was pouring coffee in the dining room, and there he was." Ingeborg hung up her coat and reached down to hug Thorliff, who'd thrown himself against her skirts as soon as she crossed the threshold. "How's my Thorly? Have you been a good boy for Tante Kaaren?" She stroked the curls back from his forehead and patted his cheek.

"Ja, I been good." He eyed the pocket of her coat.

"Then, Mrs. Johnson sent you a treat." Ingeborg pulled a napkin-wrapped square from her pocket and laid back the white cloth corners.

"Cake." Thorliff looked up at her, his eyes dancing. "Mrs. Johnson is a nice lady." He took the sweet with a whispered "mange takk." Crossing his legs, he sank to the floor to devour every crumb.

꒰ ꒱

When the train left in the morning, it rattled the dishes as usual. Knowing Gould was heading west on that train rattled Ingeborg's heart, but only for a moment. After all, friends did not need to be together to remain friends. Later she would send prayers after him, but right now she had breakfast to put on the table.

She took a few minutes after the noon rush was over and, taking Mrs. Johnson's mail with her, headed for the post office. She told herself today was the day they would hear from home. Here it was March, and they'd not had any letters from family back home. Surely between the three families left in Norway, there must be someone who had written.

She stamped the slush from her shoes on the steps and entered the post office. "Hello." She spoke her English carefully. "Is there mail for Bjorklunds?"

The man behind the counter looked over his half spectacles and nodded. "Came in today." He reached behind him to the wall of small cubbyholes. "Ah, here it is." He handed Ingeborg a thin envelope with a postmark from Norway.

She blinked rapidly, the film on her eyes making reading difficult. "Mr. and Mrs. Carl Bjorklund." Did she dare open it?

"Ma—thank you." She turned and nearly skipped out the door.

With a deep breath, she settled herself back down to a more ladylike fashion and hurried back to the hotel. The letter gave her wings for the remainder of her day. Dark had long blanketed the earth when she reached the boardinghouse they called home.

"Kaaren, a letter." She burst through the door to find her sister-in-law laying a sleeping Gunny in the cradle loaned them by the house owner. "For you and Carl."

"What does it say?" Kaaren met her in the center of the room.

"How should I know, silly? It's your letter." Ingeborg handed the precious missive over, dreaming that she could smell the pine-scented air of home on the envelope.

Kaaren carefully slit the envelope with a knife from the table and withdrew the paper with trembling hands. She looked up at Ingeborg, fighting to keep the tears inside.

"Read it."

Kaaren wiped one eye with her finger and began.

"My dearest Carl and Kaaren,

Greetings also to Ingeborg and Roald, and hug the children for us. We miss you so dreadfully and were relieved to receive your letter and know you are all well."

Kaaren sank down in the chair by the table where the light was better. She took a handkerchief from her pocket and wiped both her eyes and nose.

"How glad I am to know you and the baby are getting stronger. Your tante Gunhilde is so pleased that you named your first child after her."

Ingeborg stood next to the stove, elbows cupped in her palms. As the words created familiar pictures of home and family, she tried to swallow the lump in her throat. She, too, wiped her eyes. It was as if life in Norway existed in some other time and space. When she thought of the distance they had come, home truly was on the other side of the world. Would this flat land with its never-ending wind ever become home?

Kaaren finished the letter and laid the pages in her lap. "I miss them so."

"Ja, I know."

"Gunny will never know her bestefar and bestemor. I remember when . . ." As she told the story of her grandparents, her voice softened and a smile returned. She finished and looked up at Ingeborg. "Do you really believe this is all worth the struggle? That this land will become home to us?"

Ingeborg started. Was the younger woman reading her mind? What could she say? She knew what Roald would answer. But were those words hers also? Those thoughts and dreams? She gave herself a mental shaking.

"Yes, it will." She paused and nodded as if she needed convincing as well. "It will."

The days flew by, and each night Ingeborg and Kaaren tried to figure out where the men were on the simple map Roald had drawn for them. One thing they knew for certain: if they stood on the top of the Moorhead Flour Mill, they could probably still see the two men on their horses; the land was that flat.

Each night Ingeborg thanked her Father in heaven for the warming weather and the absence of blizzards. On one hand, she was grateful for the melting snow, and on the other, stories of the morass of the roads as soon as the ground began to thaw had her also praying for cold. It was a good thing God did what was best rather than listen to His foolish children, she decided one night.

One prayer was always consistent. "Please God, let Roald find the place for his heart, the perfect land that will make him happy."

When the horrible blizzard blew through, she and Kaaren prayed together that the men had found shelter.

By now, Kaaren was helping the landlady with the baking and with cleaning the rooms of the male boarders. She kept Gunny, as they called the baby, slung in a shawl and tied to her chest. Thorliff ran errands up and down the stairs or played quietly at her feet. He often sat with his slate and drew the English letters that the landlady taught him. Kaaren learned along with him.

By the end of the second week, Ingeborg began watching for the men. Each night she hoped to see them around the table when she entered the room, and each night she sighed with disappointment when she got home and saw their chairs empty. Roald had said not to worry or expect them back yet, but she couldn't stop hoping.

At day eighteen, Ingeborg admitted to herself that she was worried. Were they all right? Had they been trapped in the blizzard? How far did they have to travel? Was there no land left? The questions buzzed through her mind like angry bees and kept her turning in her bed. "God, Father, please keep them safe." She couldn't think what else to pray. She knew Kaaren was worrying the same, but both of them kept their thoughts to themselves. It was as if saying the words out loud might cause the unthinkable to happen.

If only the men had had money for the train to and from Grand Forks, at least.

Kaaren read Bible verses to them the next night. Her verse said, "Faith is the knowledge of things hoped for, the assurance of things unseen."

"We must have faith." Kaaren closed the book in her lap.

"Ja, we must," Ingeborg acknowledged. *But waiting is so difficult.*

Two days later, Ingeborg was busy peeling potatoes when Daniel came in with a load of firewood. "Mrs. Bjorklund, someone outside wants ta see you."

Ingeborg took one look at the dancing Daniel and dashed out the back door. Roald and Carl sat on their horses. Carl had a big grin on his face, while Roald wore his normal solemn demeanor but with the light of victory in his eyes.

"We found our land." Roald swung off his horse and grunted when his feet hit the ground. He held Ingeborg's gaze. "It will be good land."

Ingeborg clasped her hands to her breast. "Thanks be to God."

Roald nodded. "Ja, that too." He glanced around at the bare patches of dirt where the snow had melted. "We must be on the road as soon as possible. The land up there is not surveyed yet, so if we do not hurry, someone else may stop upon it."

At the question on her face, Carl continued. "We cannot file a legal homestead claim until the surveyors go through. But if we are there, then we will be able to pay the survey fee and file on our land."

"So we must hurry."

"Ja, we went to Mainwright's already and will take the horses to him tomorrow. He says he can be ready as soon as we get there." Roald stroked his hand down the horse's nose.

"Have you been to see Kaaren yet?"

Both men nodded. "Now we'll go see if someone has a span of oxen for sale. You haven't heard of anyone else wanting to leave the country, have you?" Grinning, Carl raised an eyebrow, and Ingeborg knew he referred to her earlier discovery.

"Sorry, no. Just many people coming in. Mr. Adams of the railroad came by and asked when you'd be back. He said anytime you want a job with him, you will have one."

"That's good, but we will be farming our own land." Carl slapped his brother on the shoulder. "Won't we, brother?"

Roald winced and nodded at the same time. "God willing. But for now we must find another wagon and a team of oxen, and then tomorrow begin the repairs on Mainwright's wagon." He remounted and leaned forward slightly. "You will tell Mrs. Johnson that you are leaving?"

"Ja, but since we are not sure of the day yet, I will work as long as I can." Ingeborg felt the familiar knot in her chest. Saying goodbye to people she'd come to care about was never easy. There had been too many goodbyes this year.

"Hopefully we will be leaving by Saturday," Roald said.

As the two men rode off, Ingeborg returned to her labors with a heavy heart. She thanked the Lord they'd made the trip all right and found land they were pleased with, although how they could tell it was good when it was covered with snow was a puzzle to her. Was it a good idea to start out before the snows were all gone? Was it even safe?

"Please, God," she muttered as she picked up a knife to slice potatoes.

"So, you will be leaving in the next few days?" Mrs. Johnson stopped by Ingeborg's cutting board. "I almost kept hoping they wouldn't find anything this season and would be content to come back to Fargo to work on the railroad."

Ingeborg agreed, but loyalty to her husband kept her mute. "Working here in Fargo was just a temporary measure. I told you that when I first came to work for you."

"I know you did, but then I didn't know what a marvelous cook you were, or that I would come to depend on you so much. Hard workers like you are few and far between."

"Mange takk and more." Ingeborg forced herself to switch to English. "Thank you. I like it here, and . . ."

"And we better get this meal out before both of us are salting the stew with our tears." Mrs. Johnson leaned over and, opening the oven door, checked on the simmering roasts. Her face glowed bright red from the heat when she stood again. "These railroad men go through more food—you'd think I was feeding an army."

During the next few days, Ingeborg was grateful she worked at the hotel instead of having to help organize the rapidly growing mound of supplies for their trip. The major thing still missing was the yoke of oxen. No one had any to sell.

"We'll have to keep the load to one wagon and look again in Grand Forks," Roald said one night after Ingeborg returned home.

"But you already have two wagons." Ingeborg felt like collapsing on the bed. Her back ached more than usual, which had made the day seem longer and the work more difficult.

"We will sell one. We've already done enough repair on it that we should be able to make a few dollars on it." Roald paced the narrow confines of the room.

"I wish we . . ."

He whirled and caught her gaze. "You wish what?"

"Only that we could go by train or wait until the paddle boats are running, or even take a barge." Ingeborg sighed.

"You think I am not doing what's best?" His clipped words gave evidence of his thoughts.

"I know we do not have the money for such luxuries, but it doesn't hurt to wish, does it?" Ingeborg looked up from watching her fingers pleat the wool of her skirt as if they had a mind of their own. One glance at her husband's face made her wish she'd kept her dreams to herself. She trapped the sigh she felt coming with an abrupt rising to her feet. "Good night, Roald. I must go to bed now."

With each passing day, Roald became more restless. The weather turned warmer, and with the ice leaving the ground, the streets of Fargo turned into ruts filled with muddy water.

On Saturday morning he ordered Ingeborg to tell Mrs. Johnson this would be her last day. They would leave in the morning with one wagon.

Through the early hours at the hotel, Ingeborg kept Roald's order secreted in her heart, as if hoping something would happen to change it. A new woman had started in the kitchen two days earlier, training to take her place. After breakfast had been served, Ingeborg and Mrs. Johnson sat for a few minutes with their cups of coffee.

"This is your last day, ain't it?" Mrs. Johnson said after a lull in the conversation.

Ingeborg nodded. "I don't know what to say."

"Not goodbye, for we shall see each other again. I feel it in my bones. Just God bless and keep you in His grace."

Ingeborg reached across the wooden table. "Thank you for hiring a green immigrant like me." She patted Mrs. Johnson's hand, then reached in her pocket for a handkerchief to dab her tear-filled eyes.

"Smokey in here, ain't it?" Mrs. Johnson smiled around her own bit of cloth. "Here we sit, as close to blubbering as two Norwegians like us can get. You know how to write to me and let me know where you are. One of these days there'll be mail shipped all over this territory, you just wait and see."

Later, when Ingeborg opened her final pay envelope, she sniffed again. Inside she found an extra week's wages.

They left just as the first rays of daylight cracked the horizon between the endless prairie and the low-hanging clouds. Seated high on the front seat of the wagon, Ingeborg gave a silent farewell to the rising town of Fargo. The wagon could now be called a prairie schooner, since Carl and Roald had stretched canvas over the curved ribs of oak and firmly lashed it to the creaking wagon box. A rooster crowed off to their left as they slip-slopped their way north on Broadway. The street lay ankle deep in mud that some called gumbo because of the way it stuck to everything that tried to make its way through. Already the horses' hooves were three times their normal size.

Ingeborg huddled into her warm wool coat. Spring might be here, but it had frozen the night before, and all the puddles were rimmed with hoarfrost. She glanced down at Thorliff, who was standing on a box in the wagon so he could lean his elbows on the seat between his father and mother.

"Would you like to sit up here?" Ingeborg dug in her pocket and produced a handkerchief to wipe his nose. She sniffed herself, not sure if from the cold or the sorrow of leaving, then helped Thorliff scramble up to sit beside his father.

Roald glanced down at the squirming boy. "I thought you would sleep awhile like Gunhilde is doing right now."

"Gunny is a baby."

Ingeborg hid a smile in her handkerchief. Ever since they'd set the time to leave, Thorliff had let them know that he'd grown up. Even the set of his shoulders, straight and square, matched that of the man beside him. Roald held the reins in relaxed hands resting on his knees.

"Far, how did you know that was our land?" The words carried the same quiet pride as when Roald said "our land."

Roald hesitated. He'd answered this same question more than twice the last few days, more like every hour.

"The water was high in the rivers, and there were many trees and plenty of flat ground ready for our plow."

"But how could you tell under the snow?"

"The snow lay deep to melt down in the rich earth and nourish our fields. Snow is important to farmers."

"But what if there are rocks there?"

Roald shook his head. "They say there isn't a rock in the Red River Valley, nor a stump to dig out. Just rich land waiting under the prairie grass for our plow. You will plant seeds in the garden that will sprout as fast as you can put them in the ground."

"But I want to help you plant wheat and corn in the fields."

"Little boys help in the garden. When we have a cow and some sheep, you will herd them so they get plenty to eat but do not graze too far."

"All by myself?"

Thorliff's voice squeaked, either in joy or fear, Ingeborg wasn't sure. *Roald has said more to his son in these last few days than he has in the boy's entire lifetime*, she thought.

"Ja, you are getting to be a young man now."

Thorliff shot a look of pride up at his mother. Ingeborg took the opportunity to wipe his nose again. As he twisted away, she glanced back in the wagon box. A pallet had been made for Kaaren and the baby on top of the trunks and boxes they'd brought from Norway. She sat propped against another box, nursing Gunny and watching out the rear of the wagon, where Carl alternately rode on the endgate or walked along beside.

If only they had been able to find a team of oxen, this wagon wouldn't be so heavily loaded and so difficult for the horses to pull. She knew Roald had planned on buying or trading for more machinery too. Would they be able to find what they needed in Grand Forks? Someone had said prices were higher up there.

From the Minnesota side of the icebound Red River, a train whistle wept across the prairie. How much easier this trip would have been on the train or on the riverboat when the thaw finally set in and the ice went out in the river.

She closed her mind on those kinds of thoughts. Could one covet a train ride?

Only an hour up the trail, Roald stopped the team for a rest. He and Carl took sticks and knocked the mud off the horses' hooves and legs, and then cleaned between the spokes of the wheels. Next they scraped the gumbo from beneath the wagon bed.

"There, that should make their job easier." Carl straightened and stuck his stave behind the water barrel. He held the bucket under the spigot and, when it was half full, gave each horse a few swallows. While he was doing that, Roald checked the harnesses and the horses' hides for sore spots from rubbing.

He'd spent hours working on the harness, repairing strained places and oiling it so the cracks wouldn't go below the surface. More than once he'd grumbled about the way Mainwright had abused his farming implements. "That man had the sense of a flea," he muttered.

Ingeborg watched from her place on the seat. Maybe they should all walk to save the horses. Should she suggest such a thing? The narrowing space between Roald's eyebrows warned her to keep her opinions to herself.

The day and the miles dragged by as they repeated the mud-scraping stop about every hour. Yet, still the horses drooped from pulling all the extra weight.

Roald had hoped to reach Georgetown, but they were far short of that by the time they stopped for the night.

"Pray for a good hard frost and cold days," he muttered as he and Carl shuffled their goods to make better sleeping accommodations. They had hoped to find a farm where they might stop the night over, but in this land of bonanza farms, the home places were few and far between. At least the travelers had plenty of firewood. Cottonwood, willow, and occasional oak trees bordered the river and offered both protection from the never-ending wind and a good supply of dead branches that burned hot and crackling.

Coffee had never tasted so good. With the pot steaming to the side of the fire and mush frying in the pan, the snowbanks seemed to fade away. The sound of horses cropping dried prairie grass where Carl and Roald had cleared away the snow made camping out seem less a burden and more like an adventure. Thorliff dragged more branches back to the fire. The adults sank knee-deep in the snow with every step, so the boy had an easier time than any of them since he was small enough for the snow crust to hold him.

Ingeborg closed her eyes, the better to enjoy the savory steam from the mug in her hands. With her eyes closed, she pretended they were on an evening skating party in Norway. She pictured the pine and fir-clad hills that rose to granite mountains—hills, that when skied, connected one farm to another by minutes.

"Mor." Thorliff's question brought her back to the windswept prairies.

"Ja, den lille?"

"Tell me a story."

"Nei, not tonight. You must go to sleep right away." She rose from her overturned bucket by the fire and led him to the wagon. After tucking him in and saying prayers with him, she returned to the fire. Roald had found a piece of oak that he was carving into a handle for some implement. Carl was putting more wood in the flames, and Kaaren had just finished nursing the baby. The three of them sat snuggled with a quilt over their shoulders. Off in the distance the coyotes' mournful song floated across the snowdrifts.

For a fleeting instant, Ingeborg felt a piercing sadness so intense she caught her breath. When the pain struck again, it turned heavy, a load too much to carry. Maybe that's why the coyotes sing—to bring some life to the windblown loneliness of snow and the emptiness between it and the sky.

She shook her head at the fanciful thoughts. The coyotes no doubt were hunting, and she hoped they found something to eat far away from the Bjorklund camp. Now, if it were wolves, she would be concerned. And how could she call this lonely—-there were four of them around the fire, and two children who could always be counted on to ask questions or to need something.

Ingeborg fought against the desire to look over her shoulder. There were no eyes watching them. They were safe here with their wagon and with one another. Both horses grazed peacefully. If there'd been something out there, their sharp ears and eyes would have caught it long before the people did.

Ingeborg was glad they had a gun.

But a gun wasn't what they needed in the days ahead. Strong backs and stronger wells of patience were far more necessary. The weather continued warm and sunny, with the wind now a breeze and green shoots springing up with every passing breath. Only the deepest drifts remained and some scattered snow in those places shaded by bare-branched trees.

One afternoon, the driver of the stage bound for Grand Forks and Pembina hallooed them from behind before passing in a rush of waving arms and shouted greetings. Passengers rode both inside the coach and up by the driver, filling the rocking vehicle to capacity. The Bjorklunds waved back, and their horses picked up the pace for a few minutes, as if wanting to race.

In the few places where the track was dry, Ingeborg climbed down from the wagon and walked beside it, sometimes playing tag with Thorliff and other times just watching the cloud patterns on the prairie or lifting her face to the warm sun. As the snow continued to melt, the rich, fecund aroma of dirt and plants burgeoning to life made inhaling a pure pleasure.

During the long hours of riding, Ingeborg and Kaaren knitted and taught each other English words and phrases they had learned. Thanks to the little boy Thorliff had played with at the boardinghouse, he could add words, too. It became a game for all of them, learning this new language. The only problem was, they weren't sure what was right and if they were pronouncing the words correctly.

Carl had bought a language book, and they took turns puzzling out the words. On the slate, Kaaren wrote the alphabet, and they went over it until they could all recognize the English letters and numbers.

"You are a good teacher," Ingeborg said to Kaaren after one of their lessons.

"I always wanted to be a teacher, but my father said educating women was a waste of time. We just get married, after all."

"Ja, and who would teach the little ones if it wasn't for the mothers?" Ingeborg had never believed such a silly statement.

"I know. Maybe sometime in this new land I'll be able to teach at a school." Kaaren leaned her head back to let the sun warm her face.

"Starting with our own children." Ingeborg put a hand protectively over her middle. The ache in her back from working the long hours at the hotel had disappeared, as did the morning sickness, and she felt better than she had for weeks.

Roald asked about oxen and a wagon as they passed through the stage stops of Grandin, Caledonia, and Buxton. Thanks to the riverboat traffic, all were growing towns. At each stop they received the same answer: Sorry, no oxen available.

"I'm beginning to think we're making a mistake in wanting only to farm the land. We should buy up breeding mares and cows and raise draft horses and oxen. We could break just enough land to prove up our claims," Carl muttered after one more turndown. "There is such a need that we could set our own prices."

Roald stared at his brother. "But that would take more money than we have."

"Farming will, too. You know we plan to borrow from a bank just like everyone else."

"I hate the thought of borrowing money."

"I hate not having the things we need even more—like another team." Carl shifted on the hard wooden bench of the wagon.

"You've never trained oxen."

"Ja, but I've never come to America before either, and here we are."

"I suppose you think we should build the wagons too." Roald slapped the reins when the horses slowed. At the moment they were driving a fairly dry stretch and could make better time.

Carl stroked his whiskers. "That's not a bad idea. We could . . ."

"Carl, we are farmers, and we will farm."

"I am not saying we would not farm. I think we could add raising livestock to sell and make a better return sooner."

Roald's voice carried like a whiplash. "I will not talk about this anymore. We are farmers who till the soil. And that is that."

"Remember, brother. We are in this together," Carl spoke softly, but his words carried all the weight of his determination.

Ingeborg listened to the discussion, her hands busily knitting the sock on her needles, but her mind racing beyond the men's discussion. Talk about two hardheaded Norwegians. Couldn't they see they were both right? They needed to have some income the first year, before the prairie sod could be broken and the crops planted. She had heard about the breaking of sod, how it could break both a man's back and his spirit. She had also heard that when you stuck a seed in the ground, it sprouted and grew before you could finish the end of the row.

Even Ingeborg could recognize a tall story when she heard one, but she thought there must be some basis for the tale. She shivered in spite of her coat as the clouds above grew blacker. Without the sun, the temperature dropped in pace with the plodding horses.

The storm began with a chilling mist that soon turned to pounding rain and finally to snow. By the time they'd unhitched the horses and made camp for the night, Ingeborg felt chilled clear to her bones. How had the weather changed so quickly? Just a short time ago, the sun's warm rays had felt like summer, and now winter had returned. Cold coffee and leftover mush filled their stomachs but did little for their spirits.

By morning, six inches of snow had fallen, making land and trees sparkle as the sun rose. But with a south wind and warm sun, it soon turned to slush and melted off by midafternoon.

"I guess winter wanted to get in one last lick," Carl said, swinging his feet as he sat on the endgate of the wagon.

"Let's just pray that was the last one. All the men are saying spring came too early, and winter'll be back in time to freeze everything." Roald flicked the reins over the horses' backs. "Come on, you lazy bags of bones, let's pick up the pace. We have land awaiting us."

They spent the day sinking in potholes and wrenching the wagon out again. When evening fell, they had covered a grand distance of two miles. Both Carl and Roald wore frowns that looked to permanently crease their foreheads.

Before she fell asleep that night, Ingeborg prayed for a drier journey on the morrow. It couldn't get much worse.

Worse didn't happen, but more of the same brought shortness of temper, and only their wisdom and care for their team kept them from using the whip. After being yelled at several times, Thorliff huddled in the back of the wagon. He leaned his head against Kaaren and finally fell asleep. With only a cold evening meal again, no one had much to say before falling into bed like trees felled by an ax.

By the time they finally reached Grand Forks, they felt as though they'd been on the trail for half a lifetime.

They unhitched the team and set up camp along the riverbank. There were few trees left; others who'd come before them had stripped the banks bare.

Ingeborg and Kaaren looked at each other and shook their heads. "How will we cook?" Kaaren asked.

"I'll take Belle and return to where I saw some trees," Carl said. "We'll drag something back." He quickly added some rope and a chain to the harness and leaped on the mare's back.

Roald handed him an ax. "We might be here a couple of days, so bring in a good one." He tied the whinnying Bob to one of the wagon wheels. "I'm going into town to see if anyone has a team of oxen to sell."

"Can I go?" Thorliff looked up at his father, every line of his face and body a plea.

Roald shook his head, then changed his mind. "Ja, if you think you can behave yourself."

"I can, I can. I'll be the goodest." The little boy spun around, his arms flung wide as if his father had just given him the sun, moon, and stars rolled into one.

Ingeborg felt her throat tighten. It took so little to make the boy happy. A shame it was that his father didn't do such things more often. But then, she was trying to learn to be grateful for each little gift they received. This was such a one.

She and Kaaren shook out the beds and set Bob on a long line to graze the harsh grass that hid the tender green shoots springing up everywhere. After getting the coffee ready, they mixed cornmeal and water together for mush. What a treat it would be to have warm food with some of their precious dried meat for supper.

Ingeborg stared across the land, her eyes squinted against the setting sun. Even so, she could see the haze of green. In another week or two, the horses would have real grazing.

"God surely paints the most glorious sunsets here, doesn't He?" Kaaren came to stand beside her.

"Maybe He's trying to make up for the lack of mountains and evergreen trees."

"Inge, we must be grateful for what we have. Surely we will come to love this land as we do Norway. It is our home now, after all."

"Ja, after all." Ingeborg sometimes wondered what might be included in that "after all."

At least one wish came true that night. Carl returned with a tree for firewood and two rabbits. After he'd skinned them out, Ingeborg dusted the meat with flour and laid the pieces in a pan over hot coals. The wonderful smell of frying meat set all their juices flowing.

"I think you should teach me how to shoot the rifle and hunt. Then we wouldn't have to wait for you to find the time." Ingeborg made the surprising statement as she poured the last cups of coffee for the night.

Kaaren groaned, and Roald shook his head. But Carl gazed at her, speculation in his blue eyes. "Have you ever shot a gun?"

Ingeborg nodded. "My brother taught me when I was young. But when my father found out about the shooting lessons, he put a stop to them—quick. Who knew at that time I'd be moving to Dakota Territory where game would be so plentiful." She paused, readying herself for the arguments she could sense coming. "You heard the ducks and geese flying north. They have to set down somewhere in the evening. Maybe they even nest around here."

"I think that's a good idea," Carl stated flatly and glared at his brother to quell any argument.

Roald looked startled, as if a favorite dog had suddenly turned and snapped at him.

Ingeborg sat without moving, sensing the discussion could go either direction at that moment. Would Roald let Carl make a decision? She glanced at Kaaren out of the corner of her eye. Her opinion could be read off her face like a page in a book. Women did not shoot guns and hunt game. Women cleaned and cooked game when it was brought home.

Roald shook his head.

Ingeborg held her breath, then let it out in a whoosh. She rose to her feet, squared her jaw, and looked her husband directly in the eye. "I will go hunting with the rifle and so give the two of you more time in the fields. All I need is some practice and a bit of advice." She swallowed and straightened her back further, as if preparing for an onslaught.

The silence stretched, broken only by the snap of a log in the fire.

Roald rubbed the side of his nose with one finger, a gesture he'd copied from his father. "I guess it wouldn't hurt." He turned and looked directly at her. "But if you waste too many shells . . ." His unfinished sentence threatened louder than if he'd said the words.

Ingeborg looked at him as if afraid her hearing had gone bad. Had she heard him right? She ran the words through her mind again. She could learn to hunt—with the gun. She repeated them for good measure, then tucking her smile carefully out of sight, thanked him in a prim and gentle voice.

There were no oxen available in Grand Forks, much to Carl and Roald's dismay. They questioned everyone they met but to no avail. They left the town with the suggestion that they might try up in Pembina, which was the last stop of the Red River carts before they entered Canada.

"That's who's buying up all the oxen from around here," Carl said, shoving his hands into his pockets.

"And also the bonanza farmers, though most of them are using horses." Roald took his hat off, rubbed his head, and secured the brimmed homburg back in place. "So the question is still the same. Besides which, we need another wagon and a plow." Why was nothing going the way they'd planned? Returning to the camp empty-handed each night was beginning to weigh on him.

On top of that, the weather turned cold again. For the next two days it didn't rise above freezing, and the cold wind came from the north.

"We're going on," Roald announced the morning of the third day. "At least on our homestead we'll have the protection of trees rather than being at the mercy of the wind out in the open like this." Since they'd run out of wood again, they had to do without their coffee, so Roald and Carl harnessed up the team and headed on up the road.

Carl walked ahead of them, sounding the swamp and creek ice for strength. In spite of their care, the rear wheels cracked through the ice in a thin spot, but the horses managed to dig in and pulled the wagon out and up the shallow incline.

A short time later, the horses stepped onto the ice again, dragging their load across the winding creek once more. With a mighty snap that reverberated like the crack of doom, the heavy wagon sank into icy water deep enough for the pitch-tarred wagon bed to float. It pulled the horses backward as the ice split in all directions. The horses screamed and flailed, trying to regain their footing. The wagon tipped precariously to the right. Ingeborg clutched the seat with both hands, trying to lean to the left to help stabilize the teetering wagon.

"Here!" Roald thrust the reins into Ingeborg's hands and leaped onto the wagon tongue, working his way up to the horses' heads. "Easy now, Belle, Bob, easy. You're going to be fine." Roald spoke in soothing tones, trying to keep the animals from panicking.

"Just keep a firm hand on those lines," he cautioned Ingeborg.

Carl waded back, up to his pockets in the frigid water. "Throw me that lead rope, and I'll pull from here. We have to get them out of the water before they freeze to death."

"Ja, and you too." The water crept over the tops of Roald's boots and up to his knees.

Ingeborg could hear Kaaren in the back praying and comforting Thorliff, who had begun to scream.

"All right now, let's get out on solid ground again." Roald swung on top of Belle's broad back and slid off into the water. He grabbed the lead rope that he'd tied to her collar and pulled her forward. The mare took one step, then another, forcing the wide-eyed gelding to follow suit.

"All right, now, give 'em a touch of the lines," he instructed Ingeborg.

Ingeborg flapped the reins over their backs. "Gee-up," she hollered at the same moment. With the men scrambling backward up the bank trying to keep from being run over, the horses threw themselves into their collars and, hooves scrambling for a purchase in the slime, rocked the wagon out of the slew and up onto solid ground.

"Thank you, God." Kaaren said aloud what they all were thinking.

Ingeborg stepped down from the wagon, then clutched the mud-dripping wheel when her knees threatened to give way. Mud had splattered her skirt, coat, face, and into her hair. As soon as her knees stopped quivering, she reached up to lift Thorliff down.

"You go get us some wood, small pieces for a fast fire. Kaaren, hand out the winter coats and dry clothes for the men. They must change right away. We can rub the horses down with that sacking we saved." As she spoke, Ingeborg unhooked the traces on one side and rehooked them up onto the harness as Carl was doing on the other. Roald led the horses away from the wagon tongue.

"Here, take these and I'll get the rest." Kaaren handed out the men's clothing and turned back inside the wagon.

Carl and Roald shivered so badly they could hardly speak. Ingeborg handed them the warm clothing and took the lead lines for the horses. Tying them to a nearby tree, she turned back to assist Thorliff in his hunt for dry wood. He'd been on the trail long enough now to know to break dead branches off the trees and bushes, since anything on the ground was saturated with the melting snow.

"I'll help him. You start the fire." Kaaren handed Ingeborg the knife for shaving tinder and the flint box.

Thorliff brought in an armful of dry sticks and immediately Ingeborg began the tedious job of shaving the wood fine enough for the spark to catch. She could hear Kaaren caring for the men, the horses stamping and blowing, and the snap of tree limbs as Thorliff continued his search. Her hands shook so she could hardly aim the sparks. Finally, a spark caught and a tiny eye of red appeared. She blew on it gently until the eye turned into a minute spiral of smoke, and the fire caught. Carefully she added tiny twigs, increasing their size as they flamed, then added larger sticks, all the while blowing on it and nursing it along.

"I have the coffeepot ready."

Kaaren appeared at her elbow, startling her. She'd concentrated so on the fire, she hadn't heard the younger woman approach.

"Ja, that is good. Bring their boots here so they can dry, too. Hurry, Thorly, our fire is gobbling up your sticks too quickly."

Roald and Carl spread the quilts like wings to trap all the heat from the fire. They didn't wait for the coffee to finish boiling but drank the hot water first.

"Heat some for the horses, too," Roald said, stamping his feet. "We'll mix it with the oats and give them a real treat. I hate to stop this soon, but we'd better." He eyed the sun which was just beginning its afternoon descent.

"That was close." Carl glanced over to where Kaaren was rubbing down the horses. She'd pulled in some willow branches so they could eat the tender tips.

"Ja, a good thing we took the time to tar the seams in that old wagon. I don't think anything got soaked." Both men looked up as the train whistle mourned across the prairie. By the looks on their faces, they all were dreaming how simple the trip would have been if only they could have afforded the train fare. But "if only" were words they must forget.

"We should be on our own land tomorrow," Roald declared, greeting the day two mornings later. He stood facing east, watching the horizon for the first gold rim of the rising sun. The cloudless sky brightened from cobalt to lavender to flaming gold when the sun finally burst from its bed to begin the upward climb.

"If all goes well." Carl stopped beside his brother.

"Ja, God willing." The two watched the sun rise for a few moments more, then turned as one. "Let's be on the trail."

The next afternoon, Roald knew how Moses felt when he stood with God and looked over the promised land. Only this land was Roald's to give to his descendants. He would not be kept from taking possession of it as had the patriarch. He looked to the west, shading his eyes with his hand. One mile square, he and his brother would be filing on. Bjorklund land. Free of ice now, the Red River flowed behind him north to Winnipeg. Once the surveyors arrived, he could place cairns of stone at the four corners of their land, and then return to Grand Forks to file the official papers.

He picked up one small stone and tossed it in the air a couple of times.

One of the horses whinnied and, with ears pricked, looked toward the river.

14

If the woman who stepped out from the trees was as old as she looked, she'd have been a compatriot of the Moses Roald had been thinking about.

He stood beside the horse's head, watching her stride across the winter-flattened prairie grass. Hair gone nearly white and tied back with a string, a face so seamed it resembled nothing more than a dried apple left too long in the barrel, and a stocky build somewhat stooped by age but still spry all blended to create a character similar to the trolls he'd heard of as a child. Bright black eyes returned his scrutiny as she approached.

He nodded when she stopped a few feet from him. He sensed Ingeborg to his left with Kaaren between her and Carl. Was this an American Indian? He'd been told all the Indians were confined to reservations. What could he say?

He nodded. "God dag."

Her answer was incomprehensible. He shrugged to show he didn't understand, then pointed to his chest. "I am Roald Bjork-lund."

"Metis" was the only word he could understand, so he assumed her name to be Metis. She spoke swiftly and gestured with one arm. Where had he heard that word before? *Ah yes, Probstfield spoke of the Metis, a cross between the Indians and French Canadian trappers. Is she one of them?*

Roald shook his head and raised his hands, again to signal he had no idea what she was saying.

She spoke louder and more firmly, pointing to the ground and sweeping her hand in an arc. She finished with one finger pointing to her chest. Then she raised her hand palm out, nodded, and turned, walking off with the pace of a younger person and holding her head high.

"What was that all about?" Carl stared after their strange visitor.

"I wish I knew. She certainly was adamant about something. But she didn't seem hostile. If she's an Indian, I thought all Indians wore skins, you know, tanned leather and feathers." Roald rubbed the bridge of his nose, a sure sign he was perplexed. But he was afraid he knew what she had said. She thought this was her land.

"We must make our camp for tonight. Maybe tomorrow we can scout the riverbank and see if she is camping there."

"Then what?" Ingeborg failed to stifle her question.

"We'll tell her to leave. This is now Bjorklund land, or at least it will be when we prove it up."

But what if her family has lived on this land for generations? Ingeborg thought. *Can't we all get along together?* She stared after the woman who disappeared into the trees as quickly as she had appeared. "I wonder what language she speaks?"

"I think some was French." Kaaren stepped next to Ingeborg. "Remember the family I worked for a couple of years ago? They spoke French, and I learned a few words from them. But this woman's words ran together so fast, I can't be certain."

"She gave me a strange feeling." Ingeborg rubbed her elbows with both cupped hands. "I wish we'd had the coffee ready and could have offered her some. She might be our closest neighbor."

Within a short time, they had a good fire going and supper started. Thorliff had refused to go after wood by himself, keeping a cautious eye on the woods in case the old woman might appear again. Carl accompanied him, while Roald took the rifle and set out to see if he could raise some game.

Within a short time, he returned from the swampy area with two ducks in hand.

"Oh, how beautiful." Kaaren ran one finger down the shimmery green neck of one. "Let's save the feathers. I'll cut off the wing tips to use for dusters."

"When will we need dusters out here, living in a wagon?" Ingeborg looked up with a smile.

"I know." Kaaren smiled in return. "But I can dream, can't I? One day we will have stoves again and shelves for the dishes, and then we will have need of a bird's wing and a dustpan."

The women set to plucking the feathers and stuffing them into a sack. They would make good pillows or eventually a feather bed.

By the time the ducks were spitted and sizzling over the fire, shadows stretched across the winter-brown prairie.

While supper was cooking, Roald and the horses dragged a dead tree out of the woods and up to the fire. The ring of ax against wood sounded comforting in the deepening twilight as Carl stripped off the branches for firewood.

Thorliff stacked the smaller pieces of wood underneath the wagon, all the while keeping up a barrage of questions. "How much wood will we need? Where will we build our house? Do other people live around here? Does that Indian lady have children? When will we get our cows and sheeps? Are there buffalo around here?"

The adults took turns answering him until Roald said, "Enough."

When they sat down on the log to eat, Ingeborg cleared her throat. "I think we should say grace. We have much to be thankful for."

Roald nodded and bowed his head. "I Jesu navn går vi til bords . . ." Everyone joined in, including Thorliff. The sound of their gratefulness rose like the smoke of their fire, an incense to their God.

"We will begin breaking sod in the morning," Roald announced as they made their way to bed. "And as soon as the ground dries enough, we can sleep on our own land too. But in the meantime"—he turned over on one side so there would be room for all of them in the narrow space—"we'll make the best of this." Somehow the wagon bed seemed more comfortable on Bjorklund land.

The lilting song of a bird woke them well before sunrise.

Roald lay listening to the predawn hush. The bird sang again, music trilling from its throat. Unable to lie still a minute more, he picked up his pants and shirt, scooted to the end of the wagon, and pulled on his clothes over his wool long underwear. Carl joined him as he fumbled for his boots. The pearl gray tint of first light bathed all the earth in luminescence—the trees shimmered, the remaining snowbanks glittered. Even the horses' coats shone as they calmly grazed on last year's grass, hobbled by short thongs around their front legs to keep them close. He sucked in a deep breath of the chill morning air as if breathing for the first time. For him it was a first. The first morning on his own land. The new day bringing new life with every thrust of a blade of grass. If this prairie could grow such thick grass that the horses could find plenty to eat even now, surely it would grow the wheat and corn seed he had in the wagon.

Ingeborg joined them, and as they stood there gazing across the land, they could hear Kaaren murmuring to the nursing baby. Morning sounds, sounds of life both continuing and new. The bird sang again. Carl stirred the banked ashes from the night before and began blowing on the coals, adding small sticks. Ingeborg finished braiding her hair and tied an apron over her skirt and around her growing waist. Somehow the apron made her feel as if she were indeed in their own home, and this was a day like any other.

"I'm going to feed the horses and check over the plow and harness. I'll eat as soon as the meal is ready," Roald tossed over his shoulder as he headed for the timber line.

"I'll call you." The repeated birdsong made her heart sing. So much to do and so much to learn about this new land. What was the singing bird called here? What were the new words for all that she saw around them? While she went about the morning's chores, her mind surged far ahead.

Overhead, she heard the honking of geese and looked up to watch the V formation fly northward, their dark bodies etched against the blue sky. The coffee bubbled, sending a welcome aroma into the air. She mixed the leftover duck with the cornmeal and set it to simmer. How wonderful cream would taste over the porridge. Surely there were berries here to make jellies and syrups.

"Today I bake bread," she announced as Kaaren joined her at the fire. "I will use the fat from the ducks. And if we get some of those geese, we'll have more. Then we can fry the mush for a change."

"Have you laid out the house yet and planted the garden? What about . . ."

Ingeborg turned with a laugh. "Ja, I know I run ahead of myself, but how can I help it? There is so much to do. When I close my eyes, I can see a fine white house, a big barn, fruit trees, a garden, cattle, my chickens, and some pigs to make fine hams. Can you not see it?"

"Ja, and another place just like it over there." Kaaren pointed to the quarter section to the north. "If we both put our houses near the property line, we will be close enough to call out the front door. We will have flowers: tulips and lilac for the spring, lilies in the summer, and sunflowers for the fall. Our children will run back and forth and help their fathers in the fields. And during the winter, we will have school, and music, and we will teach our daughters to knit and quilt and cook and sew."

"Besides keep a fine house." Ingeborg clasped her hands in front of her. "Please, Lord, let it be so."

"Amen," whispered Kaaren.

Ingeborg stirred the mush one more time and called the men to breakfast.

"I will go hunting after we get started breaking sod. The plow is different than what we've used before." Carl spoke between spoonsful of hot food.

"Did you see that place over by the trees? There has already been a garden or small field there; the sod is broken for a couple hundred feet or so, each way." Roald pointed over toward the trees. "Someone has been living here; I am sure of it."

"But we will be the first to file on the land, so legally it is ours." Carl finished his bowl and poured another cup of coffee. "You think it might be Metis? That old woman?"

"I don't know. But I plan to walk every inch of this section. I want no surprises." Roald handed his cup and bowl to Ingeborg and turned back to the waiting horses. "No surprises."

Carl followed him a couple minutes later.

Ingeborg watched the two of them hitch the horses to the front of the plow and knot the reins to hang around the plowman's neck. With both hands on the handles of the plow frame, Roald clucked the horses forward and guided the point of the plowshare as it bit into the sod and folded a furrow over. The horses angled to the left.

"No, straight on," Roald called as he pulled them back to the right. They went too far, and the black dirt curved behind them. Roald pulled on the reins and looked behind him. No self-respecting farmer would allow crooked furrows. But breaking sod out on the prairie was different than plowing a furrow in a previously tilled field. He bent down to examine the black gash. The top of the cut was still packed with grass roots. How far down did the sod go? They'd been told they wouldn't be able to plant any of this newly broken land until next year, and now he understood why. They would have to replow, or backset, the field in the fall, going crosswise to the present furrows. Uff da.

The two brothers stared down at the ground and then at each other. Reading about breaking sod and actually doing it were as different as June and January.

Carl tried picking up the laid-over sod. While only two inches deep, the strip weighed heavy. He lifted it and tried breaking the section apart. The interwoven grass stems and roots refused to part.

He slammed the sod down on the ground, startling the horses.

"Easy, Bob, just trying to understand this land of ours." He placed the piece back on top of the ground where it had turned. "No wonder we have to come back in the fall and backset it. The grass needs that long to disintegrate." He dusted off his hands. "Let me lead the horses for this first strip, and then you can use that as a marker for the rest. If that's as hard to do as it looks, we can spell each other."

Roald started to say something and obviously thought the better of it. He put the reins back around his neck and grabbed the plow handles. Surely this first row was the hardest.

Ingeborg watched the exchange, feeling the tension emanating from her husband. He was so used to always being the leader, the one who made all the decisions. How would he handle his younger brother having ideas of his own, and good ones at that? Could the two become a team as the two horses, both pulling the same plow but each with their separate harness?

She watched the black sod roll over for a few more feet, then turned back to the wagon. If she was going to start bread to bake by suppertime, she'd better get to it.

She took the bubbling sourdough starter from the night before and divided it in two—half for the bread today and half to grow for the next time. After mixing in melted duck fat, a dollop of molasses, salt, and more flour, she stirred vigorously. When the dough was stiff enough, she began kneading, using the endgate of the wagon as a table. With each turn, roll, and press with the heels of her hands, the dough gained texture. Air bubbles began forming within the dough as if it were alive, making it feel and smell rich and yeasty. She kneaded more, rejoicing in the pull at her shoulders and the stretch in her back. Kneading bread used the entire body.

After she formed the finished dough into a ball and set the bowl next to the fire where it could rise in the heat, she stood back. Not quite the kitchen of home or the Headquarters Hotel, but it was theirs, and it was on their own land. Their food might not be as plentiful as she had served at the hotel, but she could make it just as tasty. Today they would have fresh bread. She would take some of the dough and fry for dinner, and they'd still have bread for supper.

"That smells heavenly," Kaaren said, bending over to sniff the bowl of rising dough after buttoning her shirtwaister. She'd been nursing Gunny while Ingeborg started the bread. "Where's Thorliff?"

Ingeborg pointed to the small form trudging along beside his father. While the women watched, the boy bent over, picked up something from the ground, and showed it to his father.

"Probably a worm." Ingeborg shook her head. "He loves the things of the earth: rocks, sticks, worms, bugs. Having cows and sheep to care for will be a big change, but a welcome one."

"Ja, I think today we forego the slate and let him study nature as it is."

"As long as his father can stand it."

When Carl returned to the camp, the women were shaking out the bedclothes and rearranging the interior of the wagon.

"Anything special you want from God's larder, ladies?" Carl reached for the rifle and pocketed a few shells.

"A deer would be nice. We could dry some of the meat, and you wouldn't have to go out each day." Kaaren adjusted the shawl sling that kept Gunhilde tight against her body. "And if you could bring in several geese, we would soon have a feather bed."

"As you wish. You know, I was thinking we could set snares for the rabbits, and soon the fish will be biting in the river, so we can dry those too." He caught Ingeborg's eye. "You want a lesson in snares and shooting this afternoon?"

"Of course," Ingeborg said, smiling at his offer.

"Good, because once we have that second team, neither Roald nor I will have time to hunt." He hefted the rifle, settling it under his arm with the barrel pointed to the ground. "I'll be back as soon as I can." He set off, the tune he whistled floating back like a friendly wave.

Later, Ingeborg took the water bucket and headed for the river. Their water barrel was nearly empty. She made her way carefully over the broken branches and fallen trees, trying to find the best path to the water. When she finally made it to the bank, she could see the hoof prints of deer and tracks that looked like a dog's, so there must be coyote or fox nearby. But the rounded and smeared footprints were certainly not animal.

15

Ingeborg could feel eyes staring at her.

She hated the feeling of looking over her shoulder every minute but couldn't make herself quit. In desperation, she turned around and studied the trees behind her. Bare trunks left little room for concealment, but many of the tree trunks and lower branches were large enough to hide a good-sized person. She felt a twinge of fear and wondered if there were animals in the region that could or would attack?

"Wolves wouldn't be out in the daytime." She spoke loudly, just in case something needed to be frightened away. She made her way carefully over logs thrown up by the spring flood, through brush covered with mud from the spring thaw, and between trees that had captured debris from those same floods. Everything wore a coating of dull brown gray dirt that matched the water flowing between the banks. Ingeborg wrinkled her nose. They were going to drink water from this so-called river?

On the bank sloping down to the water she saw more prints left by their wild neighbors. She studied them: waterfowl, deer, coyote, maybe fox, nothing large enough for wolf. She breathed a sigh of relief and dipped her bucket. She would have to let the mud settle out before it could be used. Returning to the wagon, she followed the narrow trail left by the animals, finding it much easier to travel. Halfway back, she looked down and stopped. The tracks again included the softly rounded prints of a human.

Were these the tracks of the woman who'd visited them? Was she nearby? Ingeborg looked to the surrounding trees again but couldn't see or sense a presence nearby. No longer feeling as though eyes were drilling her in the back, Ingeborg strode back to the wagon, chiding herself all the way for letting the sensations bother her.

When she set the bucket down, Kaaren took one look at the muddy water and wrinkled her nose. "I certainly hope we can find a spring with clean water soon, but until then, we must strain this." She lifted her face to the sun. "I am sure we should be grateful we have water nearby. And wood." She stopped and looked closely at her sister-in-law. "Something is bothering you."

Ingeborg shook her head. "You are far too observant for such a young woman. I saw human tracks down by the river. And while I was there, I felt eyes watching me." Ingeborg shrugged, as if to say it meant nothing. "Silly of me, wasn't it?" She looked toward the river. "And I keep looking for wolf tracks. Ever since my brother was attacked by wolves on his way home from town, wolves terrify me. We were so thankful that he lived."

"Have you ever seen a wolf yourself?"

"No, but I've heard them howl, and I'll never forget it. My father said it must have been an entire pack. And you know the stories they tell about being set upon by wolves in the winter." Ingeborg made a dismissing motion with her hand. "I'll get over it, I'm sure." She could still feel the hair rising on the nape of her neck at the memory.

The morning passed swiftly as the two women went about setting up a permanent camp. They dug two pits for fires, one to be used as an oven. They pounded in iron bars to become a tripod on which to hang their pots and to use as a spit for roasting meat. They would also use the spit for drying any meat that Carl would be fortunate enough to bring in.

Ingeborg checked the pot where her bread was rising. The dough grew slowly in the warmth from the sun and the smoldering coals beside it. The yeasty smell of working sourdough carried the fragrance of home as it rose to her nose. She breathed deeply and felt a smile begin down about her toes and work its way through her body, up to her lips and eyes. A bird flew overhead, its song rippling on the breeze as it passed. Another answered.

"Mor, Mor." In his excitement, Thorliff stumbled across the thick dead grass remaining from last season. He picked himself up again and, with a grin as wide as the prairie, held up a fat, wriggling worm. "Now we can go fishing. Far said."

"I think we need more than one worm, don't you?"

He shook his head, setting the blond curls tumbling across his forehead. "Nei, one for a fish."

"What if the fish eats our worm and swims away?"

Thorliff frowned in thought. "Then I need more worms." He laid the worm on his cupped palm and studied it as if he'd never seen one before. "He is so big he could catch two fishes." He giggled when the worm wriggled out of his hand and flopped on the ground. Squatting down, he retrieved the worm and put it in his pocket. "I get more." He headed back for the field, his giggles sending back sheer joy.

"I hadn't the heart to tell him that the worm probably wouldn't live in his pocket." Ingeborg watched his progress with a smile.

"We must braid some grass or willow branches into baskets for just such a thing." Kaaren sat down on the log by the fire and unbuttoned her dress for the whimpering baby to nurse. "When I think of all the food and utensils we had at home and now we must replace somehow, I feel like twenty-four-hour days are far too short."

"Ja, and the sooner we get a garden planted, the sooner we will have more to eat. I found the patch of land where someone has already broken the sod. When you are finished, I will show it to you." Ingeborg walked over to the wagon and, retrieving two mugs from the cooking box, poured them some coffee. Sipping the hot liquid, she watched as Roald and the team turned a corner and continued with the grueling sod breaking. *How fortunate that he is so strong*, she thought. *Keeping a firm hand on the plow so the sod lies over evenly would wear out a lesser man.*

As the sun neared its zenith, she hung the kettle with last night's supper remains over the now crackling fire. Having finished nursing the baby, Kaaren helped with the meal preparations.

"I wonder how far Carl had to go to find game."

"I haven't heard a rifle shot, so he's probably stalking something." Ingeborg sliced off a section of the rising dough and, after setting the skillet to heat, cut the dough into smaller pieces and patted them flat to fry for their noon meal. The simmering stew and sizzling bread made her mouth water. One thing about increasing as she was, she felt hungry all the time. Thank the Lord she'd passed the sickness stage. Straightening from turning the frying bread, Ingeborg searched the sky for the geese she could hear honking their way north. If only one of the flocks would set down near them for the night. The meat, the feathers, and the rich fat would all be welcome.

The jingling harness brought her attention back to the moment. Roald was on his way in from the field.

"Mor, see me!" Thorliff hollered from the back of the white horse. "Far let me ride."

Ingeborg felt a burst of love for this man of hers. Such a small thing, letting Thorliff tag along while his father plowed, and now giving the child a horseback ride. At home there had been no fields of their own to work, no time that a small boy could dog his father's footsteps and collect fishing worms at the same time. She'd teach him to make a basket tonight.

Roald lifted Thorliff down and unhitched the team. "Carl is not back?"

"Nei, but your dinner is ready. I could take the team down to drink while you eat."

Roald nodded and continued stripping off the harness, checking for sore spots. The horses needed a break as badly as he did. "Don't let them drink too much, and then they can graze while I sharpen the plow. This sod wears the plowshare down as if it were made of wood instead of iron. Far would be amazed at this land."

After dishing up a plate for him, Ingeborg took the horses' lead shanks and led down to the river. They needed to cut a decent trail, she decided, just one more thing that needed doing right now.

"Walking with you two is certainly different than walking by myself," she murmured as she led them between trees and around a fallen log. "The back of my neck no longer says someone is watching." Bob nudged her in the back as if to say "stop talking and walk faster." She kept a tight grip on the lead lines as they reached the edge of the river. Both horses waded in fetlock deep and drank. Ingeborg jerked on their leads after only a few deep swallows. Bob jerked back, insisting he should drink more. Belle lifted her head, water dripping from her muzzle and, ears pricked, stared at the opposite bank. Bob copied her. Ingeborg felt a shiver run up her spine. What was over there? Was the river deep enough to protect them if it were Indians? Or wolves?

Both horses snorted and dropped their heads back for another drink. Whatever had gotten their attention had left. Ingeborg let them drink a little longer and pulled their lead shanks. Reluctantly the horses followed her. After they passed out of the tree line, she hobbled them on a patch of prairie they hadn't already grazed. Letting the horses clean up the dried grass from the summer before allowed the new grass to sprout up sooner. Soon they'd be able to graze on the rich green shoots.

"The horses saw something across the river, but I couldn't see anything." Ingeborg walked over to Roald and Kaaren.

Roald looked up from sharpening the edge of the plow with a file. The whine of metal against metal stopped. Right then the pop of a distant rifle shot made him nod and Kaaren smile. "Carl found something." The rifle popped twice more and fell silent. "Bird most likely." The whine of file on blade drowned out anything else they might hear.

"Onkel Carl said he'd bring us a deer to eat."

Ingeborg looked over at her son, sitting with his back up against the log they used as a bench. In spite of himself, his eyelids drooped, and his head wobbled on a weary neck. "Did you find more worms?" she asked.

He nodded and dug in a pocket. The worms lay limp in his hand. "They don't look so good."

"No, they can't breathe very well in your pocket. Worms need dirt to live."

"Oh." Even the single syllable sounded exhausted.

"If you sleep for a while, you'll be able to help Far again."

"Or Mor." Roald put his file carefully back in its place in the tool box and rose to his feet. "Mange takk for maten."

"Velbekommen," Ingeborg responded. He had appreciated the meal and said so. It seemed like forever since she'd heard those words. She watched him go to the horses, calling their names as he approached. Belle raised her head and nickered, then pricked her ears and looked up the river. All three turned to look where the horse did, just in time to see Carl step out of the woods. He raised one hand that clutched two geese by the necks in salute, while his other hand helped balance the deer carcass he had slung over his shoulders.

Thorliff darted out across the prairie to meet his uncle. "You shot a deer and gooses. Let me help." But when Carl laughed and handed the little boy one of the geese, Thorliff dragged it on the ground. "It's heavy."

"They're beauties, they are. Here, you take this instead." Carl pulled a rabbit carcass from his coat pocket and gave that to Thorliff instead. "Now we can have rabbit stew for supper. What do you think of that?"

Thorliff stroked the soft fur and proudly carried the still-warm body over to the fire. "Here, Mor, feel. You could make mittens for me and Gunny from this, couldn't you?"

Ingeborg smiled at him as she took the rabbit by the hind legs. "Ja, we could. If we can find time to tan the hide." She looked at the deer with admiration. "Now you won't have to hunt for a long time. And I only heard three shots."

"I set a snare for the rabbit. There are trails all over the prairie. Soon I'll have to teach Thorliff how to trap and snare. He can keep us supplied in meat that way." Having laid the deer on the ground, Carl straightened up and stretched his shoulders. "That got heavy. Guess I'll hang it from the wagon hoops to dress it out." He turned to Roald. "How's the sod busting going?"

"Slower than I'd like, but the horses can't go any faster."

"You want me to work the plow for a while, and you dress this deer out?"

Roald flexed his hands. "If you'd like." He picked up the harness again and headed for the horses. "You eat while I get them ready."

Kaaren bustled about to fill Carl a plate while he washed his hands at the basin. "You made every shell count. Such variety: rabbit, goose, and venison. We'll be busy now."

Ingeborg looked longingly at the garden spot she wanted to work over with the mattock. Just the night before, Roald had finished carving a handle for the heavy, broad-headed tool, shaped something like a two-headed hoe. When she had asked Roald if they should leave the garden place for the old woman in case it was hers, he'd shaken his head as though she were losing her mind. It was Bjorklund land now. Ingeborg stifled the fear of reprisals. Roald's word was law. She straightened her back. The garden would have to wait, since they couldn't let any of the meat go to waste. "Come, Thorliff, you can help me pick the geese. Soon there will be a feather bed for you to sleep on."

Roald swiftly skinned out the deer, being careful not to slit the hide in the process. Carl had bled and gutted the animal where it fell, keeping the heart and liver for them to eat. With the hide pulled free, Roald stood back to look at the carcass. "He wintered well, even has some fat left. If only we had a tree here to hang it from." He glanced to the woods. "Maybe we should move camp closer to the trees."

Ingeborg and Kaaren swapped an "oh no" look. Not after all the time they'd spent digging the cooking pits! Ingeborg went back to stripping the feathers and stuffing them in a cloth bag that already held those of the duck. A goose feather caught on the air and floated up to her nose. She sneezed, making Thorliff laugh.

"Feathers all over!" He blew at one that escaped his hands, sending the bit of down across to Ingeborg, who blew it back. The boy clapped his hands, floating more tiny feathers.

By the time they finished, they both looked as though they'd bathed in goose down. Ingeborg picked several feathers out of Thorliff's hair. "You have been a big help, son. See how full our bag is?" She held up the puffy sack. "Now we need more firewood to dry all this meat. Think you can find some?"

The laughter left Thorliff's face as he glanced over his shoulder to the trees. His look pleaded for her to help him, but he took a deep breath and nodded.

"You must stay where we can see you, so only pick up branches along the edge." At that his face brightened again.

"I can get plenty of wood." His voice sounded like a younger version of his father's. "I can drag big branches back."

Ingeborg tickled his nose with a feather she plucked from his shoulder. "I know you can." *Such a brave little boy*, she thought. *What a miniature of his father. Would that the elder could see it.* She sent a plea upward, along with a heartfelt sigh.

While he marched off, she cleaned the geese and hung them alongside the deer on the wagon box. "That would make a good deer robe even though he was already shedding." She turned back the hide that Roald had rolled with the hair side in. "I have never tanned one myself, have you?"

"Ja, though we sold most of the pelts we trapped as young men." Roald looked up at the sound of a bird call. "You know, deer aren't so plentiful in Norway anymore. But when we killed a steer, we tanned the hide and used it for making harnesses and shoes. My father was an expert at making boots and shoes. One day I will have to make a last to form the boots over."

"Is there nothing your father could not do?"

Roald appeared to think for a moment. "I don't believe so." He began cutting thin strips of meat off the haunch to hang over the spit to dry. "Best you bury those entrails so we don't draw coyotes."

Or wolves. Ingeborg tried to stop the thought and the accompanying shudder. She picked up the mattock and the goose residue and headed for the garden plot, where she ran into Thorliff. He was dragging a branch behind him and carried sticks in the crook of his arm.

"That is good, son. Why don't you go help with Gunny when you are finished. I think she needs a nap." Thorliff just nodded, making Ingeborg aware how exhausted he was. When Thorliff was too tired to ask questions, he was really tired. But he still protested the thought of a nap. Naps were for babies, not for big boys. However, watching Gunny was becoming one of his assigned chores. If he fell asleep too, so much the better. She watched him trudge back toward the fire pit before she set off to bury the entrails. They would make good fertilizer for her garden.

But by the time she'd swung the heavy mattock over her head, slammed it into the soil, and then drawn it back to loosen the soil a few dozen times, she could feel the familiar ache in her back, compounded by the weariness in her arms and shoulders. Would that there was time to plow this patch, but the horses were needed more in the field. If only she knew which of the sprouting plants were safe to add to their diet. Surely that was a dandelion at her feet. She fingered the green, serrated leaves, always recognized at home as the first taste of spring. Pinching off one leaf, she rubbed it between thumb and forefinger and sniffed.

"Dandelion—I'd know that smell anywhere." She bent again to pick the leaves and searched out others. When her apron was full, she returned to camp feeling as though she'd been gardening after all.

Kaaren was setting the bread to bake when Ingeborg returned to camp. Fat dripped from the drying meat and sizzled on the coals below. The rising smoke would help the meat-drying process.

"Oh, look what you found." Kaaren picked out a small, tender leaf and bit the tip off. "Now we'll recover from the winter quickly. Mother always said dandelion was the best physic around. She picked the first of the greens herself and cooked them with bacon. What I wouldn't give for a side of bacon or ham. Maybe by next year we'll have a smokehouse."

"Use the strips of dried venison to flavor these. I keep wondering what roots around here are edible, what seeds, which trees and bushes will have berries and fruit to eat." Ingeborg dumped the dandelion leaves on a cloth at the back of the wagon and leaned the mattock against a wheel. Then, kneading her lower back with both fists, she turned to watch where Roald had joined Carl at the ever widening square of broken sod. To think they couldn't plant the black earth as they would an ordinary plowed furrow. The laid-over sod would now rest and rot, to be backset again in the fall. With plowing and dragging the following spring, the ground would finally be ready for planting. *No wonder so many homesteaders fail to prove up their claims*, she thought. *There is far too much time before they can reap a harvest.*

She turned toward the river and studied the piece of already broken land. Roald said it was about an acre and a half in size. He planned to plant it to wheat and oats—wheat flour for them and oats for the livestock. The plot looked too small to do all that it needed to, especially since some of it would be in corn and potatoes. She let her gaze sweep the land. If what they said about the prairie grass growing waist high was true, they wouldn't have a shortage of hay; that was for certain.

"Ja, if those two men have their way, we will see many changes here by next year. I, for one, look forward to a roof over our heads." Ingeborg nodded toward the western horizon. "I have a feeling those clouds are carrying a bellyful of rain, and it will be here before supper. We'd better put everything under cover, especially the wood. I'm going for more."

The rain held off until the geese were roasting on the spit, and the rabbit stew was bubbling on the coals. When it began to sprinkle, Roald and Carl hurried to unharness the horses after they'd left sod busting for the day. They hobbled them and dashed for the wagon when the downpour hit.

Kaaren poured coffee, and everyone sat in the wagon sipping the hot liquid and listening to the rain drumming on the canvas.

"We have to get those plow handles sanded down," Carl said loud enough to be heard above the rain. He grimaced when he studied the palms of his hands. "That Mainwright certainly knew nothing about caring for his belongings."

"Let me see." Kaaren took his hand in hers. "My goodness, your hands look like ground beef. Roald, how are yours?"

Ingeborg groaned when her husband turned his hands palm up. Blisters, open sores, and crusted blood mingled with the dirt of the field.

Y ou need to turn that deerskin into gloves as soon as you can." Carl studied his sore hands. "Tomorrow I'm wrapping those handles with leather."

"In the meantime, you get those hands scrubbed and let me bandage them. You'll get infection if you're not careful. Both of you." Kaaren's hands were planted on her hips, and the set of her eyebrows warned everyone that she wasn't backing down.

Carl looked at Roald and shrugged. "You know how she is when she gets her dander up."

"Can we wait until it's done raining?" Roald raised his hands in a plea. Thunder rolled overhead, and in a few seconds, lightning flashed to the east. "The storm's passing." He looked over at the smoldering fire. Steam rose in billows from the raindrops drowning the blaze. The strips of venison hung dripping in the steam clouds. "When it rains here, it could put out a burning barn, let alone a cooking fire."

The crescendo on the canvas reduced to a patter, then to intermittent drops. Ingeborg sat on the end of one of the trunks, lost in the celestial show. "Oh, look, a rainbow!" She pointed to the full arc that stretched clear across the sky. *Do you suppose God is giving us a sign too? He'll not flood us out and will always remember His promises?* She rested her chin in her hands. *God, help us to keep our promises, just as you do.*

Thorliff leaned against her, his head on her shoulder. "The thunder woke me up."

Ingeborg put her arm around him. "Were you frightened?" He shook his head. "Good, because thunder never hurts anyone. But we must be careful of the lightning out here on the open prairie.

There are no trees like in Norway to attract the lightning strike. Remember that lightning always strikes the highest point."

"You must lie down on the ground if you are caught out in a thunder and lightning storm," Roald said, joining in the conversation. "Never stand up and run."

"But I run fast." Thorliff caught his father's stern look. "Yes, Far."

"That is a good boy." Ingeborg patted his bottom. "You can help me with the fires while Far and Onkel Carl scrub their hands." She swung off the endgate and turned to give him a hand so he could jump without slipping. "Good thing we brought in so much wood. You go under the wagon and pull out some small sticks for me."

Thorliff ducked low and handed her the small branches broken in short pieces. After finding some hot coals in one of the pits, they stirred them, blew on them, and added small bits of wood. Within moments, a wisp of smoke trailed upward, followed by a bright orange flame licking the bark and sticks.

"Now, how will I start the other fire?" Thorliff asked.

"Take one of the burning sticks and put it over there."

"There?" Thorliff pointed to the pit under the dripping meat. Ingeborg nodded. "I can build the wood just right." At Ingeborg's nod, he retrieved more kindling from under the wagon and, after pushing the soaked firewood to the sides, laid several sticks, then inserted the tip of the burning branch.

Ingeborg nodded each time he looked up at her. "You are doing a fine job. Soon we'll put you in charge of the fires."

Thorliff drew a long branch from the burning fire and squatted beside the other. He poked the burning tip into the sticks and watched the flame catch. Doing just as his mother had, he added ever larger sticks until the fire burned brightly, the pitch snapping and crackling in the rising flames. Arms crossed over his knees, he stared into the fire, careful not to sit on the ground and soak his britches.

"You did well." Carl sat on the log behind the squatting child.

Thorliff threw a smile over his shoulder and continued his study of the flames until the fire grew too hot. He retreated to the log where Kaaren had set up her bandages. After wrapping the men's hands, she lifted the lid of the iron spider; the aroma rising from the rabbit stew mingled with the clean fragrance of newly washed air and land.

Ingeborg saw the look Thorliff sent his father. *Why can Roald never tell the boy he's done well? It would take so little.* But Roald's gaze appeared locked to the strip of cloth wrapped and tied around his hand.

"Uff da, the bread wasn't baked enough before the fire went out." Kaaren turned the fallen loaf out of the lidded iron pot and onto the wagon endgate. Using the hem of her apron as a pot holder, she broke the round loaf into pieces. "We'll just have to eat fallen bread tonight. Sorry, Inge. I know you were so pleased to bake real bread."

"That is the least of our worries." Ingeborg stepped back from turning the cooking geese when the smoke blew in her eyes. "We would do well to dig a long trench and make racks for drying the meat. Like the ones we had at home"—she corrected herself—"back in Norway, for drying the fish." She wiped the tears and sniffed. "But right now, we all need to eat."

"We'll take the deer and hang it from a tree branch first. We don't need visitors tonight." Roald rummaged in the wagon until he found the rope they'd brought. "One of these days I'll have pulleys carved, but a tree branch will do for now."

"Can I help?" Thorliff leaped eagerly to his feet.

"No, you stay here. Come on, Carl." Roald hoisted the deer hide and head, the rope, and the ax. "You take the deer."

Carl shot Ingeborg an apologetic smile and followed his brother into the deepening dusk.

Ingeborg kept the frown she felt from showing on her face. *It would take so little.* She reminded herself that Roald *had* let the boy ride on the workhorses.

By the time the men returned from their task, dusk had long since deepened into night.

"When you are ready to cut off more strips of venison, Carl or I will lower it for you." Roald took the plate Ingeborg had prepared for him and sat down on what had become his favorite spot on the log.

Tired from the long day and hard work, they ate supper in silence and then went to bed.

During the night, Roald moaned in his sleep every time he rolled over on the hard wagon surface. Ingeborg lay and stared at the canvas above. Her shoulders and back ached as though she'd been beaten with the handle of the mattock rather than turning the ground with the heavy tool. And when Roald groaned, she knew he must be in pain, whether he would admit it or not. Toward the front of the wagon, Carl snored. The baby whimpered, and Kaaren settled her for nursing. All were sounds she'd heard many times before—

and knew she would for months to come. She turned on her side and pillowed her head on her bent arm. Now she could see the bright stars out the back of the wagon.

She rose for the second time and added wood to the fires to keep the meat drying. No sense in waking anyone else when she couldn't sleep anyway. She shivered in the predawn cold. While spring was blossoming during the day, night seemed to want to stay in winter. She had the coffee hot and ready when the others climbed from their beds.

"Mange takk," Carl said, accepting the steaming cup. "Did you not sleep at all?"

"Ja, but"—she carefully schooled her face—"all of you were sleeping so peacefully that I decided to take care of the meat myself. It was nothing."

"It was more than nothing to me. I needed the sleep, in spite of the hard bed." Carl stretched his arms over his head and rotated his body, trying to stretch out the kinks. "We worked so long on the railroad and then on the trip coming up here, I thought all my muscles were strong enough. But bucking that plow uses different ones, all right."

"How are your hands?" Kaaren propped the baby on one hip and inspected the wrapped hands of both men. "You said you'd wrap the handles with leather for now?" At their nods, she glanced at Ingeborg. "How long will it take to tan the deer hide? That's not something I've ever done, but I can make gloves when the hide is tanned."

"It depends on how much time we can find to work it." Ingeborg stretched her shoulders up and down. The mattock had done for her what the plow had done to the men. "Breakfast will be ready by the time you harness the horses."

"You want first shift or afternoon?" Roald asked Carl, his mouth full of mush, flavored with roast goose.

"You start, and I will clear a trail down to the river. That will make it easier to get water. Then I'll work on the garden if I have time," Carl responded.

Roald nodded. "Perhaps by next week I can go to St. Andrew and see if anyone there has a team of oxen to sell, or knows of one. If not there, we'll have to go back to Grand Forks."

"That's a three-day walk."

"I know."

"How far is St. Andrew?" Ingeborg took her usual place on the log.

"Depends on how high the Little Salt River is running."

"Is there a ford?"

Roald shrugged. "We didn't go there when we were scouting. Just heard about it." He rose to his feet and, after handing Ingeborg his empty bowl, headed for the horses.

Walking in the opposite direction, Carl shouldered the ax and took one of the buckets for water. Ingeborg carried a bucket for water and one to put the strips of venison in. With the longer drying rack, all the venison would be dry in a day or two.

"When do you think you could give me a lesson on the rifle?"

"Tonight. You know Roald's not too pleased with the idea of you using the rifle. We didn't do things that way in Norway." Carl flashed her a smile.

"I know." Ingeborg heaved a sigh. There were many things that would have to be different here. If she could do some of the men's chores, then they could both be breaking sod, or plowing the garden, or cutting sod for the house.

"Look at the size of those tracks." Carl knelt on one knee, his hand gripping the ax handle. "That has to be a wolf." He traced the large paw print with one finger. "He's missing a toe. Must have been in a fight."

Ingeborg forced herself to watch what Carl was doing. By ignoring the pounding of her heart, she could nod and look up to make sure the wolf hadn't taken their deer. The cloth-wrapped carcass still hung about eight feet high, held in place by the rope knotted around the trunk.

"Look, he even tried getting at the rope." Carl studied the scene. "With all the rodents and such available, you wouldn't think he'd be after our meat."

Ingeborg followed his finger. Sure enough, toenails had scraped the tree trunk. "You say 'he.' What if it's a female needing to feed her pups?"

"Too big. But you never know." Carl lowered the carcass to where Ingeborg could easily reach to slice off strips. "I'll get a bucket of water and bring it back. Tomorrow will be easier with a trail cleared."

"Mange takk, Carl. I nearly slipped on a log yesterday." She grabbed her knife out of the bucket and began slicing the haunch, dropping the strips in the bucket. She hummed a tune under her breath, trying to ignore the fact that the wolf could be watching her right now. She'd learned since childhood to make noise in the woods to scare the animals away. But the wolf had crept this close to their camp. If only they had a dog to bark and warn them. They must all have slept so deeply that the horses' snorting didn't wake them. She shook her head. *She* hadn't slept that soundly. All the while slicing and dropping the meat, she let her thoughts continue their path. The wind must have blown in the other direction, and the horses were hobbled west of the wagons.

"I will not look around. I will not."

"You can if you want, Inge." Carl pushed through the bushes with a teasing grin. "Don't worry about feeling afraid. Pay attention to everything around you—it's safer that way." He set the bucket down and made a face at it. "We better collect all the water we can next time it rains. This water doesn't look clean enough to wash in, let alone drink."

"We've been letting it set before straining it through a couple layers of cloth. Comes clean that way. I'll get these strips drying and come back for more."

"Send Thorliff down for wood as soon as he's eaten. He can haul the short pieces up. Later, we'll drag the trees with the horses." He looked out across the prairie. "See that hawk? He's probably grateful for all the mice we scared up." Just then the hawk dove, snatched a small animal with its talons, and beat its way back into the clear sky. "See, I told you. I saw him do that yesterday, too."

Ingeborg felt a burning in her chest. *So free and so powerful. What a magnificent sight.* She picked up the buckets and headed back to camp. Watching birds wouldn't get her work done. She heard the trill of a meadowlark, lifting its song on the morning breeze. At least she could listen to the music of God's world and walk at the same time.

"Mor, I was missing you." Thorliff leaped from the sitting log and darted across the camp, dodging the drying rack as he ran. "Can I go to Far and help him plow?"

"No, Onkel Carl needs you to bring up firewood. He's clearing a trail to the river for us." At the stubborn set of her son's chin, Ingeborg continued. "He needs your help. You can take a jug of coffee out to Far later."

Thorliff's face brightened. "Then I can ride the horses."

Ingeborg laid the strips of meat over the drying rack. "Hurry now."

Kaaren finished tying the baby into the shawl sling. "She's fussy today, crying whenever I put her down. Do you think there's something wrong?"

"Nei, babies need to fuss sometimes. She doesn't have a runny nose or anything, does she?" At Kaaren's shake of the head, Ingeborg continued. "And you have plenty of milk for her?" A nod. "Then not to worry. At least that's what my mor would say, along with 'let the day's own troubles be sufficient for the day.' She had a Bible verse for everything."

"You're right. I shouldn't worry, but it's not easy. She's so small, and we're so far away from any help."

To that there was no answer.

"Mor, Mor, come! Come quick!" Thorliff ran shouting from the woods a short time later.

Ingeborg and Kaaren looked at each other and, gathering up their skirts, ran toward the river. *Is Carl hurt? What can be wrong? Dear God, please help us.* Her thoughts and fears kept pace with her feet as she ran. But the look on Thorliff's face wasn't fear as she'd supposed. A grin that split his face in two and a finger pointing to the river let her stop to catch her breath. Kaaren did the same, almost bumping into her.

"Why did you frighten us so?"

"Onkel Carl said to hurry. There's a big boat in the river." He grabbed her hand. "Come and see."

A piercing whistle, followed by another, rent the air. Kaaren and Ingeborg shared looks of delight and hurried down the trail Carl had cleared. They found him standing on the bank, waving to the passengers lining the rail of the paddle boat as it beat its way up the swollen river. The whistle blew again.

The boat glistened with a new coat of white paint, trimmed in bright red. Smoke rose from the stack and drifted behind them. The sloshing beat of the paddle wheel nearly drowned out the halloos of the passengers standing on deck and waving.

People, real people. There were others alive in the rest of the world after all. Ingeborg blinked repeatedly, the sheer joy of it bringing tears to her eyes. She waved along with the others, calling "god dag, god dag" until finally remembering "hello, hello." So much had happened since she'd tried her English, she'd nearly forgotten it all.

Thorliff danced beside her, waving both arms and shouting his delight. As the boat cruised around the river bend, the boy looked up at his mother. "Someday, Mor, I will ride on the steamboat." His arms dropped to his side. "Someday."

Ingeborg rested her hands on his shoulders. "Me too, son, me too." She listened for the fading slosh and thump. "Would the captain stop here if we needed them?" she asked Carl.

"Not sure. I know they put in at St. Andrew. Roald and I plan to cut wood this winter for their fireboxes, if we can find the time. Then when spring comes, they'll stop for sure. As the river drops, you will see more traffic here."

Ingeborg sighed and turned back to her work, picking up pieces of wood as she went until she had an armload. "Thorliff, you bring back a sack and gather all these chips. They're good and green for smoking the meat." She glanced up to check the position of the sun. "Far needs his coffee jug, too."

Thorliff dashed ahead.

"Pick up some wood as you go." Her call stopped his running feet and brought out a frown that disappeared almost before it reached his face. He obediently picked up an armload and carried it to the stack under the wagon.

"Hurry, Mor. Far is thirsty." As soon as she poured the hot coffee in the metal container, he charged off toward the field.

"Oh, for that energy." Ingeborg turned the drying meat. Her back ached again, and she'd noticed that her shoes were getting tight from her swelling feet. "Uff da," she muttered under her breath.

That afternoon, Carl relieved Roald at the plow, turning row after row of sod. Certainly none of the fieldwork they had done in Norway had prepared them for this backbreaking job. But it would be worth it all next year when they could plant their precious grain. Even now he could picture the wheat bending and rippling like waves as gentle winds blew across the fields. *Ja, this hard work will eventually pay off for us*, Carl thought.

Several hours later Carl stopped to rest a bit, wiping his brow with his shirt-sleeve. Though the work was tedious and exhausting, the rows of laid-over sod that lay behind him showed the harvest of his labor. Turning and looking toward their camp, he could see Ingeborg and Kaaren bending over the fires, preparing the evening meal. Just thinking of food made his stomach rumble in anticipation. Soon he could quit for the day.

After cleaning up the supper dishes, Ingeborg sat near the fire and scraped the remaining fat and tissue off the deer hide. Periodically the rising stench reminded her stomach of the days of morning, afternoon, and evening sickness. Usually she could control the reaction, but once she had to leave the fire and heave into the growing prairie grass. When she finished this side, she planned to rub a mixture of brains and watered wood ashes on the outside, and then leave it set to loosen the hair.

"You all right, Mor?" Thorliff appeared at her side as she wiped her mouth with a cloth.

"Ja, I will be. You can help me scrape if you want. Then we will be finished more quickly." She stood for a moment and looked heavenward. The great swath of stars that made up the Milky Way lightened the skies above them. She could hear the wind sighing over the grass that seemed to grow a foot a day. Carl's laughter swung her gaze back to the camp where the men were working on the plow, one sharpening the share, the other smoothing the handles they had carved. Sparks shot skyward when Kaaren stirred the fire and added wood.

Ingeborg cupped the back of Thorliff's head with her hand. "Come, den lille, let us be back to the deerskin."

⚶ ⚶

Two mornings later, Roald slung a sack of food over his shoulder and set out for St. Andrew. If he didn't find a team there, he would take the paddle boat to Grand Forks. While he hated to spend the money for passage on the boat, he knew he was needed back at the homestead as soon as possible.

Carl drove the team out to the plow, taking Thorliff with him.

Since Kaaren was busy nursing the baby, Ingeborg picked up the buckets and trudged toward the river to get the day's supply of water. She checked her pocket. The hook and line were still there where she'd secreted them the night before. The thought of fresh fish for supper made her mouth water—she'd roll the fish in cornmeal and fry it in venison fat. But she'd have to catch them first; surely they'd be biting by now. Cutting a sapling, she stripped off the small branches and leaves, then tied the line at the narrow tip.

She stared out across the muddy water. How would any fish see the worm, let alone smell it? She'd caught many a trout and salmon at home, but there the creeks ran sparkling clear with deep pools for the fish to lie in. What a surprise fresh fish would be for supper.

She worked her way upstream from where they usually dipped their water until she found a log to sit on at the water's edge. Tucking her skirts under her legs, she took the prairie grass nest she'd made for the bait and removed one wriggling worm. Baiting a hook had never been her favorite part of fishing, but if fish didn't like them so well, God wouldn't have led man to use them—or so her reasoning went. She tied the string around a small rock and tossed the line out as far as it would go.

Her brother would say no self-respecting fisherman sits on a log, but instead walks the bank, the better to jerk the line when one felt a fish nibbling at the bait. She smiled to herself. But then she'd always caught more fish than he did. She batted away a pesky fly and smoothed a strand of hair up into her braids. How heavenly to sit here and fish all by herself in the quiet.

When she felt the bump of fish against the bait, she paused and jerked the pole. A fish broke the surface of the river, and with another jerk she landed it flopping on the muddy bank. She removed the hook from its mouth and stuck a stick through the mouth and a gill to hold it while she took another stick and knocked it on the head. "Sorry, fish, but I can't stand to see anything suffer." Her voice sounded strange against the stillness.

The stillness. There was not a sound in the air. Even the birds had quit their singing. The hair rose on the back of her neck. She felt eyes watching her. Slowly she turned. Not far away a gaunt gray wolf sat watching. He lifted one side of his lip, baring a fierce incisor.

Ingeborg slung the fish at him and turned to run, but her skirt caught on a branch. She slipped, fell backward, and slammed into a log. Pain arched through her back. At the same moment, her head crashed against another log.

17

"But I don't want to borrow more money!" The words burst forth, shocking him with their intensity. Roald shifted the sack of supplies he carried on his back and shook his head. Was he going crazy, talking to the wind?

He strode through the calf-high prairie grass like a ship's prow breaking the waves. While aware of the rising sun gilding the dew-laden blades of grass, his thoughts continued to wrestle with the problem ahead. He needed to find a team of oxen, but he didn't have sufficient money to pay market price. The thought of going back to Grand Forks if he failed here burned like the stings of a hundred bees. He should have talked with Probstfield again. He should have made more of an effort in Fargo. He should have, he should have, he should have. The thoughts beat time with his striding feet.

"Uff da!" He reached up and wiped his brow, frustrated that he hadn't planned better. Breaking sod now meant the possibility of a crop next year, so they couldn't put off buying another team. Yet, if they waited, they might have more money. They could earn extra by cutting wood for the steamships paddling the length of the Red between Grand Forks and Winnipeg. Back and forth went the internal argument and carried him closer to the small port town of St. Andrew.

He heard a rifle shot somewhere to the north. The sound made him think of Ingeborg and her determination to hunt. A wedge of ducks quacked their way northward. If she had her way, she'd be bringing them down with that rifle. Who would think that behind that gentle smile—he shook his head. Ingeborg, the woman who had brought light back into his life and dumfounded him so often. He fingered the coins in his pocket. Was there some little thing she would like from the store? Something that would bring the laughter to her eyes. He jingled them again. Something he could afford. With a snort he picked up his pace.

When the sun reached its zenith, Roald sat cross-legged in the prairie grass and dug in his sack for a flask of water, bread, and strips of dried venison. Hat pushed back on his head, he studied the sky while he chewed on the dry meat. Ducks and geese still beat their way north almost daily, long V-formations etched against the cloudless sky. The music of the prairie settled around him: the sighing of the wind rippling and bending the prairie grass like waves on a lake, the wild cry of geese overhead, a cricket sawing away on a grass stem, and a meadowlark adding the melody. Roald let his gaze wander the horizon. To the east, the woods bound the river; in the west a cloud pile climbed into the sky; northward, he could now see the trees of the Little Salt River; to the south, a man could get lost in the limitless expanse.

In a rare moment of ease, he crossed his hands behind his head and lay back, cushioned by the thick grass. The sun felt blessedly warm on his face and painted circles on the backs of his closed eyelids. He stretched his legs out flat and sighed, letting his body mold itself to the earth. Opening one eye, he watched a butterfly flit above him, dipping and fluttering from a stalk of grass to sip at the golden heart of a flower, yellow as butter churned from cows fed on fresh spring grass.

Off in the distance, he heard the cutting whistle of the riverboat. St. Andrew must be closer than he thought. He leaped to his feet, a twinge of guilt making him brush the seeds and grass off his pants with more vigor than necessary. It was a waste of time lying in the grass watching the geese fly north. *They*, at least, were going somewhere, while he drowsed the afternoon away. He slung his sack over his shoulder again and started out at a dogtrot to make up for lost time.

Before the sun had dipped halfway down the sky, he strode down Levee Street in the river port town of St. Andrew. Wagons lining the street in front of the general store reminded him that this must be Saturday, the day the farmers came to town. That was good—more people to ask about a yoke of oxen. He eyed a fine pair standing patiently in the sun, white tails swatting flies. If they were his, they would not be standing here wasting time in the sun. They would be home in front of the plow, turning up the rich black soil.

Boot heels ringing on the wooden stairs, he mounted the entry to the general store. He blinked in the dimness and inhaled the mingled fragrances of kerosene, pickles, harness, and boot leather. Barrels, tubs, bins, and boxes lined every shelf, while the ceiling was festooned with hanging harnesses and hay rakes. Pitchforks and shovels dangled from the rafters, while housewares covered the walls. Bolts of bright calico and blue dimity draped beside needles and thread, with a variety of lace to please any woman's heart. If that weren't enough, a straw hat with a cabbage rose nodding on its brim perched next to a man's straw hat. Behind the counter, spices lined the shelves, along with nostrums and cans, coffee beans, the grinder and pot, plus barrels of sugar and flour.

Roald stared at all the bounty surrounding him—clear out here in the wilds of Dakota Territory. His heart beat faster; people must be wresting a good living from this rich black loam if a store could manage to carry the necessities and all these luxuries, too. He looked around for the proprietor and heard a voice from behind a length of shelves that divided the chockfull room. He followed the sound.

The storekeeper, round as he was tall, nodded vigorously while pointing out the finer qualities of a pair of boots to a customer who looked as out of place as Roald felt. He waited until the man shook his head and the clerk shrugged, then put the boots back in their place.

"God dag." Roald hoped that someone spoke or understood Norwegian. He was certain the two men had been speaking English.

"God dag." The farmer stepped back and nodded, letting the aproned man take over.

"I am looking for a yoke of oxen and could not help admire the pair outside. Do you know who owns them?"

"He does." The man translated for the other customer.

"Please ask him if he is willing to sell or has others to sell."

The proprietor nodded. "You are new here."

Roald nodded in return and looked toward the waiting customer. When the man shook his head, Roald asked, "Do either of you know someone with oxen?"

After a brief murmuring, the other farmer shook his head, while the shopkeeper scratched a red spot on his chin. "You might try up in Pembina. Those Red River oxcart drivers get their stock somewhere. If anybody would know about a team, they would."

Roald nodded. "Mange takk." He started to leave but turned back. "When does the riverboat go north?"

"Sometime before nightfall. They don't keep much to a schedule; the one to Grand Forks left some hours ago."

Roald thanked him again and turned to leave.

"I didn't catch your name."

He stopped. "Roald Bjorklund."

"Wal, I'm Ross MacDonald from Ohio. This here's Abe Jeffries. He's homesteading out west a'here." He waited, but when Roald didn't volunteer any more information, asked, "You homesteading, too?"

Roald nodded. "Most of a day's walk south. We arrived a few days ago—my brother and I."

"Just the two of you?"

This time Roald answered with a shake of his head. "We have wives and children. You know anyone with an extra plow or wagon?"

"You can order them from Grand Forks, if you like. I take orders right here. They'll get here in a couple of days on the riverboat if they're in stock. We can get most anything here."

"Except for oxen?"

Ross grinned, showing a blackened right front tooth. "Yep, that's about right. Livestock's hard to come by, what with so many settlers wanting 'em. You wouldn't do half bad going into the breeding business, if'n you had a mind to."

"Mange takk," Roald said again and tipped his hat. Why was everyone pushing him to raise livestock to sell instead of wheat? Granted, they needed horses and oxen, but the world needed bread. When he stepped out into the bright sunshine, he let his eyes adjust and looked to the east. The dirt street ran right to the river's edge, where a wooden dock continued out into the river. Pembina it was, instead of Grand Forks.

He turned and headed up the street, his boots kicking up dust puffs as he walked. Past the Riverfront Hotel where the aroma of roasting beef and apple pies with cinnamon wafting out made his mouth water, past the livery with the ringing of the anvil, past the saloon, until finally he reached the river.

Deep shadows cast by trees overhanging the shallow western bank turned the mud-brown river to black. He sat on a piling and, after checking both directions, let his gaze wander the opposite bank. A point of land stabbed into the river's belly, causing the slow-moving current to swing to the west. A flash of action caught his eye, and he turned to see an eagle beating huge and powerful wings against the air and lifting from the surface with a fish clutched in its talons. The eagle turned and headed for a broad stick nest in the top of a dead snag directly across from him. The eagle dropped to the edge of the nest. Roald pictured the eaglets eager for food, beaks wide and with shrieks demanding a turn.

As a young man, Roald had climbed the mountains of Norway and watched an eagle's nest below him on a ledge. He'd never forgotten either the sight or the thrill of a creature so wild and free in a continuous fight for survival. He'd never told anyone, as if keeping this secret gave him a kinship with the creature.

He shook his head at the fanciful thinking. Glancing at the sky, he wondered how soon the boat would arrive. Roald did not think they traveled at night.

He heard the boat approaching long before it nosed around the western bend in the river. The whistle cut the air, causing a flurry of activity in the town. People hurried from the hotel, general store, and from their houses, quickly congregating on the shore and dock. Between the noisy shpluck, shpluck of the approaching paddles and the babble of townsfolk, a little boy jumped up and down on the edge of the dock. His vigilant mama snatched him back from a certain dunking.

Roald could tell the boy was getting a tongue-lashing by the tone of his mother's voice and the hangdog look on the child's face. Thorliff would look like that, Roald thought, and Ingeborg would pull him back just as this mother had. Thorliff and Ingeborg would have enjoyed the sights of this town so much, if only he would have brought them. Surprised at the thought, he watched the paddles reverse and bring the boat to a stop precisely where the gangplank would be lowered at the end of the pier.

"Mail!" one of the deckhands shouted, and Mr. MacDonald of the general store excused himself past the onlookers and took the leather pouch.

"I'll have this laid out at the store in just a jiffy," he promised, making his way back up the street.

"Your crates'll be right here, waitin' yer return." Two deckhands trundled boxes, crates, and sacks labeled flour, sugar, beans, and coffee down to the dock and stacked them off to the side. Sacks of seed wheat, oats, and corn followed. At the same time, two other hands loaded the stack of wood from the end of the pier onto the steamer.

A young man with a trunk on his shoulder, his wife and children at his side, threaded his way between the commotion and onto the land. He left his wife on´the side of the street and returned to the boat for more of their baggage.

When all the supplies were unloaded, Roald and another passenger made their way up the gangplank and, after paying the man at the railing, strolled past the kegs and crates to the bow. The timbre of the engine changed, the boat shuddered as the paddle wheels began a sluggish rotation again and, with a farewell blast of the whistle, moved out into the middle of the river and proceeded downstream on its way to Winnipeg.

Roald leaned his elbows on the mahogany railing, feeling the vibrations of the engine up through his boot soles. He watched as ducks dipped for their dinner along the banks, tails pointing toward the sky. A great gray heron looked like a tree branch until his beak stabbed the water at the river's edge, then, before his neck straightened to its full length, he'd swallowed the fish. A swimming muskrat created a V-ripple behind him as he breasted the current.

Dusk slipped over the land, softening the angles and shadows until Roald nearly missed the sight of a doe and her fawns coming to the water's edge for a drink. Feeling hungry, he dug in his sack for a piece of dried venison and, after biting off a chunk, chewed thoughtfully. Traveling by riverboat put the land route to shame. As the boat swung around each of the winding bends in the river, he waited for new sights. A spiral of smoke told of a cabin off to the Minnesota side, and a young boy hallooing and waving on the west bank let him know of another family turning the prairie into a home.

Roald waved back.

Night had almost blackened out the dusk by the time they docked at Pembina. Deckhands secured the steamer for the night as Roald threaded his way back to the gangplank and down to shore. Where should he start his search for oxen?

Lamplight fell in a square from the saloon door, and Roald peered into the smoky room before pushing through the swinging doors. Off to the left, a man tended the polished walnut bar, while another plunked out a tune on the piano. Men in the black pants and jackets of farmers rubbed shoulders with others dressed in the bright red shirts and black suspenders of a darker-skinned group who sang in a language Roald recognized as French, even though he had no idea what they said.

"Good evening," he said to a man leaning against the bar. The fellow shook his head and pointed to the bartender.

"So you're a Norwegian. What can I get you?" Bald as the glasses he polished with a stained dish towel, the man smiled around a gold tooth.

Roald raised a hand to forestall the pouring of whiskey into a glass. "I'm looking for someone who might have a yoke of oxen for sale. Can you help me?"

The bartender rolled his eyes upward in thought, but after a moment shook his head. "Not sure that I do, but you could check with Pierre St. James. He has a farm 'bout four miles west of town. He was in here earlier today, but he's prob'ly home by now. I'd wait 'til mornin' meself, then take the road west about two miles, go north on the cross road, and you'll see his place off to the left 'bout a half mile up. You could miss it in the dark."

"Mange takk." Roald tipped his hat and turned to leave.

"Sure you won't have a bit to clear the dust from yer pipes?" The barman raised the amber-filled bottle and reached for a glass.

Roald shook his head. While a drink might set the fire burning in his belly and drive the worries away for the moment, he needed the money too badly for other things. Once outside, he headed west out the road, guided by a full moon just creeping up its arc. Sleeping in the open wasn't a hazard at this time of year, especially since the red sunset had promised a fine day on the morrow. Unless one counted the mosquitoes. He swatted one off his neck and kept on walking. He'd get as close to the turn this night as possible without going by it.

When he grew too tired to continue, he slept with a blanket covering his head rather than his feet, making sure that every bit of skin was hidden from the bloodthirsty stingers. The birds heralded the dawn and woke him the following morning. He ate while he walked, reaching the farm before the dew had entirely left the prairie grass.

Two friendly dogs barked at his heels as he strode to the yard between the sod house and a barn surrounded by corrals. Cattle grazed in a pasture fenced with barbed wire strung between crooked fence posts, while pigs grunted from a pen next to the sod-roofed barn.

A woman stepped from the door of the soddy and yelled at the dogs, which slunk away.

Roald tipped his hat. "God dag. Is your husband here?"

The woman shrugged and pointed to the man plowing the field to the west.

Roald thanked her and set out across a five-acre seeded field. Green shoots were already defining the rows, so he walked carefully to keep from stepping on grain. The man waved, then wiped his forehead with his sleeve. Off to the north, Roald could see a second team, and beyond that, a third. Was that another farm, or had this man broken this much land already?

"I am looking for a yoke of oxen to buy, and in town they told me to talk with you." He spoke slowly, praying the man could understand Norwegian. If only he had spent more time on the boat learning the language. He eyed the two oxen, one brindle, the other white with red spattered throughout its coat, placidly waiting instructions.

Roald sucked in a deep breath and tried again. "Mr. St. James?"

The dark-haired man with tired eyes nodded. "Sprechen zie Deutsch?"

Roald breathed in a sigh of relief and offered a silent prayer of gratitude. The man spoke German. "Nei, Norwegian, but we can understand each other. I am looking for a team of oxen." He pointed to the team. "Do you have any for sale?"

At the man's head shake, Roald felt his heart sink in his chest. "Do you know who might?"

Roald forced himself to stand still as St. James studied him. He wanted to walk away and vent his frustration in private. There had been no oxen for sale in Grand Forks when he was there less than a month ago. Why hadn't he started looking earlier in Fargo?

"There is . . ." St. James paused and shook his head again.

"Ja?"

"I have a team that I have just begun to break. They are not fully trained yet, and I do not like to let a team go until I know I can depend on them. I have a reputation, you see?"

Roald only heard the words "have" and "team." His heart soared with renewed hope.

"You have a team?" Roald said the words reverently and with relief. Now, if the man would accept his limited cash, everything would work out.

"Yes, a young pair, they are not yet strong enough for a full day's labor."

"Please say again."

St. James did as asked and nodded. "Have you worked with oxen before?"

"Some." Roald flinched inwardly. His "some" was an exaggeration at best. He *had* driven a yoke around the railroad yard once. He kept his gaze steady, looking at the man with as much honesty as he could. *Please, God, we must have this pair.*

St. James nodded. "I have carved a yoke for them, but you will need a larger one within a few months. Have you one?"

Roald shook his head. "I will by the time it is needed." He walked to the front of the two animals and studied the size and shape of their yoke. It would require a big tree. Had one that size been blown down on his land? Where would he get seasoned oak? He looked up in time to catch a flash of doubt on St. James's face.

"What do you want for them?"

The farmer named a figure half again as much as Roald carried. "That's because they are not fully trained. In a few months they will be worth twice that."

"Can I see them?"

St. James looked at the land he had yet to plow, looked up at the sun standing in the ten o'clock position, and then back at the land. "Well, I guess we can use a break." He unhitched his team, turned them, and headed for the barn. "I don't see no wagon. How'd you get here?"

Roald pointed to his feet.

"You have breakfast this morning?"

Roald nodded.

"Coffee?"

Roald shook his head.

"Well, let's see if we can remedy that. I'll water these boys here while you look over the young'uns. Then we'll discuss the deal over coffee."

Roald watched everything the man did with his oxen, from the voice commands of "gee" and "haw" to "whoa" and "easy now" to the way he checked under the yoke for hot spots that could lead to sores.

"You got to make sure the yoke fits right with no rough places. You can ruin a good animal by rough spots. Remember that oxen need rest, just like a man does. In fact, from the look of you, I'd guess your animals need more rest than you." By the time they reached the corral, Roald's mind was reeling with all the oxen lore St. James had shared with him.

Roald listened so hard he stumbled over a dirt clod. At the well, Roald cranked the rope up so St. James could water the animals, and then cranked it again. What a luxury, this clear, clean water. He drank as deeply as the oxen had. In the shade of the sod barn, he helped St. James remove the yoke, taking those moments to study the heavy wooden piece more closely. He ran his hands over the curves, imprinting their shape in his mind so he would remember for his own carving.

Together they leaned on the fence, watching two young steers graze. They were both white with red patches. One looked as if someone had flicked a red paint-filled brush over him.

"So." Roald forced his fingers to lie relaxed on the fence post. "You said you wanted ninety dollars. All I have is sixty."

When St. James started to shake his head, Roald added, "For now."

"Come on, young man, let's go have that cup of coffee." St. James turned from the fence.

Roald started to add something, then thought better of it. Right now he could hope. The man hadn't said no. Roald glanced over his shoulder at the two oxen. How long would it be before they could work the way he needed? Maybe he should look elsewhere.

Besides the coffee, Mrs. St. James set a plate with corn bread smothered in syrup in front of him. Roald nodded his appreciation. "Mange takk."

After a few bites and another swig of coffee, he could feel life returning to his tired body. Would the man never speak? Roald looked around the room of the soddy. Whitewashed walls, bright red curtains, a braided rug upon the polished dirt floor, even a cast-iron stove for cooking. Soon Roald would have such a house. A log one built from the trees on their own land. Maybe next year. A noise caught his attention. A child in a long dress with bare feet played with a kitten near the doorway.

"More coffee?"

Roald didn't need to understand the language to recognize the gesture. He nodded and held up his cup. "Mange takk."

"Well, son, you said you only have sixty dollars. I just can't let 'em go for that, since they'll be worth so much more and all." St. James smashed a crumb of corn bread beneath one finger and lifted it to his mouth.

Roald swallowed. *Well, that is that.*

"But, I will hold a note, due in two parts, if you agree to pay five dollars for the yoke. Or you can take a loan at the bank and pay me as soon as you can. You can mail it to me by way of the general store in Pembina. What do you say?"

"I say thank you, and I will pay in two parts. You can trust me."

"I know that, or I wouldn't have offered." St. James extended his hand, and Roald met it with a handclasp full of gratitude. He now had a team of oxen, but he still needed a plow. Maybe he and Carl could make one by the—he shook off the idea. They needed one now. But how and where would they find one?

"If'n you drive them home, by the time you get there, you and them'll pretty well understand one another." St. James pushed away from the table. "Let's get 'em yoked. I got ta get back to the field."

"Ja."

Roald counted out the bills. All he had left were a few coins to jingle in his pocket. But that didn't matter. He and Carl now owned both horses and oxen.

A short time later, Roald walked down the lane behind his team, holding the lines snapped to the ring in each animal's nose. One day they would be voice trained and he wouldn't need reins.

He carried two sets of hobbles and a renewed supply of food for his trip home.

⚘ ⚘

Two days later he walked into the empty Bjorklund camp. Where was everyone?

18

W hat was all the hollering about?

Kaaren looked up from stirring the stew set for dinner. She could see the old woman running from the woods and waving. She yelled something, stopped, beckoned Kaaren to come, and ran forward again.

Kaaren listened carefully. Yes, it was the French word for help. What could be wrong? At the same moment, Ingeborg's name flashed through her mind. Something had happened to Ingeborg. *Oh, dear God, don't let her die. Please, please, whatever is wrong, be with her and us.*

She started toward the woods at a run, but the old woman waved her back. Kaaren stopped. She listened for all she was worth, and suddenly she knew what to do. "I'll get Carl. My man." She shouted the French for man and spun around. Gathering her skirts up around her knees, she headed for the field.

"Carl! Carl!" She waved her arms as she shouted.

Carl lifted the plow from the furrow and clucked the horses toward home. Kaaren met him halfway.

"Ingeborg is down at the river. Metis said to call you. Please hurry."

"You bring in the horses." Carl handed her the reins. "If I'm not right back, unhitch them and drive to the river, in case we need them."

"Ja, I will. Hurry."

Carl headed for the river at a dead run.

"Mor, what is the matter with Mor?" Thorliff started to slide off the back of Belle.

"Stay there," Kaaren ordered. She grasped the plow handles and clucked the team forward. All the while her *please God, please help us* silently pounded the doors of heaven.

Carl ran as if his life depended on speed. Leaping logs and brush, he slipped and slid his way to the riverbank. He looked downriver but spun the other way when he heard a halloo to his right. Moving as quickly as he could through the trees and brush, he found Metis bending over a figure on the ground.

"Ingeborg." He dropped to his knees beside the unconscious woman. With one hand he reached to touch the woman's head. A square of cloth seemed to have stopped the bleeding, but blood stained the ground under her.

Metis continued to hold the material in place, at the same time motioning Carl to lift Ingeborg and carry her back to camp.

A shudder racked Ingeborg's body, but it wasn't sufficient to force her to regain consciousness.

If only I could understand the woman, Carl thought as he lifted Ingeborg in his arms. *Does she know what happened here?* How he wished he had brought the horses. Carrying Ingeborg's dead weight through the trees and underbrush set his muscles straining, and he could hardly get his breath.

Ingeborg's body spasmed again.

Carl leaned against a tree. Metis checked the head wound, now dripping blood down Carl's arm. Warm water gushed from Ingeborg's skirt and down his pant leg.

He looked to Metis, who stood shaking her head. She muttered a few more words and shook her head again.

"Go . . . Kaaren . . . horses." Carl spoke slowly and distinctly, using the little English he knew.

Metis nodded. She motioned him to keep the cloth on the wound and set off at a run.

⋈ ⋈

Kaaren unhitched the horses with shaking fingers. "You go watch Gunny, Thorliff. I have to hurry." She hooked the traces up on the harnesses. "Here, tie Bob to the wagon wheel." She handed Thorliff the halter shank.

"But Mor is hurt. I want to see Mor." Thorliff stood in place, the lead shank clutched in his hand.

"You will see her later. Please, Thorly, do what I say right now." Kaaren jerked on Belle's rope. "Come on, girl, let's go." The mare rolled her eyes and jerked back on the rope. *Please, God, help me.* Kaaren took a deep breath to calm herself and clucked again. This time Belle followed her, trotting more quickly as the woman ran faster.

She met Metis at the edge of the woods. Together they wound their way back to where Carl stood leaning against a tree somewhat closer to the camp.

"Thank God you are here." He closed his eyes, still fighting to get his breath. Ingeborg was a solidly built woman, of that he was certain after trying to carry her so far.

"Oh, Ingeborg." Kaaren laid a hand on her sister-in-law's shoulder. "How should we do this?"

"Metis, here, can give you a boost on the horse, and then we'll hand Ingeborg up to you so you can hold her upright. With one of us on either side, we should make it back all right."

Working together as though they did this every day, they soon had Ingeborg on the horse, leaning against Kaaren, and were heading back to camp.

"She's slipping," Kaaren cried halfway back.

Carl reached up to hold them steady while Metis took the horse's head. "She's having some kind of fits."

"No, no." Metis shook her head. "She having baby."

"Oh no!" Kaaren tightened her grip on her unconscious friend. "Oh, Carl, she's losing the baby."

"Better that than her life." Carl clucked Belle forward.

By the time they had Ingeborg bedded down in the wagon, the contractions were coming more consistently. The wound on the back of her head continued to seep.

"We sew head." Metis pointed to the bandage.

"I . . . ah . . ." Kaaren swallowed hard. She'd never stitched through skin before.

"Now, while she sleep." Metis paused. "Needle you have? Thread?"

Kaaren nodded. "I'll get them."

Once they clipped the matted hair away, sewing the lips of the skin together was no more difficult than stitching a quilt. Kaaren ripped up several strips of material, and after folding one several times, she tied the pad in place.

"Carl, could you please bring us coffee?" She stuck her head out the back of the wagon to see Carl and Thorliff mending harnesses by the fire.

"Ja, that I can do."

The two women sat on trunks and sipped the warming brew, keeping a close eye on Ingeborg at the same time. "How did you find her?" Kaaren asked.

"Wolf come me get."

"Wolf?"

"He my fran. Me pull him from trap, save foot, lose toe." Metis set down the cup and placed a hand on Ingeborg's contracting belly. "Baby come soon."

"Did Ingeborg see the wolf?"

Metis shrugged. Along with a shake of her head, she added, "Wolf no hurt me fran."

"Maybe not, but Ingeborg is terrified of wolves. If she saw him . . ." Kaaren shook her head. Would they ever know what really happened?

The baby was born as the blazing red sun sank in the west. Blood as red as the clouds continued to flow in spite of Metis' best efforts to staunch it.

"Must bury," she said to Kaaren, pointing to the pan. "Bring hot water."

Kaaren stepped down from the wagon to do as she was bid. The tears stung her eyes and the smell of blood made her sick. She set the pan to the side and walked around the campfire, breathing deeply of the clean, pure air. *God, here we are saying "please" again. Now that she has lost the baby, bring Ingeborg back to health. She is suffering much and will do so more. Father, help us out here in the wilds with no doctor or midwife. No, we do have a midwife.* She thanked her heavenly Father for that and went to pick up the mattock. She would do this herself and pray over this tiny soul as if it had been born when the time was right.

When Carl started toward her, she waved him away. "You stay with Thorliff."

"God be thanked," was all she could say sometime later when Metis announced that the bleeding had finally stopped.

"I go home, get medicines. Come back." Metis stood upright for the first time in hours. Her head didn't even touch the oak ribs of the canvas.

"You should eat first."

"No, eat later." She stepped off the endgate and trotted across the field.

Kaaren watched, the moon so bright it seemed like noonday.

"Is she going to make it?" Carl brought her a plate of food and a cup of coffee.

"I think so. At least the bleeding has stopped." Kaaren leaned against Carl's solid body. "How am I going to tell her?"

"God will give you the right words."

"Where's Thorliff?"

"Asleep by Gunny. I fixed him a bed there." Carl wrapped his arms around his wife's waist. "Poor little fellow is scared as can be. You don't think he remembers his mother dying, do you?"

Kaaren shrugged. "I hope not."

Even with the herbs Metis used in both tea and poultices, Ingeborg slept on—through the next day, the next night, and through the following morning.

"When will she wake?" Kaaren and Metis were sitting on the logs around the fire, drinking coffee and watching Carl, with Thorliff on the horse, plowing the field.

Metis shrugged. "Better be soon, or . . ."

"ho are you?" Ingeborg forced the whisper past the bar in her throat.

The woman's black eyes smiled along with her mouth, but the words that flowed from her like a spring freshet meant nothing to Ingeborg.

Still, she felt comforted. There was something about the gentle smile. She looked above her to see the familiar canvas of their wagon, even to the patch above the middle hoop. What had happened? When she tried to turn her head to follow the movements of the stranger, a sharp pain shot from the back of her head, so all-encompassing she could only close her eyes and pray for it to pass.

Those strange words came again fast, but soft and accompanied by an arm to lift her shoulders enough so she could drink from the cup held to her lips. The bitter taste and the motion of rising made her begin to wretch; but a sharp "No!" helped her stop. "No" she understood.

"You're awake." Kaaren leaned on the side of the wagon. They'd rolled the canvas up so a breeze could blow through.

"Ja, have I been sleeping long?"

"Three days."

"Nei." One small shake of her head and Ingeborg immediately refrained from further movement. *Why can't I remember?* "What happened?"

"We do not know. Metis found you down by the river, bleeding from that gash on your head. You might have bled to death if she hadn't helped you."

Ingeborg digested the words. Bled to death. One did not usually bleed to death from a knock on the head. She lay still, assessing her body. "My baby!" She knew by Kaaren's silence. "I lost the baby, didn't I?" The pain that throbbed in her head now ripped her heart in two.

"There will be others. You are strong and will be healthy again soon." Kaaren's words stumbled into silence.

Like a black cloud blanketing the land, the thought of having no baby sent Ingeborg spiraling downward into darkness.

"Fishing—I had gone fishing." With the words came the memory of the wolf she'd seen. She looked around the wagon as much as she could without moving her head. Dusk had fallen, and the light of the fire danced bright images on the canvas. *How long did I sleep this time? Has Roald returned? Oh, my—Roald. He wants another son so badly.* Tears drained from her eyes and into her ears. When a sob caught in her throat, she stifled it, afraid moving would bring on the searing pain again. When she held still, the throbbing was endurable. Why had she panicked like that? Wolves didn't attack in the daylight. The animal hadn't even moved—except for the lip. In spite of the tears, she could now remember the scene clearly.

The wagon shook with the weight of someone climbing in. "You're awake again?" Kaaren's gentle voice only brought more tears. "It is good to cry them out." She took Ingeborg's hand and settled down beside the pallet. "I brought you more tea Metis made for you. She boiled barks and herbs and said it will help you get strong again."

"How do you know what she said?"

"She speaks a dialect with some French words. Remember, I worked for a family that spoke French."

"Ja." Ingeborg forced herself to concentrate on what Kaaren was saying. Anything to keep the dark thoughts of her terrible loss at bay. "When?"

"When did I work there, or when did you get hurt?" Kaaren's smile said she was teasing, but Ingeborg hadn't the energy to smile back.

"Hurt."

"Three days ago. Oh, Inge, I was so afraid you'd never wake up." Kaaren laid her cheek on the back of Ingeborg's hand. "I couldn't have stood it here without you."

Ingeborg closed her eyes. *No baby. Why, God? Is it so wrong to want a baby of my own?* The silence deepened like the darkness falling outside. "Where are Carl and Thorliff?"

"Just coming in from the field. Carl's been using every moment of light to break the sod."

"And Gunny?"

"Asleep in the hammock under the wagon. Metis showed me how to fashion it so the baby is off the ground. Gunny loves it. When she wiggles—and you know how she loves to wiggle—her bed swings."

"This Metis seems to be a fountain of information."

"She is. We can learn much from her. She knows how to live on this land and survive."

The jingle of harness and Carl's "halloo" caught their attention at the same moment.

"We're in the wagon," Kaaren called as she laid Ingeborg's hand back down and, with a pat, rose to her feet. "I'll bring you some stew as soon as I finish serving our men."

"I'm not hungry."

"Yes, you are, at least for the broth. You are going to get well again, and the sooner the better. Metis says the headache will go away, but it will take some time."

"Why do I have such a headache?"

"Even us hardheaded Norwegians can't slam our heads against a log and not expect a headache. Now, would you like to see Thorliff? He's been so anxious."

Against her real wishes, Ingeborg agreed. She'd much rather lie in the dark and let the blessed relief of sleep lull away the pain. She heard Gunny begin to whimper in her sling under the wagon, and listened as Carl and Thorliff unharnessed the horses and brushed them down close to the wagon, allowing her to catch the whiff of sweaty horses. Thorliff kept up his usual stream of questions, which Carl answered patiently. Did the boy never run down?

Ingeborg laid her hand over her belly. It had been too soon to feel life there. She'd never felt the babe leap and kick. She touched her breasts. There would be no milk, no searching mouth to suckle. *Dear God, have you forgotten me? Did I do something wrong that you have taken my baby home before he even had breath? They say it was an accident, but your Word says you know all that happens. How can I say this is your will? Is this one of those times of discipline? How am I to understand?*

"Mor?" Thorliff spoke from the end of the wagon, his voice hesitant, as if afraid to call out to her.

"Ja, den lille, you may come sit beside me and tell me all that has happened while I slept." Ingeborg turned her head, and this time the pain didn't flame into an anvil or piercing sword. She watched him scramble over the open endgate and around the cooking boxes. On all fours he crept to her side and peered into her face.

"You sleeped and sleeped," he said reproachfully. "You wouldn't wake up."

"I know, but I'm better now." She patted the quilts folded beneath her. "So you helped Onkel Carl in the field?"

"I rode Belle, then I rode Bob, and then I slept in the grass. Far still isn't here. When will he come home?" Thorliff chattered on, and Ingeborg forced herself to make the proper responses. At least with his presence the shadows lurked farther away, more toward the horizon instead of behind her head or right shoulder.

Carl stuck his head in. "Glad to see you're back to join us. You gave us a bad scare." He tweaked one of Thorliff's curly blond locks. "Come on, farmer, let's eat."

"Mor, you coming?" Thorliff halted in his haste toward the end of the wagon. "I'll help you get up."

"Nei, you go eat. It sounds like you've earned a good supper." The wagon shook from the child's leap to the ground, causing a minor earthquake in her head. She closed her eyes against the pain. If the vile-tasting concoction that woman gave her stopped the throbbing, she'd gladly drink more. Where had the woman gone, anyway, and what did Kaaren call her—Metis? Wasn't that the name of the old Indian woman?

After the camp settled down for the night, Ingeborg lay on her pallet, waiting and praying for sleep. The draught Kaaren helped her drink hadn't brought the blessed relief it had before. Was something wrong with it too? Gunny whimpered but settled down again after a few minutes without needing to feed. Carl snored in whiffles. An owl hooted. Ingeborg turned on her side, pillowing her head on her arm. Her back ached, probably from slamming against the log, if not from lying in one position for so long. She reached up and carefully felt the tender place at the base of her skull. The swelling had disappeared, and the small cut scabbed over, so that wasn't the bleeding problem. Losing the baby had been. To think she'd been unconscious through something so terribly sad. She'd even looked forward to the pain of childbirth, because then she would hold a child of her own in her arms. The tears came again, softer this time, more like the gentle rains of spring than the torrents of summer. Finally, Ingeborg slept.

The next morning Kaaren helped her sit up, propping a flour sack filled with dried prairie grass behind her. One stalk poked her in the back until Kaaren beat it into submission. While the moving made her head pound again, she felt grateful for the change in position. Thorliff was off helping Carl in the field again, and Gunny gurgled and cooed on the quilt beside her.

The antics of the baby brought a rush of moisture to her throat and a burning to her eyes. Hadn't she cried enough already? She could hear her mother's voice so plainly. *There's no use crying over what might have been. Get on with what is.* So, like a dutiful daughter, Ingeborg reached for the baby and tickled her belly. One chubby hand clasped her finger and tried to bring it up to the baby's mouth to be chewed on. How she had grown from that fragile squalling infant aboard the ship to this roly-poly bundle who could melt the heart of one much sterner than her aunt Ingeborg!

That afternoon the babe slept in her aunt's arms.

Ingeborg awoke to the sight of Metis bending over her. Startled, she jerked and woke the baby, who instantly yelled as though she'd been pinched. "Sorry," Ingeborg muttered. Did the woman always move without making a sound? Metis nodded and laid a hand against Ingeborg's forehead. When she shook her head, Ingeborg agreed. "There's no fever. You have been a good doctor."

Metis smiled, her dark eyes hooded by lids so papery they looked transparent. The deep wrinkles that grooved her face could have been sculpted with a knife, so precise they lay. And when she smiled, Ingeborg could not help but smile back.

Ingeborg thanked her again. Metis said something, raised a hand in farewell, and slipped out the back of the wagon. Ingeborg could hear her and Kaaren talking by the fire. The fragrance of bread baking made her stomach rumble. With one hand she rocked the now gurgling infant, and with the other she fingered the long golden plait that lay across her shoulder. It was time to get up and about, but she didn't know if her legs would even hold her if she tried to stand.

They didn't.

She grabbed for the hoop above her, banged into the trunk, and sat down heavily on a box.

"What are you trying to do?" Kaaren appeared at the open wagon end and, after one look at her patient, climbed in without seemingly touching the endgate. "You should know better than to get up without help. Have you no idea how sick you've been?" All the while she scolded, Kaaren bustled about, righting the quilts and pallet and easing Ingeborg back down. "And what did this do to your head, may I ask?"

Ingeborg didn't answer—she couldn't. Between trying to keep her head from falling off and her stomach down where it belonged, she just kept her eyes closed and moved whatever way Kaaren indicated. When she was prone again, and the world had quit spinning, she opened one eye. Kaaren stood over her, hands planted on her hips. Keeping her eyes closed seemed the wiser of actions for the moment. And safer.

"Ah, Ingeborg, please be patient. Metis says head injuries take some time to recover. You will be dizzy and suffer headaches for even weeks, let alone be weak from all the blood you lost losing the baby."

"What does Metis know about all this? Is she a doctor? You treat her as if she's the voice of God." Ingeborg regretted the words the minute they were out of her mouth. She was acting like a spoiled child.

"No, she's not a doctor, but a very wise woman who is becoming a good friend, even though we are homesteading the land she says the government had given her husband."

Ingeborg tried to pay attention, but a lassitude stole up from her feet and circled her head, alleviating the pain and bringing the blessed relief of healing sleep. Her last thoughts were of Metis. God brought angels in different disguises: David Jonathan Gould in New York and Metis in Dakota Territory. Was this really the old woman's land?

20

Ingeborg, Kaaren, where are you?"

Silence reigned in the Bjorklund camp. Neither woman was busy bustling about the campfire. Where were they? What was going on?

Roald searched for clues as to their whereabouts. Off in the distance he could see Carl and the horses with a small figure astride Belle. So Thorliff was with Carl. The cooking fire had burned down to the coals, but since patches of red heat were still visible, he knew they hadn't been gone too long. The coffeepot sat on the edge but would probably still be warm. The long trench where they had dried the meat now lay cold in gray ashes. Then he saw the water bucket was missing. *Ah,* he thought, *they must be down at the river.*

Knowing the oxen needed a drink from their long walk, he slapped the reins on their backs with a strong "gee" to turn them toward the river.

"Who's there?" a quavery voice called out. "Roald, is that you?"

"Ja, Ingeborg, what is wrong?" He halted the oxen and tied their reins to the rim of the wagon wheel, tangling the leather lines in his haste. With one foot on the wagon gate, he swung into the shaded interior. "Oh, Ingeborg! What has happened to you?" Instead of the rosy-cheeked woman he had left a few days ago, his wife now lay on a pallet with a drawn face the color of pale milk, and eyes huge and lost above pronounced cheekbones. She still wore her nightclothes in the middle of the afternoon.

He slumped to his knees beside the makeshift bed. With one finger he stopped the trail of tears that seeped from her eyes. "You are crying."

The softness of his voice melted her resolve to be strong. "Oh, Roald, the baby. I lost the baby." Ignoring the headache at the abrupt movement, she flung herself into his arms and sobbed great, heart-wrenching cries against his chest.

Roald held her close, letting her cry and stroking her back. His son, there would be no son. When the sobs subsided to hiccups, he asked, a catch in his throat causing him to stammer, "How? What happened?"

Ingeborg told the story between hiccups and gasps, wiping her tears on his shirtfront. "The wolf, he didn't move, but he frightened me so."

"A wolf?"

"Ja, he sat looking at me, and when I threw the fish at him, I slipped and fell." She finished the story to his silence.

"Did Carl kill the wolf?"

Ingeborg shook her head.

"Why?"

What a strange question to ask. Doesn't he care about the baby? She closed off the question *and me?* before it could be completed. The storm spent, she drew back and looked up into his face. Brows met over his eyes, but of his thoughts and feelings there was no other sign.

"We must thank Metis. She saved my life."

"Metis?"

"The woman who says she owns this land. She came to talk with you, but we did not understand her, remember?"

"Ja, but she doesn't own this land. It is ours. I will file all the necessary papers as soon as the surveyors come through, and then we must prove it up."

"I know but . . ." She rubbed her forehead, the ache making her vision blur. Or was it the tears?

"There is no but. This land is mine." He pushed himself to his feet. "I must water the oxen and . . ."

"You found a team, then?" She lay back against the pillowed box so she could sit up. She ignored the pain.

"Ja, but no plow, and the oxen are young." He started to leave. "Kaaren is at the river?"

"Ja."

"Does she have the gun?"

Ingeborg blinked to bring him into perspective. "Nei, you know she can't shoot a gun."

"Then she will learn. I will not have a wolf terrorizing my family.

If he stayed that close, he is not afraid of humans, and that is a dangerous thing."

He stepped down from the wagon, the jolt of it making her close her eyes. *How strange. He's been so adamant that women shouldn't shoot guns, and now he is just as adamant on the other side. If I'd had the gun, would I have shot it?* She listened as he spoke to the oxen and drove them off to the river. The thought hadn't entered her mind before. *Why didn't the wolf run away? Why did it sit right there in the open as if it owned the land? What would I do if I saw it again?* The questions had no answers. But thinking back to Roald's strange reaction brought the tears again, no matter how hard she fought them. Was her dream of seeing Roald smile dying like the baby before its time?

That night Roald lifted Ingeborg from the wagon and laid her on a quilt with the log to prop her back. She looked around the campfire, feeling a part of the family again in spite of the headaches.

"It's only been four days since you fell," Kaaren whispered in her ear as she bent down with a filled plate. "You must eat and rest and continue to drink the tea Metis left for you."

"I know, and it helps the pain, so I look forward to the bitter stuff. But we have so much to do, and you cannot do it all."

"You let me worry about that."

"You never worry, that's what bothers me."

"I let God handle the worrying. He's bigger than I am." The last was said with a smile as the younger woman turned to answer a question from her husband.

Ingeborg shut her mind against thoughts of a caring God. Had she not prayed so long for a baby, and now it was gone? And she had believed He was a God of love. What kind of love was that? No. He was a God of judgment, punishing her for her many sins. And Roald going about the farming as if nothing had happened. Didn't he care at all? She closed her eyes against the tears that seemed to lurk right behind her eyelids. Refusing to dwell anymore on the painful thoughts, she turned back to the discussion between the two men.

"I must go to Grand Forks in the next few days," Roald said after a brief silence.

"But why?" Ingeborg asked.

The men looked over at her as if the log had spoken.

"We need to borrow money from the bank if we are to buy another plow and a cow, that is, if we can find one. We need seed, more plowshares, the list goes on and on."

"But we said we would not go so far into debt, and that we would pay as we go." Ingeborg clutched her head to stem the dizziness that came from speaking so forcefully.

Silence fell around the camp, broken only by the snapping sticks in the cook fire. She could feel everyone's eyes staring at her, even Thorliff's.

"That is my decision to make." The words came out flat and hard, bitten off.

Ingeborg felt as if she'd been struck. "But I . . . we worked so hard and . . ." She couldn't continue against the glacial quiet that was her husband. She set her plate to the side and gathered her legs under her to stand.

"Ingeborg, no!" Kaaren tore around the fire and to her side. "Let me help you."

Roald carefully set Kaaren aside and leaned down to lift Ingeborg. He hefted her up to his chest as if she weighed no more than Thorliff and without a word carried her back to the wagon and set her inside. Still, without talking, he climbed in, lifted her again and settled her on the pallet.

Ingeborg felt tears of frustration burning behind her eyelids. A newborn kitten had more strength than she. "Mange takk."

Roald dipped his head in response and returned to the campfire and his meal.

Or at least, that is what she supposed. She tried to find a comfortable position, but the pain was unbearable. She turned again, only to find him beside her, holding a cup for her to drink. The bitter tea slid down easily, taking the tears with it. While she said the "mange takk" in her mind, she did not release the words. Surely a man who didn't care would not handle her so gently. Comforted by the thought, she drifted off to sleep.

Roald threw himself into the sod busting as if to bury his sorrow under the turning earth. Perhaps pushing the plow through the matted grasses would keep him from thinking. No more baby. Of course his father would say, "There will be others. Ingeborg is strong and things like this are just God's will." Roald no more wanted to knuckle under God's will than the prairie wanted to roll over and become wheat fields.

They had worked hard and prayed—for what? He shut off the dismal thoughts and turned the corner to start down the south leg of the ever-growing field. If his pastor knew what he'd been thinking, he would have thrown him out of the church for blasphemy. One did not question the Lord God of Hosts.

Uff da. He stopped the horses to check the plow and, after knocking the sod away, ran a practiced eye over the share rim. So dull already it wouldn't cut cheese. With a glance at the sun peeking out from mare's tail clouds, he could tell it wasn't even midmorning yet. He wiped the sweat from his brow. The share was beyond filing; it would need to be hammered out again.

He slapped the reins. "Gee-up." Bob and Belle, heads nodding, threw their weight into the collars, and Roald rammed the plow back under the sod. It would have to do until noon. They needed another plow, let alone a plowshare. So many things they had taken for granted in Norway, and here they did without and suffered. He batted a persistent fly from drinking the moisture around his eyes. He should be wearing a fly guard like the one he'd fashioned out of an old sack for the horses.

He looked toward the camp. If only he could see Ingeborg moving around from the garden to the drying racks and bending over the fire. *Dear Lord, please make her all right. I don't think I can survive losing another wife.* The prayer flew heavenward in spite of his stubborn will.

By the time Roald left for Grand Forks, Ingeborg could walk again, even though the few steps from wagon to campfire seemed farther than a mile. The headaches continued, but she no longer became dizzy or suffered from blurred vision. She sat jiggling Gunny on her knee as Roald and Carl rode out of the camp. Carl would return with the horses that afternoon, now that they knew how close they were to St. Andrew.

"I wanted to go." Thorliff kicked a clump of grass, sending dust rising around them.

"Maybe next time. Right now we need wood. You've been out on the horses so much we've nearly run out."

"What if the wolf is there?" The boy kicked up another dust cloud.

Ingeborg felt the fear rise in her throat. "If you stay on this side of the woods, there shouldn't be any trouble." The picture of the sitting wolf sprang to mind. "Remember Tante Kaaren said Wolf belongs to Metis. He won't hurt us."

The boy stared at her, doubt clouding his round eyes.

"Maybe Tante Kaaren will go with you." How she would love to go pick up wood, get a bucket of water, or cut prairie grass to dry for the pallets. She looked across the waving grass that was beginning to head out in the spring sun. Soon it would be time to cut hay for the winter. The garden needed planting right now, and somehow they had to find time to hunt so they would have more meat to dry. And here she had made a supreme effort by simply dressing herself and playing with the baby. She felt worthless, as if a huge black cloud had taken up permanent residence right over her head, about to drench her.

She rose carefully to her feet and laid the now sleeping baby in her hammock. Whenever she stood up or bent over, her head rewarded her with a sickening series of throbs. But they subsided if she moved cautiously.

"Why not work that deer hide," Kaaren said, coming to stand beside Ingeborg. "That is something you could do sitting down. I checked it, and the hair is turning loose."

"I suppose. But planting the garden is so much more important."

"Ja, well, I will do that. Carl has worked up half of what we need. Thorliff can help me. Do you think you can watch Gunny at the same time?"

"Ja, I will." Ingeborg looked wistfully at the newly turned earth, black and steaming in the sun. Right now it looked infinitely more appealing than a hide that had been curing in wet ashes and mashed deer brains. She held out her hand for the scraper that Kaaren passed to her with a smile.

"Bring it on."

By the time the sun stood straight above her, most of the hair had been scraped from the hide, and she'd stoked up the fire. They could have hot coffee and stew for dinner. In spite of her strong will, she felt like collapsing on the smelly hide.

Carl returned in midafternoon and sat down to drink a cup of coffee and rest. When he was finished, he hobbled the horses so they could graze. That done, he yoked up the oxen and returned to sod busting.

The days ran together, with Ingeborg's periods of needed rest stretching further apart and lasting a shorter time. The tears flowed less, and when they came, she was never sure if they were for Roald or for the lost baby. She knew in her heart that Roald grieved alone, so if nothing else, she could cry for him.

Every day they listened for the signal they'd planned. Roald was to ask the riverboat captain to blow two short blasts, two long, and two short as they passed the homestead, to let them know he was back. What was keeping him?

When the signal finally came, Carl brought the oxen in from the field and removed the yoke, handing the lines to Ingeborg. "Please water them, and Thorliff will help you hobble them out."

"Take him with you, please. It would be the most exciting thing that could happen to him." Ingeborg spoke softly, only for Carl's ears. She waited as Carl thought for a moment.

"We may have to stay overnight." He grinned at her. "Hey, farmer, how'd you like to go to town with me?" Thorliff's squeal said it all. "You help your mother hobble these oxen while I harness up. Kaaren, help me get the wagon ready to roll."

When the wagon finally creaked out across the prairie, all their belongings were stacked together on the ground and covered by a canvas that stretched out to one side to make a small tent for the women in case the men didn't get back right away. Ingeborg watched them go, the team finally becoming a dot on the horizon. Never had the prairie seemed so flat or so vast.

"Well." The word seemed to evaporate in the air. The two women looked at each other, shrugged, and headed for the river. It seemed they always needed wood and water. Returning sometime later, they looked to the west. The sun was slipping behind dark thunderclouds, building like a mountain on the horizon.

The downpour struck with a vengeance. Wind slanted the rain under their canvas and sent them scurrying to fold the bedding before the driving rain soaked the quilts. The fire sizzled out under the onslaught. Ingeborg and Kaaren tucked Gunny safely between them and huddled under the canvas, keeping it from flapping with frozen grips. Lightning split the dark sky, forking in the west and to the north. Each time the thunder crashed and rolled, Ingeborg shuddered but couldn't keep her gaze off the awesome beauty of it all. All around them, raindrops smacked the beaten earth and created miniature ponds, pocked by larger drops until they formed lakes with streams running between. The grass seemed to suck in the life-giving moisture like a babe at its mother's breast. Thunder rolled now to the east, and the deluge turned to rain curtains, shimmering between them and the sun that was emerging low on the western horizon. As the storm passed over them, the patter of individual drops could be heard on their canvas covering, and soon they were left with only the drips of runoff.

Kaaren and Ingeborg looked at each other and shook their heads. Now the firewood that had been protected by the wagon would be soaked too.

"Well, I hope they don't plan on hot coffee when they get back." Kaaren stretched an arm, cramped from holding the baby close.

Ingeborg felt a giggle starting somewhere deep inside her. It erupted before she had time to stifle it. Together the two women chuckled as they untangled themselves from their canvas cocoon. When Ingeborg slipped on the ground where the top layer had instantly turned to gumbo, their chuckles turned to laughter that tugged at their bellies and brought joyful tears to their eyes.

"Wha-what are we laughing about? He . . . here we are, two women alone in the middle of the prairie, soaked to the skin, no dry firewood and I . . . I can't stop laughing." Kaaren tried to take a deep breath but hooted instead.

"M-m-me too." They leaned against the stack of boxes and trunks, wiping their eyes with the corners of their aprons. "Thank the good Lord there's no one around to see us." Ingeborg held her side with one hand and her head with the other. She wasn't sure which hurt worse, but this time she knew the pain would go away—and soon. "Coffee anyone?"

Shortly after breakfast the next morning, Ingeborg heard the jingle of harness and looked up from softening the hide. She leaped to her feet and, with a quick motion, stripped off her apron and waved the white banner over her head.

A cheery "halloo" floated back to her on the breeze. As they drew closer, she could see Thorliff jumping up and down on the wagon seat between the two men.

"Mor . . ." She couldn't understand the middle, but the last word "cow" came through loud and clear. Kaaren left her bread kneading and waved too.

"Mor, Tante Kaaren . . ." This time one of the men clamped a hand over the boy's mouth.

"You're spoiling the surprise." Carl spoke loud enough for them to hear.

To Ingeborg it felt like Christmas and birthday all rolled into one. What all had Roald done?

When Roald finally pulled the wagon to a halt, he swung Thorliff down first before the child could scramble over the wheels. He glanced up at his wife and shook his head, obviously relieved at getting the boy out of the way.

Ingeborg smothered a grin. Thorliff did manage to wear one down with all his questions.

"Mor, come. Come now." Thorliff tugged at her hand, pulling her toward the rear of the wagon. A haltered red-and-white cow, heavy with calf, had already dropped her head to graze.

"Oh, isn't she beautiful?" Ingeborg walked up to the animal to stroke the silky neck. "We will have milk again soon." A glance at the flaccid udder told her the cow was completely dry. "A month or so?" She asked Roald the question.

"Ja, maybe a bit less." He swung back over the seat and, stepping around boxes, sacks, and the plow, flipped back a canvas covering a small slatted crate.

"And chickens." Ingeborg clasped her hands in delight.

"We will have to build a coop right away if we don't want them roosting in the wagon." Carl had climbed down and joined them at the tailgate.

"Eggs to cook with . . . fried eggs for breakfast." Kaaren looked up at her husband. "I will make a cake as soon as we have two eggs."

"Then you'd better begin." Carl dug in his pocket and brought two eggs out to hold up for all to see. "I found them in the crate just up the way. Our hens didn't let a little thing like a riverboat trip or a wagon ride keep them from their duties."

Thorliff couldn't stand still. "Show them the . . ." He got the hand-over-mouth treatment again.

"There's more?"

Was that a twinkle in Roald's eye? Ingeborg blinked and looked again. She must have been mistaken. She leaned into the wagon bed, but leaped back when the bundle she'd leaned her hand on jumped away with a startled "ba-a-a-a."

Thorliff let out a shriek of delight. "A sheep. Far bought a sheep."

"I wanted to buy you several ewes and a ram, but the farmer would only sell this feeder for now. But I know where to go back and get more. I thought she could be a pet for Thorliff, besides giving you wool for yarn."

Ingeborg could find no words to thank him with; her eyes had to do it for her. He knew how much she loved her sheep back in Norway. And now he'd brought her one for her very own. Surely this was a gesture from a man who cared in spite of his lack of words. The lamb was indeed a gift. A gift that dimmed the edges of the hole left in her heart by the loss of the baby.

"We'll unload the rest while you make breakfast." Carl swung up in the wagon to begin handing out bundles, including a wooden churn that made Ingeborg gasp with pleasure again.

"Ja, your food will be ready in a minute. I knew you would be home soon." Kaaren cradled the two eggs to her breast as if they were the crown jewels.

Ingeborg took the thong tied around the lamb's neck and tugged at it until the lamb leaped nimbly to the ground. "Baaa." How friendly the sound. She looked at Thorliff, who stared up at her, his eyes dancing to match his feet. His grin stretched near to cracking his face.

"You must think of a name for her."

"Sheep." He shook his head. "No, Lamb. Call her Lamb."

"But when she grows up?"

"Lamb."

"We'll see. Maybe you'll think of something different."

"Lamb." Thorliff clamped his hand on the thong too. "She's hungry. Onkel Carl said to pound a stick in the ground and tie her to it so she won't run away."

"We'll do that later. Right now, we'll tie her to the wheel." Ingeborg did so, moving the cow's tether to the front wheel at the same time. In one trip, they'd become farmers with livestock to tend. Soon there'd be a calf, either to raise for another ox, or a heifer to breed and continue to build their dairy herd. There'd be butter and cheese, maybe even some to sell. After all, St. Andrew was only three hours away. Surely someone there would like to buy her cheese.

Roald dropped his announcement after Kaaren had poured his last cup of breakfast coffee. "That woman you call Metis has tried to file a claim against this land. The land office is looking into it. She said she had a dwelling here until it burned down last year. That is why some of the sod had been broken."

"What will happen now?" Ingeborg felt the cloud return and hover over her head.

"She's nothing but a squatter, that's all. She never filed a legal claim. Even we can't file officially until the surveyors come through." Roald took a slug of coffee. "Besides that, her husband was the one given the land, and according to her, he died a year and a half ago. She doesn't have a chance."

There must be some way for Metis to keep her plot of land, Ingeborg thought. *Surely the rest is enough for us, isn't it?*

21

I nstead of planting the rest of the garden in the plot by the woods, we'll put it next to the soddy."

"The soddy?" Ingeborg looked up from the basket she was weaving of willow branches. Roald had not mentioned building the soddy for so long, she'd given up hope, thinking that would be the last thing done before winter.

"Ja, we will seed what's left to wheat and oats, along with potatoes and corn. We'll start busting a plot right here and then use the sod to build the walls," Roald said. "We can raise the walls after dark, when the horses and oxen are out to graze." He looked over to Carl, who was carving a larger yoke for the oxen as the other would soon be too small. He'd been working on another scythe handle, since they needed two for cutting grass for hay. June was fast approaching and the prairie grass seemed to grow an inch a night. Already they were reminding Thorliff not to go beyond where he could see the wagon. They told him the tales they had heard of children who wandered off in the deep grass and were never seen again.

The next afternoon, Roald was as good as his word. While Carl took the horses out to the ever-widening field of broken sod, Roald paced out the house, twelve feet wide and fourteen feet long. He pounded pegs for the corners and then stepped back and surveyed what he'd done. With a nod, he turned to Ingeborg. "We will put the door and window here, facing south, so the sun can come in to light the winter."

Ingeborg stepped into her doorway and turned to see what would greet her each morning. Prairie rolled before her, grass rippling before the wind in unending shades of green. "I will plant a wild rose right here." She pointed to the side of the imagined door.

"And a tree from the riverbank to shade us in the summer. It will go here." She pointed to the western corner.

"Ja, well, we will see." Roald strode off to where the oxen grazed, moving slowly in their hobbles. Thanks to the grazing animals, they now had better than an acre cropped short, resembling an honest-to-goodness yard. The chickens scratched in the shade of the wagon, eating their fill each day of bugs and seeds. Both the cow and Lamb were tied to stakes that were moved when needed.

"I think tonight we need a celebration." Kaaren brought the mattock over and handed it to Ingeborg. "You scrape and I will rake, then we'll change off. We'll get a head start on the floor. Metis said to pack it and then wash it with water mixed with cow dung until it forms a hard surface. Otherwise we will have dust in our beds all winter."

Ingeborg made a face. One day they would have wood floors again, along with wooden walls and real glass windows. She pulled the blade across the ground, cutting into the soil just enough to shave off the grass tops. Within minutes, sweat dripped into her eyes and ran down her back.

"Here, it is my turn." Kaaren switched places with her, and the labor continued until nothing showed but roots and black soil. Then, using the head of the heavy tool, they tamped the ground, stamping their feet at the same time.

When Gunny started to fuss after her afternoon nap, they quit their tamping, and Ingeborg headed for the river with a bucket in either hand. Roald had spoken of carving yokes for the carrying of water also. Soon they'd be like the oxen, yoked together and pulling hard. The men had also talked of digging a well. Someday, they would have these things.

The shade from the canopy of trees kissed her with coolness. She lingered for a moment. As it always did, her gaze traveled to the spot where she'd seen the wolf. Since he said it was well-cured, Carl had taken the log she'd fallen against for carving his yoke. Thank God, her body seemed well-cured also. As ever, she thought of the babe that was no more. She would have felt the fluttering movements by now, and her waistbands would have had to be let out. She leaned against a tree trunk for a moment, still trying to accept the accident as "God's will," as Kaaren always said. She shook her head and started again down the trail.

Out on the river, two men paddled a canoe upstream toward Grand Forks. She returned their wave and dipped her buckets full of the muddy water. A turtle sunned itself on a log, and across on the other bank, two ducks dabbled in the shallows. Overhead a crow announced the news with a hoarse caw, flapping its wings and settling in the top of a cottonwood. Ingeborg checked again on the sapling she'd marked for her own. It would be easy to dig up and transplant, and she'd carry water for it if needed. She *would* have a tree by the house, and this one would be only the start.

By the time they'd watered down the floor of the yet unwalled soddy, allowed it to dry, and watered it again, the sun was slipping rapidly to its berth. Ingeborg thought she saw something moving off to the south and shaded her eyes with her hands.

"A wagon, there's a wagon coming."

Roald stopped the oxen, and Kaaren climbed on the tongue of their own wagon to look. She leaped down again like a young girl. "We will have company for supper. Quick, Ingeborg, slice more dried venison real fine so it can cook quickly. I'll make biscuits and . . . Thorliff, you see if the hens left us any more eggs." She flew around like an officer ordering her troops, much to their delight.

By the time the wagon drove into the yard, the stew bubbled merrily over the coals, a cake was baking in the cast-iron spider, and the coffee's aroma welcomed the visitors.

"God dag." Roald greeted the man who drove the wagon hooped in white, just as theirs had been.

The man returned the greeting with a smile. "So good to hear the right language. We can actually talk to each other."

His wife poked her head out over the seat. "My heaven, what a sight you are. Just like visiting at home."

"Supper's nearly ready, so the sooner you unhitch your horses, the sooner we can eat." Kaaren wiped her hands on her apron. "We were going to have a celebration tonight, and now you will make it even better. Our first guests."

Ingeborg listened to Kaaren chatter and added her own smile of welcome. *What if these people settle near here? We could have neighbors, friends.* The thought set her heart to singing. As they introduced themselves, Thorliff clung to her skirts, keeping himself behind her until two boys near his age leaped from the back of the wagon.

"Now, Knute, Swen, you two behave," Mrs. Baard ordered the two who looked like angels with not-so-angelic eyes. "Watch out for your sister." A girlish version of the other two joined them on the ground. Next came a rounded rump, covered in brown calico faded to tan, and finally a matching sunbonnet that shaded merry eyes. The woman clutched a baby to her ample bosom. "There now, children, be polite. Let the little boy, here, show you around."

Ingeborg disentangled Thorliff's hand and gently pushed him forward with a hand on his back. "Go on now. You can show them Lamb."

"My, my, that surely does smell heavenly. We been eating mostly beans for the last week. Mr. Baard said we would stop in Grand Forks for a spell, but he's impatient to find land to claim. Why I spect that's what he's talking to your men about right now."

"I am sure you are right. Won't you sit down?" Kaaren indicated the chunks of log that Carl and Roald had sawed off their sitting log. The simple act had made the clearing feel even more like a home, instead of a camp-out.

"Well, if you don't mind, we've been sitting for some time." Mrs. Baard rubbed the small of her back with one fist. She raised her voice. "Penny, you come on out now. She's my sister's daughter, come to live with us." The baby, tucked under Mrs. Baard's other arm like a sack of meal, whimpered and then let out a howl. "I'd best feed little Olaf here before he frightens the birds out of the trees. He has some pair of lungs to him, he has." She returned to the wagon for a quilt and plunked herself down on one of the stumps, flipped the quilt over her shoulder, and instantly the howl turned to suckling.

Ingeborg looked up to see a slim, older girl step shyly from the wagon, a book cradled in her arm. "Come join us. Would you like coffee?" At the girl's nod, Ingeborg fetched another mug from the cook box in the back of their wagon.

She poured mugs of hot coffee for their guests, careful not to look at the mother and baby. The sight brought her own sorrow back, burning her eyes and throat. "Here, I'm sure this will wash the dust from your throat."

"Mange takk, my dear." Mrs. Baard sipped in appreciation and rolled her eyes. "An entire day without coffee feels more like a week."

The three men joined the women around the fire, and the conversation regarding land, its location, and availability continued. Roald and Carl took turns telling of the riches of the area they'd chosen.

"There's plenty of land to the west of us, at least there was in March when we found this piece. I put money down on the half section adjoining ours when I was in Grand Forks."

Ingeborg choked on her coffee. *He did what?* He shot her a look that said they'd discuss this later.

After everyone joined in grace, Kaaren and Ingeborg served the supper, ladling venison stew onto plates and passing them around. The biscuits were oohed and aahed over as hungry people devoured them. But when Kaaren brought out the egg cake, silence fell.

"I haven't had cake since we left Ohio," Mrs. Baard said reverently.

"We ain't had eggs, period," Mr. Baard added. "Now you children say thank you to these nice people for giving us such a good supper." He accepted his piece of cake and inhaled the fragrance before taking a bite so large it left enough for only one more. "Now, that is something!"

After supper the men strolled over to the pegged-out soddy. "I see you're all ready to lay the walls." Baard nodded to the patch of cut sod. "Now where I come from, neighbors help each other. Why, I imagine that if us three strong backs got on this first thing in the morning, we could have it ready for the roof by suppertime. You cut any timbers for the braces on that yet?"

Roald shook his head. "I . . . we . . . ah . . . ."

"Say no more. You talked me into settling in these here parts, and that makes us liable to help each other out. I'll let you know when we are ready for our soddy raising."

"Mange takk and more. We are grateful."

Ingeborg clasped her hands together to keep them from clapping. By tomorrow night they'd have a roofless home and a cleared garden plot. Kaaren came to stand beside her, and she turned to say something. A single tear glistened in the dim light and meandered down to the younger woman's chin. She stood straight and silent, without wiping it away.

The work began as the first bird notes announced the coming dawn. Treating each three-foot strip of sod like a brick, they overlapped the seams. The weight of the new layers packed those below, creating walls a good twelve inches thick and solid enough to withstand any elements. As the walls rose, the three boys ran water to the workers and played tag around the wagons. Their laughter rose above the grunts of the men and the chatter of the women.

Penny minded Gunny in the shade of the wagon, leaving the three women free to cook. They even found time to exchange a packet of precious quilt pieces. To Ingeborg, it felt like home.

The men fulfilled their predictions early in the afternoon, then they headed for the riverbanks with axes and the crosscut saw.

The three women entered through the opening left for the door and turned around to check out the space. The east end still had an opening for the fireplace with a goose-down cloud floating on a blue sky that substituted for a roof. But two walls were completed to their seven-foot height, and the door lintel would be finished when they had a wooden piece to lay across the strips of sod.

"Well, it certainly looks solid." Kaaren laid one hand on a dark wall. Pieces of grass dangled in spots and sprouted straight up in others.

"It smells like the ground all right." Ingeborg jerked some of the grass loose, sending a shower of dirt onto the floor. *How will four adults, one rambunctious little boy, and a creeping infant live in these cramped quarters through a Dakota winter?*

They could hear the ring of the axes and the crash of one tree after another falling. "We'd better get some supper ready; they'll be mighty hungry after a day like this." Kaaren led the way out of the room. "Mrs. Baard, do you . . ."

"Please call me Agnes; it sounds so much friendlier. And Mr. Baard is Joseph."

Kaaren and Ingeborg nodded. "Then you must do the same. We are Kaaren and Ingeborg. The two brothers are Roald and Carl." Ingeborg pointed to herself. "And I am married to Roald, the one without the beard." As if they'd worked together for years, the three women scurried about and prepared the evening meal, with Agnes telling them of life in Ohio, where they'd farmed with her husband's brother.

When Ingeborg realized that Agnes knew some English, she felt a renewed thrill of anticipation. Perhaps this winter they could come together for schooling. Kaaren could teach the children reading, writing, and arithmetic, and Agnes would teach them all English. This all depended, of course, on the Baards finding land to homestead within a reasonable distance. It would be heavenly to look to the west and see a trail of smoke curling into the sky from a cook fire, to know that a friendly face would appear at a door if you walked that way. The thought gave her goose bumps.

The next day they raised the walls for the barn.

When the Baards drove off, the silence that fell seemed deeper and more profound than ever. But when a meadowlark flew overhead pouring out music with great abandon, the joy of the morning returned.

Roald plowed the ground, newly stripped of sod, and the dirt rolled over in curls like good soil was meant to.

Thorliff plucked a fat worm from a clump of dirt and, laughing in delight, held it up for all to see. "Let's go fishing."

"Tomorrow, den lille. Today we plant." While Roald finished the plowing and then pulled the drag over to loosen the soil even further, Ingeborg carefully cut the few remaining seed potatoes so that each small chunk had at least one eye, preferably two. When finished with that, she dug into the trunk that held their seed collection, packed so carefully in Norway. Carrots, turnips, rutabagas, beans, and oats. She dug further and found cabbage seed and onion, and finally down in the bottom, flowers: nasturtium, marigold, hollyhocks, and pansies. Would the plants survive in this harsh wind? *Please, God.* She clutched the packets tight in her fist against her breast. *Please!*

That night in the beds they had moved under the wagon when the ground dried, Ingeborg turned to Roald. "Mange takk for the garden," she whispered.

He rolled over and propped his head up on his hand. "I am glad you like it. We are so much further on now, after the help of our new friends. Soon you will have a house again." He motioned to the square box throwing shadows in the moonlight.

"Ja, soon." She cuddled closer and laid her hand on his chest. "I've missed you."

"Ja, me too." He wrapped her in his arms, and it was some time before sleep found them.

Right after breakfast, Ingeborg gathered her seeds, and while Kaaren managed the housekeeping chores, Ingeborg marked her first row in the garden. She dropped seeds and showed Thorliff how to cover them. She let him plant the beans since the seeds were easier to see, while she marked the next row with sticks pounded in at either end.

Back and forth they worked, taking moments to admire a particularly fine worm. Once Ingeborg picked up a handful of the rich Dakota soil and held it to her nose. The smell—the wonderful smell of dirt waiting to be planted. So black, so pure. No rocks and pebbles to be hauled away. Just dig and plant.

"Come for dinner." Kaaren stood at the edge of the garden.

"Already?" Ingeborg straightened and wiped the sweat off her forehead with the back of her hand. She gazed with love over her handiwork. Now for a good gentle rain to soak the ground, and with the warm sun, the seeds should sprout quickly. A garden, their first garden on their own land. Well, almost their own.

That evening she and Thorliff went fishing.

Behind them the ring of axes told of the men's labor to cut roof timbers. With all the noise, Ingeborg didn't bother to look over her shoulder for the wolf. Besides, now that she knew the wolf and Metis were friends, she wasn't quite so afraid.

She sat on her log, swatted at a mosquito on her arm, and let her mind wander over the last weeks. Kaaren had to talk fast to keep Roald from hunting for the wolf. She was right; it wasn't the wolf's fault Ingeborg fell. It was her own fault for panicking like that. Thinking of the wolf brought her mind to Metis. Wasn't there some way they could share the land? Metis didn't ask for much.

"Mor!" Thorliff's shout jolted her back to the present. "Help me. I got a fish."

Ingeborg stuck her pole in a crook of the log and leaned over to assist her son. "Easy now." The pole quivered as the fish swam upstream, then down. When it slowed, Ingeborg whispered, "When I say jerk, you pull the pole back as hard as you can, all right?"

Thorliff nodded, his eyes big as the saucers beneath her good china cups.

"Now! Jerk!"

Thorliff jerked the pole, and a two-foot fish landed on the log behind him. "Get him."

"Hang on to the pole." Ingeborg grabbed for the flopping fish and missed.

"Get it, Mor."

Their shouts brought Carl and Roald on the run.

Ingeborg grabbed again and this time got both hands around the slippery, flopping fish. She stuck one finger in a gill and hoisted the fish up for all to see.

"He's a beauty." Carl looked from the fish to the boy, who flailed arms and legs in his excitement. "You are a real fisherman, Thorly."

"Get your pole." Roald made a dive for Ingeborg's pole, which was fast disappearing, towed by a fish on her line. Soaking wet and in the water to his knees, Roald held up the pole with another fish flipping on the end of the line.

"Far, you are all wet." Thorliff stared at his father, mouth hanging open.

"But we got the fish."

"Ja, that we did."

"And you can lay money that any fish within half a mile has left the country," Carl said with a laugh. "You think two fish are enough for breakfast?"

Thorliff nodded. "They are big fish." He looked at the one his father had laid on the bank. "And mine is the biggest."

"Ja, it is. Think you can carry them back to camp?" Ingeborg took the two fish Roald had stuck on a stick.

Thorliff eyed the load. "One is yours. You could help me."

Ingeborg felt the smile warm her belly before it reached her face. She looked up to see a corner of Roald's mouth lift, deepening the crease line from nose to chin. That was definitely a twinkle in his eye. Her heart nearly burst with joy.

"Ja, I will help you just as you helped me all morning in the garden. Come, we will go show these fine fish to Tante Kaaren. She has missed all the fun."

The thud of ax on tree accompanied them back to the homesite.

The gentle rain came as if in answer to her prayers. It fell through the night and only broke with a rainbow in the rising sun. Drops turned into diamonds on the blades of grass and outlined a spider's web that festooned the wagon tongue. Ingeborg repeated her thanks as she went about remaking the fire. Thanks to the wood kept dry under the wagon, fire-starting was no longer the chore it had been, especially since right under the waterpot several coals still smoldered.

Two nights later, the cow dropped her calf. They awoke to the sight of a white tail flicking from side to side as the little heifer nursed.

Thorliff squealed and ran toward them before Ingeborg could grab his arm. The cow lowed once and lowered her head.

Roald snatched his son back, just in time. "She doesn't want you to touch her calf, so stay away."

"But, Far, Boss is my friend." Thorliff looked up at his father as if he'd been struck.

"Ja, but not today. Give her a couple of days to get used to us again. I will teach you to milk her, starting tonight."

"But then what will the calf drink?"

"Don't you worry; she will get her share." Roald gave Thorliff a pat on the behind. "You go stake Lamb out now, or she will be complaining about having nothing to eat."

That evening Roald tied Boss to the wagon wheel, and after overturning one bucket to use for a stool, he set the other bucket under the cow's swollen udder and sat down. Thorliff hung right by his shoulder. "See, now, you put your hands on two of the teats and squeeze." Twin jets of thin liquid danced on the bottom of the pail. Roald milked some more, explaining the squeeze and pull of milking. "This isn't her real milk yet. See the globs of colostrum?"

Thorliff had his head planted against his father's shoulder. "Ja."

"That's for the calf to be healthy, and Mor will make us some pudding from it." Roald continued to milk. "You want to try?" He moved his bent leg back so Thorliff could squeeze in.

Thorliff knelt by the bucket, took the two first teats in his hands, and squeezed. Nothing happened. He tried again, still to no avail. "My hands won't work."

Roald put his larger ones over his son's, and together they stripped the milk from Boss's udder. "You see how it feels?"

Thorliff sat back on his haunches and shook his head. "I have to squeeze harder."

"Ja, squeeze and pull. You will learn."

From the shelter of the wagon, Ingeborg watched the two of them. She looked forward to doing the milking, and by the time they had more cows, Thorliff would be a good assistant.

The men spent each night hewing the timbers for the sod house and barn. The ridgepoles were hand-hewn, and the beams were sawed from larger branches. Thorliff gathered all the chips and piled them under the wagon to dry for kindling, then stacked the small branches along with the larger ones cut into fireplace lengths. Keeping ahead of the cooking fire was a monumental chore, especially when Carl returned from hunting with another deer.

"I could have bagged a second one, but I didn't see how you could handle all that meat, as warm as it is."

"It's a good thing Roald brought back a bag of salt. We'll cure part of it while the rest is drying." Besides drying the meat, the smudgy smoke from the fire did one other thing—it kept the mosquitoes at bay. With warm days and nights that didn't cool much, the pests descended upon the Bjorklunds, both human and animal. Even Boss and her calf found relief around the smoky fire.

With summer, the black flies hatched and pestered them even more. Ingeborg couldn't believe that now she prayed for wind, because only then did the tormentors let up. Roald and Carl had rigged fly guards for the horses and oxen—canvas cut into strips that brushed over the animals' faces and protected their eyes.

The day after the surveyors moved on, Roald took the steamboat to Grand Forks to file on their land. Nothing was said of Metis' claim. Against her will Ingeborg kept her mouth closed.

One week later to the day, Mr. Baard rode by to tell them he'd been to Grand Forks and filed on his homestead. He said the land lay due west about five miles. Now they would begin breaking sod, and he figured he would do the same as the Bjorklunds had done and put the garden where he cut the sod for the house and barn.

"You let us know when, and we'll be there." Roald tipped his hat back and wiped the sweat from his forehead. "We sure need rain, wouldn't you say?"

"Ja, I'm just grateful we were able to find land with water on it, like you have. I heard tales of some folks having to haul water along with all the other work. If someone wanted to go into the well-drilling business, I think they could make a good living at it. 'Course they'd have to take payment in trade since no one has cash for extras."

Ingeborg listened to their discussion while she kneaded the bread and tended the drying venison. *This country also needs someone to raise workhorses and oxen, and someone to go into the black-smithing business. Pounding out plowshares is a never-ending chore.*

What she wouldn't give for a well and a springhouse to keep things cool. Carl had promised to dig a root cellar in time for harvesting the garden. They needed a smokehouse too. She had been putting the churn to good use, so she quickly fetched a sack and put a soft cheese, butter, and a loaf of bread in it.

"Here, you take this home to Agnes and tell her she knows what to do with it. I can't keep up with all the milk that cow is producing." Ingeborg stepped back and waved as he thanked them and prepared to leave. What a glorious feeling to have something to give away. To think they had friends nearby. What a blessing.

"Mange takk. You know my missus will be over to visit as soon as we can spare a moment."

Ingeborg watched him ride off. One day they would have a road between their houses.

Now instead of breaking sod, Roald and Carl spent long hours scything the prairie grass so it could dry for hay. After the golden swaths dried beneath the sun, they raked it and forked it onto a dray, a platform that dragged across the ground for the horses to haul into the yard. There they forked the dry hay up onto a fast-growing hay-stack right next to the sod barn walls. When she could, Ingeborg joined them in the raking and turning of the hay so it would dry completely. In Norway, they had draped the grass over fences to dry, but in this land of no fences, raking and turning sufficed. Thorliff helped pack the stacked hay, sliding down the hay pile when it was time to head back to the field.

"We are so blessed," Kaaren said one day, watching as the men followed the team back out after the noon meal.

"Why now?"

"We four share the work. The men out there and we here accomplish far beyond what a man and woman can do alone."

"That is true. And we have someone to talk to, also."

"And argue with?" A twinkle in Kaaren's eye reminded Ingeborg that she had not been very pleasant that morning.

"Ja, that too." Her monthly had begun again, and that meant still no baby. It always reminded her of the one that never would be. Would she ever be able to give Roald the son he wanted?

22

"Today is the day."

Ingeborg looked up at Roald with a question on her face. "The day?"

"Ja, today we raise the ridgepole." Roald dumped the dregs of his coffee on the ground and picked a bit of coffee grounds off the tip of his tongue. "You think between the four of us and the horses we can do that?"

"We could still lay the roof flat with only one side slightly higher." Carl rubbed the pad of his thumb along his jawline.

"I know. But we will need the extra space inside that a pitched roof will give us. Either that or raise the walls farther." Roald knew they could make do with the shed-style roof, but there was something about a pitched roof that said the man who lived here would go the extra mile to make his house a home. It was bad enough having to lay sod for the roof instead of shakes. For a brief instant he let himself think of the roofs in Norway. There they were covered with rows of overlapping slate or shingles, and steeply pitched so the snow would slide off. One day, one day soon, he would have such a house again.

He studied the sod walls. A house would come later. What was he doing dreaming the day away? He stood. "Let us be at it, then."

The two men hitched up the wagon and drove out to the latest sod-cutting patch. They loaded the freshly cut sod and returned to the house. Standing in the wagon bed, they set the sod into a peak formation, with the high point dead center on the west end of the structure. On the east end, where half the wall would be fireplace, they laid a beam along the top of the sod half, from wall to wall, giving them support for the post they set next. In the post, they'd notched out a bed for the ridgepole. Hammers rang as they drove into the wood the few nails they'd made themselves on the forge.

When dinner was ready, the two men stepped back from their handiwork. Roald nodded. "Ja, that will do," he said, turning to Carl. "What do you think?"

"I wish we could put an opening in that east gable so we would have more light."

"Ja, but one window is all that is required. We will make do." The two men continued their discussion over the meal, and as soon as they finished eating, they returned to the roofing. Parallel to the north side of the building, they set the wagon loaded with the beam.

"Kaaren, Ingeborg, we need you now." Roald hated to ask the wives to help, but he could see no other way, short of riding over and asking Joseph Baard for a hand. When the women stood ready, he looked from them to the beam and up to the wall. "We will hoist this up, and then you hold it in place until we get up there and can carry it to the peak. If you stand in the wagon, you will be tall enough."

"If it starts to fall, get out of the way," Carl ordered. "We do not need any broken bones."

Ingeborg and Kaaren nodded.

"Thorliff, you hold the horses' heads," Roald said. "Go get them some oats first. That will keep them happy."

Ingeborg started to say something but stopped herself. What if the horses bolted and ran over the boy? He wouldn't be able to leap out of the way. They would just have to keep the beam steady, that was all.

"On three." Carl took his end of the beam and Roald grabbed his. Kaaren and Ingeborg stood in the middle. The wagon bed felt hollow beneath their feet.

"One, two, three." With a mighty heave the men lifted the beam waist high, then chest high, and on up to the top of the wall.

"Now hang on to this." Roald made sure the women had the beam braced before he climbed down from the wagon and mounted the ladder. Carl did the same at the opposite end of the house.

Belle stamped at a fly and Bob took a step forward, setting the wagon to rocking.

"Whoa!" Thorliff jerked the reins.

The beam wobbled as Kaaren, thrown off balance by the moving wagon, lost her grip.

Ingeborg, caught in the same motion but braced more securely, pushed harder.

Kaaren regained her balance and managed to get her hands back up under the beam just as it wobbled again.

"You got it?" Carl bounded the last three rungs on the ladder and nearly threw himself over the wall to grab the beam.

"Hold those horses!" Roald sounded like the voice of thunder booming from the heavens. He grabbed the beam after Carl by only a moment. The four adults stared at each other, breathing hard.

"Thanks be to God," Kaaren whispered.

"Amen to that." Carl took a deep breath and flashed his wife a smile. "You are all right?"

"Ja. But that was close."

"Thorly, you did fine." Ingeborg dusted off her hands and climbed down from the wagon.

"They don't like flies." Thorliff looked up at his mother, hands still clamped on the reins. "It was a big fat horsefly that bit Belle. I saw it." His lower lip quivered. He looked up at the men on the ladders as if afraid Far would come down and swat him.

Ingeborg couldn't remember a time when Thorliff had been struck. He tried so hard, this son of theirs. "You did just fine, son. Just fine." She spoke the words loud enough so Roald could hear and perhaps take a hint.

"I am thinking there might be a pancake left from breakfast that would go well with molasses for a boy who did such a fine job." Kaaren stopped beside the two. "You make sure the horses are in the shade, and come with me."

Ingeborg and Kaaren walked back to the fire. "Mange takk."

"Ja, to you too. I should have been braced better." Kaaren shot a look over her shoulder. "I don't like standing on things to get higher. The way they go up and down the ladders—that is not for me." She shuddered.

Ingeborg didn't answer. She knew that if she had to she would climb ladders and roofs and whatever else needed climbing. She'd been a better tree climber than her brothers, another one of those secrets she was careful to never tell her mother.

By moving the beam a bit at a time, pounding a peg to hold it, then moving the ladder and repeating the exercise, Roald and Carl finally dropped the heavy length of wood into the cradle they had carved for it.

Thorliff set up a cheer. Ingeborg and Kaaren clapped their hands.

The men both removed their hats and wiped their foreheads with the length of their arms.

"Thanks be to God," Kaaren murmured.

"Uff da." Roald shook his head. "That is one heavy chunk of wood."

"Ja, but we did it, and on the first try." Carl set his hat back on his head and straightened the brim. "Now we will put up the rafters. They will go up much faster."

"I am going to make us a special treat for supper, unless you need me anymore." Kaaren paused in her retreat. At that moment, Gunny let out a lusty wail. "After I feed her, of course."

By the time it came to do evening chores, all the rafters, some bent and gnarled as branches tend to be, were lashed in place with crosspieces creating small squares up one side. Ingeborg and Thorliff did most of the fetching and handing of things. Ingeborg looked longingly at the ladder. She could tie off the crosspieces as well as the men, since it took nimble fingers instead of brawn. It would free the men up to return to breaking sod.

She gathered all her courage together through the good supper Kaaren had prepared and, after the coffee was poured, said, "Would not you rather be in the fields than working about the house?" At their looks of doubt, she continued. "I could tie off the crosspieces now that the rafters are in place. Thorliff would help me. Then you could return to . . ."

"I will not discuss this further. The answer is no. Tomorrow we will lay the sod on the roof. A woman's place is not on the roof." Roald spoke as though she had just suggested he cook the supper while she plow the field.

Ingeborg rose to her feet and dusted off her skirt. "If you will excuse me, I believe I will go for a walk."

She heard his muttered "confounded woman" as she left the campsite. *I was only trying to help; what is so wrong with that? Men are so bull-headed. Leaving Norway didn't change that.* She clasped her hands around her elbows. The newly fallen dew was already dampening the hem of her skirt. The stars seemed so low that if she stood on the ridgebeam of the soddy she could almost pick them from the cobalt sky and save them in her pocket. She swatted the mosquitoes and kept on walking. She didn't fear getting lost, for their campfire stood out like a beacon on the prairie. As long as she stayed out of the tall grass, she was all right.

What difference does it make who does what as long as the work gets done?

Roald and Carl were just putting away their carving tools when she walked back into camp.

"Mor," Thorliff called as soon as he saw her. "Where did you go? You missed the römmegrot Tante Kaaren made for a treat."

"I am sure it was very good. Now you be a good boy and go climb in bed. I will be right there to say your prayers." Ingeborg poured herself a cup of coffee and followed Thorliff to the wagon. She sat down beside his pallet in the wagon bed and rested her chin on her knees as he prayed. Together they said the Lord's prayer, the age-old words bringing a measure of peace to her heart. Was the order of things God's will as her mother had always preached, or did man have a hand in it? She kissed the boy good-night, got into her nightdress, and spread the bed on the ground where she and Roald slept. She fell asleep dreaming of ways to help her husband see the wisdom of her desires.

Finishing the roofing took two more days. The space had narrowed between Roald's eyebrows as his frustration grew with their missing time in the field. They tried to hurry.

Roald's pained "Uff da!" caught Ingeborg's ear. She looked up to see him pulling his leg out of a hole in the row of sod just laid. Crossbars underneath had given way. She could see the debris hanging since she was opposite the gaping open wall the fireplace would fill.

The men stripped back the laid sod, repaired the break, and continued.

"I thought that roof was strong enough to hold a buffalo," Carl said to Kaaren later.

"Thank God no one was hurt." Kaaren looked up at the soddy. "You are so close to finishing. It looks like a real house now."

"Ja, a house with a hayfield for a roof." Roald drew up his pant leg to see blood soaked into his boot. "Uff da," he muttered again and went for a washcloth and water.

"Uff da is right." Ingeborg took the pan from him, pointed to the log stool, and went to the wagon for a clean cloth to use as a bandage. *You are so stubborn you could not even look at your leg. Surely you felt the pain when this was cut.* As she cleaned and bandaged the wound, she kept her words to herself. She was getting much better at doing that.

"I think we should have a party when we move into our house."

Kaaren made her announcement the next morning. When no one bothered to contradict her, she continued. "Good then, I will walk over to the Baards and invite them. Which day do you think would be best?"

"We have no time for parties; we have lost too much time as it is." Roald kept shoveling the eggs and venison into his mouth as if the matter was settled.

"Now wait, brother. A party would be a good idea. We need to take time to thank the Lord for what He has given us, and a little laughter wouldn't hurt us either."

Kaaren came to stand by her husband's shoulder. "True."

Ingeborg kept silent, watching the scene unfold before her. Would Roald give in to his brother?

"The Baards won't take a day off. They are further behind than we are."

"It never hurts to ask." Kaaren glanced over to where the chickens were scratching in the dirt of their yard. "Those young roosters are about the right size for frying, and I imagine that if we looked under the potato vines, we would find enough new potatoes to make a meal. What do you think, Inge?"

Ingeborg shrugged, but the tilt of her head told Kaaren she agreed.

"Good, it is settled, then?" The statement ended in a question with all their eyes locked on Roald.

"If we spend all of our morning here, that roof will never get done." Roald strode back to the soddy and hoisted the first block of sod from the wagon bed up to the roof.

Kaaren looked from Carl to Ingeborg and over to Roald. "Next Sunday, then." They all nodded as one.

Several days later, they moved their boxes and trunks into the completely roofed soddy and stacked them along one wall. The men planned to build two beds along the back wall for the adults. The children would sleep on trundle beds that fit under the big beds during the day.

"Where is Ingeborg?" Roald asked when he returned for dinner the day before the party was to be.

"She took Thorliff to the river. She said it was to be a surprise, but you know Thorliff. He can no more keep a secret than that wind will quit blowing." Kaaren brushed bits of ashes off her face. Strips of venison hung over the drying racks, along with fish that Thorliff and Ingeborg brought in almost every morning. With the heat of

August upon them, they alternately blessed and cursed the wind.

They were halfway through the meal when they saw Ingeborg striding along, carrying a bucket with a tall branch, complete with leaves, in it. Thorliff dragged something with one hand.

Roald and Carl looked at each other and shook their heads. But Kaaren knew immediately what it was. That was why Ingeborg had been digging a hole by the side of the house.

Ingeborg set the bucket in the shade of the soddy and, after washing her hands in the pan, joined the rest of the family at the campfire.

"What are you doing?" Roald asked around a mouthful of bread.

"Eating. Same as you." Ingeborg handed Thorliff a full plate and fixed one for herself.

Roald didn't say a word, but his expression said much.

"Far, we dug a . . ."

Ingeborg shushed him with one finger to her lips. "That's a surprise, remember?"

"You dug up a tree?" Roald set his plate on his knees.

"Ja. For the west corner of the house. It is only a cottonwood, a small one. I want an oak, but that will have to wait until fall or next spring."

"It will die in this heat."

"Not if I shade it and keep it watered. You will see."

"Mor said I should put horse manure in the hole for fertilizer." Thorliff added, "We are going to plant more trees, all around our house."

Roald shook his head. "What a waste of time." His mutter carried back over his shoulder as he went to yoke up the oxen.

Maybe so, maybe no, Ingeborg thought. *If it dies, I will just plant another. I will have trees around the house and flowers.* She glanced over at the garden where her marigolds were just coming into bloom. The splashes of yellow and gold against the deep green of the bean plants did her heart good. She knew she'd save extra seed so she could give some to other women as they came through on their way west. Even one blooming plant made a soddy a home.

Carl took a few minutes to help her plant the young sapling. "We'll make a windbreak for it out of part of the canvas from the wagon. But it will take a lot of water."

"I know. Transplanting it this fall would have been wiser, but I wanted to surprise everyone, and . . . and I needed this tree by the house. Just think, in a couple of years it will be taller than the roof and shading us in the summer." She wiped the sweat from the side of her face. "And shade is a premium out here."

"That it is." Kaaren joined them, Gunny perched on her hip.

They let Thorliff tamp the ground down with his bare feet, the water and soil turning to mud that squished up between his toes. He giggled, splashed some more, and laughed out loud. Gunny waved a fat little fist in the air and chortled along with him as if he were having fun just to entertain her.

Thank you, God, for children who help us smile more. Ingeborg tickled Gunny under the chin for another belly laugh and chuckled along with her.

All three returned to their chores lighter of both foot and heart.

In the morning the leaves of the cottonwood drooped on their branches.

Ingeborg decreed that all the wash water be dumped on the tree. Up to now, it had been Thorliff's job to carry wash water over to the garden and water as many plants as possible with it.

The next day the Baards arrived, and the fun began. The men talked crops and sod busting nonstop; the women shared the trials and triumphs of creating a home on the prairie.

Penny took the boys off to play, promising they would bring full water buckets back with them. With the meal cooking, Ingeborg took Agnes out to see the garden. Together they picked the beans and pulled carrots for dinner.

"You ever made bean britches?" Agnes asked, holding up a particularly fine cluster of green beans.

"I do not think so. What are they?"

"You dry the beans in pairs like this so you can hang them over a rack to dry. Then when you cook them, you leave them together and add bacon, onion, whatever. I learned the trick from a woman who came up from the south. They do things different down there, you know."

"We will try it. I have pickled beans in the past, but we must make vinegar first. And we don't have the jars for canning. Oh, when I think of the pickled herring we used to make! Have you ever tried to pickle other fish?"

Agnes shook her head. "But we used to buy lutefisk in the winter. Maybe the store in St. Andrew will bring in dried lutefisk. And my mother made the best lefse."

The thought of turning some of her potatoes into lefse made Ingeborg smile. But how would they do that over a fireplace? Lefse needed a large flat surface to bake on, like a stove.

Agnes stood with hands on her hips and looked over at the small field they had planted to grain, corn, and potatoes. "That looks mighty fine. Your wheat will soon be ready for harvest."

"And the oats. Thorly and I, we dug under the vines last night and stole a few small potatoes for dinner today."

"New potatoes?" Agnes clutched the bunch of carrots she'd just pulled to her bosom. "You are a gift from God, my dear, sent to bring happiness to my soul. New potatoes. When I think of our garden in Ohio, I . . ." Agnes shook her head. "No, I won't think back. My garden is late this year, but we will have food from it. Just pray God we have a late frost."

When they had the vegetables cooking, they strolled over to the soddy.

"Now, ain't that just fine." Agnes stood in the center of the room and looked around. Just the night before, Roald and Carl had set the bed frames, using a board pegged into the wall for one side and a post for the footpost that worked for both beds. "Your men are mighty clever." She looked up at the pitched ceiling. "You can hang bunches of herbs and even meat from up there. Keep from swishing you on the head, that way."

"Once the beds are roped, we will sleep in here. I have sheeting to stuff with hay for the mattresses, or we'll use the corn shucks." Kaaren pointed to the future fireplace. "Carl wants to buy a stove, but I think we will do with this for at least a year. Have you ever cooked in an oven in the fireplace wall?"

"No, can't say that I have. I miss my stove more than anything. But it was just too heavy to bring along. Joe says maybe by winter we can get one."

After grace they all fell to the meal as if they hadn't eaten for a month of Sundays. Kaaren's plum pie was the hit of the hour.

"Looks like we licked the platter clean." Kaaren held up the two pie pans. She'd baked them in the spider in a pit of coals.

"I never thought you could turn out such perfect baking without an oven. You two are geniuses, far as I can see." Agnes shook her head. "Penny, you go on over to the wagon and bring me that parcel I packed."

When the girl returned, Agnes drew out a jar. "Here. We found us a bee tree and helped ourselves. Thought you might like some too."

"Honey." Kaaren and Ingeborg passed the jar back and forth, admiring the deep golden color.

"There'll be more where that came from. We left plenty for the bees, and they got right back to work." Agnes snagged her toddler away from the edge of the fire. "You seen that Metis woman lately? I wanted to thank her for the hammock idea."

"No, she goes farther north to be with her family she said. She will return before winter." Ingeborg looked up in time to catch a scowl on her husband's face. He hadn't asked about Metis, and she hadn't offered. He probably thought she'd gone for good.

Saying goodbye when the sun started toward the horizon was made all the more difficult after having become better friends.

"We will help you raise your soddy soon as you say the day." Roald stood by the rump of the horses now hitched to the Baards' wagon again.

"I figure September—late like. I got to get a beam cut and braces."

"We could bring one or come a day early for the cutting." Carl put one foot up on the wheel spokes.

"I couldn't ask that of you."

"You did not ask. We offered." Carl looked to Roald, who nodded.

"Well, then, we'd be obliged," Agnes said as she laid her hand on her husband's arm. "You know us Norwegians; we have a hard time accepting help."

"Ja, we know." Carl turned to flash his wife a grin. He jiggled Gunny on his hip and helped her chubby hand wave bye-bye.

"I will let you know when I am ready." Baard slapped the reins on his horses' backs. "Gidap, there. Mange takk for the party and congratulations on readying your soddy." He lifted a hand in farewell and drove out of the yard.

"Bye, bye. Come see us," the boys yelled out the back of the wagon.

The Bjorklunds stood watching until the dust settled and the rig was hidden by the tall grass beyond their property.

"Ja, well, that was a good visit." Carl turned and headed for the sod barn. "Think I'll work on the beams for the roof, here, so when we can find the time, they'll be ready."

"I will milk so you can return to busting sod." Ingeborg blinked back the moisture that blurred the sight of the disappearing wagon.

When they woke in the morning, the little tree had perked up, and the rounded leaves sparkled with dew. Ingeborg couldn't resist caressing one as she poured water into the well they'd created around the base. Like the Bjorklunds, the tree would make it. She wouldn't let it die.

The next weeks passed in never-ending toil from before dawn until well into the night. They picked and dried plums from the bushes along the swamp and turned the chokecherries into preserves. What wouldn't store fresh in the root cellar that was yet to be dug they dried. Beans, both as seeds and in the pods, corn, both on the cob and off—all lost their moisture quickly in the hot Dakota sun and incessant wind.

They harvested the wheat and oats, bundled and tied them, then hauled them to the barn to flail later when they could no longer work outside. The size of the crop astounded them. So much yield from such a small tract.

"If only we'd had twenty acres of this," Roald was heard to mumble more than once.

When they dug the root cellar, they laid the sod off to the side to use for the roof. Since the land was so flat, they had no mound to dig into, so they had to go deeper. By throwing the dirt up for walls, they cut down on the depth somewhat. By the time they finished, they had a new bump on the prairie. With the sod house, the sod barn, and haystacks, their land was beginning to look like a real farm.

One day Thorliff came running into the soddy where Ingeborg and Kaaren were stuffing corn shucks in the casings they had sewn. "Mor, company's coming." He ran in place, waving a finger to the south. Both women dropped what they were doing and ran out the door to see. Sure enough, a wagon drawn by a team of oxen was approaching.

"Go get Far." Ingeborg gave him a gentle push on his way.

As Thorliff scampered off, Ingeborg shaded her eyes. Her sunbonnet hung by its strings down her back, its normal place. "We better put the coffee on. Is there enough for supper?"

"I'll add more vegetables and make dumplings. That should be a treat for travelers."

Slowly the wagon drew nearer, and with each turn of the wheels, it became more evident that the travelers were at the end of their endurance. Or at least their equipment was.

Ingeborg was afraid they could see clear through the shaggy-faced man driving the squealing wagon. How he stood up to a good wind was beyond her.

"Good day, missus." He stopped the oxen, which stood with lowered heads, their ribs sticking out like barrel staves.

Ingeborg replied in English but prayed he spoke Norwegian. "Good day."

"Name's Abel Polinski and my wife's Caroline. Them's my boys, Reuben and Esau in the back." He gestured to each with a tired thumb. "We was hoping you could let us stay for the night." He spoke slowly in German.

"Ja, you are welcome. This is Bjorklund land." Ingeborg introduced the members of her family and pointed to the men driving the teams in from the field. "Coffee is ready if you would like to sit." She reverted to Norwegian and pointed to the stump and log seats around the cook fire.

"Ya got water for my team here?"

"Down at the river." She pointed to the trees.

"No well, huh?"

Ingeborg shook her head. Why did she feel like asking them to move on? What had happened to her sense of hospitality?

The Polinski family climbed down from the wagon, their clothes as ragged and dirty as the canvas that flapped in the wind. Mrs. Polinski only nodded in their general direction, otherwise she cuddled the babe wrapped in a blanket with more holes than threads. The boys hid behind her.

By the time Roald and Carl had unhitched and staked out the horses and oxen, the Polinskis had devoured two loaves of bread and half a pail of milk. The cheese disappeared like ground fog in the sun.

"How long do you suppose it has been since they had something to eat?" Kaaren asked when she and Ingeborg returned to the soddy for more food. "Should we send them to the river to wash before supper?"

Ingeborg shook her head. "How will they make it through the winter when they are coming so late in the season?"

"I do not know." Kaaren dug in the trunk for a blanket Gunny had grown too big to use. "This would protect the baby more than that rag she has. Do you think I dare offer it?"

After two days, they learned that the Polinskis didn't mind taking whatever was offered. In fact, it seemed they had come to expect the Bjorklunds to help them out.

Instead of wishing the company could stay longer, Ingeborg prayed they would leave. She felt guilty for the supply of food in their root cellar, the grain for their animals, and the roof over their heads. But when she had suggested the traveling family might use the soap to bathe and wash their tattered garments, Abel insisted his wife was too weak to do even that. And never once did he offer himself.

Roald had quit suggesting that there was possible land available in the area.

Carl made sure one of them was in the yard all the time. "I just don't trust anyone who will not look me in the eye," he said under his breath to Kaaren.

She gave him a secret smile. "Looking you in the eye is difficult when one of your own goes off to the side."

Carl slapped her on the bottom. "Do not get fresh with me, woman."

A throat being cleared made them both turn to the doorway. Polinski stood there, the familiar hang-dog look on his face.

"If'n you wouldn't mind, might I have another cup of coffee?" He held out his mug.

"Help yourself, the pot is out on the fire." Carl's voice had an edge.

Ingeborg swallowed a smile. The man was wearing out his welcome, for certain, if even Carl, who made friends with everyone, was tired of him.

When the newly greased wheels of the mended wagon finally carried the Polinskis north on the prairie, Ingeborg clutched her elbows with her hands. She had a funny feeling about that family. *God, please make them move on, far on, like across the Little Salt River.* She didn't wave back when Abel shouted a goodbye.

23

Thoughts of the Polinskis continued to nag at Ingeborg. Abel—
what a name for a man who acted *unable* to do anything. The day
they arrived, he didn't even lead his oxen down to water until Carl
made a remark about the animals needing a drink. Was he bone lazy
or just incompetent? And the poor children. How would they ever
make it through a harsh winter?

The thought she had resolutely locked in a box and stuffed in
the back of her mind kept unlocking the box and popping up. Why
did God let people like that have children, and she still hadn't con-
ceived? Guilt made her feel worse. She felt guilty for coveting someone else's children and guilty for judging people she hardly knew.
She knew the verse—it had been drilled into her since childhood:
"Judge not, that ye be not judged."

"I'm going fishing." She called loud enough for Thorliff to hear.
He left the slate he'd been drawing on and charged out the door.

"Me too?"

"Ja, you too. You seen any good worms lately?"

"I picked some yesterday from the sod when I was out with Onkel Carl." He dashed behind the house and returned with a woven
grass basket full of worms.

"You are lucky they didn't crawl away."

He looked up at her, blue eyes perfectly serious. "But I gave them
dirt and kept them damp like you told me."

"You did fine." She reached up and took down the fishing poles
they kept on pegs pounded into the sod wall. Off they trudged
through the garden that now only had a few cornstalks, several
pumpkins, and some squash left in it. The root vegetables were still

to be dug, but she wanted to wait until the nights turned cold, near to freezing.

Ingeborg stared up at the trees ahead. Some of the leaves were turning yellow, and a few were tinged with rust and vermillion, especially the oaks and the brush. Fall was drawing near, that was for certain. One day soon they would have to build in the fireplace so they would have heat.

Sitting on the bank with her line in the water, she let her thoughts drift back home. It had been so long since they had received a letter. Maybe there would be one waiting in St. Andrew when Roald went in to purchase supplies before winter set in. She had several pages written that she'd been adding to throughout the summer. If only she could tell them she was in the family way again.

"A fish." Thorliff jerked the line and a fat perch flopped at his feet. He stuck a finger in one gill to hold it, picked up a stick, and knocked the wriggling fish on the head. Then he shoved a forked stick through the gills and rammed the opposite end of the stick in the mud so the fish remained in the water. When he had the hook baited again, he tossed it out and looked up at his mother.

"Your turn."

"You don't need me to fish with you anymore; you do just fine yourself." Ingeborg swatted a mosquito on her neck and brushed another away from her face.

"I like it better when you are here. Do you think Metis will come back?"

"Ja, when the cold comes. What made you ask?"

"Far said she might try to take our land. He said he would run her off."

Ingeborg laid a gentle hand on his shoulder. "You let Far and Mor take care of those things. You play with Gunny, take care of Lamb, and catch lots of fish. And when winter comes, we will have school right there in our soddy—the Baards and us. We will all learn English, and you will learn to read and write and do sums. How does that sound?"

"I know my ABCs." He jerked his line again. "Fish."

He caught eight to Ingeborg's two. The grin on his face told the family at the table later that day how proud he was.

"Thorly, you're turning into a great fisherman like your great-uncle Hamre," Carl said.

Fried fish fresh from the river always put everyone in a good mood.

They had just finished supper when they heard a halloo from the south. Roald stood on a block of wood to see over the dried prairie grass. "There's a drover with sheep coming." He stepped back down, and he and Carl walked out to meet the traveler.

"You mind if I camp near here for the night?" the man asked after introducing himself as Benjamin Wald. "I'm taking these sheep out to my brother in the northwestern part of Dakota Territory."

"Of course you may camp here. The coffee is still hot, and we have cleared a good trail to the river where you can water your flock."

Thorliff stood right beside his father. "We have Lamb. She will like your sheep."

"Good for you, son." The drover whistled for his dog and waved it toward the river. "We will care for the animals first, and then I look forward to a hot cup of coffee. Three days I been without." He shifted the pack on his back and set it on the ground. "You don't mind if we graze that green patch, do you? Everything's so dry, the critters will appreciate green grass for a change. I can see you hayed it earlier."

Roald watched him walk off, not sure if he was driving or leading the sheep, but the dog certainly knew his job.

"You think he might have a young ram to sell?" Carl stroked his beard. "A ewe would be good, too. Then we'd have lambs in the spring."

"Might be." Roald slapped his brother on the back. "You feeling wealthy or some such?"

"I seem to recall it is your wife who loves the sheep. Mine likes knitting the wool, and I like wearing it."

"Spekekjøtt, cured mutton, would be a taste of home next winter, eh?"

That night they sat around the campfire listening to Benjamin's stories until Thorliff fell off the log in his sleep. Roald picked up his son and carried him to the pallet by the rope-strung beds, then returned to hear more. Wald told of the settlements of Norwegians in Minnesota, the groups of Germans who also homesteaded there, as well as the Swedes and even a few Russians. Sometimes the settlements didn't get along too well with the other nationalities, but "that is the way of folks, I guess," he said.

"I thought we all became Americans when we came here," Roald said. "I am Norwegian by birth but American by choice." Grateful the drover spoke a combination of German, English, and Norwegian, they all spoke slowly so as to understand one another.

"Ja, me too. My father came from the old country when he was a young man. He farms in Wisconsin, but my brother and I, we want the free land to build for ourselves."

"We too," Carl added. "It is good when brothers can help each other."

"Ja, for being here such a short time, you have done much. Others are not so fortunate."

When the man left two days later, a ram and two ewes remained. "They should lamb in February. God's blessing on your house for taking in a stranger like you did." He patted the pack that now held bread and cheese and dried venison.

Behind their harnessed teams, Carl and Roald walked with him as far as the edge of the field they were backsetting. They hooked the horses and oxen to their plows and set to turning the sod as they did every day.

"You will have to herd the sheep now," Ingeborg told Thorliff when she let the small flock out of the barn after milking Boss. "They need to get to know your voice, so when you call, they will come."

"Lamb comes."

"I know. And the others will too. Soon we will need to fence off pasture, but for now, make sure you keep in sight of the soddy. You know you can always find your way back by following the line of the trees too."

"Mor." Thorliff looked at her as if she'd lost her memory. "I know that."

"I know you do, but it never hurts to be reminded." She walked with him as far as the garden and pulled a couple of carrots. "Break these up and keep the pieces in your pocket. If you give the sheep dessert once in a while, they will like you sooner."

"Tante Kaaren gave me bread and cheese. I have full pockets."

Ingeborg helped him break the carrots and waved at him when he looked back. Such a little boy for such a big responsibility. But he had cared well for Lamb, and Roald insisted his son do his part with the family chores.

When the morning chores were finished and the noon meal was cooking, Ingeborg took the rifle and headed for the target she and Carl had fashioned. With all the rush of summer, he hadn't taken time to show her how to shoot their rifle until a short time earlier. The new gun Roald bought made shooting her brother-in-law's old rifle seem like digging in the ground with a stick instead of a plow. No more muzzle loading and black powder. Here they used real bullets and could load six shells at a time.

She could hear Roald's words ringing in her ears. "Do not waste shells."

She lay on the ground and sighted carefully. With the weight of the gun and her inexperience, Ingeborg had learned she could be far more accurate in this position. Carl had also suggested using a branch or tree trunk as a brace. How she looked forward to bringing in her first deer. Or even a rabbit or two. She resettled the stock against her shoulder, lined up the sights on the target, and slowly squeezed the trigger. The resulting bang made her flinch. The gun barrel flew up, her shoulder felt as though she'd been kicked by a horse, and the powder burned her eyes. But she hit within the circle.

Six shots later, she stopped to rub her shoulder and walked up to the circle cut in the tree bark. Four out of six. Not bad. But Roald would say it was not good enough. She had wasted two shells. She fingered the brass casings she had put in her pocket and glanced up when she heard ducks calling each other. They were flying high, the V-formation etched against the rich blue of the autumn sky.

That night around the supper fire, Roald said more with his eyes than his mouth. Ingeborg knew he was not happy with the idea of her, a woman, hunting. With Carl it was a different story.

"I will take you hunting late tomorrow afternoon so we are ready for the deer when they leave their bedding places and go to the river for a drink."

"Can I go?" Thorliff looked up from his supper plate.

Carl shook his head. "Not this time, but soon I will teach you to snare rabbits. If you know how to snare rabbits, you never have to worry about going hungry. There are always rabbits in the country."

Thorliff's shoulders slumped.

"You can help me with Gunny when you get back from herding your sheep." Kaaren patted his shoulder as she walked by on the way to put the baby to bed.

"My new sheep followed Lamb. Even down the trail to water. Sure wish I had a dog like Mr. Wald."

"Ja, we will have to think about either a dog to herd the cattle or fences to keep them from wandering too far. Hobbles work fine for a small number like we have now, but soon . . ." Roald paused as dreams lit up his eyes. "But not until next spring. We have hay enough for our stock now but not for many new ones."

Besides, no money to buy more. Ingeborg kept the thoughts to herself. But if Roald saw a cow or other stock when he went to St. Andrew for winter supplies, he would buy it. What happened to that man who vowed he wouldn't go into debt?

The next afternoon Ingeborg and Carl set out for the woods. He showed her where the game trails ran and where he had shot many of his deer. A tumble of brush made a good hiding spot, and after they made themselves comfortable behind a log, he reminded her where to shoot.

"Aim just in front of the deer, for they will bound forward at the noise. Head shots are the best because you damage less meat, but a chest shot is easier in the beginning."

Ingeborg nodded.

"Take your time. Most people get too excited and miss the shot."

Ingeborg propped the rifle on the log exactly as he had shown her.

Quiet settled around them, but for the whine of the mosquitoes. When the forest noises started up around them again, Ingeborg felt a sense of peace, of time standing still like the hush before dawn. Two squirrels chattered above in the larger of the oak trees. Sparrows flitted in the brush around them, chirping their news and finding seeds and bugs.

Three deer appeared in the edge of her vision, a doe with her young and a four-prong buck. They tripped noiselessly down the trail, their big ears tracking for any unusual noises.

Ingeborg raised the rifle to her shoulder without a sound, each motion slow and deliberate. She sighted down the long barrel until the buck's head lined up in the two Vs. She tracked just ahead of him. He stopped and looked around.

She took a deep breath, let it all out, and squeezed the trigger.

The buck leaped in the air and dropped to the ground.

"What a shot!" Carl jumped to his feet and over the log, drawing his knife as he went.

Ingeborg used the rifle as a prop and got to her feet, shaking as though she had the palsy. She had killed a deer—on her first shot. Joy made her want to leap. Her eyes filled with tears. The buck had walked so proud and beautiful and free.

She forced herself to walk over to the fallen animal where Carl waited for her.

"You want to slit the throat as soon as possible so the animal can bleed." He looked up for her nod. "I know you know these things, but it never hurts to have a reminder. Where's your rifle?" When she pointed to the log, he shook his head. "Always bring it with you in case you only stunned him. He could get up and kill you or seriously injure you. Those horns are wicked."

The pride she felt vanished like smoke caught on the wind. She should have known better than this.

Taking his knife, she knelt beside the fallen animal. They would have food and another hide to tan for either a cover or clothing. She should be grateful. She cut the jugular with one swipe and turned away to get the gun.

By the time they had the deer gutted and were heading back to the homestead, darkness hid the ruts, and vines and branches slapped her in the face. Why was she so weary? It was as if her strength had drained out with the blood of the deer. While Carl could sling the deer over his shoulder, how would she drag a carcass back to camp? Did she really want to become the hunter for the family?

The awe on Thorliff's face made her smile again.

"I only heard one shot." Kaaren looked at her, her mouth half open.

"Ingeborg only needed one shot." Carl tied the back legs to the tripod they had fashioned for dressing game. He looked toward his brother, who was drinking coffee by the fire and hadn't yet said a word. "She didn't waste any shells, you know." He waited a moment for an answer that didn't come, then set about skinning the deer.

After finishing his supper, Roald returned to the forge where he had spent many evenings pounding out plowshares. But that night when they had collapsed into their bed, he rolled over and put his arm around Ingeborg. "That was good," he whispered in her ear, his breath tickling the hair around it.

Ingeborg felt as though he'd given her the moon and stars. "Mange takk."

⚘ ⚘

The days ran into weeks, with the Bjorklunds hurrying to prepare for winter. Ingeborg went out hunting nearly every day, and Thorliff's snares kept the stewpot bubbling with rabbit. He stretched out the rabbit skins so he could tan them, imitating the continuing work of Kaaren and Ingeborg with the deer hides. All the animals fattened on the rich prairie grass, even after the late frost.

The day Joseph Baard rode over and asked if they could raise his soddy the following day gave them all a sense of relief. "I got the beam cut and all. Ivar and Margaret Weirholtz from just north of me are coming too. We should have a regular party together."

"Ja, that is good. You want we should bring the sod cutter and both teams?" Roald tipped his hat back. A line marked his brow like all the others, separating the tanned skin from the white.

Ingeborg left off slicing strips of venison from the haunch. "I'd better get more bread made, then. Kaaren, there should be enough fat on that buck to make piecrust. I remember Mr. Baard here is partial to your plum pie."

"Don't want you to go to no trouble, now." Joseph nodded his thanks when she refilled his coffee cup. "Agnes has been cooking the last two days, too."

As he rode off, Ingeborg and Kaaren couldn't stop smiling even if they had wanted to. Other women to talk with, and a new neighbor to meet. Such excitement.

The day of the soddy raising became the high point of the fall. While everyone worked hard, laughter made the load lighter, good food and plenty of it refueled their energy, and when the sun sank, Ivar Weirholtz brought out his fiddle.

Ingeborg hadn't danced since the previous fall when the neighbors at home got together to celebrate a good harvest and listen to tales of the new land from one who had returned. Then the group had been larger, but the spirit here felt the same.

They danced the hambo, the masurka, the reinlender, and pols. All ages together, they shuffled, spun, skipped, and clapped, some with partners, more often without. The children paired with adults and with each other. Everyone danced, even Gunny in the arms of her father.

"We have to start them young," Kaaren teased back when Joseph made a remark. "We do not have that many times to play here on the prairie."

"There will be more when we have a school to meet in and a church to worship in," Roald promised. "The southwest corner of Bjorklund land is waiting for the buildings."

Ingeborg sent him a special smile. Here was another of those surprises he enjoyed springing on her. He was determined to build a community here for his family and others. So easy it was to forget the dreams when they lived in the present moments of backbreaking toil.

When Roald took her in his arms for the vals, Ingeborg looked up at his strong face, moisture glistening in the firelight. Would he mind if she said "I love you"? She kept the words in her heart but returned the steady pressure on her hand and sent him the message with her eyes.

After they returned home that night and finished the evening chores, it was a long time before they fell asleep.

Several weeks later, Ingeborg realized she was late with her monthly. She hugged the secret to herself, unwilling to mention it in case she was wrong. When she started throwing up in the morning, Kaaren guessed immediately.

"Have you told Roald yet?" she asked one morning when Ingeborg returned from her retching bout behind the soddy. Ingeborg shook her head. "You'd better soon, or your pale face will give you away."

"I want to be certain."

Kaaren raised an eyebrow.

"I know, but what if I. . . ?"

Kaaren raised a hand, shaking her head at the same time. "That was not your fault, Inge. Accidents happen."

But in spite of the joy that swelled her heart that a baby was on its way, Ingeborg couldn't shake the gnawing fear that clenched her stomach.

After she told Roald, he only said, "When?"

"In June," she replied, but she could tell by the light in his eyes he was pleased.

"June is a good month for babies." He nodded once more and raised a warm, calloused hand to touch her cheek. "A very good month."

When the temperatures dropped to freezing several nights in a row, the men took time off from the field work and hauled stones from the river to build the fireplace. Rock by rock, the soddy grew darker. They fashioned a mantel above the firebox and continued up to the eaves with the chimney sprouting above. After the mud and rocks had time to dry, Carl laid a fire and brought in a stick from the campfire to light the wood.

Would it draw? They all stood in the soddy, watching the flames lick the kindling. The smoke drifted straight up.

"That is good." Roald let out a held breath, as did the others.

Thorliff hunkered down in front of the raised hearth and stared at the flames. He looked back around the room. "This fire is friendly. See, it makes colored pictures on the walls."

Ingeborg followed his pointing finger. It did indeed. Maybe dark walls were good for something, reflecting dancing red-and-gold flames.

The day they set the door, though, Ingeborg felt as if she'd been sent to prison. The soddy walls seemed to close around her, stealing the light and air she needed to live. She took the gun and headed for the woods. They'd dried the last of the venison; it was time for another deer.

She'd about reached the woods when a familiar figure stepped from the trees.

"Metis! How are you?" Ingeborg felt as though the sun had just come out after a long rain.

The old woman nodded, her face wreathed in a smile to match Ingeborg's. "You well?"

"Ja. Welcome home." Out of the corner of her eye, Ingeborg saw a gray shadow disappear back into the woods. Wolf was back too. But this time, she ignored the twinge of fear. Wolf would never hurt a friend of Metis. The old woman had assured her younger friend of that before she left on her trek last summer.

"You want to go hunting with me?"

"Your man let you shoot?"

"Ja, but Carl taught me to hunt," Ingeborg said, holding up the new rifle she carried.

"Ah." Metis held out the dead rabbit she gripped by the ears. "This yours." She nodded over her shoulder. "In snare."

"Thorliff has been so busy helping set the door, he hasn't checked his lines yet. Can you use it?"

A nod.

"Then, you take it. Thorliff has been keeping us well supplied." A chill wind tugged at Ingeborg's coat. "I'd better get going. I am glad you are back."

"Yes. Good to be home."

What will she do for a home? Ingeborg thought as she strode south along the tree line. Last year Metis had lived in a cave in the riverbank. Would she want to build something more permanent again? Would Roald let her?

She returned to the soddy empty-handed and chilled clear through. "I saw some large hoof marks on one of the trails farther south," she told Carl when he sat down for supper.

"Elk. We sure could use a couple of elk hides for the winter. I've heard that with the hair left on they are almost as warm as buffalo robes."

"Perhaps you could hunt for elk while I take the team and drive into St. Andrew for supplies," Roald interjected. "We could have snow any day from the look of the sky tonight. I think we have put this trip off as long as we dare."

"Good." Carl turned to Kaaren. "You make up a list of what we need and make sure you include coffee." He winked at her. They'd been out for over three weeks. Roasted and ground wheat just didn't take the place of coffee.

Both men left in the morning after doing the chores, which included bringing in an extra load of wood. The fireplace devoured wood like the steam engine of a train.

Ingeborg stood at the side of the campfire and watched them go. The sky had lightened just enough for her to see the man high on the wagon seat off to the north. She laid another round of venison strips over the drying fire and started to rub the ashes and brains into the hides. While not her favorite chores, she'd rather do anything outside than be cooped up in the soddy. The thought of a long winter within its dark walls seemed beyond her capabilities.

She shivered in the wind. A snowflake landed on her nose. If only she could call the men back.

By midafternoon, Ingeborg could no longer distinguish the sky-line.

"Roald will most surely stay in St. Andrew," Kaaren said over the whimper of a fretful Gunny. They kept taking turns walking with her or rocking the hammock tied between the bedpost and the side of the rocker. The baby rubbed her ear and upped the pitch of her crying.

"Ja, I am sure he will." Ingeborg stopped at the window. If Carl were lost out hunting, how could they let him know where home was? If only she had a gun to shoot every so often to guide him. One of the bells that the lead cow in the herds of home wore would work also.

She looked around the kitchen. What could she use? The cast-iron spider sat on its three legs in the coals in the front of the fire-place. "What do you have cooking in the spider?"

"Bread, why?"

"Will it be done soon?"

"Ja, I could probably take the lid off now. Inge, what are you planning?"

"We have to make a bell to guide Carl home if the snow turns into a blizzard. You can't see the barn from the door right now."

When she picked up the lid, yeasty perfume filled the room. Eyes closed, she inhaled the fragrance for a moment. The round loaf already wore the tanned crust of nearly done bread.

"Good." She tied a dish towel through the handle on top of the lid so the metal circle hung suspended. What to beat it with? It had to be iron to ring true.

"Where are you going?" Kaaren asked as Ingeborg grabbed her wool coat off the peg by the door.

"To the forge. I will go ahead and milk now before this gets worse. Thorliff, you come help feed the other animals."

Thorliff looked up from the book he was reading in the lamplight. "Now?"

"Hurry, son." She tossed him his coat and knit hat. Taking a spill from the mantel, she lit it in the fire and held it to the lantern wick. The flame flickered and then flared into the cheerful golden glow that would light both their way and the barn.

The sod barn huddled into the ground, as if hiding from the onslaught of the driving snow. The outline was barely visible until they had walked about ten feet from the house. Snow drifted about their ankles and settled on their eyelashes. The wind tugged at their scarves and made their noses run.

Once inside, Ingeborg breathed in the warmth, the quiet, and the rich mixture of odors. To her, the barn smelled almost as good as the baking bread. Boss turned her head and mooed softly. The chickens clucked from the spots they'd found to roost upon, and one of the sheep bleated. The oxen were outside in the corral Carl had finished just two days before.

"It is good in here, isn't it?" Thorliff said in the dimness.

The barn had been built with openings under the rafters to allow air circulation and light, but the storm had blown out the light. Ingeborg turned to hang the lantern on a hook from the rafter. Along one wall, Roald had a box with pieces of iron. She took out a solid bar about twelve inches long and, with the dish towel in one hand and the bar in the other, stepped back outside. She walked about three feet beyond the end of the barn and held the lid out from her body. Beating three times on the metal, she waited between each for the ringing to stop.

"Why are you doing that?" Thorliff stood by her side.

"To let Onkel Carl know where home is, in case he is lost in the snow. If we had the rifle, we would shoot it three times like this."

"And waste the shells?"

He is his father's son, she reminded herself. *But, Thorliff, never put things before people. People are always more important than things.* She listened for a shout or a shot. Nothing. "Is not your Onkel Carl of more value than a few rifle shells?"

"Mor! I did not say that." The child stood with his hands planted on his hips and a look of utter shock on his face.

Ingeborg rang the pot lid again. Three times it bonged. "You go feed the animals, and then you can ring this while I milk the cow."

"I will," Thorliff said, then scurried off.

Ingeborg followed the wall of the barn to the lee side so she would be protected from the wind. Like a foghorn, she banged the lid every few minutes.

"I am finished." Thorliff returned in a while and took the lid. He held it up and pounded it manfully.

Ingeborg left after reminding him to stay close to the barn. As warm milk streamed into the bucket, she could hear the ringing. "Please, God," she murmured, her forehead pressed into the cow's warm flank. "Please bring them back home safely." After checking to make sure all the stock had hay and water, she took down the lantern and started for the door.

The door burst open and Thorliff tumbled inside. "I heard him, Mor. I heard Onkel Carl."

"Keep ringing, then, so he can follow the sound."

"Thank you, thank you, thank you" rang with the improvised bell.

"That is enough, boy. You want we should all go deaf?" Carl loomed out of the snow, looking more like he'd rolled in it than walked through it.

Thorliff threw himself at his uncle, the lid and bar tossed to the ground.

Once in the house, Carl stood as close to the fire as he could, a cup of hot wheat drink in his still-mittened hands. "Thank God for your quick action, Inge. I went right by our place. Next stop would have been St. Andrew or the Little Salt River, I'm afraid. That is, saying I would have made it that far."

Kaaren bustled about, serving him a plate of hot venison and vegetables. Every once in a while she dabbed at her eyes with the corner of her apron.

He sopped his bread in the juice and rolled his eyes in appreciation. "I thank my God for this hot food, I tell you. When I prayed for help, He sent an angel with a spider lid. All the bells of heaven will sound no sweeter than that ringing."

"Should we keep ringing for Far?" Thorliff started to button his coat again.

"No, no need. He will stay in St. Andrew. He and I, we have a pact. If the snow starts to fall, stay where you are."

Unless he was already on his way home. Ingeborg smothered the thought. Roald had stayed in St. Andrew; he wouldn't have had time to get there and do the buying of all their supplies in so short a time.

A yell from baby Gunny made them all look at her. She sat with a dish towel tying her to the chair, a gummied crust of bread in one hand and a spoon in the other. She banged the spoon on the table and yelled again.

Carl leaned over and untied the knot. Gunny tangled one fist in his beard and whacked at him with the spoon. "No you don't. Little girls don't hit their far." He swung her up in the air and yelped when she didn't let loose of his beard.

Kaaren laughed with the rest of them, untangled the baby's fist, and laid her hand on Carl's shoulder as if reassuring herself he was real and not an apparition. "That will teach you to throw a girl around."

Gunny waved her fat little fists and shrieked in delight when Carl tossed her gently in the air. Looking down at him, she drooled and chortled some more.

"If she can't beat me, she spits on me. What kind of child do we have here?" He brought her down and cuddled her in his arms. "Thank the good Lord and His angels for bringing me home." He sent Ingeborg a smile of gratitude.

"It was just the spider lid." She looked over at Thorliff. "Besides, the one you heard ringing is sitting right there. He kept it up for you."

"Ja, I know. Bet you haven't been called an angel before, huh, Thorly?"

Thorliff shook his head. "Tomorrow we will ring for Far."

Just before she fell asleep that night, Ingeborg reminded herself of the pact the two men had made. To be safe, she again committed her husband to God's keeping.

A quiet, white world greeted them in the first light of the morning. The rooster crowed from the barn. The cow mooed.

"Now this . . . this is the day to go elk hunting." Carl made the announcement when he returned from the barn.

"Not again." Kaaren ladled ground cornmeal mush into a bowl. The cream and molasses were already on the table.

He ate quickly, kissed his wife goodbye, and after bundling up for the cold, he took the rifle down from its pegs and out the door he went.

"Men!" Kaaren sat down at the trestle table Carl had made and cupped her hands around the mug of bitter brew.

Ingeborg served herself some mush and joined Kaaren at the table. While the children slept, only the snapping fire broke the silence. Ingeborg drizzled some of the precious molasses into her imitation coffee and spooned the mush slowly. She knew why Carl went hunting. If he hadn't said so first, she would have volunteered. Outside was crisp, cold, bright, glorious. Inside was dark and smelled like dirt. Good dirt to be sure, but dirt nonetheless.

While Kaaren set the water kettle boiling to wash diapers, Ingeborg took out the deer hide and, laying it over the table, set to working the life back into it. She rubbed it back and forth over the edge of the table, a handful at a time, moving around the skin. Slowly, the stiffened hide became soft and pliable.

Kaaren fed the children, and as soon as he finished eating, Thorliff ran outside to play in the foot-deep snow.

Ingeborg's back began to ache from the way she was sitting and from pulling the hide up and down. She rose up and kneaded her lower back with her fists. "I heard the Indian women used to chew on the hides to make them soft." She made a face. "Can you imagine that?" She smelled her hands. "Ugh."

Kaaren took the clean diapers out to hang on the clothesline Carl had strung up for her. She and Thorliff were laughing about something. Ingeborg could hear their happy voices and wished she were with them. Pull and pull. She stopped for a moment, listening intently at a distant sound. Chimes? Bells? Jingling harness!

She leaped to her feet and flew out the door. Belle and Bob were within sight. Ingeborg and Thorliff jumped up and down, waving and shouting. The boy tore across the open field and met the wagon. Roald stopped and helped his son up, then let him drive the rest of the way up to the house.

"You were not worried, were you?" While he tried to frown, Ingeborg could tell he was as glad to be home as they were to have him. When they shook their heads, Roald wound the reins around the brake handle and climbed to the ground. Reaching behind the seat, he grabbed a white bag and hefted it high. "Coffee beans." He pulled an envelope from his pocket. "And a letter from Norway." He looked around. "Where is Carl? Did he not make it home last night?"

"Oh, he made it home, thanks to Ingeborg, but he went elk hunting again this morning. Said tracking would be easy and the elk did not have a chance." Kaaren sounded a bit put out. "So, I will make the coffee, and he will have to do without."

LAURAINE SNELLING

Roald raised an eyebrow. "Thanks to Ingeborg?"

Ingeborg shook her head. All she could think was how glad she was to see this stern-faced man. "I will tell you later." She clutched the precious bit of paper to her bosom. They would read it this night when they were all together, if she could wait that long.

The sun had started its afternoon descent when Carl puffed his way to the door, dragging the haunches of an elk on the hide. "I strung the rest up in a tree," he said as he collapsed on the bench in front of the fire. "It'll be frozen solid by tomorrow, but I couldn't drag any more and make good enough time. Sure wish I'd had one of the horses."

"He must have been a giant," Thorliff said.

"Wait 'til you see the head. I will carve you a special spoon out of one of his antlers." Carl looked up to take the cup of hot coffee Kaaren handed him. "Mange takk. What do you want me to do with the meat?"

"We can cut it up and let it freeze. We'll use it all by the time it warms up again in the spring." Ingeborg stroked the thick pelt. "This one would make fine boots."

"Or harness leather," Roald added. "But I think we should keep it for a robe. We're going to need more to keep us warm this winter."

"There are plenty more where this one came from. If I didn't spook them too badly, they'll stay in the wooded area along the river. There are signs of them everywhere."

The thought gave Ingeborg a deep sense of security. They would have plenty of food and, with extra hides, some of the other things they needed. God was indeed good. After reading the letter and talking of the family news, she had more to thank her God for.

With the snow now covering the ground, their days and evenings fell into a pattern. While the men spent much of the day in the barn at the forge, repairing harness, or building the many things needed on the farm, the women kept busy cooking, caring for the children, working the hides, washing diapers—a never-ending job it seemed—and sewing or knitting to keep everyone in clothes. When Thorliff got restless in one place, he was sent to the other.

The evenings were spent together in the soddy, with the men carving on bits of wood they declared were secrets. Thorliff carefully saved all the shavings for starting the fires and spent hours at his slate, forming the letters assigned him by Kaaren.

One evening Ingeborg looked up from her knitting. The children were already in bed, sent there when the adults grew weary of their noise. Roald held a length of wood in his hand, shaping it with his knife, then smoothing it with the elk horn. Carl was putting his piece away.

"Would any of you like a cup of coffee and a piece of bread before bed?"

At their nods, she tucked her needles and the sock she was forming into the basket at her feet. "Good. I certainly do." While the wind moaned outside, she hooked the coffeepot on the tripod and swung it over the flame. While it heated, she sliced and buttered the bread. Taking a hunk of cheese from the larder, she sliced that and laid the pieces on the bread. The act filled her heart with gratitude. Such riches: a snug house that kept out the storms, food in abundance and variety, and one another. She shook her head. She hadn't been too appreciative of some of the others earlier in the day. Thorliff and his questions, Gunny whining with her teething, and . . . she sighed and called the others. The coffeepot bubbled over—it must be hot enough.

As the days passed and Christmas arrived, it seemed to Ingeborg as though the holiday had already been celebrated when Roald brought supplies from St. Andrew. But Christmas presents were all handmade in secret and brought out after the roast goose had disappeared in lightning fashion. The special moment of the day was the peppermint sticks Roald had bought and hidden. Thorliff sucked on his with such delight that Ingeborg felt guilty. While there hadn't been much money in Norway either, at least there they had a large family and small treats for the children.

When each had received a present, Roald and Carl winked at each other, got up, and left the room.

"They're going for the . . ."

Carl swooped back, clapped a hand over Thorliff's giggling mouth, and took him outside with them.

Ingeborg could hear his shouts of laughter above that of the men. What was going on?

"I don't know." Kaaren shook her head and shrugged at the same time.

"Close your eyes," Carl shouted through the closed door. The women shared a look of excitement.

"More presents?" Kaaren whispered.

"Are your eyes closed?" Roald pounded on the door.

"Ja, closed tight," Ingeborg answered.

"You go see," Carl said as he pushed Thorliff in the door.

"They are." The little boy ran to the women and then back to the door.

Ingeborg could hear shuffling, something being set down, and the door closing.

"Open your eyes." Thorliff grabbed Ingeborg's hand. "Look what Far made."

Ingeborg clasped her hands to her breast. "A spinning wheel!" She reached forward and stroked the delicately carved spindles on the wheel, the way the joints met so perfectly on the wheel itself, the pedal to make it spin. After each minute stroke and discovery, she looked to Roald, her heart in her eyes. "Mange takk is far too small a word."

"You like it." His deep voice raised the statement into a question.

"Like it? Like it?" She rose from her chair and wrapped her arms around his waist. He had given her his heart, carved in golden oak and turned black sod. Beneath her cheek his heart thudded its steady rhythm while his hands found each other around her back. She raised a finger to smooth the pulse that pounded in his neck. So hard he worked to keep his feelings inside. "Mange takk."

"Tante Kaaren, you are next." Thorliff left his mother's skirts and went to pull on Kaaren's hand. "Come and see the . . ."

"Nei, do not say it." Carl stopped the boy again. "Close your eyes."

"Again?" Kaaren pleaded.

"Ja, for only a moment."

Ingeborg kept one arm around Roald's and a hand on the spinning wheel.

"Open them."

Kaaren couldn't talk. Tears took the place of words. She, like Ingeborg, smoothed the carved wood, this time of a rocking chair. At Thorliff's urging, she sat in the chair and set it to rocking.

"Gunny will like it," Thorliff said, head cocked to one side. "See the arms. I helped smooth them. Onkel Carl said I am a good woodworker already."

"Yes, you are." Kaaren stroked the silky wood. She wiped away the tears and reached up to hug her husband. "You two and your secrets out in the barn all those nights when you wouldn't tell us what you were working on. Hutte meg tu. Such men." She looked at Thorliff standing right beside her. "You think this beautiful chair might hold the both of us?"

He nodded vigorously.

"Good, then you come right here, and we will read the Christmas story from the Bible Gunny's bestemor sent."

When Kaaren finished reading, the men got to their feet. "We will do the chores now."

"Ja, and we will clean up the dinner things."

"So we can eat again."

"You are hungry already?"

Thorliff nodded. "I know we have a good dessert."

"Then you bring in the wood while we take care of the animals." The two men went out the door as Thorliff was shrugging into his coat. Silence fell for a few moments.

"I know we should be thankful we have plenty to eat, but . . ." Kaaren said softly under the sounds of washing dishes.

"But you miss home, just like we all do." Ingeborg dried and put away the china plates she had brought from the old country. This was the first time they had taken them from the trunk and used them. Roald promised to build a shelf so they could be enjoyed between special occasions.

"Think how wonderful it will be when we have a church nearby. I think I miss the services as much as I miss our families." Kaaren's face wore the dreamy expression she usually kept hidden. "The hymns with so many voices; when I remember, I am sure it sounded like angel choruses."

"We can sing the songs when the men come in from chores."

Kaaren sighed. "I know."

"And we will have julekake with our coffee." Ingeborg had hoarded the cardamon, the spice that made the fruited bread taste so different from everyday loaves. She had made the bread, ignoring the twinges of guilt over using the precious sugar for such a luxury. Next year, they would have a real Christmas.

After supper and the singing of several carols, Carl motioned them all to put on their coats and follow him outside. "Sh-h-h." He put a finger over Thorliff's questioning mouth. "Listen." He pointed to the north where the northern lights danced in unearthly splendor. When they all held their breath, it seemed they could hear an ancient song by the lights snapping and sizzling on the frigid air.

Ingeborg slipped her hand under Roald's arm. This time next year, she would bring their baby out to see the lights.

Thorliff leaned against her side. "So pretty. What makes them?"

Ingeborg looked up at her husband. Together they said, "God does."

After a mild blizzard in January, the weather stayed fairly clear. The Baards and the Bjorklunds took turns having the school at their houses. Agnes taught everyone to speak English; Kaaren taught the children to read and do sums.

"I wish we could meet every day," Kaaren said on the way home one afternoon.

"Ja, well, Roald and I will have to learn our English from you in the evenings. Both of us need to be down at the river cutting wood, not just one of us at a time. In the spring, those steamboats will take every cord we can cut."

"Ja, so we can pay off our debt at the store." Ingeborg still felt a stab of resentment that Roald had put so much of their supplies on credit. The shopkeeper had taken the wheels of cheese, butter, and eggs in trade for some of the staples. Next year they would buy more cows, and she would start supplying the bonanza farm across the river.

"Will the Baards always come to our house if you are cutting wood?" Thorliff asked, sticking his nose out of the pile of quilts on the hay in the back of the sled.

"No, you can take the team over there. Your mother and Tante Kaaren know how to drive the horses," Carl answered the boy's question.

"Oh." They could almost hear him thinking, *I could drive the team.*

"When you are bigger." Carl slapped the reins. "Come on, Belle, Bob. Pick up your feet a little faster. It's getting cold up here."

Ingeborg cuddled Thorliff against her side in their nest in the wagon bed. "You will drive the team soon enough. Now, show me what book you brought home today."

Thorliff dug under his coat and handed her a tattered copy of *A Wonder-book for Girls and Boys*. "In English. I will read it to you when we get home."

The clear weather held, and since they were no longer dependent upon the men, the families met every day.

Until the snowstorm arrived. With all of them trapped in the soddy, each day seemed to last longer than a week.

"Can you not make the baby quit crying?" Carl asked for the third time.

"She has the earache. What can I do?" Kaaren put a warm cloth on the baby's ear and continued to rock her.

"I'm going to work in the barn." Carl took his woodworking tools, the wooden chair pieces, and stalked out the door. Roald had pleaded the need of forge time already.

With the men gone, the room seemed larger.

"Can I go with?" Thorliff begged. "I'm tired of the house."

"Ja, me too." Ingeborg looked up from her knitting. If only she could go hunting, but the continuing snowfall made that impossible. The weather could turn into a blizzard at any moment. After what had almost happened to Carl, it was too risky. She wondered how Metis was in her cave by the river. They hadn't seen her for weeks. The baby's fretful crying grated on her nerves, making her want to scream. The poor thing, it wasn't her fault.

"Thorliff!" Kaaren barked. "Watch what you are doing."

"I . . . I did not mean to." The boy stared at the cup shattered on the stone hearth.

"Why can't you be more careful?"

"Don't yell at him like that. It was an accident."

"That's the last china cup. How could you be so clumsy?" Kaaren shook her finger at the child's nose.

"Kaaren, leave him be." Ingeborg's tone cracked like the trees shattering in the cold.

"Don't you tell me what to do." At the sound of their yelling, Gunny let loose with a shriek that rattled the pots. Thorliff's tears turned to wails.

It was all Ingeborg could do to keep from screaming herself. She grabbed her coat off the peg, stuffed Thorliff's arms into his and, slamming the door open, fled.

What had gotten into them all?

No one said anything that night. Ingeborg tossed on the bed, and each time she rolled over, the ropes creaked and the corn shucks rattled. She could hear the same sounds coming from the other bed, along with snores that matched Roald's. At least the men slept. But then, they would sleep through anything.

Ingeborg clenched her teeth and her mind against the unwelcome thoughts. God forgive her, but right now she would gladly toss someone out in the snowdrifts.

Gunny whimpered. Kaaren rose and, taking the baby, went to the fireplace, where she had a potato in the spider keeping warm. Putting it against the baby's ear helped more than anything else.

Ingeborg finally fell asleep to the creaking song of the rocker. And even that made her growly.

When the sun finally shone again, the men left for the riverbank to cut more wood. Ingeborg took the rifle down from the pegs. "Come, Thorliff, you can go hunting with me." She gave Kaaren a brief nod and headed out the door.

She could hear her mother's voice as clear as if she walked right beside her. *Do not let the sun go down on your anger.* Then she would quote the Scripture passage. Ingeborg shook her head at the memory. The sun hadn't even shone its face, let alone gone down. The days had run together, but she was sure it had been a week since the shouting match.

And neither woman had spoken to the other.

"Mor, are we going to get a deer?"

"I pray so. Fresh venison would taste real good, don't you think?"

Pray. That was part of the problem. Why pray about a petty problem like this? With time, all would be right again. Perhaps they could go see Agnes tomorrow. That would help.

"When do I get to shoot?"

"When you are bigger."

"I *am* bigger." Thorliff walked beside her on the frozen crust of snow. "I snare rabbits and catch fish. Why can't I shoot the gun?"

"Thorliff, if you want to be a hunter, you have to be quiet." One glance at the woeful expression on his face and she regretted her sharp tone. Maybe she should have left him with Kaaren, but she wouldn't ask any favors. He could have helped his father cutting trees, though.

A deer jumped up in front of them and bounded through the trees before she could raise the rifle to her shoulder. Could she do nothing right?

They returned home tired, cold, and empty-handed.

"The men aren't back yet?" She hung up her coat.

"No."

"Mor, listen." Thorliff opened the door again.

Faintly they could hear someone calling for help. Ingeborg reached back in for her coat and ran toward the river, shrugging into the garment as she ran.

Roald waved at her from the edge of the trees. "Get Belle. Carl is hurt."

Blood soaked the right leg of Carl's pants and ran into his boot. Ingeborg stopped the horse right beside the injured man. She looked to Roald. "How bad is it?"

"Would have bled to death but for the belt I cinched around it. We will get him to the house, and you can stitch him up."

Carl groaned, his face the color of the snow.

Ingeborg helped Carl to his feet, and between them, she and Roald set the injured man on Belle's broad back. "How did it happen?"

"Ax slipped. Not surprising on frozen wood, but . . ." He shook his head. "You lead and I'll hold him up there."

"I will make it." Carl spoke around gritted teeth. "Stupid dumb-fool thing to do."

Ingeborg took the lead and headed for home. One look at the gash had been enough. The bone glinted white in the bloody cut.

Carl passed out just as they stopped at the house. Roald caught him and carried him inside. He laid his brother on the bed and turned to Kaaren. "Get your sewing supplies. Can you stitch him up, or do you want Ingeborg to?"

Kaaren looked at all the blood and sucked in a deep breath. "I sew better than she does. I will do it."

"Good. Is there hot water?" At her nod, he continued. "We'd better heat that poker to cauterize the wound. Can't have him getting infection and losing the leg."

Ingeborg hurried into the house after putting Belle out in the corral. "How is he?"

"Still out. That is for the best." Roald waited to loosen the belt until all the supplies were at hand. "Ready?" He looked to the women. "Thorliff, you go on out to the barn and look for the eggs. We do not want any to freeze before we can eat them."

Ingeborg shot him a grateful look. Thorliff did not need to see their repairs on the injured leg.

Roald breathed a sigh of relief when he let loose the belt. No blood spurted out from a severed artery. If only they had some spirits to deaden the pain. "Hurry."

Ingeborg brought the white-hot poker and handed it to Roald. "You do it. I cannot."

Kaaren turned her eyes away, both of Carl's hands clamped tightly in her own. "Please, God, please help us do what is best." Carl raised up with a scream as the poker burned his flesh. The smell made Ingeborg gag. She forced the contents of her stomach back where they belonged and took the poker back to the fireplace.

Roald held Carl down while Ingeborg held the edges of the wound firmly together. Kaaren, tears streaming down her face, stitched the seared flesh together and bound the leg with clean strips of cloth.

Sweat ran down their faces.

"It is up to the good Lord now," Roald said, wiping his forehead with the back of his hand. "You have any of that tea Metis brought to help him heal?"

"Ja, and we will pack his leg in snow to help keep the fever off." Ingeborg could taste blood where she had bitten through her lip. Was Roald beginning to appreciate Metis? "I have some seeds to brew that help deaden the pain too." She left the bedside to dig in her trunk for her medicines box.

"Can I come in now?" Thorliff stood at the door. "Is Onkel Carl going to be all right?"

"Yes and yes. We will pray for him." She gave him a quick hug and took the eggs he handed her from full pockets.

"I found the nest the hens were hiding. It was under Belle's feedbox."

"We will have eggs for supper, thanks to you."

That night, Carl tossed and turned, muttering strange words and groaning when Kaaren repacked his leg in snow. He drank the tea, making terrible faces but drinking it nonetheless.

In the morning, he sat up for breakfast. The second day, he swung his leg over the side of the bed and sat up. Later in the day, Roald helped him over to the rocker.

"Here, you can rock the baby." Kaaren handed him a sleepy

Gunny. She immediately tangled her fist in his beard, and, along with a gentle tune he hummed, she fell asleep. So did Carl.

That evening Kaaren sat on one of the benches and faced Carl still in the rocker. Gunny stood between his legs, her arms hooked over his knees. She raised one foot, acted like she was going to take a step, looked up at him with a chortle, and put the foot back down.

"Go to Mor, Gunny, there's a big girl."

Kaaren clapped her hands. "Come, Gunny."

Gunny dropped to her knees and started to crawl. Carl picked her up and kept her vertical.

The game went on. Thorliff ended up rolling on the bed from laughter. Carl lost his patience and let her use his fingers to hold on while she stepped across the space. Kaaren shook her head.

"She just isn't ready to walk yet." She took the child in her arms and rubbed her face against the plump baby belly. Gunny's laugh set them all off.

Ingeborg looked across the lamplit table to where Roald worked on another of his carvings. His eyes met hers across the space and one side of his mouth lifted. Was that firelight dancing in his eyes or merriment? Ingeborg wasn't sure which.

After four more days of being housebound, Carl took the crutch Roald had fashioned from a branch with a crook in it and hobbled out to the barn.

"If you make that leg bleed, I refuse to sew it up again," Kaaren called after him.

She and Ingeborg shook their heads. "Men."

But they all were grateful that over the next weeks the wound healed so well that Carl soon quit limping. It could have been so much worse.

⚬

In March, Kaaren used some of the precious remaining flour and sugar to bake a cake in honor of their first year in America. She used the last of the dried plums for a sauce to pour over it.

"Now, if only we had real coffee." Roald made a face at the brew in his cup. "We should go to town before the frost leaves the ground. Right now we could take the sled."

"Well, I say here's to all our years in this new land." Carl raised his cup in salute.

They echoed the sentiments and Roald's opinion of the hot drink.

"But we have food." Ingeborg thought of the Polinskis who had come begging for stores the day before. How they made it this far through the winter was more than she could believe. From the sound of things, Abel had been out begging at other houses too. It wouldn't be so bad if he offered to work for supplies, but when Roald suggested he come help them cut wood, the man said his back was too bad for such work.

A week later, when Roald returned from St. Andrew, he not only had coffee, beans, sugar, flour, and cornmeal, he also had a letter from Norway. Ingeborg read it aloud, with all of them gathered around the fireplace. Tears streamed down her face as she read, making it difficult for her to see. Mor wished her blessings on the new baby that would be arriving in June. Far said the winter had been hard in Norway, too. Her brother Hjelmer was thinking of coming to the new land. There were greetings from the other families too. "And make sure you keep strong in your faith in our Lord Jesus Christ, spending time with your Bible every day. I know that must be hard without a pastor to preach the Word, but God is faithful and so must you be."

Ingeborg said the last softly. How long had it been since she read the Scriptures herself? She depended upon Kaaren to read it aloud, and since the time of dissension, that had not happened.

Roald slapped his hands on the table. "I am glad they are all well. Write and tell Hjelmer that if he can find passage, he will always have a home with us." He turned to Carl. "We can always use another able body around here, can't we, brother?"

Spring finally came to the Red River Valley, and Ingeborg gloried in the warm sun. When she checked on her cottonwood tree by the house, each branch had leaf buds showing. Like the Bjorklunds, the cottonwood had made it through the winter. As soon as the snow left the ground, green shoots shot up from the black soil. When Carl and Roald set the plow to the busted sod that had been backset in the fall, the soil crumbled, ready for the drag and seeding. They sold all the wood they'd cut to the paddle wheelers and promised them more, as time permitted. The cash from that paid off their account at the store in St. Andrew and provided extra for wheat and oat seed.

Ingeborg breathed a sigh of relief. They didn't have to borrow more money. When fall came, they could use the money from the grain to pay on their notes at the bank. One step closer to owning their own land.

In spite of her increasing girth, as soon as the garden was plowed, Ingeborg spent as many hours of the day as possible hoeing and planting. One of the hens turned broody, and they let her have a clutch of eggs to hatch. The lambs gamboled in the field, and Boss dropped another calf—a fine bull, this time, that they could trade, raise to eat, or train as an ox like its sire. How grateful Roald had been that one of the oxen he bought from St. James had not been castrated, so they could use it for breeding.

"I have some good news for you," Kaaren said one day when Ingeborg came into the house for dinner.

"What?" Ingeborg reached for a towel to dry her hands.

"I, too, am in the family way again." Kaaren laid a hand on her middle. "Perhaps this one will be a son." She looked over at Gunny, who walked now by holding on to every piece of furniture. She could get wherever she wanted to go that way, so it appeared she saw no reason to step out on her own. "Just think, two new babies."

Gunny clutched her mother's skirt and babbled her request to be picked up. When they didn't understand what she wanted, they asked Thorliff to translate. He would listen to her baby gibberish, and then tell the adults what she wanted. It worked every time.

Kaaren picked up her little girl and nuzzled the wispy curls. "How would you like a baby brother, den lille?" Gunny smiled, showing her four new teeth, and patted her mother's cheek.

Ingeborg looked around the dark, cramped soddy. "That is wonderful. When is the baby due?"

"Sometime in October, I think. We will have a fall celebration."

As soon as they had the broken ground seeded, the men started busting sod again. In spite of her big belly, Ingeborg took over the milking, turning the extra into cheese as she had before. "If we had another team, I would make a trip to town," she said one day.

Kaaren could do nothing but stutter. "But . . . but . . . ."

"We could both go. We drove to Baards. St. Andrew is only two or so hours farther. And just think, if we took our produce in, we would have a mite to put in our own purses as well. Wouldn't you love to go into a store, look at the materials, smell the spices, or buy a pair of shoes?" She studied the cracked boots that needed new soles. Roald kept saying he would get to it, but somehow he never did. As soon as it grew warmer, she planned to go barefoot like the children.

"I would buy thread and flannel to make diapers. And Gunny would look so pretty in a blue dress."

"And Thorliff needs . . ." Ingeborg shook herself. Here they were spending valuable time dreaming instead of working. But her son would love to have a new book. He had memorized the three they had. Why, he probably knew more scriptures by heart than the pastor back home did.

Metis dropped by to say she was going north with her people again. She would return in the fall.

Ingeborg watched her leave, wishing she would remain until after the baby was born. While she had Kaaren here, and Agnes would come if they asked, Metis and her medicinals were something she appreciated all the more now that she had learned how to use many of the local ingredients, thanks to the old woman's tutelage.

She ignored the cramping and low backache for as long as she could. Finally, she found herself clutching the back of a chair, her fingers imprinting themselves in the wood.

"You've started, then?" Kaaren laid a comforting hand on Ingeborg's shoulder.

"Ja, some time ago. But this one seems to be in no hurry." She stood upright again and returned to kneading her dough. "I thought to get extra baked . . ."

"I'm surprised you aren't out in the garden." Kaaren's gentle teasing made Ingeborg smile.

"Anything I can do to keep my mind off it helps. My mor used to say that pacing helped. 'Keep moving,' she would say. So when I am done here, I will go out and hang up the diapers. I am glad we were able to get the spring cleaning done before this." Ingeborg felt as though she was rambling but didn't try to stop.

By late afternoon, walking had become difficult.

"What can I do?" Roald asked for the third time, the vein pulsing in his neck. *So brave my Inge, but so big. Surely this babe will be hard to bring forth.* He pushed back the fear that gnawed like a rat at his heart. Those years ago, another woman—his Anna—was in travail like this. And then their life together was over.

"Take Thorliff and Gunny over to Agnes or at least keep them out in the barn. I don't want them to see me like this." She panted around the force ripping her apart.

"We will go do chores and make beds in the hay." Roald gathered up the sniffling Gunny and fled from the house as if wolves were snapping at his heels. Boss looked at him as if he were mad. The sun hadn't even set, and here they were in the barn already.

Carl and Thorliff came in from the field.

A sound like a cutoff moan came from the house.

"Her time?" Carl asked.

Roald nodded.

"Ahhh. Hey, Thorliff, I need you to help me here."

The boy stopped halfway across the yard. "But something is wrong, and I . . ."

"Nothing is wrong. Come here."

Thorliff looked at his uncle with distrust written all over his sweat-streaked face.

In the house, Kaaren laid out clean sheets, put water on the stove, and had baby things ready on the trunk. "Keep walking," she commanded.

Ingeborg grunted. Her jaw ached from biting back the groans. But after her water broke, the baby took the birthing into a race for daylight.

Carl Andrew came into the world yelling of his arrival and causing his mother no further difficulties.

Sometime later, all cleaned up and propped up against the goose-down pillows in bed, Ingeborg held him in her arms. She traced the curve of his cheek and put her finger in the palm of his hand so he could grasp her finger. She looked up to see a real smile on Roald's face. One that not only tugged at the sides of his mouth but went clear to his eyes.

Her own eyes brimmed with tears of joy. Roald was smiling! She handed him the snugly wrapped bundle. "Here, Far, meet your new son."

Father and baby studied each other as if memorizing faces. Roald jiggled the baby gently and sat down on the edge of the bed. "He is a true Bjorklund."

"Really? How can you tell?" Ingeborg shifted on the mattress. Sitting up was not very comfortable yet.

"The eyes. Already they are blue, but soon they will look like mine." He gazed at his wife. "Thank you for a strong and beautiful son." Just then, Andrew, as they had decided to call him, whimpered, squirmed, and then squalled. "Listen to those lungs. He will have no trouble being heard. Maybe he should become a preacher— or a politician."

"Or a farmer like his father."

Thorliff sat on the edge of the bed. "You good now, Mor?" At

Ingeborg's nod, he snuggled against her side. "Baby Andrew sure cries a lot. Do all babies cry like that? Did I cry, Far?"

Ingeborg and Roald exchanged the smiles of proud parents everywhere. Thorliff was back to normal with his questions, questions, questions. Carl Andrew was making his needs clearly known, and Gunny slept in her mother's arms in the rocking chair.

Ingeborg could no longer keep her eyes open. She accepted her son back to nurse and fell asleep while he did. Her last thought brought a curve to her own lips. Roald had smiled.

"Mor, come see," Thorliff called a couple of days later. Ingeborg dried her hands on a corner of her apron and stepped outside the door. The sun so bright after the dim soddy made her blink.

"What is it?" After a glance at Roald's face, she followed Thorliff's pointing finger. Right by the door a rosebush now thrust three canes up against the soddy wall. One bud glowed pink against the dark earth.

Ingeborg clasped her hands under her chin, then swiped away a trickling tear with one finger. "Mange takk," she breathed, staring deep into her husband's soul.

His blue eyes glistened like the high mountain lakes of home. "Velbekommen."

"Mor, don't you like it?" Thorliff gave her a puzzled look.

"Ja. Very much!"

"Then why are you crying?"

"Women do that," Roald answered, clamping a hand on Thorliff's shoulder. "It means they are happy."

Ingeborg nodded. It certainly did.

Ingeborg regained her strength quickly and soon had the baby in a shawl tied to her bosom so she could hoe the garden. She even took the baby fishing when Thorliff pleaded for a chance to try out his worm collection. As long as Andrew was full and dry, he was a happy, mostly sleeping baby, growing as fast as the lambs gamboling after Thorliff on their forays for pasture.

That summer, with pasture in abundance and plenty of land yet to hay, Roald bought more livestock: two cows, ten ewes, a sow that had ten piglets a month later, a team of mules, and a bull.

Joseph Baard bought a boar with his sow with the agreement they would trade off breeding services. During haying they exchanged labor, and when it was time to cut and bundle the grain, they did the same.

"That's just what neighbors and good friends do for each other," Agnes Baard was heard to say more than once. She, too, was in the family way again. Her little girl had been born in the last blizzard of the winter.

One day Thorliff came crying into the house. "Mor, the hawk took the chicks. I chased him off, but the mother hen is hurt too." He held a limp little body in his hand. "Why, Mor?" Tears brimmed over again and ran down his cheeks.

"Far told you not to let them out of the chicken house, didn't he?"

"Yes, but . . ."

"That is why. The hawk needs to eat, too, and now we won't have so many chickens to butcher or young hens to lay eggs."

"I'm sorry. But I was cleaning the chicken house like Far said, and the chickens were in the way. I didn't want them to get trampled on."

"I know." Ingeborg smoothed a finger down the new feathers of the three-week-old chick. "You can go bury it in the garden. How badly is the mother hurt?"

"She won't let me see. She just pecks at me and keeps her wings over the last two chicks. I let her in the barn."

"We will put her back in the chicken house after dark. You'd better check on your sheep, or a coyote might get them."

"In the corral?" He left to check on his charges.

⚜ ⚜

The Baards and the Bjorklunds worked together cutting and binding the wheat and oats in preparation for the threshers to come. Since this year they had sufficient acres planted, and Roald had seen the metal monster called a threshing machine on his trip to Grand Forks, he had contracted with the owner to stop by the Bjorklunds to help with their harvest.

Kaaren, Ingeborg, and Agnes had been cooking for the last two days.

Thorliff danced and shrieked in delight when the huge rig, pulled by twelve mules, clanked its way to a halt south of their sod barn. As soon as the men had eaten breakfast, they lit the firebox and soon steam puffed from the stack. When the long belts began to turn, the men forked the grain bundles into the clattering mouth where chain belts pulled the bundles inside. Straw blew onto a growing stack on the south side, and golden grain poured into the gunny sacks at the other end.

Roald had a hard time keeping his stern demeanor. Inside he felt like dancing in delight like his son.

"Far, come see." Thorliff's shout could be heard above the clamor of the machine.

Roald came and watched the man sew the full grain sack closed after hooking another on the metal frame that held the sack open. He helped oil the monster and tossed more wood into the firebox. All the while, he dreamed of owning one. Surely the two families could buy one together.

At dinnertime, the three women set venison stew, fried chicken, new potatoes, bread, cheese, pies, and gallons of coffee on boards covering sawhorses for tables.

"Your two wives sure know how to fill a man's stomach," Lars Knutson, the owner of the machine, said to Roald as they sat together on one of the long benches. "You'll have no trouble getting machine help with a table set like this."

"Mange takk. We are indeed blessed here with good crops and our growing families."

"Ja, coming to America was a good thing," Carl, on the other side of the man, added. "I have never seen such a thing." He nodded toward the machine.

"You ought to go watch or work harvest on a bonanza farm. Lasts for days." Lars held his cup up for a refill as Ingeborg made her way around the table. "Mange takk for maten, Mrs. Bjorklund. That was right tasty."

The next day they repeated the process at the Baards'.

Thorliff and the two Baard boys ran after the thresher for a time as it left and then came panting home. "Someday, I want a machine like that," Swen, the older of the Baard boys, said. "I want to travel all over the country and bring home bundles of money."

The adults looked at one another and shook their heads. Ja, their children understood the American way already.

With the threshing done, Roald and Carl sat at the table the following morning for a second cup of coffee. "We'd better get started on that soddy of yours pretty soon," Roald said, rubbing the side of his nose with his finger. "If'n we want it all finished before it gets too cold."

"Thanks be to God!" Kaaren clasped her hands to her breast. To have the new soddy built and ready in time for the baby—such a blessing.

⁂

Ingeborg insisted that Kaaren rest more frequently now that her time was nearing. The heat of summer had not yet let up, adding to her discomfort. One afternoon as she leaned back in the rocker and put her feet up on the stool, she said to Inbeborg, "I think you were the wiser." She wiped the sweat from her brow with the edge of her apron.

Ingeborg looked up from carding the wool they had sheared from their own sheep. "Why is that?"

"You gave birth to Andrew before the heat and the flies came."

"Ja, but the screen door has made a big difference. At least we can leave the door open now." She heard Andrew fussing and immediately her milk let down. She put the carding paddles down on top of the fleece and went to pick up the baby. "You surely do have your mother trained well, my son." She unbuttoned her dress front and settled him against her breast.

"You want this chair?"

"No, you need it more than I." The gurgling and suckling of the nursing babe sounded peaceful in the quiet room. Gunny slept in her trundle bed, the men were in the field, and Thorliff was out herding the sheep.

While Ingeborg sometimes wished she could be out in the woods or the garden, right now she was where she most wanted to be—nursing her son.

On Saturday the Baards came, and together they set the other soddy. Carl had marked out the house and barn about two hundred yards away, just on the other side of the property line. Now they would be completely up to the letter of the homesteading law. A dwelling met the requirements. The sod barn was extra.

"Here, I made this for you." Agnes handed Kaaren a wedding ring quilt, the colored patches glowing in the late afternoon sun. "And these should help, too."

"Curtains for the window." Kaaren held them up with delight. "What riches."

By the time they moved half the meager furniture into the new soddy, both houses looked empty. They left the big bed for Thorliff and Andrew, so Ingeborg had sewn a new sack for the corn husk mattress for Kaaren and Carl. "This goes to your house too." She took the down quilt and folded it into Kaaren's arms. "Now you will be plenty warm. And with more elk robes this year, we can keep all of our beds warmer."

The first night she and Roald were alone felt strange. With the boys asleep, they sat in front of the fireplace, Ingeborg carding wool, and Roald smoothing the wooden legs for a new chair. She watched him as he rubbed his calloused hands down the satiny chair leg. Most men used whatever branches they could find to fit for chair legs, but Roald, craftsman that he was, turned each piece of wood into a thing of beauty. The shelves on the wall that held her precious china were testimony to his skill. She leaned her head against the curved back of the new rocker she so enjoyed using. Roald had finished it late last spring, so that she would have one too when they moved the other to Carl's soddy. Roald thought so far ahead, sometimes she wished she could look into his mind and see his plans.

"Ja, what is it?" He caught her staring.

"Nothing. I . . . I . . ." She had almost said, "I love you." Would that be such a terrible sin, since they were here alone? "Would you like a cup of coffee before we go to bed?" At his nod, she got up and poured their cups full from the pot always set just off the fire. She rested one hand on his shoulder as she handed him the cup.

"Mange takk." He touched her fingers with his. That night sleep took a long time coming. Such freedom within their own four walls.

Three nights later, Baby Lizzie joined the family in the other soddy. Like Andrew, she let out a gusty wail, so they all knew she had arrived.

Ingeborg kept Gunny for the first few days and cooked the meals for the men. When she thought of the previous fall and her hunting days, she felt a pang of loss. This year, the closest she got to the woods was to haul water. If only they had gotten a well dug this year. Roald had promised, but always the fields came first.

Andrew began to cry and woke Gunny from her nap. She crawled into Ingeborg's lap and stuck her thumb back in her mouth.

Oh, for a few hours to walk the trails and admire the turning leaves. She hadn't even been fishing since before Andrew was born. And winter, the long dark days of winter, were nearly upon them once again.

The blizzard struck on Christmas Day.

"We won't be going to the Baards', that's for sure." Roald stomped his feet and brushed the clinging snow off his coat. He'd just returned from following the rope he'd strung to the barn so he could care for the livestock no matter how fierce the blizzard might become.

"Can we get to Carl and Kaaren's?" Ingeborg placed bowls of steaming mush on the table and set the coffeepot back on the cast-iron stove to keep warm.

Roald shook his head. "I would rather not take the chance. I'm sure the wind has drifted the path full of snow, so we could get lost between here and there. Glad we made that last trip to town before this hit."

"But how can we have Christmas without Onkel Carl and Tante Kaaren?" Thorliff looked from one adult to the other as if pleading would change the weather. "I carved a doll for Gunny."

"We will go as soon as the storm quits." Roald sat down and dug into his breakfast. "Eat up now and maybe Mor will give us one of her fatigman for a treat." The shriek of the wind tearing at the stovepipe made him look up at the roof. "Thank God, we have such a snug home and our animals are all under cover too. It isn't fit for man or beast out there."

Ingeborg sat in her rocking chair nursing the baby and thinking of home. Christmas in Norway meant that all the family would be together, gathered about the huge round oak table. Sisters and their husbands whom she knew only through letters, new babies and children growing so fast she would no longer know them. She dropped a kiss on the down-covered head of the son for whom she'd waited so long. At seven months, Carl Andrew had learned to get up on all fours and rock back and forth. It wouldn't be long before he was creeping and getting into everything. He belched and stared up at her with the same blue eyes of his father and brother. A smile tugged one corner of his mouth and milk drizzled out the other.

"Had more than you need, I take it?" His smile stretched further, and he reached up to pat her cheek with one chubby fist. She nibbled on his finger, causing a chortle that made them all laugh. She smiled back in response and nibbled again when he stuck his finger in her mouth. Dimples came and went as he laughed at her and repeated the gesture again and again, until she tired of the game.

Ingeborg looked up to see a smile flit across Roald's face at the sound of the baby's laughter. The smiles came more easily of late, not only because of the baby but because the farm was earning enough money to pay their debts and buy some of the things they needed. She knew he was more content now that things were going so well. Such a sense of duty he had.

She glanced gratefully at the cookstove, her Christmas present that had arrived in the back of the wagon last week. As cold as it was outside, they might be more than just a little grateful for the increased warmth. Now the wood sent more heat into the room instead of up the fireplace chimney, since Roald had boarded up the fireplace to keep it warmer in the soddy.

"Mor." Thorliff leaned against the arm of her chair. "Tell us a story."

"Ja, that is a good idea." Roald picked up the wood he'd been shaping into a large shallow bowl, rounding the edges with care. He settled back in his seat, made one slice through the wood, and held his blade up to the light of the kerosene lamp, running his thumb along the knife edge. With a grunt he put the wood down, picked up the whetstone, and spit on the center before smoothing the edge of the knife blade round and round to sharpen the edge.

Ingeborg watched the ritual while she paused to decide which story to tell. The way her men had settled into their seats warned her that one story would not be sufficient, so she began. "In a time long ago there lived a young boy named David, who guarded his father's sheep up in the hills of a faraway desert country."

Thorliff sat cross-legged at her feet, his elbows on his knees, his chin propped on the heels of his hands. He flashed his mother a grin. "David and Goliath—my favorite!".

Ingeborg kept one eye on the window as she continued the story.

By the end of the second story, a drift had blocked out what little daylight remained.

When she rose, Roald followed her actions and put away his carving. "I am going to dig out the door before it is stuck so fast we are trapped in here. Thorliff, you fill that big pan with snow so we can melt a bucketful for the cattle. I brought in extra water earlier so we would be prepared."

Ingeborg felt a surge of admiration for this man who took such good care of his family and farm. She rose and checked on the goose roasting in the oven. The heat flushed her face and teased her nose with the heavenly fragrance. Cooking in the stove rather than the fireplace made her life so much easier, she almost felt guilty. They'd planned such a feast with all the Bjorklunds and the Baards. And now the bounty was all for themselves.

"Thorliff, would you please peel the potatoes, and then we'll set the table."

"When are we going to open our presents?"

"You think we have presents?" She tried to look surprised but ended up smiling into his upturned face.

He nodded, his eyes solemn.

"After your father takes care of the livestock again. We'll play Hide the Thimble while he milks the cow, and then I have a surprise for you."

"Presents?"

"No, something so delicious you won't believe it."

"Better than cookies?"

Ingeborg nodded.

"Better than lefse?"

Another nod.

"Candy?"

"You might say that."

"Tell me." Thorliff's eyes danced, enjoying the age-old guessing game as much as she.

"When the time comes." Ingeborg stirred the pot of dried green beans she'd seasoned with chunks of bacon and onion. What a feast they were about to have. Only having their family and friends all together could have made it better. She wanted to see Gunny open the doll Thorliff had carved and for which she'd sewn clothes. At two, Gunny would be such fun to watch.

For a change, Roald volunteered to say grace when they were all seated at the table. Usually he began eating before anyone could begin, and because he obviously didn't want grace said, she'd let it go, too. Today, they said it together, "I Jesu navn, gar vi til bords . . ." At the end Roald added, "And thank you Lord for this land and bounty you have given us. Amen."

Ingeborg stifled the look of surprise she felt moving over her face. She dished up and passed their plates of food, served on the china she'd brought in the chest from Norway. She saved them for only the very best occasions, and the rest of the time they lined the intricately carved shelves Roald had built. Under the shelves stood the trunk painted in the rosemaling pattern of the Valdres area. While some of the paint was worn and chipped due to the hard wear, in the trunk she kept her linens and quilts. There, too, she saved her treasures, such as a curl from Thorliff's first haircut, the first rose she'd picked from the bush by the door and dried between the pages of their English/Norwegian dictionary, and pieces of fabric she'd collected for a quilt.

She watched her two men devour their Christmas dinner as if they had to rush back to the field work. None of them were accustomed to a holiday; that was for certain. Ingeborg savored the mashed potatoes and rich gravy, the slices of crispy goose that she'd shot herself, the rolls and chokecherry jelly. Thorliff passed his plate again and again, as did Roald.

"Coffee?" She rose to her feet and returned to the table with the pot in hand. As she poured, she glanced again toward the window as if hoping something had changed. She could just see light filtering through the snow. Anytime there was a lull in the conversation, the wind whistling around the corners of the soddy, pleading for entrance with the wicked cold, made her shiver. For weeks now, she'd been more aware of the wind, especially since it always seemed to come from the north.

The first Christmas had been crowded with all six of them living in the one room, but they'd managed. Now, with all their added belongings, the same room was hardly big enough for four, and one of them wasn't out of the cradle yet.

"Mor?" Thorliff's question brought her back to the present. "Andrew is crying."

"Sorry, den lille," she murmured, picking up the whimpering baby and holding him up for a kiss. "You will have to holler louder to be heard over the wind and your mother's dreamings."

Roald finished the last sip of coffee and pushed his chair back. "I will take care of the stock now so we can have a peaceful evening."

He put on his coat and boots, wrapping the long wool muffler over his face before he opened the door. The drift had blocked it halfway up again since the last time he'd shoveled it away.

Thorliff brought the pan, and before going farther, Roald filled it again with snow to melt.

"Put as much as you can in the reservoir. Since the water is already hot, it will melt the snow quickly." How she loved saying the word reservoir and dipping hot water from the tank on the end of the stove. Maybe by summer they would have the well dug and no longer have to carry water from the river. One good thing about melting snow, she hadn't needed to make the trek with two buckets hooked on a shoulder yoke for weeks. Nor did she have to strain the mud out. She glanced over at Thorliff, scraping the snow from the pan into the reservoir. At seven, he'd become such a good helper. Since it already showed he was going to be about the size of his father, or taller, a lot of responsibility fell on his growing shoulders.

This afternoon she would make sure he had time to read, something he'd almost rather do than eat. She settled into her chair to feed the nuzzling baby. "I'll do the dishes in a bit. You find your book and read to me if you will."

Thorliff's eyes lit up, and he dived into the box under his bed where he kept his treasures. Roald had brought a copy of *Pilgrim's Progress* from town for the boy's birthday last fall. Already the pages were beginning to look worn, he'd read it so many times. Once Kaaren had started teaching the children last winter, Thorliff had taken to reading as though he'd known it all his life and hungered for every written word. He could even read parts of the Bible. He'd started with the stories of his hero, David.

Thorliff flipped eagerly to the page marked carefully with a bit of paper and began reading about Pilgrim and his trials. Once in a while he became stuck on a word and spelled it out, bringing Ingeborg back from her land of recollections to answer him. She looked across to the boy seated at the table next to the lamp, which, at best, gave poor light. If she didn't know there was a window, she couldn't tell by looking at the wall. Roald was taking an awful long time. She shivered again at the howling of the wind; it was worse than the wolves'.

When Andrew lay sleeping in her arms, she rose and put him back in his cradle, then picked up her knitting and sat again, one foot on the rocker to lull him back to sleep. She pulled her shawl more snugly around her shoulders. With the temperature dropping, even the cookstove didn't keep the soddy warm.

When Roald finally blew in with enough snow to fill the pan again, he stomped his feet. "Sweep me off, Thorliff, before we have a mud puddle here." He looked across at Ingeborg. "This is the worst I've seen. I couldn't see my hand in front of my face, and if it weren't for that rope, I never would have made it back to the house. The trail filled in behind me that quick." He shook his head. "I wish I had marked a trail over to Carl's. Now that I think of it, we could have set six-foot posts and strung a line between them to follow. Why didn't I think of that sooner?"

"Because you never expected a storm like this. One good thing, the snow covering the soddy will help keep us warmer." Without her seeming to pay attention, her fingers kept looping the yarn over the needles as if they had a life of their own, round and round, the sock length growing by the minute.

"Mor?"

"Ja." She smiled at the question on Thorliff's face. "I know, the presents."

"And the special treat?" He closed his book and rose to store it safely away.

"That too."

Roald finished pulling off his boots and set them by the stove to dry. "I wish I had a way to see if Carl is all right."

Ingeborg looked around from where she was fetching supplies from the shelves curtained by a length of gathered calico. "Why are you so concerned?"

Roald rubbed the side of his nose. "You know last week when we were in town?"

Ingeborg nodded, measuring sugar into the pan she'd set to heat.

"Well, there was talk about many people succumbing to the influenza. They called it an epidemic."

"But you weren't there long."

"No, but Carl said the baby had been up all night, and he was coughing himself. What if he is too sick to care for his stock?"

"Not Carl. Nothing would keep him from chores." Ingeborg stirred as the mixture began to bubble.

"What is it, Mor?" Thorliff stood at her elbow, watching everything she did.

"You'll see."

"Do you know, Far?"

"I'll never tell."

"It's candy!" Thorliff breathed in reverence as Ingeborg lifted the spoon to watch a fine thread reach back to the pan.

"Quick, fill the pan with snow and pack it down tight." Ingeborg moved to the cooler part of the stove and kept on stirring.

Roald held the door to keep it from slamming against the wall while Thorliff scooped the tin pan full. Shutting the door against the wind was more of a problem. Snow drifted through the opening in spite of their best efforts. Roald threw his weight against the stubborn door, and Thorliff dropped the bar in place.

While Thorliff watched in awe, Ingeborg drizzled the sweet syrup on the snow, making circles, loops, and figure eights.

"At home we called this snow candy. It tastes best at Christmas."

While the hot syrup melted down into the snow, the pattern remained when she lifted out a section and broke it off to share between Roald and Thorliff. She grinned and closed her eyes to better savor the treat. Were they making snow candy in Norway today? Last year she hadn't dared use the precious sugar for such a frivolous thing. So much to be thankful for.

"Now the presents?"

"Now."

Each of them scurried to a different part of the room where they had hidden their treasures. Ingeborg dug in her knitting basket for hers. Late at night she'd cut pieces from Roald's worn-out shirts and sewn one for Thorliff. After bleaching out any stains, she had dyed it yellow, using the onion skins as Metis had shown her.

He held it up to his chest. "And the sleeves are even long enough." His eyes lit up. "Thank you, Mor."

"This is for you too." Far handed him a small, oblong package. Thorliff carefully removed the paper and stopped stock still.

"My own knife." He stroked the mother-of-pearl handle and opened one blade, testing the edge with his thumb as he'd seen his father do innumerable times. He glanced up.

"No, it is not sharpened yet. You and I will do that together, and then you must always keep a good edge on it. That way it will be ready when you need it. And if you keep carving like you have been, you will need to sharpen it regularly."

"Thank you, thank you." Thorliff folded the blade closed and put the knife in his pocket.

"And for you." Roald gave Ingeborg a wrapped package also.

"But I already got my present." She looked from him to her stove. "You said that was Merry Christmas." All the while she deftly untied the string and smoothed out the paper. "Oh." She could think of nothing else to say. Words just weren't enough. Folded in her lap lay blue silk, the color of the summer prairie sky when the blue of the sky and the green of the new grass made her eyes and heart ache with the beauty of it. She lifted the fold of fabric and held it to her cheek. Silk. Such a silly, useless fabric for life on the prairie, and yet so wonderful. She quickly wiped a tear away lest the treasure be stained.

She looked up at Roald to catch a small smile tugging at his lips. "I hoped you would like it."

"Like it!" She shook her head, keeping the fabric to her face.

"You maybe could wear it to church—when we get one, that is."

"Ja, to church." She couldn't keep her hand still, stroking the fabric as though she'd never felt such richness. "Oh, such a wondrous gift made me nearly forget." She handed Roald a parcel she dug out.

"New gloves." He immediately pulled on the deerskin gloves, smoothing them down snugly over his fingers. "Perfect fit."

"And this." She added a second package.

"Mittens?" These were also of deerskin, but this time with the hair left on and fashioned on the inside.

"You can wear both of them at the same time to keep your hands really warm. Or you can wear these woolen ones as inner lining." She gave him the third gift. "I rubbed the gloves with bear grease so they should keep out the water."

"Your mor wants to make sure I have warm hands," Roald said, removing the mittens. "Here, you try them on."

Thorliff giggled when his hands as well as part of his arms disappeared in the huge mittens. "My turn." He took off the mittens and laid them in his father's lap. Taking two small packages out from behind the rocking chair, he gave one to Mor and the other to Far. "Mor, you go first."

Ingeborg slowly unwrapped the bit of fabric. "A butter paddle! How perfect." She rubbed the smooth, curved surface over the palm of her hand. "You know I needed one. Thank you, Thorly."

"Far, your turn."

"A belt. Did you carve this too?" .

"Onkel Carl helped me. He tried it on and said if it was big enough for him, I should make it this much bigger." He held two fingers about two inches apart. "It would fit you. Does it?"

Roald measured it around his waist. "Did you make the buckle also?" He stroked the metal.

"No, maybe next year. I am not so good at the forge yet. Onkel Carl said to tell you I did it, but I didn't."

"You did a fine job, son. You have many talents, just as a good Bjorklund man should."

Ingeborg could feel the joy radiating from the boy at his father's words. Smiles and words of praise from her husband. Those alone were enough to make her thankful this Christmas.

After a meal of leftovers from the feast, the family went to bed early to conserve on the firewood. Ingeborg lay beside the gently snoring Roald, hugging the pleasures and wonders of the day close in her heart, like Mary of old. The beauty of the words Thorliff had read rolled through her mind. "And Mary wrapped him in swaddling clothes and laid him in a manger, for there was no room for them in the inn." If she closed her ears against the wind's howling, could she hear the angels singing?

The storm took two more days to blow over. The silence awoke Ingeborg sometime in the night. *Thank you, heavenly Father, that you have kept us safe through this storm.* She fell back asleep, nestled close to the warm body of her husband.

In the morning, as soon as Roald finished the chores, he headed across the frozen drifts for Carl's house.

Ingeborg set bread to rising and rinsed the beans she'd been soaking to make baked beans. After adding the molasses, onion, and chunks of salt pork, she placed the bubbling pan in the oven. Perhaps the Baards would try to come today, and they would all have dinner here. With that thought and hope in mind, she set the goose carcass to boiling for soup. The Baard young'uns could about eat them out of house and home.

Roald came bursting through the door. "Ingeborg! Oh, Ingeborg! Come help me, quick! Carl and Kaaren are too sick to get out of bed, and little Gunny is gone."

27

"N o, God, no. Oh, Father God, be with us." She murmured the prayer as she dried her hands on her apron and reached for her coat. "Thorliff, you stay with Andrew. He should sleep for several hours. I will come home to feed him. You tend the stove and stay indoors. It is too bitterly cold out there for man or beast." She tucked a jar of honey in a basket along with some herbs for cough and fever that Metis had taught her to use. All the while, thoughts of Gunny, their bright-eyed laughing child, tore through her. She couldn't be dead. Not like this. She just couldn't.

But she was. When Ingeborg walked in the room, the smell of death and putrid sickness nearly brought her to her knees. Roald was already sponging his brother's body, trying to bring down the raging fever. And raging was the only word to describe Carl. He screamed at whatever demons tormented his mind and took a swing at Roald that was mocking in its weakness.

Kaaren lay comatose with baby Lizzie beside her, both of them lying in a pool of vomit and urine. Ingeborg took the baby, cleaned her up, and wrapped the quiet form in another quilt. Lizzie's tiny chest barely rose with each breath, the skin so hot Ingeborg could only think to dunk the baby in a cool bath.

When she tried to dribble warm milk in the flaccid mouth, Lizzie gagged, and the milk ran down her cheek. Ingeborg gave the baby a sponge bath and laid a cool cloth on her chest. Unable to think of anything else to do, she returned to care for Kaaren.

But before she began stripping the sheets, she bent over Gunny's trundle bed. The small form lay still and cold, her skin waxen, colorless. Ingeborg touched the small perfect lips with one finger in farewell. She covered the child's face with the patchwork quilt Kaaren had so lovingly made.

Ingeborg could hear her mother's voice, clearer than she had for some time. *Tend to the living. Where there is life, there is hope.* For Gunny, hope was no longer needed. The little girl now rested in the Father's arms.

She rolled the soiled sheets in a ball and struggled to work Kaaren's nightgown over her head. Even though it wasn't proper, Roald would have to help put a clean one back on. After sponging off Kaaren's hot body and repeatedly changing the cold cloth for another, she could feel Kaaren's burning temperature begin to subside.

From across the room as she checked on the baby, she could hear the rattle in Carl's chest. Would an onion plaster help? If only she had two more pairs of hands. But first, if she didn't get some liquid into these people, they would burn up.

Her back ached, and she knew Andrew must be screaming his head off by now, but still she kept on. Finally, she put the baby back in bed with Kaaren so she could care for the two of them together. Lizzie was still unable to swallow, and milk just drooled out the side of her mouth. Over and over she dipped the cloths in cold water, wrung them out, and laid them back over hot skin. Finally Kaaren swallowed a bit of water, then some of the tea Ingeborg had brewed from willow bark.

Roald was having less success with Carl. After the first bout of delirium, Carl had slipped deeper into unconsciousness, responding to neither Roald's voice nor the changing of cold cloths. At times he shuddered and gasped, choking on the mucus draining down his throat. Other times, his shivers shook the entire bed.

"I must leave and feed Andrew. I don't want to bring him here."

"I'll care for them while you are gone. When you come back, I will do all the chores." Roald looked up, his eyes filled with hopeless despair. "If only we had a doctor near here. Maybe he could do something."

"Perhaps." Ingeborg got into her coat and shawl. "I'll be back as soon as I can."

Ingeborg returned as quickly as she could, but felt hopelessness surge through her when she saw that there was no improvement in Carl or Lizzie. The baby died just before suppertime. Ingeborg put Lizzie's still body next to that of Gunny's and, wrapping them both in a quilt, placed them in the coldest corner of the soddy. They wouldn't be able to bury them until spring. Two precious little ones. How could they be gone so quickly? Ingeborg's heart weighed so heavy she thought it would burst.

"I'll watch tonight, and you go on home," Roald said after he returned from feeding the livestock and milking the two cows that wouldn't freshen until late spring. He looked so weary, but he would have to stay.

"I haven't told Thorliff how bad things are," Ingeborg said.

"No, no need to yet."

She checked on Carl one last time. His breathing had grown more shallow as the evening passed. Kaaren remained the same except to swallow when they spooned liquid into her mouth.

"If only I had come sooner." The cry tore from Roald's throat, all the anguish of his heart bursting out with the words.

It did no good to remind him he would not have made it through the blizzard. "Ja, I know," was all she said.

Back home, she washed her hands and changed her dress before picking up her own dear son. Andrew, red-faced from screaming, latched on to her breast as if she'd been gone a month. His hiccups lessened as he relaxed against her chest. Ingeborg looked down at him, feeling the love within her swell so greatly that she clutched him to her. The baby flinched and grunted. How would she tell Kaaren that both her beloved children were gone? Would Kaaren ever revive enough to even know? And Carl?

"Andrew wouldn't quit crying, Mor. I tried to give him mush like you said, but he spit it out."

"I know, but you did your best, and going hungry for a time isn't the worst thing that can happen." Visions of the two small bodies wrapped in a quilt made her lips quiver and tears burn on her eyelids. She ducked her head, hiding them against the quilt she'd thrown over her shoulder and the nursing child. "It smells good in here. You've been a good cook today."

"All I did was stir the beans like you said. The soup kettle is sitting on the back of the stove."

"Oh, the bread." For the first time, Ingeborg remembered starting it, those eons before.

"I punched it down two more times like you do. The loaves I made do not look too good, but you can bake them now."

"Oh, my son, how good you are. Is the fire plenty hot?" At his nod, she continued. "Take the beans out of the oven and put the bread pans in."

He smiled up at her and dashed off to do her bidding.

How do I keep that sickness out of our house? It is so close. How to protect these two innocents?

"When is Far coming home for supper?"

"He'll be staying with Carl and Kaaren. They need him more than we do right now."

"Did Gunny like the doll we made?"

Pain struck in her heart. "Ah . . . no . . . I don't know. I didn't take it over there yet."

Thorliff studied her face, his eyes serious, and his mouth pursed. "Gunny is sick too?"

"Ja . . . no." Tears welled in spite of her attempt to hold them back. "Oh, Thorliff." She reached out to take his hand in hers. "Gunny has gone to heaven to be with God. Baby Lizzie, too."

"She died like the baby chickens?"

Ingeborg nodded. She had no words to say.

Thorliff sighed, his lower lip quivering. "I want Gunny to come back."

"Me too. Oh, Thorliff, so do I. Poor Tante Kaaren and Onkel Carl. They are too sick to even know it yet."

"Will they die, too?" A tear overflowed, and others quickly followed, coursing down his cheeks. He brushed them away with the back of his sleeve.

"Pray God they won't. We must keep praying for them."

⚜ ⚜

But when Roald returned in the morning, the slump of his shoulders and the devastation in his eyes told her what she'd feared.

"Kaaren?" He shook his head. Unable to say the precious name, she asked instead, "Do you think she will pull through?"

"I don't know. Oh, Ingeborg. My brother is gone, and I could do nothing to save him." Roald slumped in his chair, head in his hands.

"I will go there now."

He shook his head again. "I will bundle Kaaren up and bring her back on the toboggan. Then we will leave the others and let the house freeze up. I have no lumber to build boxes for them." Dry-eyed, he looked up at her. "I should never have brought him to this land."

"This death is not your fault. You didn't create sicknesses such as this. People die from illness in Norway, too." Ingeborg tried to reason with him, but he was past hearing or understanding. She laid a hand on his shoulder, and he rested his cheek against it.

Sounding as if a far way off, he finally said, "I didn't do the chores yet."

"I will do them. You sleep for a while." Ingeborg put on her outer garments and, filling the bucket with water, headed for the sod barn. Later, Roald could walk the team down to the river, if he could re-open the hole where he'd kept chopping out the ice for a drinking hole. Maybe that, too, had frozen so solid they'd have to melt snow for all the animals.

The red-and-white cow turned her head and bellered when Ingeborg opened the door. "I know, you're hungry and thirsty and your bag hurts. Be patient, and I will get to you."

Later, carrying a bucket of milk, cooled so it no longer steamed, and with six eggs tucked in her pockets, she stopped at the side of the soddy. Across the narrow field separating their two places, she looked for the familiar plume of smoke. Faint, it hovered a moment, then dissipated in the breeze. Soon, it would be no more. She bit back the tears again and entered the warm room. Thorliff was stirring, and she could tell by the tenor that Andrew had entered his second stage of demanding food. The next would be a caterwaul fit to scare birds from the trees.

As soon as she'd hung up her things, she shushed the baby and quickly changed his diaper. She needed to wash diapers this morning, too, and when Kaaren came, caring for her would take every available minute. Ingeborg sat down in the rocker and, unbuttoning her bodice, fed her son.

"I'll bring her now." Roald stirred from the brief sleep he'd collapsed into and rose to his feet, looking more like a man of sixty than thirty-seven.

"You must get some sleep so you don't come down ill yourself."

"Ja, and I must check on our neighbors too. I haven't seen sign of the Baards or the Polinskis."

"As to them, they are probably frozen to death in that thing they call a house. If he weren't so lazy . . ."

"Ingeborg."

"I know, but you have helped and helped him, and we have all donated food and clothes for those poor children." Ingeborg couldn't believe she was saying such things. Didn't the Bible say the poor would always be with them? And to love your neighbors as yourself?

"I don't wish them ill, but . . ."

"I will leave as soon as I've brought Kaaren over here and tended to their animals. I'd bring them too and put them up in our barn, if we only had room."

By the time he returned with the barely alive young woman, the wind had picked up again and dark clouds had gathered on the northern horizon. As soon as he'd settled Kaaren in Thorliff's bed, he turned to leave.

"I will go to the Polinskis' first, since they are closer, and spend the night there if I have to." At the frown wrinkling Ingeborg's brow, he shook his head. "I am aware of the clouds. I will be careful."

He took the words right out of her mouth. She hugged her shawl tightly around her shoulders. *Polinskis! Roald, we need you here.* But she kept the thoughts to herself, knowing that trying to keep Roald from a course he had set was like trying to stop the blizzard. That dedication to caring for those around him was one of the things she so loved. Except for now.

"Go with God," she whispered into the rising wind.

Kaaren's fever broke late in the evening. She breathed more easily too, sleeping now rather than lying in the comatose state as she had been.

"Thank you, Lord," Ingeborg prayed. "And please protect Roald, wherever he is." She milked the cows and fed the stock early while there was still light. Thorliff helped her, so they finished more quickly. They brought in extra wood and set snow to melt in the barn. By dark, snow had begun to fall, hard driving pellets swirled by the wind.

"Mor, I don't feel good," Thorliff said as she tucked him in Roald's side of the bed.

Fear made her throat go dry. "You sleep now. You will be better in the morning." She kissed his cheek. Was he running a fever?

Baby Andrew, too, seemed restless, nursing a bit and then whimpering. "You haven't eaten all you need," she said, stroking his cheek. He rubbed his eyes with his fists and went back to nursing, only to stop again. *Where, oh where, are you Roald? Please, dear God, keep him safe. We need him so, right here, right now.*

When Andrew finally fussed himself to sleep, Ingeborg checked on Kaaren one last time. As she put the spoon of broth to Kaaren's mouth, the sick woman's eyes fluttered open. She turned her head slightly, and a faint smile eased the lines of pain.

"Inge, I thought you were an angel." Kaaren took the half cup of the venison broth, one spoonful at a time, before drifting off to sleep again.

"Thank you, God." Ingeborg laid a hand on Kaaren's cheek. Cool and warm both, just the way skin ought to feel. She breathed the prayer of thanks again and crawled beneath the quilts of her own bed.

Andrew awoke in the middle of the night, fretful and hungry. He nursed again and went back to sleep, but Ingeborg could not. Thorliff kept coughing and was starting to wheeze.

By morning, the wind still raged, and Ingeborg made it to the barn, thanks only to the rope Roald had strung. She took care of what chores she could, making two trips with water, but still the horses were thirsty. Her body felt as though she'd been fighting the plow sod busting for a week without rest. Her head hurt, her throat felt raw, and she was tired, so tired she fell asleep feeding the baby.

"Mor, I'm thirsty." Thorliff's plaintive cry, combined with a retching cough, startled her awake.

"I'm coming." She set Andrew down, only to have him fuss and begin to cry. He howled louder than the wind while she cared for Thorliff and Kaaren.

By that evening, after chores that took twice as long as usual, she kept seeing double and dragged herself from chair to chair around the room. Her hands trembled so severely, she could hardly feed Kaaren, and when she tried to coax some soup into Thorliff, he just turned his head away.

"Hurts."

"I know. But please, eat this anyway. You must eat." Ingeborg rested her throbbing head on her hand. The spoon clattered to the floor.

That night, she took Andrew to bed with her. She was afraid she wouldn't have the strength to carry him later. "Please, Father in heaven, if you love us, let Roald come home in the morning."

28

Was the pounding inside her head or from somewhere else?

"Ingeborg, the door. Someone is at the door." Kaaren's faint voice came from near her left ear.

Up out of the fog, out of the swirly place where she'd hidden, Ingeborg dragged herself, foot by reluctant foot. But when she raised her head from the pillow, the tilting room made her retch. How to get to the door? Why don't they just come in? She struggled to her feet, fighting back the nausea, the pain, and the terrible heat. How could it be so hot in here? She knew it was winter, that much hadn't changed.

Andrew whimpered like a newborn kitten. Thorliff choked and coughed in his bed.

The pounding again. This time she knew for certain the head-splitting noise was coming from the door.

Ingeborg leaned against the edge of the table. It seemed a mile to the door. *Place one foot in front of the other. Move!* A draft from around the door blew across her feet, up under her soaking wet nightgown, and bit her legs. The chill made them move. When she finally rested her forehead against the cold of the door, she stared at the bar that kept intruders out but now barred the way for help to enter.

"Ingeborg, open up!"

Ingeborg jerked her head back as the pounding rattled the door and the shouting penetrated her mind.

"Metis." *Oh, Lord, thank you, it's Metis.* She hardly recognized her own voice, it rasped so sharply. The bar. *I must raise the bar.* She lifted with both hands. Her fingernails scraped down the bar; her head banged on the door. She scrabbled for a handhold and, by a supreme act of will, remained upright. "I . . . can . . . not . . . open the door."

"You must! I not help you otherwise."

Ingeborg understood enough of the accented words to respond. Summoning strength from she knew not where, she heaved on the board. The wind slammed the door open, throwing her back against the stove—the now cold stove. Slowly that fact registered on Ingeborg's befuddled mind. The stove was out. They would freeze to death. Were her babies still and lifeless? No, those were Kaaren's babies, from how far back? Where was Roald?

Metis threw her body against the door, fighting the wind until it gave and slunk back to howl a protest from the eaves. With the bar dropped in place, she turned to Ingeborg. "Ah, as I feared, you have failing sickness I hear attacking white men. Go to bed; you need milk for baby, no?" She helped Ingeborg back across the room and saw Kaaren sound asleep again on the other side of the bed. Metis looked at Ingeborg with a question in her dark eyes and shook her head sadly at the silent answer. "You cover up. I start fire. Cows bellering. Much to do."

Grateful to leave the reins in someone else's capable hands, Ingeborg lay down and was barely awake when Metis put Andrew to her breast. He felt even hotter than she, but he nursed. She stayed alert enough to drink something that Metis offered and then let herself sink back into the swirling fog.

Save Andrew and Thorliff. The thought kept Ingeborg responsive enough to do all within her power to obey Metis when she ordered her to drink or to swallow.

Three nights later in the still hours just before dawn, her fever broke, and even in her haze, she knew Roald hadn't returned.

In the morning, she opened her eyes to see Kaaren staring vacantly at the wall. In the way of children who recover so quickly when they are on the mend, Thorliff sat down on the bed beside her.

"You are better."

When her throat refused to respond, she merely nodded. Just then Andrew let out a lusty yell, and she felt relief flood her system. The children were all right. But Roald? She tried to sit up but couldn't muster the strength. She heard someone come in the door and hope flared until Thorliff ran across the room.

"Metis, Mor is better. She is awake."

"Is good. I thought it be soon." She peered into Ingeborg's face and nodded. "You soon be strong, my daughter. Little one needs you. He not like cow's milk."

It took all of Ingeborg's concentration to follow the words. So long since they'd practiced their English. "Slow down." She croaked the words, bringing a grin to Thorliff's anxious face.

Metis chuckled. "You soon be well. See, you give orders. Come, Thorliff, help mama drink so she get strong."

"Will Tante Kaaren drink too?"

"Yes, we make her."

Ingeborg listened to the exchange. She was alive, alive to see her babies grow up, alive to wait for Roald to return. Surely he was still helping some other family. A surge of bitterness caught her by surprise. He should have stayed here with his own family. What if he were lying somewhere, sick himself, with no one to nurse him? *Please, God, not that.*

The next day, a knock at the door brought her out of an afternoon slumber. When Thorliff hurried to the door, he opened it to find Petar, the Baards' nephew who had arrived the previous summer.

"Is Roald here? My uncle needs him."

"No, Far has been gone for a long time." Thorliff stepped back and motioned the young man inside. "Come talk to Mor."

Petar removed his hat and stood by the bed, turning the knitted stocking hat in his hands.

"Didn't he come to your house just before the storm?"

"Yes, but when he found we were managing, he said he would go back to the Polinskis'. We tried to get him to stay, but he said someone had to see after them. We wasn't so sick, you see, like some."

"Would you go to the Polinskis', please, and ask for him there?"

"Ja, that I will. They wouldn't have nothing to feed his mule, though. They was burning all their hay in twists, last I saw."

"Mange takk, Petar. Why don't you have some soup Metis made before you leave. I am sorry I cannot serve you."

"Never you mind, ma'am. I can look out for myself." He looked over to Kaaren, who sat perfectly still in the rocking chair and appeared not to see anything around her. Her face was blank, her body motionless. "Is she gonna be all right? Aunt Agnes is just getting back on her feet and wants to know about everyone."

Ingeborg shrugged. "I certainly hope so. We will all pray to that end."

"And the little 'uns?"

Ingeborg mouthed the word "gone." The pain caught her again.

No more Gunny or Carl or Lizzie. And what about Roald? He would be here if there were any way that he could. She knew that for all she was. She glanced again at the motionless figure. What about Kaaren? Did she suspect or know what had happened? Had the knowing been too much to bear?

Ingeborg forced herself to do a bit more each day, but by evening, she fell into bed exhausted. However, she was never too tired to look out the window every time she passed, hoping for the sight of a tall man riding a stubborn mule. Or to listen for the jingle of the bit and reins. Something—anything to tell her that Roald had come home.

Each night Ingeborg went to bed praying for Roald and his return. And each morning, the day and its unending labor brought no word. Joseph Baard returned each day to help with the outside chores, leaving Ingeborg with more time than ever to think. They all knew Roald had spent several days at the Polinskis', but when Mrs. Polinski got back on her feet, and the first storm had cleared, he said he was heading home. But he had never arrived. Had the following storm caught him in the open? Had he been attacked by wolves or gotten so sick he couldn't ride and fell in a drift and never made it out? In the quiet of the night, the questions pounded away at her, magnifying the night noises and chasing away her sleep.

Was there reason to hope? Yet without hope, what was left?

One afternoon Ingeborg found Thorliff curled up in his bed trying to stifle the tears running down his cheeks.

"What is it, den lille? Do you hurt somewhere? Are you sick?" She sat down and gathered him into her arms.

"I w-an-t Far to c-come h-home."

"Oh, Thorly, so do I." Her tears matched his. "You have been such a big boy, I sometimes forget you are my little son."

"Wh-when is he c-c-coming?"

"I do not know. We have to prepare ourselves." She bit her lip and sniffed back the tears. "He might never come back." Saying the words made the hole in her heart gape like a septic wound.

"But I prayed that God would bring him back."

"I know, son. I did too. And we must keep on praying." She rested her wet cheek in the soft hair by his forehead. "But always know that Far loves us, and that he would come home if he possibly could."

When their tears finally stopped, Thorliff looked up at his

mother. "I will take care of you, Mor. I will."

"Mange takk, my son. We will take care of each other."

⁂

Several weeks later, she heard a harness jingling and looked out the window to see the Baards packed in their sleigh, surrounded by quilts and buffalo robes. Ingeborg threw open the door and stepped out into the weak winter sunshine. Arms clasped to keep from shivering, she called them in.

Agnes gathered the younger woman to her shrunken bosom and held her close. "Oh, my dear, my dear. Such a time of it you've had. And the never knowing." At the loving words, Ingeborg sagged in her friend's arms, and the tears broke forth in deep, body-shaking sobs. Agnes turned her and led her into the soddy. The three boys had already greeted one another and were heading back out the door.

"We're going to the barn."

Agnes sat down on the bed with her arm still around the sobbing Ingeborg.

Thorliff returned and stood in front of them. "Will Mor be all right?" His voice held a note of fear.

"Ja, you go play. Sometimes we women just have to cry."

Thorliff patted Ingeborg on the arm and slowly backed off, as if not sure he wanted to leave.

"Come on, Thorliff, let's go see the sheep."

With another last look to see if his mother needed him, Thorliff sighed, as if grateful to transfer the burden of caring for his mother to someone else, and ran out the door.

As quiet settled around the women, the only sounds were that of the soup simmering on the back of the stove and Ingeborg's now subdued sniffs and gulps. She dug in her apron pocket for a handkerchief and, after blowing her nose, mopped her eyes. She sighed, and the sound called forth all her longing, worry, and fear.

"He's dead somewhere, isn't he?"

Agnes Baard laid her cheek against Ingeborg's hair. "I'm afraid so. No one for ten miles around has seen him in over ten days. We checked in St. Andrew and at all the farms we know of. The last to see him were the Polinskis."

The softly spoken words snapped Ingeborg's last thread of hope.

"I prayed and prayed for him, except when I was too sick to be aware, but I think even then I was praying."

"I know."

"But God took him." The words lay flat in the silence. Ingeborg stared across at Kaaren sitting still frozen in the rocker. "And Carl and his two babies. What kind of loving God would do such a thing? If that is love, I want no part of it."

"Ingeborg! Do not say such things. God knows best. This was His will, and we must accept His will for us. The Bible says . . ."

"I do not care what the Bible says! Is the Bible going to bring Kaaren back to us? Is the Bible going to milk the cows, birth the lambs, plow the soil, plant the wheat, and break new sod?" She turned fiercely to her friend. "No! I must do all'that. This land is for Roald's and Carl's children . . ." She stammered to a halt. "For Kaaren's children, if she should ever have any more, and for my children. I *will not* lose it. Not after all the blood and sweat we've poured into this earth."

She drew away from the comfort of Agnes's arms. "We *will* farm this land. I will farm it myself." Her vow echoed in the quiet room. The ring of it woke Andrew with a start, and he began to whimper. Ingeborg rose to her feet and crossed the room. Bending over the cradle, she lifted the baby and buried her tear-stained face in his sweet chest. "Sorry, den lille, but you are not ready to eat yet." She changed his diaper and crossed to the rocking chair, laying him in Kaaren's lap. She picked up the limp hands and wrapped them around the baby, locking them together. "Kaaren, you rock this baby. Now." Authority rang in Ingeborg's voice.

She stepped back, ready to leap forward if Andrew should start to fall.

Slowly, ever so slowly, one foot pushed against the dirt floor and set the rocker in motion.

"Thank you, God," breathed Mrs. Baard.

Ingeborg shot her a withering look. "I will pour the coffee if you want to call your husband. There are cookies and milk for the children."

As the company left to get home before sundown, Ingeborg stood in the door and waved a last goodbye. She sent her vows into the sky, painted all the colors of flames by the setting sun. The time for grief had passed. *I will make it here. I will farm this land and Carl's land, and I will prove up the homesteads. I will! And there will be no more tears.*

29

I have been in a far land, ja?" Kaaren asked, her voice a cracked whisper.

With her mouth open in shock, Ingeborg looked over at her sister-in-law. Kaaren had been putting on her own clothes when they were laid out for her. She ate when food was put in front of her, and someone, usually Thorliff, put the spoon in her hand. She had even been rocking Andrew when the baby was placed in her arms. But these were the first words she had spoken since the terrible sickness.

"Ja, that you have." Each day Ingeborg had been hoping for a response, but every time she studied Kaaren's eyes, she felt as though she were looking into an empty abyss. She stepped to the door and threw out the dirty dishwater. A warm wind blew from the south, even now just before bedtime. While winter surely wasn't over, at least they were having a reprieve from the howling rage of the bitter northern storms.

Ingeborg finished putting the dishes away, banked the stove, and closed the draft so the fire would leave coals for the morning. Her nights were so short; she didn't allow the stove to go out anymore. She sat in Roald's chair for a blissful moment. If she sat too long, she would fall asleep right there and wake up freezing before morning. She knew, for she had done that more than once.

Kaaren kept the chair moving, the squeak of the rocker the only sound but for the dripping of the icicles. "How long have I been gone?" Kaaren spoke again, stronger of voice but still staring into space.

"Since right after Christmas. That was when the influenza struck." Ingeborg picked up her knitting. No sense letting her hands stay idle. "That was more than two months ago."

The rocker sang its song.

"Carl and my babies?"

"Gone."

"And Roald?"

"He went to check on the neighbors, and we never saw him again." If she spoke carefully, the words no longer carried feeling. They were just words.

"Was there a funeral?"

"No. We will have one when the ground thaws. Nearly all of the families in this area lost someone. We are among the fortunate. Some entire families were wiped out."

The rocker faltered to a halt.

Ingeborg looked up to see a solitary tear slide down Kaaren's face.

"God help us."

"No. We will help ourselves. God is too busy elsewhere." Putting her knitting aside, Ingeborg went to undress. After pulling on her nightgown, she checked on Thorliff and Andrew, tucking the covers more securely around them. "Are you coming?" She leaned over the lamp chimney to extinguish the light.

"You can blow it out. I don't need a light for getting into bed." Kaaren got to her feet, undressing as she went.

As the weeks passed, Kaaren returned more and more to her former self, but a sadness remained in her eyes, even when she laughed at the antics of Thorliff as he entertained Andrew. The sickness hadn't altered the baby's deep belly laugh, sometimes so infectious that even Ingeborg smiled.

Slowly Kaaren took over more of the household chores, especially when the lambing began. She also returned to her job as schoolmarm, allowing Thorliff to spend several hours a day at the books he so loved.

"Read this," Kaaren said one afternoon, handing Ingeborg a piece of paper, precious since it was so scarce. "Thorliff wrote it."

Ingeborg stepped to the window to see better. She looked up after reading the closely printed words of the poem. "He draws pictures with words." She read it again. "But he is only seven. You are a very good teacher."

"I believe Thorliff has been given a gift. It will be our place to see that he develops that gift."

"Ja, someday. Right now he needs a new pair of pants, and his boots are too small. It is a good thing spring will soon be here, and he can go barefoot. I never did learn how to make boots." Thoughts of Roald, who did all things so well, flitted through her mind, but she snapped the window shut on the memories immediately. Thinking of Roald only made her day weigh heavier.

Ingeborg spent half her nights out in the lean-to that housed their flock of fifteen ewes. The ram was locked in the other barn for now. She had moved the oxen, the dry cows, and the horses over there to make room in the lean-to so she could separate the ewes in labor from the others. Only one cow had any milk left.

Thorliff helped by feeding the animals in the other barn and by leading the livestock down to the river to drink so they didn't have to haul water for them.

"We have twenty-five healthy lambs," Ingeborg announced one night.

"And one bummer." Thorliff sat cross-legged by the basket where the lamb that had been rejected by its mother lay sleeping near the stove's warmth.

"Now if we can just keep the wolves away, we will have a cash crop come fall, maybe earlier. If only we had been able to cut wood this winter as the men did last."

"Are you keeping any lambs for breeding?" Kaaren sat rocking Andrew to sleep. He'd been fussy lately because he was teething.

Ingeborg glanced up from the journal where she kept the farm records. A pang made her catch her breath. The only time she held the baby anymore was when she nursed him.

"Ja, I'm keeping the finest of the lot. And I'll trade the best ram for another so we will have a new bloodline." She couldn't breed the young stock back to the old ram who was their sire, so she would have to find another stud. Not many people in the area raised sheep.

This year they would also have wool to sell, and Ingeborg hoped the sale of it would bring enough money to pay back the bank. If only she could afford to buy more cows. There was still a big demand for oxen, and she knew she would be able to sell all that she could raise at a good price. But a cow took nine months to calve, and then the calf needed a year to grow before it could be sold. It was nearly two years before it was strong enough to pull a wagon or a plow. Horses needed the same amount of time or more. The return was definitely faster with sheep. Over and over, the many decisions to be made ran through her mind. She needed Roald. How dare he leave them?

"I think we'll raise more chickens this spring," Ingeborg announced, making a sudden decision.

"Chickens?"

"Ja, we can sell all the eggs the hens can produce, and come spring planting and harvesttime, the bonanza farm across the river will take all we can supply for frying. If we had a ferry or a raft, I could take the food stuffs over there without the long trip to St. Andrew . . ."

Kaaren shook her head. "As if we don't already have enough to do!"

⚜   ⚜

Several nights later, Ingeborg awoke with shivers coursing up and down her body and the hair on the back of her neck rising. She listened to one long howl and then another, followed by the yips of a wolf pack on the hunt. Closer they came, and then there was silence.

She started to settle back down, but something made her get up and grab the woolen wrapper she kept at the foot of the bed. She went to the window but, even in the bright moonlight, saw nothing. Was it safe to open the door? Wolves had been known to burst into a soddy if they were hungry enough.

She shoved her feet into boots, put on her coat, and picked up the rifle.

"Inge, what is it?" Kaaren's low voice came through the darkness.

"Wolves, a pack of them. I'm going out to stay with the sheep."

"But, you . . ." Kaaren stopped. Ingeborg could hear her admonition without the words.

"I'll be careful." She slipped open the door and let her eyes adjust to the brightness. Moonlight on snow carried much of the brilliance of early day. Her boots crunched in the snow crust, her breath creating a cloud as she tried to breathe without making a sound.

A snarl sounded from close by. Much too close. She stepped around the corner of the soddy in time to see four shadows slinking toward the sheep shed. She raised the gun, but before she could fire, another shadow flew across the drifts, snarling like a beast gone mad. The dark form leaped on the leader of the pack, and within a breath's time, the barking, snarling, and growls sounded loud enough to wake the dead.

"Inge, are you all right?" The call came from the half-open door.

"Ja, but I sure don't know what is happening. You stay inside."

She could hear the sheep bleating and charging around the pen. The fool things didn't need a wolf to attack them. They could die of fright or trample the lambs in their fear.

The fight was out of her sight, behind the barn. If she could get to the barn door, she could get in and calm the sheep. Suddenly the snarls turned to yips, and three wolves streaked off across the prairie. She turned the corner of the barn and found one wolf lying motionless on the bloody snow. Another sat nearby, looking at her with that same steady yellow gaze she'd seen before.

"Wolf?"

He whined just a bit in his throat. Then, as if leaving her a gift, he turned and trotted back toward the river and Metis' cave. Ingeborg stared after him, not sure when she was only seeing shadows. She entered the barn and went through the barred gate into the sheep fold. The cow lowed and the sheep bleated. Small bars of moonlight came through the opening between the sod walls and the roof. She walked among the sheep, talking to them in a soothing voice. As they calmed, she tried to check for injuries but without a lantern found nothing. At least there were none lying trampled on the floor.

She paused for a moment longer, savoring the night barn sounds. A chicken must have fallen off her roost in the other lean-to and was squawking her disgust. One of the lambs bleated softly, and its mother answered. The cow lay down again with a grunt and a whoosh of breath. Ingeborg closed the door and dropped the bar in place. She would have to see about getting a dog to warn them. She thought again of the avenging Wolf. He'd nearly cost her her life at one time, and now he'd saved a major part of her livelihood. Strange.

Back in the house, she removed her outer clothes and then her nightgown, the hem and halfway to her knees now sodden with snow. As she dug in the chest for a dry one, she told Kaaren what had happened.

"God sent us a guardian."

Ingeborg snorted and pulled her nightgown over her head. If Kaaren wanted to believe God was watching over them, she could. "It was just Metis' Wolf."

In the morning, she dug again in the chest, this time removing

Roald's woolen pants that she'd packed away. She held them up to her waist. They would need major altering, but that she knew how to do. She would begin as soon as she'd finished the morning chores.

"But, Ingeborg, you can't wear those."

"Ja, I can and will from now on." She hung her skirt on a peg in the wall. "You can use this for yourself or make something for the boys. The wool is still good. But I will never trip over my sodden skirts again. If I have to do a man's work, I will dress like a man."

She ignored the horrified look on Kaaren's face, and feeling more free than she ever had, she headed for the barn. She'd fire up the forge and work again on the plowshares. How would she ever keep them sharp enough once the ground warmed up sufficiently to be turned over? And busting sod was worse. Roald had filed that iron monster every few hours and hammered it back into shape at night. So far, her hammering made dents rather than smooth, sharp curves.

She felt a familiar surge of fury. It had not been Roald's job to take care of the entire world, for heaven's sake.

⚜ ⚜

Her milk ran out at the same time the cow calved.

"Andrew will have to learn to drink from a cup, that is all." She glared at the whiny baby who could crawl across the room faster than a beetle could scoot.

"If you'd . . ." Kaaren stopped at the glare now directed at her.

"Well, at least we'll have plenty of milk for him. When he gets hungry enough, he'll take it."

But Andrew had inherited stubbornness from both sides of his family. By the third night of his crying and fussing, Ingeborg was about out of her mind. They'd tried dipping a cloth in milk and letting him suck. They'd spooned in gruel made of cooked oats and milk. They added molasses, then sugar. He'd drink just enough to take the edge off his hunger and then turn away. He pulled at her shirt, nuzzling her breast and crying until Ingeborg didn't even want to hold him.

She fled to the barn, now understanding why the men had sought solace out there the first year in the soddy. No babies cried in the barn.

After all the chores were finished, she and Thorliff returned with milk buckets brimming. Another cow was due to freshen soon. They would have plenty of milk.

When they entered the soddy, all was quiet. Kaaren sat knitting in the rocker that had become hers. Andrew played with a sock full of beans on the rug at her feet. The aroma of bread baking and beans cooking filled the air.

"What did you do?" Ingeborg set the milk pails on the table.

Kaaren smiled up at her. "A glove and honey."

Ingeborg stopped. She looked from the smiling baby to the woman who also wore a smile.

"You know those deerskin gloves you made for Roald?"

Ingeborg nodded.

Kaaren held up a cup with a funny-looking cap. "I cut a hole in the thumb, sealed the seams and stretched it wet over the cup. See, here's the thong I tied it down with. Now he can suck. The honey made him like the milk and"—she raised her hands in the air—"we have one happy baby who already has a sweet tooth, just like his father and his uncle did."

"How clever of you." Roald had never worn the soft gloves she'd made so carefully. Instead, he'd chosen the knit ones inside the deerskin mittens. Ingeborg pushed aside both the thought and the lump that swelled in her throat at the mention of Roald's name. There was no time for any more useless regrets. Besides, she'd vowed never to cry again.

⚜ ⚜

Spring finally did come, and as soon as the ground thawed enough, they had the community funeral. Kaaren sobbed as they lowered one long box and two smaller ones into the ground. But there was no raw timber box for Roald. Dry-eyed, Ingeborg stood beside Kaaren, holding Thorliff's hand. They'd chosen the southwest corner of the Bjorklund land, the place where Roald and Carl had agreed that one day they would build a school. Kaaren had insisted they build a church also, and finally the brothers had agreed. But instead of the two buildings so needed by the growing group of settlers, they started with a graveyard.

The prairie wind carried away the voice of Joseph Baard as he read the words. "Dust to dust, ashes to ashes . . . ." He finished with the Twenty-third Psalm. Everyone joined in, their voices drifting across the burgeoning prairie. All, that is, but Ingeborg. As soon as the men began filling in the graves, she turned and headed for their wagon. She had spring plowing to do. The acres closest to the river were dry enough to work. Let the others get together over food and talk if they liked. But she had no time; she had better things to do.

⁂

Day after day, Ingeborg plowed in the fields as though driven by an invisible force. She discovered that she could begin work with one team as soon as dawn lightened the sky, even before the first rooster crowed. She could drive them straight through until dinnertime, then hitch up the oxen and keep going until it was too dark to see the furrow. On bright moonlit nights, she could continue even longer. Her body grew hard as whipcord, and with the straw hat pulled down over her forehead, she could have passed for a man any day.

"There's talk, you know." Kaaren set the plate in front of Ingeborg with a thump. The children were long in bed, and she wanted nothing more than to be there also.

Ingeborg paused with her fork in the air. "Talk?"

"About you wearing men's clothes and working the fields."

Ingeborg snorted and dug into her stew. While she chewed, she buttered a thick slice of bread and took a bite. "What do they expect me to do? Give up the land and move to town so I can be nice and respectable like?"

"That isn't a bad idea, you know."

The fork clattered on the table. "Are you losing your mind?" She cut it off before adding "again." "I don't want to hear such talk ever again. We will prove this land or die trying."

That night before undressing, she stood looking down at her sleeping sons. Was she losing them, too, in this battle for the land? She never had time for them anymore. She shook her head and breathed in a sigh of resolve. The land—she would save the land. That much she could control.

As spring passed into summer, Ingeborg withdrew into a world of her own making. She never spoke except in monosyllables, and then only when absolutely necessary. She never asked for help from her neighbors, and when it was offered by the Baards, she shrugged, and said, "Suit yourself."

But Ingeborg did accept the help of Kaaren and Thorliff. It took all three of them to do the work of their land. As soon as Ingeborg finished plowing and dragging a five-acre section, Kaaren and Thorliff threw out the seed, and then she followed behind with the drag.

By the time they called it quits, they had twenty acres of wheat, ten of oats, and five of corn. Their garden covered another acre and a half.

No sooner had she finished the planting than Ingeborg began shearing the sheep. By the end of the day, her back ached so fierce she walked bent over, locked in the same position she stood for shearing. They kept enough to spin for their own yarn and shipped the remainder off on the riverboat to Grand Forks.

The Baards dropped by on their way to Grand Forks just before Ingeborg started to cut grass for hay.

"I have a proposition for you," Joseph Baard said after they'd had the ritual coffee and Kaaren's now famous egg cake.

Ingeborg nodded.

"How about we buy one of them ride-on mowers together? We could split the cost, and it would cut so fast we could both put up more hay than before."

"How many horses to pull it?" Ingeborg broke off a corner of her cake and put it in her mouth. Sitting here was costing her precious hours.

"Two. By using both our teams and the mules, we could go about all day. They have a new fangled rake too, if you think we could manage it. Petar could probably get our money back hiring out after we done ours."

Ingeborg stared at him, nodding her head. "You have a good idea. That way we could buy a couple more head of cows knowing we had the hay and grain for them."

"Good, then I'll bring it back out with me if they have one in stock. You want to do the rake too?"

Ingeborg looked over at Kaaren. Could they afford this without taking out more of a loan at the bank?

Kaaren nodded. "I have the egg and cheese money, and the young chickens are about ready to butcher. Mr. Hemlicher at the bonanza farm said he'll take whatever we can bring him. I say let's do it. Anything to make Ingeborg's life out there easier."

"Knowing her, she'll just find more to do," Agnes muttered, who was large with child.

Ingeborg refused to let the comment bother her. Agnes was a good friend, even though a mite outspoken at times.

Haying went so well that she had two stacks by each sod barn when they had finished. How much more pleasant the labor was when the two families joined together. She caught herself almost smiling at the three boys and their teasing. Though the youngest, Thorliff held his own both with wit and brawn.

One day shortly after the haying was finished, Ingeborg came back to the soddy for the noon meal just as a rickety wagon drove up, pulled by a horse that looked as if it might fall over at any time.

"Halloo, Miz Bjorklund." Abel Polinski pulled his wagon to a halt.

Ingeborg turned from the grinding wheel where she'd been sharpening the sod-busting shares. She planted her hands on her hips and glared at him from under her hat brim. What a mistake his parents had made giving this sorry excuse for a man the name Abel.

Looking as rickety as his horse, Polinski climbed carefully over the wagon wheel and lifted a sack from the bed. "I found this when I got to plowing that stretch of land by the creek. I thought of you, that . . ." He stuttered to a close, stepping back from the fierce glare she didn't bother to conceal. "Well, I thought you might recognize it." He quit fumbling with the sack and held it out to her. "But then again, it coulda been something else."

Ingeborg accepted the sack, a feeling of dread weakening her knees. "This is all you found?" Pulling out a warped and twisted bridle, she recognized it instantly. Carl had always braided the noseband a certain way. He said it gave the horse a better fit, but they all knew he just liked the look of it. "How closely did you search the area?"

"Wal, you know I ain't been feeling so good, so I . . ."

Ingeborg took a step forward, her hands itching to loop the leather around his scrawny neck and twist. She understood now what people meant by seeing red. Rage roiled, red and black and shot with sparks like those she pounded off the iron.

"Show me!"

"Yessum." He looked toward the house from which the smell of cooking floated, then turned and climbed back in the wagon. "You want to ride with me?"

"No, I'll catch up." She opened the door and told Thorliff not to bother with the horses today. He could go fishing if he liked. At his shout of delight, she added, "I'll be back later." She shut the door on Kaaren's questioning look and went to the corral and bridled a horse. Throwing herself on Belle's broad back, Ingeborg rode out.

As she'd suspected, Polinski hadn't gotten far ahead of her. Should she have asked Kaaren to come help? But what if Thorliff found—no, she'd done the right thing.

After they'd been traveling for about an hour, Polinski pointed to a spot by the creek. "There it is. If that was your husband's bridle, I figure he got caught in that there whiteout, and—"

"Thank you, Mr. Polinski. I'd like to be alone now," Ingeborg interrupted. She couldn't stomach the whine of his voice any longer. When he drove off with a reproachful look over his shoulder, she slid to the ground and tied Belle's reins to a willow tree.

She quartered the ground with long strides, wishing she could have been there before the grass grew so tall. Knee-high and more in some places, it dragged at her boots and hid whatever tales it had to tell. She paused under one of the cottonwood trees to rest a moment. Pushing her hat back, she wiped her wet forehead with one sleeve. Then back and forth she walked until the sun had lost its heat and was slipping down toward the horizon. Had he really been here or had some animal dragged the bridle to this spot? She sank down beside the trunk of the largest tree, its lowest branches a good six feet off the ground. Could he have found shelter here, waiting for the storm to pass? She slammed her fist repeatedly into the fallen leaves and broken twigs. *Roald, you . . . you . . . we needed you. Why did you leave us? Why . . . why . . . why?* The heel of her hand slammed against something hard. Surely there were no rocks here. A larger branch perhaps. Absently she brushed the leaves aside. Roald's pocket knife, the one he kept honed for carving, lay amongst the leaves, its bright shine dimmed from months of exposure to the elements of nature.

30

Roald's dead. I now know that for certain." Ingeborg's words were heavy as she dropped the bridle on the table. The weight on her shoulders seemed to push her right into the ground. She hadn't realized that she'd still been hoping, hoping that somehow, somewhere, Roald was still alive. *He's gone. I know he's gone.* If she thought or said the words often enough, surely she would begin to believe them.

"You found this?" Kaaren ran the warped noseband of the bridle through her fingers. "Carl made this for the mule. No one else braids leather thongs in this decorative way."

"No, Polinski did. I found this." She laid the knife on the table. She would clean the knife and save it for Thorliff. Someday, owning something of his father's would be important to him. She described to Kaaren what she'd done and seen. The words still seemed make-believe somehow.

"You found nothing else?"

Ingeborg shook her head. "The grass is nearly knee-high. I only found this by accident."

"Or by the grace of God."

Ingeborg stared at her sister-in-law. *How can she still believe that?* "Ja, well, think what you will. It matters not to me."

The heavy feeling continued to grow as the days passed. Ingeborg scolded herself as she followed the horses and oxen back and forth across the field breaking sod. *You knew he was dead a long time ago, when he didn't come back. So let this go. Many people have died in this*—she corrected the thought before she finished it—*godforsaken land.* She stared out across the prairie. This was her land, land for Thorliff and Andrew. It was good land, and it was not the land's fault that Roald, and Carl, and all the others had died. She knew where to lay the blame.

⁕ ⁕

One evening Kaaren flew to meet Ingeborg at the door as she dragged herself into the house. Excitedly, she blurted, "A pastor is holding services tomorrow at the Baards'. We'll have to hurry so we can talk with him before the service. It has been so long since we've had real Bible teaching and communion. I've missed the hymns more than anything. When we have a church, I shall learn to play the organ, I . . ." Her words trailed off at seeing the expression on Ingeborg's face as she dished herself up a plate from the kettle warming on the back of the stove.

"Ingeborg, what is it?"

"I am not going. I have sod to break, and the threshers will be here soon."

"So?"

Ingeborg laid down her fork and looked up, something unknown blazing in her eyes. "So—I—am—not—going." She clipped each word and punctuated them with the heel of the fork on the table.

"But, Ingeborg, we *need* to hear God's Word so terribly."

"You go."

"But . . ."

Ingeborg rose to her feet and slammed the heels of her hands on the table. "Listen to me and do not talk of this again. I am not going—not now—not ever." She stalked to the bed and sat on the edge to pull off her pants and boots. "I will use the oxen in the morning, so you can have the horses." The heaviness settled down around her shoulders like one of the stacks of hay out by the sod barn.

The next morning, she had already turned over many furrows before she saw the wagon leave for the Baards', and she only came in from the field to exchange the oxen for the horses when they returned. She never spoke of it again, nor did Kaaren.

⁕ ⁕

After dinner one noon, Kaaren sat down at the table with Ingeborg. Andrew was down for an afternoon nap, and Thorliff had gone fishing. "Fish will taste mighty good for supper tonight."

Ingeborg made no response but continued eating the baked beans and bread as though she hadn't eaten for a week.

"You think you might take some time to go hunting? We are running low on meat, and I need to start the drying now to get enough to last the winter."

"What's wrong with the pork in the smokehouse?"

"Nothing. This would just give us more variety." Kaaren sipped her coffee. "When could you go?"

When Ingeborg didn't answer, Kaaren leaned forward. "There's something else."

"Ja?" The sound of the fork scraping the plate sounded loud.

"We need a well."

"What's wrong with the river?"

Kaaren sighed. "You know that having a well would make everything easier. Carrying water for the chickens, and—I thought if we had it in before the harvest starts we could handle the threshing crew better when they come."

"So, instead of hunting, I should start to dig the well. Do you have a place in mind?"

"You can't do that too." Kaaren thumped her mug on the table.

"Who do you think will do it, the good trolls?"

Ingeborg saw Kaaren flinch at the venom in her voice, but she didn't bend.

"Joseph and his boys will help us. They already said they would."

"You asked them for help?"

"They volunteered. They said that having the well has made a big difference for them. Agnes said she'd bring dinner over, and—"

"Do what you will," Ingeborg cut in. "It looks like you have it all planned out already." Ingeborg stalked out the door without another word.

Ingeborg worked in the north section of Carl's homestead the day the Baards dug the well. She knew that if she didn't get more of that land broken, they might not prove up the homestead. Besides, she planned on forty acres of wheat for next year's planting. The sun beat down, and the black flies plagued both her and the horses. At least now they had fly guards attached to the bridles and tails to swish across their bodies. Sweat poured down Ingeborg as she struggled to keep the plowshare at the right angle to cut evenly and turn the dense sod over so the grass would die. She was busting the acreage they'd hayed not too long before. Already the grass was coming back, green shoots among the dry stems.

She had left the oxen out in the pasture by Carl's soddy so she wouldn't have to interrupt the well-diggers. That way, when she brought the team back in the early afternoon, she could change the share and yoke up again quickly. Thorliff would be over in a minute to take Belle and Bob down for a drink.

She led the oxen under the suspended yoke. Since the wooden bar was too heavy for her to lift over the two oxen necks, she'd devised a pulley, rigged over two posts, from which she could raise and lower the yoke. She'd been pleased with the arrangement. This way she didn't have to wake Kaaren or Thorliff in the early hours when she began work.

"Easy, Red," she ordered the darker red-and-white steer. "I know the flies are bad, but once we're moving, it'll be better."

"So, you talk to the animals but not to your friends."

Ingeborg whirled around to find Agnes standing like an avenging angel not three yards away. Ingeborg's heart pounded like a hammer on an anvil. "What are you doing, sneaking up on me like that?"

"I didn't sneak, I walked firm as you please. Don't you go side-tracking me now. I come to say my piece, and that I'm going to do." Agnes stepped closer. "Ingeborg, are you all right?"

"'Course I am." Ingeborg adjusted the neck hoop on Red. She refused to ask why. If you let Agnes take off, your ear would go with her.

"'Cause you look like you're working yourself right into the ground. Dirty and skinny, so sunburned you got skin like tanned leather. And that man's hat don't do nothing much to protect you from the sun." Her tone softened. "Don't you think we know what you're doing?"

Ingeborg walked around the team and adjusted the other hoop. Without a glance at the woman watching her, she began attaching the doubletree to the yoke. She could feel Agnes staring at her, could feel the woman's thoughts boring into her brain.

"I got work to do."

"Am I stopping you?"

"No, yes . . ." Ingeborg threw up her hands. "What is it?" She spun around and glared at Agnes.

"Taking a day or two out and helping with the well or at least enjoying the company of your friends won't make a whole heap of difference for next year's crops. But killing yourself from overwork before you're thirty would mean those two little boys wouldn't have no mor neither. Bad enough their far is gone." Agnes stepped forward. "For the love of God, Ingeborg . . ."

"God is not love." Like the hiss of a snake, the words whipped across the grass separating them.

Agnes stepped back, one hand raised to deflect the attack. "Oh, my friend, He is so much more than that. Turn and let Him carry your sorrow. The load is far too heavy for you."

Ingeborg threw the last pin into place, picked up the reins, and looped them around her neck, leaving her hands free to grip the plow handles. "Gee-up," she called, and the team plodded off on command, leaving Agnes standing on the prairie with tears streaming down her face.

"Lord, forgive her, she doesn't really know what she's doing," Agnes prayed brokenly.

Ingeborg didn't ask Agnes to repeat what she had said. She was afraid she knew what it was. *Go ahead, waste your time praying if you want. I did and look what happened.* She blocked out any further thoughts and concentrated on returning to the field and getting the plowshare angled just right for the first bite of the furrow. Her stomach growled. "Uff da, I got so flustered, I forgot to eat." The white ox with red spots flicked his ears. Together the oxen leaned into the yoke and dragged the plow and frustrated woman behind them.

It took all of Ingeborg's willpower to not look back at Agnes. One day, when she had time, she would have to call on her. And just as she refused to look back, so also she ignored the voice that had somewhat dimmed in recent months. Her mother had always said that next to family, friends were one of God's greatest gifts. But then her mother had said many things that Ingeborg no longer believed.

Each night after she'd hammered out the plowshares, she entered a silent house lit by a single lamp. Everyone was sound asleep, or so it seemed, for she suspected that Kaaren merely acted as though she were. Ingeborg ate the food Kaaren left for her, checked on each of the boys, and dropped like a boulder into bed. Some nights she managed to get her clothes off, and others she didn't.

She was reluctant to admit it, but the high rock wall surrounding the well did look mighty friendly. And when the bucket dangled from the rope on a winch, she was tempted to let it down and bring up clean water—water that could be drunk right from the bucket without having to be settled out and strained. Just think, clean water was finally to be had on Bjorklund land, thanks to her neighbors. How would she ever repay them? They'd be insulted if she offered money, she knew that. As if they'd even talk to her after the way she had behaved the other day.

Even the coffee tasted better, now that they were rid of that muddy residue.

Each night when she silently said good-night to the sleeping children, guilt flooded her entire being. What kind of a mother was she who gave the raising of her children over to someone else? Andrew, the son for whom she'd waited so long, went to Kaaren now when he had a bump or bruise. It was Tante Kaaren that he laughed with and followed around—not his mor. And Thorliff, such a good little boy, was still missing his far.

Just that day he had ridden out to the field on the back of Belle and followed behind her, picking up worms for fishing. When he walked up the doubletree between the horses and mounted again to return for dinner, he said with a look over his shoulder, "Do you miss Far?"

"Ja, but I try not to think about it."

"I want him to come home. God has lots of other angels. I need my far here." A fat tear slipped down his cheek, only to be backhanded away. The dust streaked and made him look dirtier and sadder than before.

"Me too." Ingeborg tightened her jaw. She was too tired for tears. They had all been shed.

She wished there were something more she could do for her son. But unable to think of how to help him in his grief, she did the only thing she knew to do: she threw herself into the farm work harder than ever. She had to make the payments and meet the requirements for proving up the land—this land that one day would belong to Thorliff. She would save the land for him. That much she could do for him.

Ingeborg hadn't spoken with Kaaren for over a week, and one night the younger woman waited up for her.

"I need the wagon tomorrow to deliver the cheese and produce to the bonanza farm. I thought you might like to go along with me. We could do the shopping for the harvest on the way back."

"No, I . . ."

Kaaren sat carefully down at the table, as if her temper might get the best of her if she moved too quickly. "Ingeborg Bjorklund, you listen to me. I will not have you killing yourself for me or for your children. If you don't slow down before you collapse, I will take the boys and move into town. My half of the homestead can be sold or let go. I cannot farm this without you, but you look more like a bag of bones about to fall apart every day. Look, your hands are shaking so badly you can hardly eat."

"Pounding out the plowshares is what does that. Goes away before long."

"Inge, please listen to me. We need help. We could write home to Norway and send the money for someone to come. We both have brothers, and Carl and Roald did too. Hjelmer said he wanted to come."

"Ja, well, he has not shown up, has he? I suppose you have planned all this without asking me, like you did the well?" Ingeborg tried to get an edge to her voice, but it took too much effort. Suddenly, the food she'd swallowed felt like a block of worms in her belly. She pushed the plate away. "Do whatever you must, but it will be months before one of them can arrive here. We have to get through the harvest now."

"You'll come with me tomorrow?"

Ingeborg shook her head. "I'll plow for half the day, and then I'll go hunting."

Kaaren studied her in the lamplight. "All right. But I do wish you would come."

"You'll take the boys with you?"

"Of course." Kaaren looked at her as if the sun must have stewed her brains.

Even "mange takk" had become difficult for Ingeborg to say. But she muttered it and turned away. Sometimes the guilt she felt for neglecting them all nearly brought her to her knees, but she didn't think she had any other choice. Someone had to keep the homesteads going, and though both she and Kaaren were doing their part, hers was the solitary one.

Or am I at the point of wanting it that way? The thought made her stop, but only for a moment. If she stayed in one spot for too long, she'd fall asleep—standing, sitting, or lying down, it didn't really matter.

The next afternoon, when she sat down by the game trail where she'd bagged several deer in the past, she fell sound asleep and didn't wake until the moon rode high in the sky. Her back ached from the hard ground, and she felt as though every mosquito in the valley had used her for a supper stop. She trudged home, rifle in hand and itching until she wanted to scrape her skin with a stick. Maybe some buttermilk would help, both to drink and put on her skin.

To keep Kaaren from being embarrassed the morning the thresh-ers were to come, Ingeborg donned a skirt with a shirtwaister and an apron. When she tried fastening the waistband, it nearly slid off her hips. With a muttered "uff da!" she tied a strip of cloth around her waist like a belt to hold her skirt in place and rolled up the sleeves of the top. Kicking the skirt out of her way, she joined Kaaren at the stove.

"I don't know how you stand milking cows and working in the garden in these things. No wonder men can get more done than women. They are able to walk faster. Now that I know this, I'll never go back to wearing skirts all the time." She grabbed a knife and be-gan slicing the smoked haunch of venison. "Just glad I milked before I put this contraption on." Her muttering kept time with the knife.

"Well, I am grateful you dressed like you ought. Those men would have been so horrified they might not have threshed our wheat. They'd call us those two crazy Bjorklund widows."

"Just one. You have never been anything but proper."

"They're here!" Thorliff came bursting through the door.

The sun had just broken the horizon when the first wave of har-vesters arrived with three binders pulled by four horses each.

"Show them where the wash bucket is and invite them in," Kaaren said, looking first over the pans of hot food crowded to-gether on the stove and then at the table all set in readiness for the crew. They'd fried the meat, sliced the bread, fried the gelled and sliced cornmeal mush, and the biscuits were nearly done. The eggs were scrambled and set on the back of the stove to keep warm.

After watering their horses and tying them up to the wheels of the machines, three men walked up to the door. Behind them, Inge-borg could see Thorliff scurrying about, bringing hay and grain for each animal as she had instructed him.

The men doffed their hats as they entered and took their places at the table. The meal was largely silent as they rapidly consumed the food, speaking little other than "pass the eggs" and "toss me one of them biscuits." Ingeborg kept the coffee cups full while Kaaren refilled the bowls and platters of food. All three said "thankee ma'am, ma'am," ducking their heads in a show of respect as they filed out the door.

"There were only three of them, but they sure could eat!" Inge-borg sank down on the bench with a cup of coffee and a slice of bread. She let Kaaren have the remaining biscuit.

By evening, the crew had cut and bundled all the wheat. Joseph Baard and the boys did the shocking and set three bundles leaning together in order to stay upright and prevent the grain from getting soaked by the dew or rain.

Ingeborg stared longingly as the men moved down the field. She would much rather be out there with them than be trapped here in the soddy where the temperature surely had left a hundred far behind. She could drive one of those contraptions as well as the men. She lifted her face to the wind. Next year, she promised herself, they'd go in partners with Baards as they did with the mower and buy their own binder. Agnes and Kaaren could feed the crew—she'd be out in the fields.

"Drinks!" she hollered loud enough for the men to hear her over the squeak and chatter of the cutting blades.

Two days later, after the oats were cut and bound, the main crew of harvesters pulled in. A twelve-up mule team pulled the steam-powered thresher into the cleared area by the sod barn. The huge metal contraption looked like something out of a nightmare, and the enormous iron wheels made enough noise coming across the prairie to scare every animal for miles around.

Thorliff's eyes were dancing in excitement. "Just like last year, Mor?"

No, last year Roald was here to take care of all this. Ingeborg banished the thought and made herself concentrate on Thorliff. "What did you say?"

"Do you know how it works?"

She shook her head. "Do you?"

"Ja. You put the shocks in that end, and straw comes out another, and the wheat goes into those burlap bags."

Ingeborg stared at her son. Amazement made her mouth drop. "You remember all that?"

"Ja! Can I help?"

"The best thing you can do is to stay out of their way. But I know Joseph will let you drive our wagon after Belle and Bob get used to this . . . this monster." She turned back to the house. "You go pull up water for the trough. Those mules will be mighty thirsty."

Kaaren answered the door when they heard a knock. "God dag. Ah . . . hello . . . ah . . ." She stopped in midsentence.

Ingeborg turned from the oven to see what was the matter. A man, with eyes the softness of a cloudy day and a smile to break hearts, stood in the doorway holding his hat in his hands.

"Mrs. Bjorklund, I don't know if you remember me from last year, but I'm Lars Knutson, the man responsible for this crew. Can I ask you a few questions?" He'd obviously learned Norwegian at his mother's knee.

"Ja, but you should talk to Ingeborg . . . ah, the other Mrs. Bjorklund." Kaaren turned and pointed to Ingeborg.

Ingeborg could see Kaaren's cheeks were flaming red, and her hand shook as if she had the palsy. What was going on here?

31

One month later Kaaren and Lars announced they were getting married that week.

Much against her will, Ingeborg helped with the preparations. Together they cleaned out the other soddy and moved some of the livestock back to the barn there. One afternoon as the young couple were in town buying supplies, Ingeborg fingered the blue silk Roald had given her that last Christmas. Would she have time to sew it into a wedding dress for Kaaren? If she and Kaaren worked together, they might be able to get it done in time. She tucked the soft fabric back in the trunk and shut the lid. She'd ask her when they returned.

Sitting for a moment in the rocker, Ingeborg thought back to the night Lars and Kaaren had announced their intentions.

"But . . . but, you've only known each other a few weeks. How can you think to make a marriage of that?"

Kaaren straightened, and sparks glinted from her eyes. "Life is too short and too unpredictable to waste time making up my mind. Lars says he loves me, and I knew I loved him before the threshers left our place the next day. It was as if God put a sign above his head that read 'this is the man I have chosen for you.' We will be fine."

When she and Ingeborg had climbed into bed that night, Ingeborg tried to reason again.

Kaaren's words came clipped and hard through the darkness. "I will *not* turn bitter and angry like you—a machine that works from long before dawn until long after dusk. Lars and I will have a good life together, and the farm will have a man again." She flipped over on her side and appeared to fall asleep immediately.

Ingeborg could think of nothing to say, and she had turned and tossed a long time before falling asleep that night.

"Look what we bought," Kaaren called from the wagon the next day. "Come with us to the soddy and help us move it all in." Excitement flowed from her voice.

Ingeborg strapped Andrew into the sling she wore to hold him and joined them outside. A rocking chair shared space with a four-lid cookstove, the metal glinting in the setting sun. Sacks of flour, beans, sugar, and other staples took up more space, but the piece that drew Ingeborg's eyes stood roped against the back of the seat for support. A lovely kitchen cabinet, with glass doors fronting the upper shelves, carved wooden ones covering the lower section, and a work space in between, took her breath away.

"Oh my." She touched the white paint with a reverent finger. It had been a long time since she had seen such a fine piece. Roald's father built wonderful furniture in the old country, but here, in America, they had been much too busy working their homestead to think about grand furnishings. Ingeborg ran her fingers over the smooth surface again. "How beautiful." A decal of pink flowers with vines and leaves graced the carved trim on the top. The counter space of speckled enameled metal begged for a cook to roll cookies there.

"See the bins for flour and sugar." Kaaren leaned over the edge of the wagon to point them out. "Have you ever seen anything so fine?"

"No, never," Ingeborg said, shaking her head.

"And look at this." Kaaren unwrapped the corner of a soft package. "Blue and white dimity. I hoped we could make my wedding dress from it. Will you help me?"

"Ja, of course." Was it relief she felt, or regret? Ingeborg wasn't sure.

Thorliff climbed up in the wagon. "Look, new plowshares and a bucket." He heard a funny noise and, after looking up at Kaaren for permission, climbed over the sacks and opened a box that had holes in the sides. With a squeal of delight, he picked up a brown puppy with white spots on its back and chest. Both front feet sported white toes, and to the laughter of all, one eye was ringed in white. The puppy licked the boy's chin with a pink tongue and peed down his shirtfront.

"Put him down to do his business," Ingeborg ordered. Why hadn't she thought to find a puppy for her son? The look on his face told her she should have. She would have to remedy that.

Thorliff set the fat ball of fluff on the ground, and it immediately whined to be picked up again. "He already did his business"—he held his shirt away from his body—"on me." When he picked the puppy up again, he got a nose lick that set him giggling.

"Do you like him?" Lars stroked the puppy's soft back.

"Like him?" Thorliff hugged the little dog. "Like him?" His voice squeaked.

"Well, we thought as how you'll be watching Andrew more of the time, you might need a helper. And this little feller's mother and father are good sheep dogs. He'll help you round up your flock." He turned to Ingeborg. "That is, if it is all right with your mother."

"Mor?"

The hopeful, pleading look on her son's face would have melted a heart of Norwegian granite. "Ja, that is a fine idea." Ingeborg reached for the puppy. "You will have to come up with a good name for him."

"Paws."

The three adults looked at the little boy in astonishment. "Paws?"

Thorliff held up the two front feet. "The spots, see. I don't want to call him Spot or Shep, but Paws fits."

"It surely does." Ingeborg held the squirmy body up to her cheek, which also got a quick swipe. "He will be a good watchdog and sheepherder."

Andrew babbled at them and reached for the puppy with a pudgy fist. His belly laugh at the quick doggy kiss made them all smile.

"I found a farmer who has a mule to sell, so we will have three teams again. And Baard said he wanted to buy a binder next fall with us. I saw something today, Ingeborg, that you will like. A plow you can ride on, like the hay mower. They said you can plow two acres a day with it instead of one, and it's easier on the team."

Ingeborg raised an eyebrow. "What is this world coming to?"

"You should take a trip with me to the bonanza farms. You wouldn't believe the different kinds of machinery I saw in my threshing days. Some say we will be doing all our field work with steam engines one day soon. Horses, mules, and oxen will become obsolete."

Ingeborg snorted. "I have a hard time believing that."

"Wait and see." Lars swung back up on the seat. "Jump on back, and we'll go unload all this."

"I have supper ready," Ingeborg reminded them.

"Good, then we can come back here to eat. Are the chores done yet?"

"Mor and me, we finished them already." Thorliff held the puppy close to his chest. "I have to show Paws the way to your house."

"You better wait 'til he's a bit bigger, or he'll get lost in the grass. You ride along."

Ingeborg sat with her feet dangling over the edge of the wagon. *Don't be selfish*, she ordered herself. *It is a man's place to take over the charge of our farms.* But part of her mind whispered, *But you've been running things just fine. We don't need a man around here. What if he tries to take over everything?*

"Oh, Ingeborg, I nearly forgot." Kaaren dug in her reticule when they reached the other soddy. "Here's a letter for you. I was hoping for one from Norway, but not to be." She handed Ingeborg the crumpled envelope. The return postmark said New York.

While Kaaren and Lars hauled their supplies into the soddy, Ingeborg leaned against the wall and read her letter.

Dear Mrs. Bjorklund, I think of you often and wonder how my friend is doing on the Dakota prairies. I learned of your tragic loss and want to tell you how my heart aches for you. I know that our God is watching over you and keeping you safe and strong. Ingeborg looked up at the cloud puffs so white against the cerulean sky. Mr. Gould thought of her. Wasn't that a miracle? She continued reading.

My biggest news is that I have married in the last year. My wife's name is Elizabeth, and we have known each other since we were children. My father is very pleased with the union, as Elizabeth is of a fine family. He closed with, *Please accept our condolences. Your friend, David Jonathan Gould.*

Ingeborg put the letter in her pocket. She would read it again later.

When she answered it a few days later, she wished Gould well in his new life and thanked him for his concern. The long-overdue letter to her mother was much more difficult to write. In the end, she kept it brief also, knowing that her mother would read between the lines.

Ingeborg wrestled with thoughts about Lars over the days and weeks after the wedding. She tried not to feel resentful when he started taking over things, but it was difficult for her to realize that she was no longer responsible for everything. She *had* done a good job running the farm since Roald and Carl had died. The only antidote she found was the one she'd always used: hard work, and more hard work. It wasn't difficult to find plenty of that. While she preferred to be out busting sod, she now had a house to care for, cows to milk, and most of all, one crawling baby and a young boy to care for. Both of them needed meals and clean clothes and all the other things a mother usually did for her children, things which Kaaren had been doing the last months. While Kaaren repeatedly offered to help, Ingeborg stubbornly refused. After all, the new-lyweds needed some time to themselves, and they had plenty to do on their own homestead.

Lars had cut trees down at the river and sunk posts for a corral adjoining their sod barn. He had started digging them a well, and the day the Baards came over to help, Ingeborg made sure she was out working in the field, just as she'd been the afternoon after re-turning from St. Andrew where the marriage had been performed in the church. She still felt pangs of guilt for not helping serve at the wedding party the Baards had hosted. She knew the entire com-munity had come. Thorliff told her all about it, whether she wanted him to or not.

Would Agnes ever speak to her again? Did she care anymore?

As the days passed, the load felt heavier, and the cloud surround-ing her grew darker. She helped with the fall butchering, drying and storing the produce from the garden, snapping corn off the dry stalks and tossing it into the corn crib Lars had built. She filled a bin in the barn so she could shell the corn for the chickens through-out the winter.

Cheese wheels were ripening in the root cellar, and since they now had a well, she could keep milk and butter cool in a bucket down there.

One day she left Thorliff and Andrew with Tante Kaaren and, taking the gun, set out to shoot a deer and hopefully some ducks and geese as well. The birds had been flying in trailing Vs, pattern-ing the skies on their way south for weeks and setting her mouth to watering for roast duck or goose. They could use more feathers for feather beds to help keep them warm during the cold winter.

Sitting along her favorite game trail, she heard a twig snap be-hind her and turned to see what it was. Metis stepped from the brush into the small clearing; Wolf was pacing not far off to her right. She sat down beside Ingeborg and rested her arms on her knees. Between the two of them, they'd learned enough of each oth-er's language, mixed with a little English, to be able to communicate.

"My friend not well," Metis said after the greeting.

"Ja, I am fine," Ingeborg said softly so as not to disturb the game. She didn't bother to ask Metis how she had found her. Wolf, lying under a bush and nearly invisible, would have seen to that.

Metis gave her a look that spoke volumes of disbelief. "You need a husband."

"Who are you to talk? You're alone and have been far longer than I." Ingeborg could feel her anger stir.

"Me old, you young. You have young sons, need father." Metis looked at her friend out of the corner of her eye.

Wolf raised his muzzle and sniffed the wind. Ingeborg caught his move and shook her head to signal silence. Two deer ambled down the trail, pausing on the edge of the open space. Downwind from them, Ingeborg knew that unless the deer saw the hunters, they wouldn't detect them. She raised her rifle slowly and sighted down the barrel. If she waited a few seconds longer, she might be able to bring down both of them. One she would give to Metis.

The deer started forward. Ingeborg fired the first shot, dropped the leader, and fired again as the second deer leaped at the sound. It, too, fell.

"Good shoot." Metis sprang to her feet at the same moment as Ingeborg, and together they ran to the fallen deer. One struggled to get up at their arrival, but Ingeborg shot it again while Metis slit the throat of the first to bleed it quickly.

With each of them working on a deer, they gutted them, being careful to remove the musk glands without nicking them. Being far from home, they threw the guts out in the brush for the scavengers. Once the deer were finished, Metis removed her hatchet from her belt and cut two long sticks for a travois. They lashed some crosspieces on with willow and loaded the deer aboard.

On the way back to the farm, Ingeborg made several detours to bring down three geese and a brace of ducks, leaving Metis to pull the travois.

"You need some rabbit or fish too?" Metis pulled steadily.

Ingeborg looked at her, ready to defend herself at the implied criticism, but shook her head. Metis wore that glint in her eyes that said she was teasing. "Not today. But some rabbit pelts would make a fine coat or vest for Andrew."

"I make that, hood lined with fur. Keep him warm."

"Thank you. You will take one of these deer."

"No, you need."

"Metis, you have done many things for our families, just say 'thank you' and take the deer home with you. I don't have time right now to work with two deer."

"You give to . . ." Metis stopped and a smile tugged at the corners of her mouth, disappearing into the wrinkles that grooved her cheeks. "Thank you."

"You are welcome." For some reason the ever-present cloud seemed to have lightened just a little.

But as the days grew shorter and colder, and Ingeborg could no longer take Andrew out of the house with her, her temper shortened too. Everything seemed to grate on her nerves: the wind whistling about the eaves, Andrew's whining with cutting new teeth, the stove going out in the middle of the night, snow that didn't come to cover the ground, and snow that didn't quit falling for days when it did. Paws got under her feet, as did Andrew, and Thorliff looked as if she'd struck him when she told him to keep them away while she was cooking. The space that had seemed so large when Kaaren moved back to her own soddy now closed around her like a pit. At least in the barn, the animals didn't argue or cry to be fed or held.

When the neighbors gathered to discuss building a school and also using it for a church until they could build one, she resolutely refused to go. "I donated the land, that's enough," she told Lars when he came to offer her a ride with them.

By now, the man knew the folly of arguing with her. "Suit your-self." He shook his head, and after patting Thorliff's head and tweak-ing Andrew's nose to bring forth the belly laugh, the man left.

Thorliff stared wistfully out the window. "Can we go to Tante Kaaren's?"

"No, the weather is too bad for Andrew to be out. Maybe when it warms up a bit we can go."

"Can I have a cookie?"

"You know they are all gone."

"You could bake some more."

Ingeborg looked up from the harness she was mending. She pounded one rivet in place and then the next. Andrew, now walking, toddled into her legs and clung. His nose was running, and he had a bruise on the right side of his forehead where he had fallen against the corner of the trunk the day before. When he rubbed his face on her pants, she made a sound of disgust and, digging a bit of cloth from her pocket, wiped his nose and then wiped the smear off her clothing.

"Uff da," she muttered and picked up the child. He was soaked again, so she changed his diaper, using the next to the last clean one. She hadn't taken time to wash any for several days. She set him back down in the middle of the bed.

"Come play with Andrew while I haul water," Ingeborg said to Thorliff. *How could I forget such an important thing? Every woman knows babies come first.* But lately, it seemed that everything needed to be done first. She was falling more behind every day.

Lars stopped by Ingeborg's soddy on his way in from the fields one day. "Kaaren wants you and the boys to come for dinner today. She's made something special for Thorliff's birthday." Lars stood on the rug by the door so his boots wouldn't drip snow on the dirt floor.

Ingeborg looked up from the bread dough she was kneading at the table. "I have too much to do." She pointed to the boiler on the stove where she was washing the never-ending diapers and nodded at her bread.

"Surely you could come for an hour or so. You haven't been to our house for weeks."

"Please, Mor, can't we go?"

"I better not take Andrew out in the cold. He had the earache again last night."

Lars sighed. "Well, can Thorliff come? He doesn't have the earache, or the stomachache, or any other complaint, does he?"

Ingeborg ignored the irony in his voice. "Yes, he can go with you." Her shoulders and back ached from chopping wood this morning and the cramps from her monthly didn't help any. She kept up the steady rhythm of push with the heel of the hand and fold the dough over on itself. She could feel the man's studious gaze, but she refused to look up.

Andrew set up a wail when he saw Thorliff putting on his coat. How wonderful it would be to send the baby too. A few hours with no demands would be bliss.

"I'll bring him back later," Lars said, opening the door.

"Ja, mange takk." She heard the door slam and Paws yip around them as they strode off for the other soddy. Andrew raised his wail to a shriek and pounded chubby fists on the door. Finally he sank down, leaned his head against the wood and stuck his thumb in his mouth, the tears still trickling down his cheeks as he sniffed.

"Oh, you poor thing." Ingeborg scooped him up as soon as she had set the bread by the stove to rise. She tied him on a chair with a dish towel and gave him a crust to chew on while she dished up soup from the kettle simmering on the back of the stove. She sat down beside him and, blowing on each spoonful until it cooled, fed him his dinner. When he refused any more, she changed his diaper and put him in the trundle bed for a nap. "Sleep now, and when you wake up, brother will be home." Lashes drifted down over his blue eyes, more like his father's every day. Ingeborg pushed herself to her feet again and went to wring out the diapers. If only she could lie down like that and fall asleep without a care. But, tired as she was, she feared she'd never wake up.

She looked longingly at her knitting needles. It had been so long since she'd picked them up, because when she did she either fell asleep or thoughts of Roald returned with a vengeance. She had had nightmares of him in that last blizzard, lost and calling for her to find him. One night she awoke with her voice hoarse, as though she had been screaming. She'd shuddered at the words of anger she remembered from the dream. What was the matter with her? Was she going daft in the head? *Why, oh why. . . ?* She cut off the thoughts before they could go any further. She would use this time the baby slept to fork straw in for the cows and sheep. When she was outside working, the voices in her head didn't scream so loudly.

What could she give Thorliff for his birthday? What kind of mother was she to forget her own son's birthday? And then to not go over there when Kaaren had prepared something special. A thought that had been recurring more and more often of late surfaced again.

Maybe I should ask Kaaren and Lars to take the children. They would give the boys a good home. Much better than I am giving them.

32

Christmas of 1883 brought little cheer to the soddy on the prairie. Ingeborg made gifts for Andrew and Thorliff, but for no one else. She turned down invitations to Kaaren's and the Baards' and only glared when Lars said he'd bring the wagon by, now outfitted with runners, to take them all to church. Service was being held at the Baards' new house.

All the other neighbors had participated in the house-raising, but Ingeborg couldn't force herself to go. She pleaded a sick child, but that was only half right, since Andrew seemed to have a runny nose much of the time.

She couldn't help thinking back to last year. It was just one year ago that the blizzard that destroyed their lives had struck the Red River Valley. She had kept her mind off the memory as much as possible, but when things grew quiet—when the children were asleep, or she had her head butted against the warm flank of a cow and milk was streaming into the bucket—it was there. And each time, the load grew heavier.

If only Roald hadn't felt responsible for everyone around them. If he'd just taken care of his own family and his brother's family. If he'd waited to be sure the storm was over. If he and Carl hadn't gone into town and contracted the influenza. If . . . if . . . if. Such a simple little word to hinge a life upon.

"Mor?" Ingeborg dragged her thoughts back to the present. She felt as though she were swimming up through a murky cloud that threatened to suffocate her.

"Ja?"

"Andrew is crying."

Ingeborg turned toward the sound she should have heard and

hadn't. Poor Thorliff. He deserved better than this. He had lost his father, and his mother couldn't keep her mind on the moments at hand.

"There, there." She picked up the soaking wet child and made a face at the smell. He'd been wet and dirty for some time. No wonder he was crying. After changing him, she propped him on her hip in the curve of one arm and fetched a loaf of bread to fix them something to eat. She needed to get out to the barn, and Thorliff had better luck keeping Andrew content if he wasn't hungry. She'd heat up soup for their supper when she got back in.

"Here, let's take Andrew to the barn with us. The bin is low on oats, and he can play in there while we do the chores."

The look of relief on Thorliff's face sent another pang through her heart.

But by the time they'd finished forking in hay and straw, fed and watered the oxen, cows, sheep, and chickens, and had milked the cows, the baby had gone from fussing to screaming to finally falling asleep, completely worn out with the waiting. As it was, Ingeborg didn't take time to clean stalls or take the oxen out for some needed exercise. They'd be so soft come spring they wouldn't be able to work half a day at first. She needed to check on the ewes. Lambing would begin in less than a month, and she needed to build a separate pen for the rams.

Maybe Kaaren should take the boys, at least during the lambing season.

⚒ ⚒

January seemed to last clear through to the next December. Ingeborg could never remember a longer month in her life. Every day she promised herself she would spend time with Thorliff on his reading and numbers, and each night she tucked him in bed wanting to apologize for her lack. Andrew clung to her skirts, when she wore them, whining and crying, "Mor, Mor."

"What is it he wants?" Ingeborg lifted the fretful child up and settled him on her hip. "How can you understand him, when I can't?"

"He wants a piece of bread." Thorliff looked up from his slate where, for a change, she had written a few sums for him to do. "A cookie would be good."

"We don't have any. There's corn bread left. I'll put syrup on it for johnnycake."

Within minutes Andrew wore syrup from the top of his curly hair to the soles of his knit slippers. It kept him quiet for a good half hour, and the grin on his face made the mopping up worth it all. While he'd babbled at Thorliff, Ingeborg had wrung out diapers and brought in another bucket of water.

The storm hovered on the horizon like a hawk ready to swoop down on its unsuspecting victims. But Ingeborg knew to read the signs. She checked the rope she'd restrung to the barn, brought in extra wood and water, and made sure all the animals had a good drink and extra feed. The thin gold of twilight lay restless over the land—and over the woman who watched the joining of land and sky.

The blizzard struck like the howl of a train bearing down on a station. Safe and warm in her bed, Ingeborg listened to the roar and shuddered in spite of the warm covers around her. It was too much like a year ago. Nightmares stampeded through her mind, many repeated from previous nights and added to new, more ferocious horrors. In all the dreams, she was lost and alone, attacked and left for dead.

She awoke exhausted, and the day went downhill from the start. Andrew fretted and whined until she felt his forehead and realized he was burning up. Terror struck her heart like the wind striking the soddy. She tucked him into bed, making sure he drank cool water, and bathed his feverish forehead and flushed cheeks. Ingeborg dug through her packet of herbs, pulling out willow bark to make a tea drink for him. Should she put a mustard plaster on his chest? All the lore she'd learned from her mother and Metis seemed crowded into a place in her mind that was guarded by a closed door. She couldn't think what to do.

Pray first, and then do. Her mother's words echoed faintly in her mind.

"No!"

"What is it, Mor? Are you all right?" Thorliff stood at her elbow. "You didn't answer me."

How long had she been gone? It felt like hours. Where had she been? Was she losing her mind? She had no answers, and the wind just howled more wildly. Andrew whimpered in his sleep, rolling his head from side to side. When he scrubbed his ear with a fist, she knew that his ears hurt again.

"You take care of Andrew. Wipe his face with a cold cloth and get him to drink. I'll get the chores done as quickly as I can. Put several potatoes in the oven to bake, and when one is done, wrap a cloth around it and put it under his ear. That will help the pain go away." Ingeborg put on her outside clothes as she gave the instructions. "Make sure you keep the fire going. I have a feeling it is going to get terribly cold tonight." She wrapped the long wool muffler over her lower face and pulled the knit hat down until only a slit for her eyes remained. "Make sure you keep melting the snow so we have water." She raised the bar on the door and leaned against it to keep it from slamming against the wall. Snow had drifted halfway up the door, but she couldn't take time to shovel it now. "Make sure you drop the bar in place or the door will never stay closed. I'll pound hard when I get back." She picked up the two full buckets of water and stepped out into the swirling snow. Locking the rope under her arm, she followed it to the sod barn. She knew she'd never have made it without the guide. She couldn't see down to her feet.

The barn wrapped arms of warmth around her, and the animals all greeted her in their own language. Ingeborg poured out grain and gave every animal a bit of the water. The two milk cows needed the most or they wouldn't be able to produce milk. The sheep trough that she'd filled earlier had an inch-thick layer of ice, and when she broke it, the sheep crowded around for a drink. One ewe brought her lamb.

"Oh, heavens, you've started." She checked the others, feeling distended bellies and full teats. Why couldn't they wait until after the blizzard?

She milked the cows and slogged her way back to the house. The snow had filled in her footsteps from the hour earlier. The drift nearly covered the door. If she hadn't had the rope, she never would have found the house. The soddy looked more like a deep drift than a home. Only the smoke from the chimney would tell anyone there was a house here.

"Thorliff!" She pounded the door and yelled at the same time. The wind seemed to take her words and puny efforts and whirl them away with the snow.

"Mor?"

She could barely hear his voice. "Ja! Open the door."

The wind and cold blew through her as if she stood there naked. She dug at the snow, pushing it aside, wishing she had the shovel. "Hurry, Thorliff."

"I can't get the bar up."

"What?" She yelled into the crack of the door frame.

"I can't raise the bar."

"Keep trying." Was that Andrew screaming or the wind? She dug faster, throwing the snow as far as she could, digging like a dog after a rabbit. Finally she had enough cleared away that the pressure could be relieved against the door.

She nearly fell into the soddy when the door sprang open. Thorliff had tear tracks running down his cheeks, and he hiccuped from crying.

She stepped back outside to retrieve the milk buckets, and together they leaned against the door to shut it. A two-inch crack remained. "Get the shovel." Thorliff handed her the shovel and like a mad woman, she threw the snow away from the door. She had to get the door closed or all the heat in the house would be gone. When they tried again, the bar slammed in place, and the wind howled as if furious with them for flaunting their puny strength in its face. But at least the howling was outside, not in.

Ingeborg leaned her head against the door. She wanted to sag down into a heap by the stove and not move for a month. But the look of terror on Thorliff's face made her reach up to take off her muffler. "You did a good job, son." She knew she had to put a smile on her face, but now the burning of her face told her how close she'd been to frostbite. She leaned down so he could inspect her skin. "Are there white places on my face?"

He nodded and touched her right cheek and the tip of her nose. "Here and here." He went to the door and scooped up a handful of the snow that still lay where it had blown in. Rubbing her face gently with it, he tried to smile. "Are the sheep okay?"

"We have one lamb, and who knows how many more will come tonight. Just like sheep to pick the worst storm of the year to drop their lambs." Ingeborg cupped her hands over the stove and opened the oven door to let more heat into the room. She could have frozen to death right outside the door, and her children might have died too. How much longer could she hold on?

She knew she should check the sheep before going to sleep, but the memory of the last trip kept her from it. Thorliff and Andrew were sound asleep now, and she would be too, standing upright, if she didn't lie down first. She spread another quilt over their bed, wondering if she shouldn't take both of them in with her. But after filling the stove with wood and turning down the damper so it would last longer, she crawled into bed with her clothes on. If the storm let up, she would go check on the sheep.

But it raged through the night. Each time Ingeborg got up to put more wood in the stove, she could hear it screaming for entry. When she woke again, she could see the sky had lightened from black to deep gray. Or was the window so covered with snow that she couldn't see out? She listened carefully. It was too quiet. The storm had blown itself out—at least for now.

She shoveled her way out of the soddy to find snow still falling, but the wind had returned to its lair. They had three more lambs and one dead ewe. "If I'd been here, maybe I could have saved it." She dragged the carcass outside and away from the barn. The wolves would have a feast. *If Roald had been here, we probably wouldn't have lost it. He could have opened the door. But not me. I almost let my children die when I couldn't get back in.* She scolded herself all through the chores and back to the house.

Lars pounded on the door just as she served breakfast to the boys. Snow blew in with him. "Are you all right? I did not dare try to come during the blizzard."

"Ja, we are fine." She told him about the sheep.

"Ingeborg, you are an amazing woman. I will tend the sheep tonight so you can rest."

"Not if the storm comes back, and it could." She looked at him from eyes that burned for want of sleep. "I will not be responsible for another of our men to die in a blizzard."

"We will see."

She drew water for the sheep trough, brought in extra wood, and dug down to the root cellar door to bring in a ham and vegetables. Storms had been known to follow right on the heels of each other, as they had last year. She wanted to be prepared.

Snow continued to fall all day, and by late afternoon the wind had started to rise again. While Andrew was better, he wanted to be held and rocked. Every time she returned to the sheep pen, Thorliff took her place in the rocker with the baby on his lap. Paws took turns going with her or staying with the children. It was as if he knew his place as watchdog and couldn't decide who needed him most.

Since Lars couldn't return, she was up most of the night with the sheep again. One lamb needed assistance coming into the world, and another ewe was in distress but wouldn't lie down for help. *Why*, Ingeborg wondered, *couldn't they have their lambs in the day-*

time? She knew that some did, but most came at night.

By the time she'd finished chores in the morning, she knew that if she lay down, she wouldn't get up again. She catnapped in the chair while Andrew slept and Thorliff whittled on a chunk of wood with his father's knife. The storm had again let up when she returned to the barn, but the cold only felt more intense. Each trip back to the barn that night felt longer than the one before. She could hardly put one foot in front of the other.

"Mor, Mor." Was that Thorliff crying? Had she fallen asleep in the barn?

"Ingeborg. Ingeborg!" She felt someone shaking her, grabbing her hands. Was it another nightmare?

She forced her eyes open. No, not a nightmare, but the look on Lars' face said something was terribly wrong. "What is it?"

"Thorliff and Paws were on their way to get me when I was almost here. They couldn't wake you."

Ingeborg raised her head to see Thorliff, his lip quivering, standing beside the bed. "Mor, I didn't know what to do."

"You did fine." She patted his cheek. "I must have fallen asleep."

"You wouldn't wake up." Tears started again.

Full awareness hit her like the storm had struck the door. "The sheep! The cows." She pushed herself up on one elbow.

"Let me take care of them." Lars touched her shoulder. "I would have been over long ago if I could have made it through the storm."

"I know. I'm glad you didn't try." She swung her feet over the bed. "But I'm all right now. Besides"—she pointed at his hands—"if a ewe needs help, your hands are too big."

Thorliff had picked up the baby and brought him to his mother. "Andrew won't quit crying. I gave him some bread and milk, but he wouldn't eat either. I don't know what else to do."

"How long has he been like this?" Lars asked.

Ingeborg tried to think. It seemed like it had been forever.

"How about if I take the children home with me and then come back to help you? Kaaren has been frantic with worry and maybe this is the way we can best help you."

Ingeborg nodded gratefully. "I'll get some of their things together."

"Good, and I'll milk the cows while you do that. The oxen can go outside."

She shook her head. "The storm drifted right over the corral fence. They could get out and get lost on the prairie."

LAURAINE SNELLING

Lars just shook his head as he picked up the milk buckets and headed out the door.

"I can help." Thorliff leaped to follow, sending a look of pleading over his shoulder to his mother.

"Ja, you go ahead. You've been cooped up in here far too long." With Andrew now quiet on her hip, she gathered some of their clothes together. She took the two remaining diapers down from the line she'd stretched from stove to fireplace. She needed to wash diapers again. She found the dirty ones frozen in one corner. No wonder the house smelled. Setting the wash water to heat, she also made a pot of coffee and started a pan of cornmeal mush. They were out of bread too.

Andrew whimpered and lay his head on her shoulder.

"My poor baby, you will be so much better off with your Tante Kaaren." She smoothed a rough hand over his curls. "I know you will."

But when she shut the door behind them, she felt as if that scabbed-over hole in her heart ripped open once again. Crossing the snow to the barn, she was certain if she looked back she would see drops of blood gleaming on the white surface.

Back and forth, barn to house, house to barn, she dragged her body on in spite of the weariness that only deepened with each step. The house was so quiet she couldn't stand to be in it. Even Paws had deserted her and remained at the other soddy.

Night, daylight—it made no difference. Had days passed, or was it only hours?

One ewe lay down, strained for a time, and got up again. Ingeborg moved her into a stall by herself and tried to get her to drink. The ewe refused and got up to pace again. This seemed to go on for hours.

Ingeborg did the milking, took the milk to the house, grabbed a cup of coffee, and returned to the barn. This time when the ewe lay down, Ingeborg managed to get an arm up the birth canal and find what felt like a back. As she'd suspected, the lamb lay in the wrong position, and she needed to turn it. Contractions squeezed her arm. She felt around, searching for the feet. Instead she felt another head. Twins. And one was blocking the birth canal. The ewe strained, but after all this time, Ingeborg could tell the animal was weakening.

"Easy, girl, let me help you." She tried to talk, to calm the mother, but the ewe struggled to her feet again. Ingeborg thought of going for Lars to help, but the wind had returned, and she couldn't take the chance of getting lost. Not after losing Roald to last year's blizzard. If he, strong as he was, couldn't conquer winter's rage, she never would be able to make it. At least, here, she was safe from the storm outside.

The ewe lay down and Ingeborg lay with her. She reached inside again, trying to turn the lamb. She found the feet. Her hand felt numb. She waited for a contraction to help turn the lamb but none came. Then she felt a faint one begin. She pulled, trying with all her might to bring at least one lamb into the world. If she could save it, the long night might have some worth. Another contraction, and she pulled the lamb out, laid it on the straw, and reached inside for the other. The ewe lay quiet. Ingeborg couldn't tell if the animal breathed or not.

But the lamb didn't. She left the one inside and, grabbing the face of the other, cleaned the mucus off its nose and blew into the nostrils, gently pressing the rib cage at the same time.

Nothing.

She tried again, and again, each time hoping for a response and each time more sure it was too late. Finally, she laid the dead lamb down beside the dead ewe. "Three! I lost three!" She tried to get to her knees, but one leg had fallen asleep while she'd struggled with the sheep. She pitched forward, catching herself with only a chin scrape on the stall wall. She hung there, her hands clenched on the bar.

Eyes feeling on fire, and a rock in her throat that may have been her heart, she hung there. Slowly releasing fingers cramped with the strain, she sank down into the bloody straw. Her nails scraped down the wall, picking up slivers as they went.

"Oh, God, if you are real, why do you torture me so? They say you are a God of love, but I feel no love. Do you hate me so? Am I so bad you must take everything from me?" She rested her head against the manger. Wouldn't death be better than this? All she needed to do was step outside and lie down against the barn wall. With the cold, she would just go to sleep.

Sleep. What a comfort. To fall asleep and not have to work again. No more dying sheep. No more crying children. No more.

"God, help me." She could only whisper the words, but they came from deep within her being. A dry sob wracked her body.

"God, help me," she rasped again. A burning lay at the back of her throat, and she convulsed with the agony of her utterance. Tears clogged her throat and overflowed her eyes.

Ingeborg wept.

Epilogue

Mor, Mor, come quick!"

Ingeborg looked up from the pan of soapy water. She'd moved the dishpan outside into the sunshine to wash the kerosene lamps. She couldn't seem to get enough of its warmth after the long winter. Snow still covered most of the ground, but right here at the south wall of the soddy, even the icicles had all melted. The chinook wind felt like the kiss of heaven. She returned the still-stained chimney to the soap suds and followed the laughter. Andrew and Thorliff were up to something again.

As she walked, she raised her face to the sun. "Thank you, Father," she murmured, as was so often her litany these days. So many things to be thankful for, and so much time to make up. She'd asked forgiveness for her year of rebellion and knew for all she was worth that the Father had heard and lived up to His promises. The months since the lambs were born in February had been long and difficult as she bounced back and forth between learning again to seek God's will and battling hours of blackness when all seemed hopeless. But at least the dark times, when they had come, had lasted only hours instead of days, or weeks, or months.

It seemed the tears had flowed for weeks. Things such as finding Roald's old hat out in the barn behind the grain bin, being reminded each time she opened her Bible that God loved her and forgave all her sins, the sweet smell of Andrew when he leaned back in her arms and patted her cheeks, all made her weep and sometimes laugh through the tears. Laughter again filled their house—how good, and cleansing, it felt. And when the meadowlarks returned to the prairie with their lyrical songs, she knew she had some mending to do. Not mending of clothes—that was a never-ending chore—but the mending of friendships.

One morning she took her courage in hand and followed the well-worn path to Kaaren's soddy. Andrew hung on her hip, while Thorliff and Paws ran back and forth, kicking up what snow they could find and sliding in the muddy spots on the path, their shouts and barks adding joy to the morning music.

"Ingeborg, come in, come in." Kaaren opened the door with a smile and a raised eyebrow that showed her surprise.

"Is the coffee hot?" Ingeborg forced the words past the lump in her throat.

"Ja, and I'll toast some bread to go with it."

"Good, but let me say what I must first."

At Kaaren's turn of the head, Ingeborg raised her hand. "Not to worry. This is good—I think." Ingeborg sucked in a deep breath and let the words out in a rush. "Please forgive me for the way I have treated you this past year, for being so hateful and angry. I am so sorry, and if you can let me back into your heart as a sister, I will be . . ."

Kaaren didn't let her finish. She threw her arms about Ingeborg, including Andrew in the hug. "Oh, Inge, you are back with us, and that is all that matters. Of course, you are forgiven. We went through such terrible times, and God has brought us safely out on the other side. Thanks be to God!"

"Ja, thanks be to God." Ingeborg took the seat at the table and cradled the cup in her cold hands. One down, the most important one.

Lars reacted the same when she asked him to forgive her out in the field. "Oh, Ingeborg, I am just so grateful you are better, I don't know what to say."

"Kaaren has said it best. 'Thanks be to God.' "

Lars nodded. "That sounds like my Kaaren. And I agree." He turned away and, pulling a handkercheif from his pocket, blew his nose. "There now, we are family like we should be. Hey, Thorly, you want to ride?"

At the boy's shout of delight, Lars smiled again at Ingeborg. "Thank you."

"I am the one to be saying 'thank you.' "

"Ja, well, guess it can't be said too often." He slapped the reins on the backs of his team. "Hup there." With Thorliff waving down at his mother, they began to cut another slab of sod and roll it over to continue breaking the prairie.

Ingeborg watched, knowing she should be home doing the same, but she had one more place to go first. Was she like the prairie, only slowly yielding to God's plow in her life? She needed busting, then backsetting, and finally after snow and sun and rain, the seeds could be planted that would sprout into living wheat. She shook her head at the fanciful thought, but it would stay with her through the weeks to come.

After dinner, she hitched Belle and Bob to the wagon, gathered up a wheel of cheese and a loaf of bread along with the boys, and set out.

Agnes welcomed her with open arms and tears in her eyes. When Ingeborg stuttered out her plea for forgiveness, Agnes broke down along with her. When they mopped their eyes, she drew the coffeepot to the front of the stove and pushed Ingeborg into the rocking chair.

"Now that we have that out of the way, you are to put it all behind you, like our good Lord says, and look forward." With a firm and loving hand on her shoulder, Agnes handed Ingeborg a cup of coffee. "Oh, Ingeborg, I have missed you so." She sniffled once more, dried her eyes on the corner of her apron, and gave her friend a tremulous smile. "Look at us, two tough Norwegians and blubbering like babies."

"Mor, they have a new calf, come and see." Thorliff and the boys piled through the doorway.

"You go on out and play," Agnes said with shooing motions. "We have some catching up to do here."

"I will come later," Ingeborg promised.

The boys grabbed cookies from the crockery jar and pelted back out the door.

"Such energy. Uff da." Agnes shook her head. "They are growing so fast I cannot keep them in clothes. Thank the good Lord that pretty soon they can go barefoot again."

On the way home, Ingeborg let her gaze roam the prairie. Off to the south, she could see a spiral of smoke from a farm home and another off to the north. The land was indeed getting settled. As they'd been saying, a schoolhouse was needed. Could she afford to donate some of the wood? Or could they make the first one of sod, as they had the houses, and then build a wood structure later?

She clucked the horses into a trot. So much to do.

Winter made one more effort, blanketing the valley in a blizzard that caught many unawares. Ingeborg made it back just in time from a hunting foray. While Lars was an adequate hunter, she rarely missed a shot and knew where all the game trails lay, so he continued to work the land, and she continued to hunt. She dragged the deer carcass into the barn and hung it from the rafters. She would finish dressing it out after chores.

Later, the house seemed so empty with the boys still over at Kaaren's. Ingeborg didn't dare brave the whiteout to bring them home. *This is what it would have been like had I given the boys away.* The thought struck her with the force of a falling tree. She could feel the darkness, heavy as a haystack, pushing her down again, smothering her and taking away her light.

She lit the kerosene lamp with shaking fingers and added wood to the stove, leaving the front lid open so she could see the firelight too. The darkness lurked in the corners of both the soddy and her mind, ready to take over.

Ingeborg paced the room, her arms clutched around her midsection. Was it all to return? Would she never be able to find the light again?

"Oh, my God, help me!" Her words met the shriek of the wind, note for note. "I cannot go through this again."

The lamp flickered in the draft, the glass chimney darkening with the smoke of it.

Recalling them from the depths of her being, Ingeborg repeated the age-old words. "I will praise the Lord. I will thank you, my God. I will sing a song of praise. The Lord is my refuge, whom shall I fear? I will praise the Lord." Over and over, she echoed the words of the psalmist.

Finally, Ingeborg stopped and listened. The wind, that howling wind, had died.

When at last she slept, she lay secure in the arms of the everlasting God, and morning brought the sunshine.

One of many things she had learned was that it was better to cry together than to cry alone. Now she could remember Roald without the terrible pain and guilt. Asking for help still took every ounce of her gumption, but even that grew easier with practice.

"Mor!" The boys' shouts brought her back to the day.

She felt like twirling in place. The joy the day brought was almost too much to contain.

"Mor!"

"I'm coming."

The two boys, Andrew still in the dress of babyhood, crouched by the south wall of the sod barn where the sun had melted the snow.

"See?" Thorliff pointed to a ridge of sod protruding from the wall, just above ground level.

"See?" Andrew mimicked his brother. Sometimes his words were total gibberish, but this word he had conquered.

Ingeborg put an arm around each wriggling body and squatted down with them. A tiny purple violet, framed by round green leaves, nodded at them.

"No, don't touch." Thorliff caught his brother's hand before the violet could disappear in the baby's clutch.

"Oh, how beautiful!" Ingeborg leaned forward and, nose nearly touching the perfect petals, inhaled. The violet lent her its fragrance. She closed her eyes, savoring this promise of spring. "Smell," she told her boys.

Thorliff bent over and sniffed. "Smells good."

Andrew crouched close, stuck his nose over the flower, and blew.

Ingeborg and Thorliff looked at each other and burst out laughing. Andrew looked from one to the other, unsure what the joke was, and then his belly laugh poured forth from his grinning mouth.

Paws, always the boys' companion, leaped to his feet from where he had been snoozing at the corner of the barn. Something had caught his attention.

Ingeborg, each hand holding that of one of her sons, followed the sound of the barking dog. Paws stood stiff-legged about a hundred feet from the barn, hackles raised on his back and one front leg in the air. He wagged his tail but continued barking.

The sun turned blond hair to golden on the tall man striding through the ankle-deep snow. Between the pack on his back, and the ax balanced on one broad shoulder, he reminded Ingeborg of pictures she'd seen of the Vikings of old. He, too, had shed his dark coat in honor of the sun and wore the sleeves of his loose-fitting white shirt rolled up to his elbows.

"It's all right, Paws. We can see him. He's company arriving just in time for dinner."

"God dag, Mrs. Bjorklund?" He nodded to her and smiled down at each of the boys.

"Ja." His eyes. They had to be Bjorklund eyes, so intense was the blue.

"I'm Haakan Howard Bjorklund, recently of Minnesota." He set his ax on the toe of his boot and extended a calloused hand. "My mother wrote and said one of our relatives needed a hand. Since the logging was done for the season, I came to see if I could help."

"You have the same name as us." Thorliff stepped forward and looked up—way up.

"Ja, your father is my cousin two times removed."

"Was." Ingeborg could talk about it now without crying. After all the tearless months, it seemed she had cried for weeks. Those tears were over now, except for an occasional freshet when something triggered the memories.

"I know." He looked into her eyes, compassion bringing the tears to the surface. "I'm sorry."

Ingeborg nodded. "I have the coffee hot, and dinner is nearly ready. Would you like to join us?"

"Most certainly." Haakan swung his pack to the ground and, after a nod to Thorliff, dug into a pocket. "I have something here I thought a young boy might like." He pulled out a stick of red-and-white striped candy. "What do you think?"

"For me?" Thorliff looked up at his mother. She nodded.

"Ja, for you." Haakan gave Thorliff the treat. "And one for your brother." Andrew received the same. He watched Thorliff and copied his actions, only licking the candy before putting the end in his mouth.

"Not so trusting, is he?"

"No, he always tests the waters first." Ingeborg swung Andrew up on one hip and led the way to the soddy. "Thank you."

Thorliff removed the candy from his mouth long enough to mind his manners and say thanks.

Andrew waved the candy in the air. "Tank oo."

Ingeborg grabbed his fist and lowered it before the candy got stuck in her hair. Once inside the soddy, she motioned Haakan to sit at the table, tied Andrew on a chair across from him, and, after lifting a mug from the warming shelf on the stove, poured their guest a cup of coffee.

Haakan took the cup and sniffed the aroma, his eyes closing in bliss. "Now *this* is how coffee should smell. Thank you." He took a sip. "And taste."

Ingeborg smiled at the compliment. Why was it this man seemed so perfectly at ease here, as if the chair had been waiting for him? She felt a tingle of anticipation race up her spine.

"It looks like spring is really here," he said.

"Ja, I think it is, too." She removed the loaves of bread from the oven and set them on the sideboard. If spring could be inside one, it certainly had come to this untamed land. Maybe it took the terrible winter for God to tame her heart.